MW01287057

TALLAHATCHIE

Rick DeStefanis

ISBN-13: 9781533028877
ISBN-10: 1533028877

A Note for My Readers

Thank you for sharing your time with me. I have done my best to ensure you will feel it is time well spent. If you enjoy this story, please write a review and post it on Amazon. com or your favorite retailer's site. This increases readers' awareness of my work and frankly, helps with sales on occasion. Those sales help me to afford publishing more of my books. Your support is deeply appreciated. I also wish to express my deepest appreciation to those who helped bring this book to print. My special thanks to Ellen Prewitt, Chris Davis, Carol Carlson, Margaret Yates, Melody Bock, Cover Designer Todd Hebertson, bookcoverart.webs.com and Editor Elisabeth Hallett, soultrek@montana.com. Learn more about Rick DeStefanis at: The Word Hunter, www.rickdestefanis.com.

CHAPTER 1

THE MISSISSIPPI DELTA

"THE ESSENCE OF LOVE DENIES rational explanation because it is predicated on dimensions beyond reason." Jack Hartman had read those words once—he couldn't remember where, but their summation best explained his journey. Jack knew he was a fool. He was leaving the Gulf Coast to come live in the dusty Mississippi Delta. Who else would leave a life of sunshine, sand, and margaritas for cotton fields and shotgun shacks? But it was something he had to do.

Despite his weariness, he was alert with anticipation as he exited Interstate-55 and headed west down a rural highway into the Delta. The love of his life, Acey, had walked out on him because of Cici Cannon, a talented young Blues singer. Acey little realized Jack's unflinching love would never allow him to be unfaithful, but attempts to please both women had shattered their lives. With Acey gone, he was spinning in a flotsam of bad decisions, and left only with his debt to Cici to repay, part of his reason for coming here.

It was nearing dawn, and a yellow moon hung low and pregnant far across the fields of cotton. The August summer heat owned the South, leaving the air heavy with a humidity that hung as a haze visible in the moonlight along the shadows of the distant tree lines.

Jack had driven through the night, the green interstate signs coming and going in his headlights. A litany of names, Vicksburg, Yazoo City, Greenville, all Mississippi towns he had visited while traveling for Hartman Manufacturing. Yet he had never been to Tallahatchie—his destination. Other than an aging furniture factory, there wasn't much there, but in nearby Clarksdale there was "The Crossroads," the heralded birthplace of the Blues, an art form he had recently begun to better understand.

Lowering the window and letting the nighttime odors filter inside, he inhaled the musty odor of insecticide when he passed a yellow crop duster sitting beneath a drooping wind sock, and the acrid odor of creosote rising from the timbers as he slowly crossed a railroad track where the waning moonlight reflected on the silvery rails extending as far as the eye could see. The radio was tuned to an R&B station, but the further he drove the more it faded as he strained to hear Sam Cooke.

"If you ever change your mind—about leavin', leavin' me behind..."

The static-splinter lyrics were interrupted with jolts of Spanish from some radio station—God only knew where,

Mexico or Cuba maybe—but like his memories of Acey, Sam Cooke's voice kept returning.

"Bring your sweet lovin'—Bring it on home to me..."

The Delta stretched to the horizon, across the Tallahatchie, and all the way to the Mississippi River— miles of cotton and bean fields, extending to distant tree lines or to the edges of sawgrass-lined swamps. Like the two women in his life, the Delta was as alluring as it was mysterious.

As the flat terrain slipped by in the predawn darkness, Jack found himself trying to apply logic where there was none. Acey and Cici were beautiful women, but they were total opposites. Acey was a blue-eyed blonde from Atlanta with a business degree and a love for the sun and surf. She was also an up-and-coming executive superstar at Hartman Manufacturing, his family's business near Mobile, Alabama.

Cici was a green-eyed Blues singer with raven hair, the daughter of a black mother and a Cajun father from Louisiana. She loved the smoky Blues clubs where she performed with a voice like none Jack had ever heard. Besides being beautiful, both women had one other thing in common. They both now hated him.

The sky was beginning to glow with a hint of pre-dawn orange when his pickup finally rolled to a stop outside the gate of the Fernwood Furniture Factory near

Tallahatchie. Shutting off the engine, he gazed up at a rusted water tower. One of those ancient numbers shaped like the Tin Man's head, it rose above the weathered metal buildings of the factory, a lonesome sentinel to what must have been better days long since passed. A guard shack, still padlocked at 5:55 a.m., stood at the main gate. And for what purpose, other than keeping out stray possums, Jack couldn't imagine, because behind the rusted chain-link fence were the most dilapidated buildings he'd ever seen.

Gazed at the sight before him, he exhaled slowly. His Uncle Tuck had warned him about coming here, and the wisdom in that argument was now evident. The Fernwood home office in Tupelo where Jack had gone for the interview was a gleaming façade of brick and glass, manicured green Bermuda and three new flags whipping in the breeze. Perhaps, because it had come so easy—this perfect job—he should have expected what now lay before him.

Instead, he had ignored an interviewer's suggestion that he might want to drive across the state and visit the factory before accepting the position. If the job was in Tallahatchie, that's all that mattered. Working at this furniture factory made sense, because it gave him the opportunity to be near Clarksdale, where Cici now lived with her aunt. If she would allow it, he hoped to visit her there, and perhaps help her get back on her feet and resume her singing career. He owed her that much.

Everything in his life had come apart in recent weeks. Cici had nearly been killed, and Acey had walked out on him. She had taken a leave of absence from her executive position at Jack's family's business, Hartman Manufacturing, and gone home to Georgia. And to hear his Uncle Tuck tell it, Jack was on a quest to fix things that weren't fixable. Tuck, the eternal realist, simply didn't understand. It was the day of Jack's departure that he told his uncle about the plan. They were on the veranda at Tuck's club in Orange Beach, The Gulf Sunsetter.

"So, let me see if I understand," Tuck said. "You're leaving your position at Hartman and walking out on Acey because you're pissed at the family and hell-bent on saving this drunken excuse of a Blues singer?"

Quelling his anger, Jack stood with his back to his uncle as he inhaled deeply from the breeze blowing off the Gulf of Mexico. Slowly he turned to face Tuck, who was sitting in the shade of the veranda.

"Tuck, she's human, and I was the one who talked her into coming down here. I think with this life of privilege we sometimes forget other people aren't as fortunate. I can't simply walk away. I owe her something."

Tuck was not only his uncle, but more importantly, he had always been Jack's best friend and confidant—at least until now. With a glass of bourbon in hand, Tuck was normally laid back, but not today. Like the rest of the family, he had suddenly become a judgmental jerk. Taking a chair, Jack sat beside him and stared out at the Gulf where a ghostly-gray ship passed slowly on the horizon.

"I still say this is crazy, and you really don't owe her anything," Tuck said.

There was little use arguing with him. How could he understand? Managing the Sunsetter kept Tuck busy, and he never fully engaged in the family business, Hartman Manufacturing. As he put it, making woodworking machines for furniture factories wasn't the sexiest job in the world. But he was getting older now, which was probably the reason for his sudden change, and he was vehemently opposed to Jack leaving his position as head of sales.

"You need to stop and think this over," Tuck said. "You're still upset about the wreck and Acey leaving."

Wiry and tanned, Tuck was wearing his wardrobe of preference: blue jeans and a T-shirt. Although in his late fifties, he looked like a man in his forties, which probably explained his latest thirty-something flame, Carol. She was staying out of this fight—back inside tending the register. Jack sucked down a deep breath and tried to remain calm.

"Look, I've already told you this once. Dad and the rest of the family blame me for Acey taking that leave of absence."

"So, screw them."

"No, I'm leaving Hartman so Acey can come back to work. And helping Cici recover from the wreck is something I have to do, anyway. So, it all works out for everyone, okay?"

Tuck shook his head. "No, not okay. You hear me? It's *not* okay."

Tuck seldom drank more than a couple glasses of bourbon, but he was on his third.

"You want a drink?"

Jack shook his head. "No. I'm leaving tonight."

Tuck lit an unfiltered Camel and lay back in his chair. He had always been more like a big brother than an uncle, except now he was acting like the rest of the family.

"Cigarette?" Tuck said, offering him the pack.

"Sure."

Jack lit up and waited.

"You know your grandpa treated me a lot like your daddy treats you. He had plans for me, but he thought I was too much of a dreamer. After I graduated from high school he sent me to a military academy up in Georgia. Hell, I was supposed to be his golden boy, graduate, then do a stint in the Army Reserve and take over the family business, but it didn't work out that way."

Tuck's crystal-blue eyes squinted at the glittering waters of the Gulf.

"You see, there was this girl I met in high school, and even after I left for college in Georgia she came to see me, and I would come back here on the weekends to see her, but the year I graduated she broke up with me. Pissed me off so bad, I volunteered for active duty. Showed her, I did—ended up spending a year in Vietnam as a platoon leader."

Jack knew about Tuck's Vietnam tour. Tuck was hard-core—had more medals than a Russian czar. He also had shrapnel scars on his chin and across his chest, spidery little white lines that never tanned. Still, they only added to his rugged physique.

"You're going to end up like me when I went to Nam," he said.

"How's that?" Jack asked.

Tuck gave a little grunt and a laugh. "I was a love-sick fool till I found myself face down in a rice paddy being plowed by a North Vietnamese machine gun. After that the girl thing was no longer an issue."

Jack squinched his lips sideways. "I don't think Tallahatchie, Mississippi, will be quite the same as Vietnam."

Tuck sat up, pinching his cigarette hard between his thumb and finger. "Try not to be a smart-ass, Jack, and listen to what I'm saying. It's the principle of the thing. You're ruining your life."

"I don't have a choice. I have to go."

"You *do* have a choice," Tuck said. "You're just pissed about your dad and uncles still treating you like a kid. You're pissed because Acey assumed you were having an affair with Cici, and you're too damned stubborn and proud to tell any of them they're wrong."

"Has nothing to do with it," Jack said.

"Hell, it doesn't," Tuck shouted. "You think you can prove something to everybody by walking out?"

Jack didn't answer as he stood and walked across the veranda toward the steps, but Tuck only shouted louder. "I got news for you, boy. What's done is done, and nothing will change it."

Stopping at the top of the steps, Jack looked back. Tuck was right in many ways.

"Take it from the voice of experience." Tuck had lowered his voice. "You're what, in your thirties now, and you want to go off on this quest like a nineteen-nineties version of Don Quixote to right the world's wrongs? Well, you can't. You can't change people, and you can't fix everything that's broke. You need to let it go and get on with your life. You hear? Just let it go."

It was almost a plea, and it would have been easy to stay pissed-off, but Tuck wasn't so different from him. When he returned from Vietnam in the early seventies, Tuck worked a few months with the family at Hartman Manufacturing, but had a falling-out with his father and brothers and bought a Harley. A few years later when he returned again, cleansed of his gremlins, they tried to cut him out of the business by giving him the beachfront club as a consolation prize. It didn't work. Tuck remained on the board of directors, eventually becoming one of the most influential members. And now, as he stared into his uncle's rock-steady blue eyes, Jack realized his anger was misdirected.

"You're not seeing the whole picture," Jack said. "This isn't simply about Acey or my dad. I need to get the hell away for a while. Besides, the Fernwood people said their Tallahatchie factory is in trouble, and they're giving me an opportunity to save it. Leaving the family business for a while, getting out from under my father and running this factory will help me as much as it will help Cici."

"I thought you said you were going to be the *Assistant General Manager?*"

"That's right. The factory manager is one they inherited through acquisition, and I'm supposed to help him right the ship."

"So, the best director of sales we've ever had at Hartman Manufacturing and heir apparent to the CEO position is leaving to save some Podunk furniture factory in Mississippi. And oh, by the way, he won't even be in total control of his destiny. You're going to be answering to a boss whose policies are apparently already failing."

Everything Tuck said was logical, and perhaps he was right. There was truly no rational explanation for anything Jack was doing.

Tuck sat upright in his lounger and pushed his sunglasses up on his head. "Tell me this is all just a bad practical joke."

Jack bowed his head. "I owe it to Cici."

"That girl made her own bed. We did everything we could to help her, but she was master of her own self-destruction."

"Okay, maybe Cici isn't the only reason I'm going. Don't you understand? My father micro-manages every move I make. I'm frustrated and tired. This little factory where I'm going is only twenty minutes from Clarksdale. I can get some R&R and check on Cici."

"So what is it with you and Cici? You sure you don't have some kind of a crush on her?"

"No, definitely not, at least not in a physical sense. I just see a person who is lost, desperate, and in need of some help. The only crush I have is for Acey, and I would say it's a hell of a lot more than a crush. I was going to give her a ring when the moment was right."

"So, at least let me contact Acey, and tell her she's wrong. You two were made for one another, and you're letting her walk away."

"No," Jack said. "I already tried, but she's too stubborn to listen."

Tuck stared back at him in silence.

"Look, you did the same thing when you got back from Nam," Jack said. "I need to do this, and I don't want to have to explain it, at least not right now."

Tuck smiled and nodded. "You know, Jack, if I didn't know better, I'd swear you were my son, because you are one hardheaded Hartman, but the more I think about it, the more I realize this might be a good thing."

"Oh?"

"Yeah. I never told you this, but I've told that asshole brother of mine all along that he needed to back off and let you run the business. Everything you've done, from the employee programs to the restructured manufacturing processes, has improved the company. Now, maybe he will see I was right."

Jack and Acey had the perfect relationship before that cold night in Memphis when he first saw Cici Cannon perform. He'd been on the road, traveling to furniture factories in Alabama and Mississippi, helping the salesmen close several large deals for the family business back home in Mobile.

Now he was tired, and the next day he would drop the rental car in Memphis and catch a flight home, but first, Beale Street promised a night of relaxation. He parked and hurried down Front Street toward Beale, but the streets were nearly empty, and not without good reason. It was a Wednesday, and a steady drizzle of sleet was falling. Signs in the windows said some of the clubs had closed early because of the weather. Icy streets were predicted by dawn.

Neon reflected silently from the wet pavement and traffic lights changed for nonexistent traffic as Jack made his way down the sidewalk to the Blues City Café. The sweet smell of barbecue hit him as soon as he stepped inside, but most of the tables were empty. Even the help looked bummed-out with the winter blues. Lounging around a table in white aprons, they were smoking cigarettes and sipping Cokes. He ordered ribs and a beer, and asked about the band.

"Our people folded up early tonight," the waiter said. "Nasty weather got most folks staying home. You might try across the street at BB's. Cici Cannon has been over there all week."

"You know that girl has herself a new recording contract?" one of the cooks said.

"You ever seen her?" the waiter asked Jack.

Jack wagged his head.

"I'm telling you, that woman ain't nothing but fine. You ought to git on over there after you eat. You ain't heard the Blues till you hear that woman sing them."

An icy rain fell as Jack ducked his head and hurried across the street to B.B. King's place. From back uptown came the distant wail of a siren, and he thought how it wasn't a good night to be on the street. People were cold and hungry on nights like this—and sometimes desperate, but as he opened the door at BB's he heard a throaty female voice singing *Call it Stormy Monday*. The cold night air disappeared as the door closed behind him, and Jack felt instantly at home. The waiter at Blues City was right: The moon glowed in her voice, soft but strong and smooth. It grabbed you by the heart and pulled you into her world.

There were only a few customers still hanging with it at BB's. A young couple sat in a booth back under the mezzanine, feeding one another barbecued nachos, while the others sat in front near the bandstand—a couple of young businessmen who'd shed their coats and ties, and an older man still wearing his.

Jack sat at a table on one side, close enough to the stage to tell the people at Blues City Café were right again. Cici Cannon wasn't just a talented singer, she was beautiful. She gave him a cursory nod and a smile as he sat down. He smiled back. A good-looking woman who didn't think she was the center of the world—that was refreshing. Her smile was eclipsed only by her intense green eyes shining beneath the klieg lights.

Cici Cannon seemed totally self-assured, yet so young. Like his Acey, Cici owned her world, and she sang as if she were in front of a packed house. Turning to the band, she gestured and smiled with a magic that had them playing like it really mattered. It was as if they were auditioning for their first show. And when she finished, Jack joined with the sparse applause.

Cici excused herself for a break and walked with the grace of a fashion model to a table near the bar. There was a big man seated there—the kind that held his beer mug as if it were a shot glass. His sports coat was draped over an adjacent chair, and his shirt sleeves were rolled halfway up his arms—arms big as Jack's legs. Probably a bouncer.

On the stage in front of the microphone was a gallon jar—an old pickle jar, perhaps. It had five or six bucks inside—pretty poor pickings for someone with her talent. Pulling a twenty from his wallet, Jack walked over and dropped it in the jar. A few minutes later when she returned, Cici noticed the twenty and turned his way, mouthing a silent "Thank you."

Jack shrugged.

Making herself comfortable, Cici sat with the microphone, adjusting her dress and locking her silvery spiked heels in the rungs of the stool.

"All right, folks, it's a dreary old night outside so let's liven things up a bit. This next song was one of Cousin Peaches' many hits, and I want to dedicate it to a true fan of the Blues."

She turned to Jack and winked. "This is for the gentleman sitting over here on my left." She pointed with the microphone. "What's your name, sir?"

The others in the club turned and looked at him. "Jack," he said, and stared down into his drink.

"Okay, Jack. This one's for you. It's called 'Shame, Shame, Shame.'"

He didn't care for the attention, but she had him tapping his foot for the next hour. The band did the instrumentals better than the original, and her vocals were perfect as she jumped from the stool and strutted across the stage, smiling and wagging her finger. When she was ready for another break, she locked the microphone in place and stepped over to where he sat.

"I hope I didn't embarrass you," she said.

He smiled. "When a lady sings a Jimmy Reed song just for me, it's difficult to hold a grudge."

Her beauty and poise were captivating, and she was in her early thirties at most. She had delicate features, sparkling green eyes, high cheekbones, and sensuous lips.

"Will you have a seat and let me buy you a drink?" Jack asked.

She glanced over her shoulder at the bouncer then shook her head. "Not now."

"Jack Hartman's my name," he said, extending his hand.

She shook his hand and smiled. "Cici Cannon," she replied.

"How about after the show?" he asked.

She raised her eyebrows and gave him an amused smirk. "You don't give up easily, do you?"

Jack shook his head. "No, no," he tried to explain. "You have me..."

She turned to walk away, but glanced back at him. "Maybe later, cutie pie."

CHAPTER 2

THE FURNITURE FACTORY

JACK RESTARTED THE ENGINE AND slowly backed away from the locked factory gate. The meeting with his new boss wasn't until 8:00 a.m. With his stomach growling, he pulled back onto the highway and drove into Tallahatchie, where he hoped to find a McDonald's. He passed Jake's E-Z Stop, a combination grocery store–gas station, and according to the sign out front it also offered a tanning bed and live bait. The shop was dark inside.

The town was still asleep as he drove up Main Street past a row of connected redbrick buildings. They were actually fronted with awnings and a concrete sidewalk, but most appeared abandoned, except for a nameless coin-operated laundry with foggy windows and a place a few doors down called Big Dog's Bar B Q Shack. A white poster-board in the window advertised chicken-fried steak, fried fish or fried frog legs for $4.75–$5.75 with fries and a drink, but there was no McDonald's.

And Jack suddenly realized he had reached the other end of town. Slowing to a stop, he glanced into the rearview mirror. A streetlight was still burning in the gray morning light, and the town seemed vacant except for a stray yellow dog sauntering down the middle of the street, no doubt that notorious candidate of choice for the local Democrats. The dog was the only thing moving anywhere.

Pulling to the side of the road, Jack closed his eyes. Hopefully, a quick nap before meeting his new boss would return some of the starch he lost during the late night drive.

It was a peculiar dream. They were far out on the Gulf in the family boat, and Acey was lying on the foredeck, sunning in a pink bikini. One could not have asked for a more beautiful day, but from somewhere there came the sound of a rooster crowing.

Jack jerked awake.

"Oh, shit!"

A car had just sped past going into town. He had been dreaming of Acey and the time he'd first seen her in a bikini. He shook his head to clear the cobwebs, and there again came the sounds of a rooster crowing. Jack glanced quickly at his watch. An almost involuntary sigh of relief escaped his lungs—perfect timing. It was 7:45 a.m.

Cranking the truck, he turned around and drove back through town to the factory. The parking lot that had been empty earlier was now full, and a security guard sat in the guard shack fanning his face with a fold of newspaper. Jack slowed, but the guard smiled and waved him through. Shrugging, he drove into the lot, pulling the pickup and trailer to the far end, where he parked and snatched the necktie hanging from the rearview mirror. It was time to meet the new boss.

The foyer in the office area was empty except for two stained vinyl chairs and a yellowed aerial photo of the plant. It was probably taken right after the factory opened, which according to the date at the bottom was 1960. There were several doors, but Jack quickly spotted the one he wanted. A tarnished brass nameplate said it belonged to Richard Nickels, Plant General Manager. His knock was met by a flurry of muted sounds from inside, punctuated by a slamming desk drawer.

"It's open," came a woman's voice.

From the moment he stepped into her office and read the nameplate on her desk, Jack knew Doris Ann Jette would be someone to be reckoned with. Plant manager's secretaries often were, but Doris Ann had a persona that manifested itself even in silence—something she was now doling out in massive doses. Without looking up, she screwed the cap on a bottle of Coke. A mild aggravation vied with what appeared to be boredom on her face as she set the bottle aside and finally raised her head and looked up at him.

"We ain't taking applications today, sweetie," she said.

As she eyed him up and down, Doris Ann suddenly broke into an open-mouthed grin, something she managed to do while chewing a wad of pink bubblegum. Her plucked and painted eyebrows slowly arched upward, and Jack was about to explain her mistake, when she interrupted him. "Wait a minute. I'll tell you what you do. You give me your name and phone number, and I'll call you the next time we're hiring." She gave him a second once-over then winked.

A bottle-blonde, probably in her mid-thirties, Doris Ann wore a thin white blouse, unbuttoned enough to display ample cleavage, harnessed by a lacey pink bra. Jack held his gaze steady and gave her a polite smile.

"I'm not here to put in an application, ma'am. I'm Jack Hartman, the new Assistant General Plant Manager, and I'm here to meet with Mr. Nickels."

Doris Ann leapt to her feet and threw her hand over her mouth. "Oh, my God! I'm sorry, Mr. Hartman, oh, lordy, I *am* so sorry. I ain't never seen a factory manager so youn—I mean—you.... you just don't look like any factory manager I ever saw. You're—well—you're tanned! And your hair, all sun bleached, where did you work befo.... I'm sorry. I'm being nosey."

Doris Ann suddenly stopped, as if she'd at that moment become aware of something. She looked back at the door to the inner office then slowly turned to face Jack again. He raised his eyebrows.

"Mr. Nickels isn't here," she said. "He told me if you showed up, I was to call one of the supervisors, Tommy Grey, and have him show you around."

"If I showed up?" Jack said. "I thought we had an appointment."

"Well..." She paused. Pulling the wad of pink bubble-gum from her mouth, she stuck it to the Coke bottle cap.

"Look, I didn't say this, but Mr. Nickels thinks the home office sent you here to take his job. The last man they sent, he ran off inside of six weeks. I mean the man just up and quit. Anyway, I reckon Mr. Nickels figured you might not even show up. You know? Maybe that's why he didn't come in early today."

Remaining silent, Jack maintained his best poker face. What else could she tell him?

"I think I'm talking too much. Let me call Tommy," she said.

She picked up the receiver and punched an extension on the phone. "The new Assistant Factory Manager is here. Mr. Nickels called and said he wants you to show him around. What? I don't know. So? I can't help it if you're busy. What am I supposed to do? Clyde? I don't know, but Clyde? Okay then!"

She slammed the phone down.

"Prick."

She looked up at Jack. "I'm sorry. Tommy is just like Mr. Nickels. They're both real horses' asses till they need something. Problem is Tommy don't need nothing right now."

"So," Jack said, "what's the plan?"

"He's sending the janitor up here to show you around the factory."

"The janitor?"

"Don't worry. Old Mr. Clyde ain't so bad. He just don't say much, but I kind of like him."

Jack glanced toward a curtained window where a credenza stood with two framed photos, one of Elvis and the other of Princess Diana. Both were draped with black silk handkerchiefs, and in front of each photo was a small votive candle. He turned and looked back at Doris Ann, who grinned sheepishly.

"Those are mine," she said.

Jack raised his eyebrows and nodded. "Nice."

The phone warbled, and Doris Ann grabbed it. "Fernwood Furniture, Mr. Nickels's office. Oh, hey, Mr. Nickels."

She pointed at the phone and silently mouthed, "Mr. Nickels," as if she hadn't just said his name.

"Yes, sir, he is. I don't know. I mean, he's kind of young, but he hasn't said hardly two words since he got here. No, sir. He's sending Clyde up—says he's got something going on back in the paint shop and can't do it right now. I don't know. It was something about Dewayne Pritchert not showing up, again. Okay. Okay. Yes, sir. I will."

Jack noticed the light go out on the phone line.

"Bye,—huh?"

Doris Ann pulled the receiver away from her ear and looked it before slamming it down again.

"Prick."

There came a knock at the door. An old black man in bib overalls stood outside the door. He held a green John Deere ball cap in his hands.

"Uh, Mister Tommy sent me up here to show the new Assistant Factory Manager around."

"There's your guide, Mr..." Doris Ann paused, obviously having already forgotten his name.

"Jack Hartman," Jack said, extending his hand toward the old man.

"Pleased to meet you, Mr. Hartman," Clyde said. Appearing to be well into his sixties, Clyde stood at least six-foot-three and his huge callused hand swallowed Jack's.

There was something about him Jack liked immediately. "Call me Jack," he said.

"Okay. You ready, Mister Jack?" Clyde asked.

"Not 'mister'," Jack said. "Just Jack." He turned to Doris Ann. "Nice meeting you, ma'am."

She had relaxed again as she pulled the wad of gum from the Coke bottle and popped it back into her mouth. "It's not ma'am. It's Doris Ann." She winked and smiled. Jack gave her a two-fingered salute off his forehead and turned to walk out.

"Clyde, you take good care of Jack, now. You hear?"

"Yes, ma'am, Miss Doris."

The old janitor led him down the hallway past a large lunchroom and several other offices, most of which were empty. At the end of the hallway, Clyde pushed open a metal door and they stepped out on the factory floor. Greeted by the roar and clatter of activity, Jack stopped to survey the production area, a cavernous room filled with a hodge-podge of machines and people. The chemical odor of coatings and glue permeated the air along with that of fresh-cut wood. Suspended from long cables, scores of fluorescent lights produced near-daylight brightness inside the building. The employees were at their machines, cutting and drilling pieces for the latest orders.

"The factory is set up like an assembly line, so the work flows from back yonder at the truck dock and supply bins around this way, then either over there to upholstery or down to that metal shed over yonder. That's the paint room."

Clyde talked loud enough to be heard over the clatter of the factory.

"From there it goes over yonder to be assembled, then down there to packing on the other end of the truck dock. We're kind of an old-fashioned factory because we still do most everything from start to finish."

They paused beside a couple men working with lathes. The machines were ancient. Jack glanced at Clyde.

"How old are those machines?" he asked.

"I reckon some of them must be over thirty years old," Clyde said.

Jack glanced around the factory. Most of the machines were layered with multiple coats of gray paint. Only a few were newer machines, and none were like the computerized equipment made by Hartman Manufacturing.

"My gosh," Jack said. "This is the most antiquated machinery I've ever seen still in use."

A young black man with his pants hanging well below his waist was working at one of the lathes. He stopped and pulled his goggles up on his head as they passed. Clyde stopped beside him.

"Pull your britches up, boy."

The young man did as he was told. Clyde smiled and continued walking.

"That's Doritoe, my younger sister's grandson," he said.

They wandered back toward the upholstery shop. The pop of staple guns and the odor of glue marked the tasks taking place there. Jack noticed a man in a white shirt, beyond a glass-enclosed floor office.

"Who's that?" he asked.

"That's Mr. Tommy Grey," Clyde said. "He's the big boss's right-hand man. We got an agreement. He don't say nothing to me, and I stay out of his way much as I can."

"Why's that?" Jack asked.

"He doesn't know how to talk to people—got no respect."

Clyde turned and pointed toward the lathes. "I know what you mean about the machines," he said. "They're all old, but they still run pretty good. That's because of Mr. Henry and the millwrights, Matt Oliver and JT. They're the ones that keep the factory going. If it wasn't for them, this place would have to close the doors."

"Where are they?"

Clyde pointed to a machine on the other side of the aisle. Parts to it were scattered about on the floor, and three men were gathered around working on it.

"That's them there. That's Mr. Henry down there under the machine. He don't mind getting his hands dirty—best supervisor we got. He's also the one that really runs the factory—gives out the work orders and handles most everything."

As they walked from area to area, Clyde answered his questions, but the more Jack saw, the more he began to worry. His only hope was that it wasn't as bad as it first seemed.

"So what do people around here do when they're not working?" he asked.

"Most of us do a little hunting and fishing now and then. You hunt or fish?"

"I deer hunted some with my uncle when I was younger. And I still like to fish, but I'm from down on the Alabama Gulf Coast. I mostly troll off the coast or fish for bonefish or tarpon down in the Florida flats."

"Nothing big like tarpons around here—mostly just catfish, bream and crappie, maybe a big gar now and then. I don't reckon you'd much like our kind of fishing."

"Fishing is fishing. I'd love to go. Is there a lake around here?"

"I like Moon Lake, up north of Clarksdale. It's got some pretty good bream."

"Let me know sometime if you don't have anyone going with you," Jack said. "I wouldn't mind catching a few bream."

"I'm going this Saturday," Clyde said, "I mean, you're welcome to go and all—I mean... I know you were probably just talking."

"What do I need to bring?"

"A sandwich, maybe, and something to drink. I've got poles and tackle."

"Book it," Jack said. "You've got a fishing partner Saturday."

Clyde led him around for several hours, explaining the various processes with such detail that Jack began wondering how a janitor could know a drill press was cutting out of tolerance, but if you adjusted the RPMs and kept the bits sharp it worked okay. There was something unsettling lurking in the shadows of a story where a man with Clyde's knowledge was sweeping floors.

At 11:30 a bell rang, all work stopped, and Jack asked the old man if he could talk with more of the people. Clyde pointed to a door near the back receiving dock.

"That little breakroom there is where some of them take their lunch," he said. "Me, I just sit out yonder on the dock 'cause they keep it like a refrigerator in there."

Leaving Jack on his own, Clyde carried his lunch in a brown paper bag and walked with the stiff legs of age out to the dock. Jack pushed the breakroom door open, and met a freeze-frame of faces, struck silent in mid-sentence.

Scarcely a potato chip bag rattled as everyone eyeballed him like barnyard turkeys watching a coyote outside the fence. He could have backed out, but what the hell, he was here now.

The painted cinderblock walls were lined with grease-smudged vending machines, the gray plastic buttons rounded smooth from years of wear, and the lettering long ago worn away. A scarred Formica counter on the far wall held a microwave and a stained coffeepot. This wasn't the large lunchroom Jack had seen up front, but a smaller one at the back of the factory. An oasis of air conditioning inside, the room was as frosty as the welcome he received.

No one said a word—except for Arlis McCallister. Clyde had pointed him out earlier, saying he'd been around a few months—moved down from somewhere in Arkansas—and he came to work each day with a Bible in his lunch sack, primed with a passage he'd found the night before. Figuring it was a pre-meal prayer, Jack paused and bowed his head, but after a few moments he noticed the others had resumed talking and unwrapping their sandwiches. Arlis continued reading aloud. Jack shrugged and began plugging quarters into the machines. He bought a pack of peanut butter crackers and a diet Dr. Pepper then pulled a chair up to the table.

Arlis had oiled black hair and the sallow complexion of a reformed drunk. He also reeked of cheap cologne. Jack was pretty sure it was an Old Spice knock-off, and there was a tattoo on his arm that depicted the head of Jesus in a crown of thorns. Depending on one's point of view, Arlis could pass for a derelict TV evangelist or an ex-con who'd found Jesus.

Clyde had explained how Arlis said he was saving money to open a church someday, and how he began lunch everyday by setting a cup on the table for donations. True to form, Arlis had set the cup on the table while he read, and his voice grew progressively louder, until he reached a witness-bearing crescendo of Pentecostal fervor. It was a passage from Revelations that ended with him slamming the book shut and glaring with coal black eyes at those around the table. That's when he went into over-drive and began a table-pounding sermon.

Today it was a tirade on the evil of porno tapes—"and DVDs, too," Arlis thundered, but his voice modulated for an aside, "except they're better quality—and you gotta have a DVD player for them." His voice climbed again. "The root of all evil is lust, lust for the female body, that soft, warm, and beautiful combination of flesh that leads men down the primrose path to hell. We must save ourselves from temptation or else suffer eternal damnation."

Lost in a fever-pitched oblivion, Arlis continued a disjointed raving that sounded as much like an advertisement for the appreciation of female anatomy as it did damnation for the ones who dared look. Jack took a pensive bite from one of his crackers while the others carried on their conversations. It was as if neither he nor Arlis was in the room. After a moment or two the guy next to Jack bent over and whispered in his ear, "You gotta ignore Arlis. Otherwise, that cracker you're eating will stick in your throat like a truck-stop biscuit."

Jack turned to him—a voice of sanity in a circus of the absurd.

"Jack Hartman," he said, grabbing the man's hand and shaking it.

"I'm Matt Oliver Tomlinson," he replied. He had honest brown eyes and a genuine smile. Matt Oliver introduced the others. "This here is JT Stoker, Paul Brantly, and Henry Smith."

Jack began shaking hands and hoping he wasn't grinning like a maniacal fool.

"Henry's our shop foreman," Matt Oliver said. Henry looked to be in his early sixties, close-trimmed silver hair, silver wire-rimmed glasses and a white shirt with a pocket full of gauges.

"Me and JT are millwrights," Matt Oliver said. "Paul here is brand new, just started today—don't know what he's going to be doing just yet."

Young, almost baby-faced, Paul didn't seem to belong. Matt Oliver pointed to a couple of black guys down at the far end of the table. "That's Cleve Thomas and Doritoe Jackson. They're machine operators."

The two black guys looked up the table at Jack. Cleve looked to be in his mid-forties, but Doritoe was eighteen or nineteen years old at best. Jack nodded and stood, stretching down their way to shake hands. Arlis continued preaching while everyone else talked and ate lunch, but after nearly ten minutes, he went suddenly silent and stood up.

Gazing about with fiery eyes, he seemed infuriated but said nothing. The others ignored him, while munching blithely on their corn chips and bologna sandwiches. The odor of stale coffee drifted from the pot in the corner, where the last quarter-inch had reduced to a sticky goo. No one in the breakroom, except Jack, seemed to notice that Arlis had stopped preaching.

Without warning Arlis turned and stalked out. Only then did someone seem to notice. "Where's that nutty bastard going?" JT asked.

JT Stoker, Matt Oliver's partner millwright, was a piece of work in his own right, with a Fu Manchu mustache and a six-inch braided ponytail. He wore a matching red and yellow Dewey Hargrove T-shirt and cap. The number "93" of the infamous stock-car driver was plastered across his back and on the sides of the cap.

"Who the hell cares where he's going?" Matt Oliver answered.

The new kid, Paul, jumped up and peeked out the door.

"If we don't watch him," Henry said, "that crazy bastard is gonna bring a gun in here someday and give us all a dose of his salvation."

Jack glanced at Henry, but the old shop foreman didn't so much as crack a smile.

Paul was still looking out the breakroom door. "He just jumped off the dock," he whispered needlessly, "and now he's walking out toward the parking lot." JT went over and peered over Paul's shoulder. There came the brief squeal of a tire from outside.

"Hell, he just got in his car and left," JT said.

"Where do you reckon he's going?" Paul asked, returning to the table.

"Who the hell cares?" Matt Oliver said. "Good riddance."

"Nutty bastard better be back time lunch is over," Henry said, "or else I'm firing him and telling Nickels to find me another finisher."

"Don't reckon that's it, do you?" Matt Oliver asked.

"That's what?" Henry said.

Matt Oliver and Henry seemed to be the two thinkers in the group.

"The paint," Matt Oliver said. "You reckon it's affected his mind? You know he doesn't wear his respirator half the time."

"It didn't take no paint to make him that way," Henry said. "There was already a leg or two missing from under his chair when he got here."

JT sat back down at the table, and Clyde shuffled up to the door. He stood in the doorway, leaning on a push broom. Clyde had amazed Jack with his knowledge of the factory and its machines. That he wasn't a millwright or machine operator seemed strange.

"You boys didn't run Arlis away, did you?" he asked. "You know we cain't make much furniture without neither of our finishing-men here."

He laughed then spat a stream of tobacco juice outside the door. Using the broom, he pushed some sawdust over the mess.

"Clyde, you ain't heard from Dewayne, have you?" Henry asked.

"Yes sir, Mister Henry. I reckon he's kinda busy."

"Hell," Matt Oliver said, "you know, it might be the paint, 'cause Arlis looks damned near sane next to Dewayne. Think about it. How long has Dewayne been applying finishes—what, nine years now?"

Matt Oliver explained that Dewayne Pritchert was the furniture factory's head coatings applicator. He started at the factory when he was seventeen, worked his way up to one of the local delivery trucks, but lost the job when a helper said he swapped a piece of furniture for some pussy up on Lamar Avenue in Memphis. Word was Dewayne left a new red-velvet Victorian couch in a room at the Motel 6, where he had bonked a big-tittied prostitute.

Dewayne was now the boss over the paint shop, which included him and all one of his employees—Arlis. The operation consisted of a metal building in one corner of the production area, a few drums of chemicals, some hoses, a mixer, and various applicators and pumps. The "chief paint-sniffer," Matt Oliver explained, hadn't shown up for work that morning, and they were already running behind.

Henry looked across at Clyde. "What's got him so busy he can't come to work?"

"Well, you know how he was planning that big barbecue this weekend, and said he was gonna butcher a hog so we could have a party at his place?"

"Yeah," Henry said, "I told him, he'd best drive up to the stockyard in Memphis and buy one already slaughtered. Is that where he's at?"

"Oh, no sir. He called me early this morning all outta breath. Said he was needin' my help, so I went down by there on the way in, and he was having all kinds of trouble."

"Yeah?" Henry said.

Clyde stopped smiling. "Mister Henry, you know that boy ain't right, don't ya?"

"Ain't right?" Matt Oliver said. "That's like saying Jeffrey Dahmer had an eating disorder."

"What happened?" JT asked.

"Well, when I got there he done gone out and got this little ol' shoat—couldn'ta been over twenty-five pounds, and calling it a hog. Anyway, when I got there, Dewayne and Miss April and all the babies, they was covered with blood from head to toe."

Jack suspected that Paul, the new kid, was from a more urban setting, because he wore a skateboard T-shirt and was clean-shaven. He sat at the end of the table, mouth half-agape and eyes wide open. He'd stopped eating his sandwich.

"The babies, they were just a-running around the trailer naked except for their diapers and covered with blood, but the little tadpoles was having a big time just a-laughing and cutting up. Poor Miss April and Dewayne, though, they was beside themselves and about give out."

"What the hell happened?" JT asked.

"Well, they done knocked the shoat in the head with a hammer to kill it and set it on some newspaper on the kitchen table. Dewayne said he cut it down the middle and was fishin' the insides out when the pig come to and jumped off the table. They got it cornered underneath the bed in the kids' room, and Dewayne figured he'd just stab it right there 'cause it was a-squealing and trying to get away. He said he poked it in the neck, and the pig charged right at him.

"That's when Miss April told the kids to catch it, and they must'a chased that pig from one end of that trailer to the other, 'cause there was blood everywhere, even up in the windows. Dewayne said with the blood and all, it was just too slippery for the kids to catch him, so Miss April finally commenced to taking the butcher knife and chasing it around herself, stabbing it till it died."

"You know," Matt Oliver said, "that Dewayne is one addle-brained sonofabitch."

"Sounds to me like he ran into the hog from hell," JT said.

"So why did he call you, Clyde?" Henry asked.

Clyde blinked and looked down at the floor as if he was embarrassed to talk about another man. Jack knew he was probably smarter than half the people in the room, but he seemed to maintain a kind of deep-seated respect for people—one that some of the same ones probably mistook for being a "good nigger." Just the same, Clyde didn't seem afraid to speak his mind.

"He said seeing's how's us colored people are good at butchering our own hogs and such, he thought I might could help him, but I told him he had the worst of it done. 'Sides, I buy my pork at Winn-Dixie now."

"You left him butchering a pig on the kitchen table?" JT asked.

"Yeah. It wasn't none of my pig. I told him as bad as I hated to, I had to get on up out of there and come to work. When I left, Miss April was mindin' off the flies while Dewayne finished dressing the pig."

"Well, it's damned near twelve o'clock," Henry said. "He sure as hell ought to be finished by now."

"That boy don't know diddly about butchering no hog, but I reckon he's finished," Clyde said. "He's probably 'tendin' to the other business that come up."

"What was that?" Henry asked.

"I was fixin' to leave when a deputy showed up outside Dewayne's trailer—said somebody done stole a pig from down the road. I told him I didn't live there, but he might ask the man inside."

"That stupid sonofabitch," Matt Oliver said. "He just went out and bought a brand new Pontiac Firebird, but then goes and steals a pig."

"He didn't buy that car," Henry said. "He leased it, and his old lady is making him take it back. She wants their old Toyota back."

"Hell," JT said. "She was the one bitching about how she couldn't see over the air scoop on the Toyota."

"Well?" Matt Oliver said. "Can you blame her? I mean, it's not like a four-cylinder Toyota really needs a humungous air scoop on the hood."

A bell rang somewhere outside the door.

"The five-minute bell," Henry explained as everyone stood to walk out. "It looks like I'll have to find a replacement for the finishers."

He cast a long glance at Paul as they walked out to the truck dock for a quick smoke. Paul may have been a kid, but he apparently wasn't stupid. Walking like a cat in a room full of sleeping dogs, he refused to look at Henry.

Even in the shade of the awning, the summer heat was stifling as Jack joined the others, gazing in silence across the parking lot, past the road, to a cotton field beyond. Orange Trumpeter vines snaked up the guy-wire of the power pole beside the road, where ruby-throated hummingbirds vied with the bumblebees for the nectar from the dangling flowers. Aged like the factory, the pole was bowed and pockmarked with gouges from pole-climbers' spikes.

Across the field, the heat shimmered beneath a cloudless sky, and Henry puffed on his cigarette while watching Paul from the corner of his eye. The veins on the boy's neck swelled and his face reddened as he ignored Henry's relentless stare. Henry had chosen his back-up finishing man, but before he could make his move, there came the roar of an engine as Arlis careened back up the road in his ancient Lincoln. Turning into the parking lot, he skidded to a stop, and jumped out with a large grocery bag.

"Lunch time is over," Henry said.

"This is *not* my lunch," Arlis answered.

He walked to the end of the dock and stood beside a big blue dumpster.

"It's my entire collection of girlie videos, and I'm putting them where they belong."

With that he emptied the bag of porn tapes into the dumpster.

"Hey," JT shouted, "don't do that. Hell, I'll take 'em if you don't want 'em."

"No!" Arlis shouted.

He whirled toward the group, and fished a book of matches from his shirt pocket. Quickly striking one, he turned toward the dumpster.

"No!" Henry shouted. There was terror in his voice. "You dumb-ass. You throw that match in with all that sawdust and paint and this whole damned factory will go up in flames."

"Oh, sorry, boss," Arlis said. The glare was gone from his eyes, and he had become instantly calm—eerily calm.

The new kid, Paul, looked around as if to validate what had just happened. Matt Oliver simply smiled. Henry shook his head in resignation. Paul's eyes sank into an unfocused stare. An uneasy silence prevailed as everyone shuffled back to their lathes and presses, back to things they could put their hands on and perhaps find distraction from what they'd just witnessed. As for Jack, he was beginning even more to understand the wisdom of Uncle Tuck's warnings.

CHAPTER 3

MESSENGER'S

WHEN JACK REALIZED HIS NEW boss wasn't coming in that day, he excused himself after lunch and went to find a place to live. By late afternoon he'd met with a real estate agent and rented a place in a pecan grove west of town. As the agent drove away, Jack stood in the shade of the pecan trees, holding the keys to the old farmhouse and wondering what to do next. He went inside. It was clean, but showed its age. The hardwood floors were time-worn and in need of a little wax, and a little dusting wouldn't hurt either. He went to work cleaning and unpacking his belongings.

Late that afternoon, with no groceries on hand, Jack decided to drive up to Clarksdale to do some shopping. Pulling his ball cap down low over his eyes, he donned a pair of dark sunglasses and gazed into the mirror. He hoped visit one of the Blues clubs, and possibly learn something about Cici, but he had to be careful. He didn't want her to know he was around until he could approach her in a controlled setting. Jack gazed at his reflection in the mirror. The disguise wasn't much, but it was better than nothing.

The sun had already set in the west as he drove toward Clarksdale that evening, and Jack thought back to that night when they first met. There were hints of trouble from the beginning—signs that were obvious if only he had heeded them. Everyone at BB's treated her like a favorite daughter, trying to own her or at least protect her from anyone who dared approach. After the show he asked if he could buy her a gin mint julep. She simply laughed, but the bouncer and the others in the band watched him as if he was about to cross a line to a place where he didn't belong.

"Sorry," he said, "I didn't mean to be pushy."

Turning, he started toward the door.

"Wait," she said. "I didn't mean to be rude. Besides, I've never had a gin mint julep."

Jack stopped and looked back. She smiled shyly, and they ended up sitting at a table long after the doors at BB's were locked. The manager and the others eyed Jack as if he were an intruder. He'd caught the fancy of their favorite girl, but Cici was the hottest thing on Beale Street, and she called her own shots.

Sitting across from him, she was on her third drink and half-tipsy, giggling at his corny jokes. After a while, the big stud with the diamond earring and a chest the size of a baby grand walked over to the table. He stared down at Jack with his best evil eye, but spoke to Cici.

"This man ain't giving you no trouble, is he, Cici?"

She rolled her eyes. "Sure, Perry, he's like a really bad dude, and he's shaking me down for my autograph. Gimme a break—will you?"

The man stared hard at Jack for several seconds before turning and walking away.

"I better be going," Jack said.

"Don't mind Perry. He's just a little possessive at times—thinks because he handles my business matters, he can tell me who I can see. So how did a traveling salesman learn so much about the Blues? I mean, you name the old Blues artists like you grew up in the Delta."

"Just an interest in the form," Jack said.

She slowly shook her head. "I can't believe I'm here after midnight, drinking and talking to a white traveling salesman about the Blues."

Jack smiled. "I have to admit I'm not just a traveling salesman. My family owns the company I work for in Mobile, Alabama, and my uncle owns a large beachfront restaurant and bar down at Orange Beach on the Alabama Gulf Coast. He books a lot of live entertainment there."

She laughed. "Oh, really?"

Her skepticism was obvious.

"Really," Jack said. "You can check it out. It's called The Gulf Sunsetter, and I've helped my uncle book some pretty big names the last few years. It has both indoor and outdoor stages and can seat up to three hundred customers. I'd love to get you down there."

Jack pulled one of Tuck's business cards from his wallet. Behind the contact information, The Gulf Sunsetter was pictured. Cici's eyes widened.

"So, how did you hear about me?"

"The people across the street at The Blues City Café told me about you."

"I don't know. The Gulf Coast is a long way to go for a gig."

Jack nodded. "Yeah, it is, but maybe Uncle Tuck can contract you for a series of appearances during the summer. He still has a lot of open dates, and we can probably find you some place reasonable to stay. We have some rental property in the area."

Cici grinned. "Do you come with the package, cutie?"

Jack felt his face flush. "Uh, no. I have a girlfriend."

Cici's grin broke. She emptied the glass and set it back on the table. "That's too bad. You could have closed the deal with that one."

"What about Perry?" Jack asked.

"Like I said, he's my business manager and sometimes plays bass with the band. But now that you mentioned it, we do need him to be part of the deal if you're really serious."

Jack glanced over at Perry who was still sitting and watching his every move.

"Let me get with my uncle and see what kind of package he can offer. I'll send you something by the end of next week."

Cici's eyes were glassy from too much drink. She reached across the table and pinched Jack's cheek. "See if he'll throw you in, too."

It was nearly 10:00 p.m. when Jack finished shopping at the Walmart in Clarksdale, and the car was filled with bags of groceries, a new coffee maker, a set of cookware and various household items. With the lack of sleep from the night before, he was almost persuaded to drive back to the farmhouse, but it was more tempting to head over to Messenger's.

That was a juke joint over in the New World neighborhood. It was on Fourth Street between Sunflower and Yazoo Streets. One of the oldest Blues clubs in town, Jack had heard Cici mention it several times when she talked about Clarksdale. Clarksdale was where it all began, where Jimmy Johnson sold his soul to the devil at the junction of Highways 61 and 49. Cici said no one was out of place at Messenger's.

The cashier at Walmart told him to drive up East Tallahatchie Street to Fourth and take a left over the old Yazoo and Mississippi Valley Railroad. Messenger's was on the rights before you got to Sunflower Street. He passed several battered Illinois Central boxcars on the rusty railroad siding along East Tallahatchie Street, and a block from the club, the street was lined with parked cars. This wasn't surprising, even on a Monday night, because posters were tacked to every pole in town advertising the return of Cici Cannon. She was performing for the first time since her accident.

Jack walked back up Fourth Street, where there came the gentle cooing of roosted pigeons in an old church tower. He arrived, to find people standing around outside and the sounds of an electric guitar vibrated through the windows. A young couple sitting on a bench outside the door smiled as he slipped inside. Standing near the back wall, he surveyed the club from behind his wraparound sunglasses. The aroma of something fried struck him, and having eaten nothing since lunch, he quickly ordered a sandwich and beer from a passing waitress.

The men at the pool tables bent with studied concentration, their faces glistening under the low-hanging lights. The bar was packed with people sitting on stools and standing between them. His eyes roamed around the room, searching for familiar faces. There were people in dress shirts with ties and people in jeans and T-shirts wearing ball caps, and construction workers in bib overalls. This was no doubt a genuine juke joint and a real home of the Blues.

As the group on stage did an instrumental version of "Bone Orchard Blues," Jack glanced at his watch. If Cici was the main attraction tonight, she should have already been on. Satisfied there was no one there he knew, he began making his way through the crowd to the bar. The woman there smiled.

"What can I get you?" she asked.

"A Miller," he said.

She was back in seconds with a long-neck of Miller Highlife. Jack put a five on the bar.

"I thought Cici Cannon was performing here tonight," he said.

"I'm sorry," the bartender said. "We announced it earlier. Cici called this afternoon and said she just wasn't quite up to it yet. She's still not doing well since that wreck, you know?"

His disappointment must have shown, because the woman gave him something halfway between a grin and a grimace. "I hope you didn't drive too far," she said. "We have people who drove all the way from Memphis to hear her tonight."

Jack shook his head. "No, not too far."

"We normally don't even have live bands till the weekend, but she wanted to start with a small crowd. She's just not doing real good. Maybe you can catch her this weekend."

"Thanks," he said.

Jack sipped his beer, but when he lowered the bottle, he spotted a familiar face. Looking directly at him from the far end of the bar was Cleve Thomas, the lathe operator from down at the factory. Behind him was Doritoe

Jackson, Clyde's nephew. Jack was busted, but hoped they hadn't heard him ask about Cici. He turned and put his back to the bar. It was time to go. Weaving his way toward the door, he had nearly reached safety when he heard a woman's voice calling from behind.

"Sir. Hello?"

He froze mid-stride and slowly turned.

"Your sandwich and beer, sir," the waitress said.

Jack breathed a sigh of relief.

"Oh," the waitress said. "I see you already have a beer."

"That's okay," Jack said, glancing over her shoulder. He'd lost sight of Cleve and Doritoe. Pulling a ten from his wallet, he gave it to the waitress.

"Will that cover it?"

"Sure," she said.

"Keep the beer," he said.

He took the sandwich and went out the door. The drive back to Tallahatchie wasn't that long, but Jack's mind was a jumble of thought and exhaustion. The self-doubt clawed at him. By coming here he might only make matters worse. If only he had been this cautious back in Memphis.

Within a week he had contacted Cici with an offer and received a verbal agreement. Perry, though, was dead-set against it, and Jack decided another trip to Memphis was needed. He picked up Cici at her apartment and drove across town. They were on their way to meet Perry for a late breakfast and hopefully to get his buy-in.

"Stop. Stop," she shouted. She was looking back at the intersection they'd just passed.

"What is it?" he asked.

"There's a store back there I want to go in."

"Store?"

"Come on," she said. "Turn around and go back."

Jack spun the steering wheel, and did a U-turn across five lanes with the rental car. Cici braced herself and stared wide-eyed out the back window.

"Damn! I hope a cop didn't see us do that," she said.

"You said turn around, didn't you?"

"You're the craziest dude I've met lately," she said, laughing.

A moment later they stopped at the intersection.

"Over there," she said, pointing at a bright yellow sign with red lettering. "That Goodwill thrift store."

"What the heck do you want to go there for?" Jack asked. "I thought we were going to meet Perry for breakfast."

Scrunching down in her seat, Cici folded her arms and pouted.

"Okay," he said. "We'll stop for a minute, but we're supposed to meet Perry in a half hour."

Sitting up, she smiled and leaned across the seat, giving him a kiss on the cheek.

"Hell, if I'd known it meant that much to you, I wouldn't have argued."

Lines of fluorescent lights burned bright inside, while a manager rolled the sleeves of his white shirt and cleaned up the litter out front. Jack parked and watched while the man righted a white trash receptacle and replaced its domed top. With that done, he picked up several empty wine bottles and fast food wrappers. Cici got out, and Jack followed her inside.

"Every August before school started my Auntie—Aunt Netta's her name—she'd gather up all us kids, me and my cousins, and drive up here in her car. There was so many of us, the little ones sat in the big ones' laps, or on the floorboard, and even up in the back window. Anyway, she'd take us and drive all the way up here to Memphis to a Goodwill Store just like this one, and she'd buy us our school clothes, and pencils and tablets."

Cici picked up a big Caribbean-style straw hat and put it on, pirouetted and found a mirror on a nearby column. As she adjusted the hat, she looked at Jack in the mirror, standing behind her.

"Aunt Netta would promise us, if we were good, she would buy us ice cream. She always stopped at the Dairy Freeze on South Third and bought all us kids an ice cream cone—'cause nobody was bad when real ice cream was on the line."

She turned and looked over the rack of hats.

"Here, try this one," she said, putting a floppy wool fedora on Jack's head. "And these." She pulled a pair of black sunglasses from a rack and pushed them on his face. While he looked into the mirror, she found a pair of sunglasses for herself.

"What do you think?" she asked, standing beside him as they stared into the mirror. "I used to wear a hat like this when Aunt Netta took us to picnic on the pier up at Moon Lake."

"Uhhh, you look good, but I look like John Belushi," he said.

She laughed. "Oh, don't be that way. You're prettier than him."

After meeting with Perry that morning, they were elated. He had agreed to the contract, and Cici wanted to show Jack around Memphis. First she made him drive back downtown to the old Stax Recording Studio, then past Sun Records—places that birthed the likes of Booker T & The MG's, Elvis, and so many other big-name artists. That, of course, precipitated the requisite drive out to Graceland, where they stared up at the house Elvis had bought for his mama. Later they ended up at a place called The Arcade where Cici sipped a lemon-lime something-or-other that she said went with her hat.

"I come here a lot," she said. "They have great drinks and the best burgers in town."

"You have a lot of confidence," Jack said. "You seem to pretty much know what you want wherever you go, don't you?"

"You think I'm confident, huh?"

"It's pretty obvious. You have your world under control."

She laughed.

"What?" he said.

"Boy, you are *so* wrong."

"Why do you say that?"

"Because confidence is the one thing I don't have. Since Perry helped me get my recording contract all I've heard from people is how I'm just a mimic, or that I'm too young and too cute to be a real Blues singer. I heard one idiot even said I wasn't black enough to be a real Blues singer—said I should stick to pop music. And the best one is the guy who wrote in the paper that I wasn't robust enough. Now, you tell me, what the hell is robust?"

Jack laughed. "Maybe they want the big mama type?"

"Well, they're gonna have to wait a few more years for that," she said.

They sat watching the traffic.

"Don't you think that's just jealous people talking?" Jack asked.

"Some of it, maybe, but that newspaper article said I haven't paid my dues, but I *have*, and they weren't cheap. You see, I come from South Louisiana. My daddy went off to Vietnam leaving my mama with all us kids. We were too young to realize what was happening till she got that visit from the Army people telling us Daddy got killed.

"I remember it like yesterday—those big tall men in their uniforms coming to our little old shack of a house down yonder. They parked their green car in the yard—didn't have a drive, just a dirt yard with some chickens scratching around. And when Mama saw them, she knew right away what had happened. She broke down crying right there on the porch. Ended up she didn't have enough money to take care of all us kids. I was the youngest so she sent me up to Tallahatchie to stay with her sister."

Cici looked over at Jack. "I was named after Mama. They called her Mama Cici, and I was Little Cici. I could tell you a lot more, but I'm not trying to sound pitiful or like I'm unhappy, but I know what it's like to feel the blues. I know. When I knew I could never sit in my daddy's lap again…"

Cici paused and wiped away a tear.

"I have this feeling like there's a big hole in my life, and it started somewhere down there in South Louisiana."

"Where are all your brothers and sisters now?"

Cici shrugged. "I don't know. We scattered like leaves in a wind. I haven't heard from any of them since I moved to Tallahatchie to live with Aunt Netta."

They sat in silence for a long time, and later when they were driving around town, she spotted a place in south Memphis called The Rack. It was a pool hall, and she wanted to stop and play a few games. Inside they found college kids in Nikes, baggy-pant gang members and bikers in do-rags. It seemed a place where trouble was inevitable, but after a while Jack began to relax as he dominated Cici in game after game of eight-ball. Outside, the sun had set and neon signs were flickering to life up and down Lamar Avenue when she again sent the eight-ball careening too soon into a corner pocket.

"This just isn't your game," Jack said.

"So?" she replied, putting her fist on her hip and sticking her chin out at him. "It's not like I hung out in pool halls when I was a kid."

"I'm glad to hear that."

She shrugged. "Not that I could have if I'd wanted to. My auntie made me toe the line. We went to church every Sunday, and she didn't put up with no nonsense. Besides, other than a little drinking and gambling, there wasn't much trouble a person could get into around Tallahatchie."

"I'd like to go down there sometime."

She wrinkled her brow and gave him a sour grin. "Tallahatchie ain't nothing but a bunch of old people and run-down houses. Besides, my auntie moved up to Clarksdale."

Jack laughed. "Cici the cynic. What about those picnics you talked about at Moon Lake?"

"Well, that's not really Tallahatchie," she said. "Moon Lake's up past Clarksdale. That would be the place to visit."

"Okay," he said.

The next morning Jack departed Memphis with the signed contract in hand. Cici and Perry had agreed to a series of appearances over an eight-week period beginning in May.

Jack saw the roadside sign for the first that night as he drove back from Clarksdale. It stood on the shoulder of the road as he approached the Tallahatchie town limit. One of those locally produced signs, it was nicely done with blue and white paint that said, "Welcome to Tallahatchie, Home of Cici Cannon." The wooden sign flashed past in the headlights, and was gone, and later Jack found he couldn't get it out of his mind. She may not have claimed this little town, but it had claimed her. Despite his exhaustion, Jack's thoughts of Cici burdened him even as he turned off the bedside lamp and fell into an exhausted sleep.

It seemed as if time had stood still for only a moment when Jack rolled over and stared at a blinding streak of morning sunlight coming through dusty venetian blinds. Squinting, he rubbed his eyes. An uneasy feeling of disorientation gripped him as he realized he was waking in a strange place, and he fought to clear his head. He glanced at the alarm clock beside the bed, and it struck him with sudden terror—he'd overslept.

Throwing the blanket away, Jack leapt from the bed, stumbled over the jumble of unpacked boxes and fell to the floor. Sitting up, he paused. He was unhurt. He shook his head as he looked back again at the alarm clock. It sat in smug silence. It was nearly 8:30, and he was already an hour and a half late his second day on the job.

CHAPTER 4

NICKELS

J ACK CONSIDERED PARKING AT THE far end of the lot and walk-ing around to the truck dock that morning, but that would fool no one. He was late for work, and there was nothing to do but meet them head on with a good alibi. He parked at the front door of the office where a rusting sign said "Operations Manager." Trotting up the steps, he forced a canned smile and walked through the front entrance as if arriving exactly as he had intended—except today, the door to the receptionist's office was open. He tried to cruise on by, but it didn't work.

"It's okay, Jack," Doris Ann called out.

Stopping, he went back and peeked inside her door.

"What's okay?"

"That you're late," she said. "Mr. Nickels isn't here yet."

She had him pegged, but he wasn't giving up that easily.

"I was unpacking and trying to get settled into my new place," he said. "Was I supposed to be punching someone's time clock?"

"Well, Mr. Henry was going to introduce you to the employees this morning, since he knows Mr. Nickels probably won't. When you didn't show up, Henry figured you must have quit."

"Sorry to disappoint him."

"Henry is one of the good guys," Doris Ann said. "I'm sure he'll be tickled to see you."

She grinned and continued chewing what was apparently her trademark wad of pink bubblegum. Making his way onto the factory floor, Jack spotted Henry. Henry Smith was the man he needed to get to know first. Henry was the one they said passed out the daily work orders. He was the one who ran things, and he was also the one the employees seemed to respect most. At lunch the previous day, when anyone made a comment, they inevitably glanced at Henry, seemingly to get his approval.

Jack made his way across the production area to where Henry and the two millwrights were once again up to their elbows in sawdust and grease—this time inside a drill press. Matt Oliver gave him a cursory smile. Henry glanced up then continued working. JT, who was kneeling under the machine, ignored him altogether. The men were already sweating as they strained to loosen a series of bolts holding a plate inside the machine.

"Can I help?" Jack asked.

Without looking up, Henry said, "Give me a ratchet and a three-eighths deep socket hex."

Jack reached into the toolbox sitting beside Henry. Retrieving the ratchet, he found the socket and pushed them together. He handed it to Henry who immediately set it atop the machine.

"Do you need a three-eighths box-end for the other side?" Jack asked.

Henry wiped some sawdust from his glasses with his shirtsleeve.

"Yeah," he said. "Give it to JT under there."

It was his first test. Albeit a small one, it was obvious. Henry had intentionally asked him to get the tools when he was within arm's reach of them himself. The men continued straining for several more minutes, until Henry stood upright.

"All right then," he said. "Now, clean that gunk out of there and replace the guides on the plate. When you get done with that, we'll pull the collar down and put the new bushings in."

He turned to Jack. "Morning."

"Good morning," Jack answered.

Henry finished wiping the sawdust and grease from his hands with a red shop-rag.

"It would help a lot if you went back yonder to the paint shed and checked on Dewayne Pritchert and the new guy."

"Dewayne?" Jack said. "Is that the guy Clyde said was butchering a pig in his trailer yesterday?"

"That's him," Matt Oliver said.

"I'd do it myself," Henry said, "but this busted press is bottle-necking the workflow. I had them call in a new employee yesterday evening. He reported this morning, and no one but Dewayne has been with him all morning."

"Scary, ain't it?" Matt Oliver said, bobbing his eyebrows.

Henry explained how Arlis McCallister had been acting even nuttier, saying the acetone and other chemicals had probably gotten the few brain cells he had left. He moved him to the upholstery department, and hired the new guy, a young Choctaw Indian named Mooreman Beaver. Henry also ordered some less toxic coatings, including a new water-based paint the vendor had delivered that morning. The vendor's rep had come in at 7:00 to demonstrate the mixing and application processes to Dewayne and the new man, but Henry had been unable to get back with them since the rep departed.

"What happened to the other new guy," Jack asked, "the boy I met yesterday, Paul?"

"Little chicken-shit just up and quit," JT said as he crawled from beneath the press.

"Didn't give much of a reason," Henry said. "When he punched out yesterday, he just said he didn't think the furniture business was his thing."

"Smart kid," Matt Oliver said.

"I'll go check on Dewayne and the other guy," Jack said.

As he made his way toward the paint shed, Jack noticed Tommy Grey standing in the upholstery department. Grey had his arms folded, watching him. Gossips like Doris Ann didn't normally sway his opinion, but Jack figured she was right about this one. Just the way Grey stood watching him said enough. He hadn't even bothered to introduce himself. She was probably right. Grey was Richard Nickels's lackey.

When Jack reached the paint shop, Dewayne and his new protégé, Mr. Beaver, were lounging on some canisters. He introduced himself, but Dewayne seemed engrossed with reading the instructions on a drum label. He didn't look up and barely nodded. The new man, who was dark-skinned, with squinty eyes and straight black hair, jumped to his feet and extended his hand.

"Mm-m-my nu-nu-name is Mo-mo-mo-moor-ma-man Bu-bu-Beaver," he said.

"Pleased to meet you, Mister Beaver. Jack Hartman."

Moorman Beaver's agonizing stutter and enigmatic name had no doubt brought him considerable grief during his life. Jack turned back to Dewayne, who was wearing a dated Marilyn Manson T-shirt and still studying the canister label with stern-faced concentration. Squinting at the label, Dewayne scratched his head. Jack waited patiently until Dewayne finally looked up at him.

"Oh, hey," Dewayne said with a grimace. "That vendor fella had me purty confused about this new water-based paint."

"How's that?" Jack asked.

"Well, he kept using them sixty-four-dollar words like viscosity, componements and proportionals, and a bunch of others I already forgot, but anyway, I think I got it now."

Dewayne, before he opened his mouth, appeared almost ruggedly handsome, but when he spoke, it was obvious he could take dementia to new and unexplored depths. His brain was no doubt an ocean trough shrouded in darkness wherein lay yet undiscovered mysteries of neuro-transmitter malfunction.

"You sure you got it?" Jack asked.

"Don't worry. I watched him, and I know what I'm doing here. Me and my little Indian buddy there'll have a batch whipped up in no time."

He picked up a scoop and began shoveling powder from a bag into a mixer tank. Tight-lipped, his head was cocked jauntily to one side as if to demonstrate his confidence and that he had matters well in hand.

"Where are your OSHA records?"

"My what?" Dewayne paused and looked at Jack, the scoop still in his hand as the last of the powder sifted into the tank.

"Your formulations, Material Safety Data Sheets, CPDS forms, your product accounting documentation—all that stuff, where is it?"

"I keep what I need right here," Dewayne said, pointing to the side of his head.

Jack shook his head. He should have expected as much, but with all the EPA and OSHA standards that had to be met, there had to be records somewhere, probably over in the floor office.

Dewayne smiled. "Don't worry. Mr. Nickels has us covered. He has the OSHA man in his hip pocket. When he comes in town, he takes him to play golf at that fancy country club over in Charleston."

He leveled off another scoop of the chemical with an ungloved hand and poured it into the mixer.

"Yeah, you really gotta know your shit with this stuff, else you can make a mess. That's why I take my time. See, an expert knows when to go slow and when to go fast. Hand me that bag over yonder, Momo."

Beaver picked up another bag and set it atop a drum. Dewayne flipped out a blade, slit the bag open and dumped it into the mixer. The blade was back in his pocket in the blink of an eye.

"Just gotta know what you're doing. That's all there is to it."

He tossed the empty bag aside while Jack used his hand to fan the cloud of dust away from his face.

"All we need now is the H-Twenty, and we'll be ready to go," he said.

"The H-Twenty?" Jack said. He cast a quick glance around the shed at the labels on the other drums. Momo stood by in grim silence, but also seemed clueless.

"Yeah, the H-Twenty," Dewayne said.

Jack knew little about mixing paint, and he'd never heard of this chemical. "Where do you keep it?" he asked.

Dewayne turned to point at something but stopped and looked back. He wore a snaggle-toothed grin, like he thought Jack might be pulling his leg. "Whatta ya mean, 'where do I keep it?' "

Jack shrugged. "I mean, where do you keep the stuff?"

Dewayne looked out the doorway, then back at Jack again. "You really don't know what H-Twenty is, do you?" he said.

"Well hell, I reckon not," Jack replied. "Why don't you enlighten me?"

Dewayne stuck the side of his jaw out at him and shut one eye. "Come on now. Don't tell me a big-shot like you don't know what H-Twenty is."

Jack shook his head. "Reckon not."

"Shiiuut, how come they don't teach y'all nothin' useful at them fancy colleges?"

He winked at Momo and walked over to the corner where he picked up a water hose. "H-Twenty," he said, "is the scientific name for water. Hell, even I know that."

"Oh," Jack said. "Yeah, H, ugh... you know, I do remember them teaching us something like that. I should have paid closer attention in chemistry class."

"I reckon so. You gotta know the names of all your componements when you're in this kind of business, and they all got special names, and you gotta use the right proportionals too, else your coating'll get too runny or too thick. That's what they call viscosity. Yeah, you can mess up in a hurry if you don't know what you're doing."

"You know, Dewayne, it's a good thing we have you back here," Jack said.

Dewayne maintained his grim countenance while nodding confidently. "Yeah, I know," he said.

A moment later there came an unintelligible garble over the intercom. It was a woman's voice.

"You understand that?" Jack asked.

Dewayne shook his head. "Nah, but it usually means somebody's in deep shit."

"Why is that?"

"That was Doris Ann's voice, and the only time she uses that old intercom is when Mr. Nickels wants somebody in his office."

Jack shook his head as he walked back across the production floor. Henry Smith was in the glass-walled floor office on the phone. Jack headed that way, and Henry hung up as he entered the office.

"Everything okay back in the paint shed?" Henry asked.

"As far as I can tell. That Dewayne—he's kind of special, isn't he?"

"Real special," Henry said. "How about the new man, reckon he's got any sense?"

Jack shrugged. "Hard to tell. Stutters like hell, and he didn't say much."

Henry smiled. "Oh well, I'll check on them again in a few minutes. Right now, you get to meet the big man we all look up to around here. That was Mr. Nickels on the phone, and he wants to see you in his office, ASAP."

Jack turned and started for the door, but paused and looked back. "Anything I need to know before I meet him?"

Henry pressed his lips together as he thought for a moment. "There's not much I can say that'll help."

"What?"

"Never mind," he said.

Henry's words ran through Jack's mind as he tapped on the receptionist's door. "*There's not much I can say that'll help,*" wasn't exactly an encouraging statement.

Doris Ann looked up and smiled. "Come on in."

She picked up the phone and punched an extension. "Mr. Hartman is here, sir. Yes, sir."

She hung up. "He said to take a seat, and he'll be with you in a minute."

Jack walked over to a chair beside the credenza where he noticed a fresh spray of flowers between the Elvis and Princess Di photos. The flowers were still in the cellophane wrapper with a red Winn-Dixie sticker.

"So, how do you like it so far?" she asked.

Jack nodded. "It's interesting."

"Have you met many of the people yet?"

"Yeah," Jack said. "Clyde, of course, and Henry, Matt Oliver, JT, and oh yeah, Dewayne, and the new guy, Mooreman Beaver."

"That Dewayne is a doofus," Doris Ann said, "but Matt Oliver is kind of interesting. He makes wood sculptures—carves them. It's his hobby, you know? He has several pieces on display down in Jackson at the Capitol Building."

"Really?" Jack said.

"Really. Now, JT, that boy is just a raving sports nut. Football, baseball, stock car racing, you name it, JT's a fan. And he just loves Dewey Hargrove, thinks he's the best stock car driver ever."

"Yeah," Jack said. "I noticed he's worn a Dewey Hargrove cap and T-shirt two days in a row."

"He'd wear one every day if Janine could keep them washed."

"What about you?" Jack asked.

Doris Ann dropped her head and affected a coy smile, but it didn't work. Shyness didn't fit her persona.

"Oh, I like to shop a little, go to the lake sometimes, and we all go up to the casinos at Tunica every other pay-day—me, JT, Matt Oliver, Dewayne and some others. It's kind of fun. We drink a little, play craps, you know? You ought to go with us sometime."

Jack gave her a non-committal smile. It sounded like a monumentally bad idea for a manager to do something like that with his employees.

"So, did you find a place to live?" Doris Ann asked.

They talked for a long while, but after nearly a half-hour Jack began wondering if Nickels had forgotten him. The phone warbled, and Doris Ann picked up.

"Yes, sir."

"Mr. Nickels said you can come in now."

Jack pushed the door open and stepped into the Factory Manager's office. Nickels was sitting in a high-backed leather chair behind a huge mahogany desk, his face aglow from the computer monitor he was studying. He said nothing for at least a minute, while Jack shifted his weight from foot to foot and gazed around the room. The walls were lined with plaques and certificates that said things like: Lowest Facility Labor Costs FY-89, Highest Corporate Safety Rate 3rd Quarter FY-91, Lowest Capital Expenditures FY-93. These were his campaign ribbons—his successes—the things that said, *"This is who I am."*

A framed print of Vince Lombardi hung on the wall behind his chair, and there was another of the regional office in Tupelo hanging above a credenza on the other wall. A single 1989 bowling trophy stood on the credenza. This was it—his domain, and Jack had been called here to stand in his presence. When he was done studying the computer screen, Nickels shoved his chair back, stood and walked around the desk, hitching up his trousers.

Nickels, was probably in his late forties, and at best five-foot-four. Jack found himself subconsciously trying to bend his knees, but not enough that it would be noticed.

"Richard Nickels," he said, extending his hand. "So, what do you think about my factory so far?"

Jack started to speak, but Nickels interrupted. "Tell you what, let's take a tour of the production area. What do you say?"

Nickels stepped into the outer office. "Hold my calls, Doris. I'm taking young Mr. Hartman for a tour."

As they walked down the hallway, Nickels talked without looking back. "So, how does it feel to be second in command over an operation this size?"

He apparently hadn't read Jack's résumé. After a brief stint with the Army in Iraq, Jack had run Hartman Manufacturing's Miami plant for almost a year, where he employed at least triple the number of employees that were here. He decided to humor him anyway.

"There's a lot of responsibility," he answered.

Nickels didn't seem to hear him as they entered the production area.

"My family's factory in Brooklyn was bought out by Fernwood in the early nineties, but the company made me move down here to whip this place back in shape. Most of the employees are fuck-offs, so I have a hell of a time staying in the black, but I do the best I can."

Jack thought back to his conversation with Fernwood's CEO after accepting the job. He told Jack that they needed a man with his experience—a man who could analyze the processes and improve productivity.

"The people at the home office seem to think the problem has more to do with the processes and workflow," Jack said.

Nickels stopped and turned to face him. "And who the fuck do you think runs the processes and the workflow?"

"Management," Jack said.

"Wrong! These people do," Nickels said, sweeping his arm in a wide arc. "We train them, and we give them the processes and the work. They simply have to do it, but they would rather bitch and whine than do an honest day's work."

Nickels spotted Henry, standing with JT and Matt Oliver at the newly repaired drill press. With it up and running now, Cleve Thomas was using the multi-spindled press to drill mounts for a table top. Henry had a gauge measuring the holes and spacing. JT and Matt Oliver looked on. As Nickels approached, Henry looked up.

"Why is it that every time I come out here three or four of you are standing around doing nothing?" Nickels shouted. The veins on his forehead were suddenly swollen and he was red-faced.

"We just got this machine going again, and I was checking the—"

"And it takes three of you to check it?" Nickels shouted.

JT and Matt Oliver, with grease and sawdust up to their elbows, were still sweating from their work, but they remained silent.

Henry tried again. "We just—"

"You just, my ass. I've told you a hundred times, if nothing is broken, make them PM the machines that aren't being used."

Henry's lips were pressed tightly together, and he avoided eye contact with Nickels as he stared straight ahead.

"Yes, sir," he said in a grinding voice.

Nickels wheeled about, nearly running over Jack as he took off in another direction. Jack glanced back. Matt Oliver was smiling as he saluted Nickels's back. JT made a face like a school kid mocking his teacher. Henry simply shook his head.

Jack could sense it. The employees saw Nickels as a buffoon—not in the sense that he was a clown, but more in the vein of a third-world dictator, whom despite his chest full of phony medals and gold-braided sleeves, everyone feared and hated. It was becoming evident that "Plant Manager" wasn't simply a job for Nickels—it was a position and a title, and you respected it or else paid a price.

Jack followed a few steps behind him as he charged across the production floor.

"You see," Nickels called over his shoulder. "That's exactly what I'm talking about. You want to talk processes? Well, here's a damned simple one: You drain the swamp, find the stumps, and you get rid of them. That's what I do. It's a simple fact. People are lazy sonsofbitches, most of them—especially the ones down here in the South. All you have to do is take them out of their comfort-zone, put some heat on their asses, and the stumps will show up pretty quick. Then all you do is fire them."

He had heard these same words of wisdom before from his father, and Jack always imagined the "drain-the-swamp" scenario was one where the employees scrambled about in little motor boats avoiding the emerging stumps as the water level dropped. When someone's boat inevitably hung on a stump, management fixed the problem. They cranked a chainsaw, waded out to the stump and promptly sawed the employee in half. Removing the stump never seemed to occur to them, and they never fixed the real problems, because intimidation always proved effective in the short term. The employees worked harder to avoid the stumps.

"Have you ever read about Vince Lombardi?" Nickels asked, calmer now. "That man knew how to rip people's asses and get results. He made them fight for their jobs."

"I thought he got results because his people respected him," Jack said.

"That's right, you put fear in them and they will respect you," Nickels answered.

"I don't mean to be argumentative, sir, but there's a big difference between intimidating people and gaining their respect. I have an uncle who was platoon leader in Vietnam, and he said you can get men to do almost anything, but you can't push them. You have to lead them."

"This isn't the army, and don't come in here lecturing me on leadership. I've forgotten more of that crap than you'll ever know, and I can tell you it's not a bunch of wishy-washy feel-good shit. It's about getting results. I create competition between departments and let the fighters rise to the top."

"Lombardi created competition during practice," Jack said. "Creating it out here on the production floor is the same as creating it during a game. Hell, if they're fighting one another—it's no wonder productivity is down."

Nickels pursed his lips and shook his head as if he was resigned to Jack's ignorance. "You've got a lot to learn about being a real leader, sonny boy."

Nickels led him back into the upholstery department. "Come over here and let me introduce you to a man who knows a little something about running a factory. You work with this man, and you'll find he's the best supervisor you have."

"Hey, Tommy," Nickels said, "Say hello to your new boss."

Jack extended his hand. "Jack Hartman."

Grey, flat-lipped and unsmiling, extended his hand as if it were an unavoidable formality. He turned to Nickels. "Yeah, I've seen him wandering around."

Jack eyed him carefully. Grey seemed sarcastically cocky for someone who was supposed to be his subordinate.

"Where did you say you were from?" Nickels asked.

Jack gave Grey a "*don't-fuck-with-me*" look, before slowly turning to Nickels. "I haven't said, but I'm from Alabama."

"What'd you do before you came to work here?" Grey asked.

"I sold computerized woodworking machinery to furniture factories."

Nickels laughed. "Really? Well, you'll find there's a lot more to actually running a factory than selling machines."

Grey gave a high-pitched laugh, as if it were actually funny. Nickels raised his eyebrows, seemingly encouraged by the laughter. "Yeah, maybe you can hook up a computer to some of these old relics around here and make them run better."

Grey let out a whoop as if it were the funniest thing he'd ever heard. Nickels obviously loved Grey's canned laughter, and the harder Grey laughed the more bullshit he came up with. They talked and laughed for another fifteen minutes, before Nickels finished. He'd made it clear in so many words that Tommy Grey was his boy.

"I've got an appointment for lunch with a client," Nickels said. "Jack, you just keep wandering around out here. If you have any questions, ask Tommy. Maybe you can pick up on some of what's going on." His sarcasm was thinly masked, as he slapped Grey on the back and turned back toward the office.

When Jack reached the back breakroom that day Henry was introducing Mooreman Beaver to the others. Momo was stuttering miserably. After the introduction the men began opening their lunches.

"So what'd you do before you came to work here?" JT asked.

Momo turned up his brown lunch bag and emptied it on the table—one sandwich. "I ca-ca-caddied," he said. "They wo-wo-wo-wouldn't le-le-let me d-d-do an-anyth-th-thing else, b-b-because I st-st-stutt-stutter."

Cleve and Doritoe scooted their chairs closer, and even Clyde had come in to meet the new man.

"You did what?" Doritoe said.

"I ca-ca-caddied at th-the Du-Du-Dancing Ra-Rabbit," Momo said.

Doritoe got a sour look on his face, like he thought Momo might be poking fun at him. "What the fuck do that mean?"

"He ain't pulling your leg," Henry said. "It's a golf club down at the Silver Star Casino near Philadelphia, Mississippi. It's owned by the Choctaw Indians, and it's called the Dancing Rabbit."

Henry's explanation seemed to disarm Doritoe. He laughed and looked over at Momo. "Man, you Indian boys got that animal name shit going on, don't you? If that don't beat all—Beavers and Dancing Rabbits, I ain't never heard so much silly shit."

Momo batted his eyes, almost shyly, but his reply was quick and the others were still laughing when he said, "A-a-at le-le-least I-I'm no-not na-na-named after a ca-ca-corn chip."

Doritoe sprang to his feet and kicked back his chair.

"You a smart muthafucka. You know that? Get your little Indian ass up and let's see who..."

Without leaving his chair, Clyde caught Doritoe by the back of his shirt and jerked him backward.

"You best pick up your chair and sit down, boy, before you get hurt."

"You gonna let him get away with that shit, Uncle Clyde? He called me—"

"You started it. Now, sit down and shut up before I crack a knot on your head."

Momo had never moved, except for dropping one arm from the table. Jack wondered if anyone else had noticed. Was he bracing himself to jump up, or was he reaching for a weapon—a knife or perhaps even a gun? Momo didn't take his eyes off Doritoe, as he casually picked up his sandwich and began eating. Momo was small, almost frail looking, but somehow it seemed the younger and more muscular Doritoe would have come out on the short end of a run-in with him.

When the five-minute bell rang, the men filed out to the truck dock for a quick smoke. Henry motioned Jack down toward the end of the dock, away from the others.

"How did your meeting go with Nickels?" he asked.

Jack shrugged. "I was hired to help this guy, but he acts like he hates me."

"That's because he didn't hire you."

"Yeah, I thought it was odd that he didn't participate in the interview. Didn't he have any say at all?"

"He didn't even know the home office hired you, until he got your employment papers."

"Yeah?"

"They needed someone to come here and fix this place, but I think there's more to it than meets the eye. I believe Nickels might be threatening a lawsuit if they fire him. They're hoping you can come in and show him how to get things running right again."

"It does seem strange," Jack said, "but—"

"If you want to get on his good side, start going to lunch with him and laugh like Grey does at his jokes. I was watching you and Grey talking with him over there in the upholstery shop. Tommy doesn't have sense enough to pour piss out of a boot, but he laughs his ass off at Nickels's jokes. You hardly cracked a smile."

"He's not funny. Why can't they fire his ass?"

"My guess is he's under some kind of protective contract clause from when they bought out his family's factory."

Henry finished his cigarette. "You can do like most of us and simply wag your tail enough to keep him at bay, or you can make your life miserable."

"I suppose I'm destined for misery," Jack said. "I'd rather get this factory back in the black, and save these folks' jobs than kiss his little ass."

Henry shrugged. "So what made you leave Alabama to come up here to work?"

"I don't know," Jack said. "Stupidity, I suppose."

Henry studied him through his sweat-streaked glasses. "You regret coming here?" he asked.

"I'm not sure," Jack said.

Henry was helping Matt Oliver and JT repair another lathe, and asked Jack to check on Dewayne and Momo again. They said during lunch that there was a pump frozen back in the paint shed. Jack saw the problem as soon as he arrived. Dewayne had made a batch of undercoat and added too much hardener. Problem was he had let it sit through lunch, and the whole outfit was ruined—pump, hoses, and sprayers.

Jack began asking Dewayne how it happened, but the "chief paint-sniffer," as Matt Oliver called him, thought he was about to be fired and began blaming it first on the new coating then on Momo, until he somehow got on the subject of his Toyota.

"You know they ruin't my Toyota, too, don't ya?"

"Who did?" Jack asked.

It was difficult to make connections between events as Dewayne saw them, but he somehow put destroying the paint equipment and the damage to his Toyota in the same genre of cause and effect. As best as Jack could determine, they were only related inasmuch as Dewayne was directly involved in the demise of both machines.

"Them damned car people that traded me for the Firebird, that's who," he said.

"Really?" Jack said. "I heard they let you out of the lease contract free and clear and gave you back your Toyota running better than when you traded it in."

"That's a damned lie JT's telling everybody. They didn't do no such a thing. They kept all the money I gave them on the head-end and messed up my car to boot."

Dewayne sat on a drum of acetone and lit a cigarette. There were no-smoking signs all over the plant along with flammable placards around the paint shed, but

Dewayne no doubt lived in the blissful oblivion of absolute ignorance.

"Don't you think it's a little dangerous, smoking in here?" Jack said, pointing to the nearest flammable sign. Momo stood by the door in monkish silence. They weren't spraying, and the ventilation fans were running, but Jack couldn't help but think what might happen if an errant spark ignited one of the many drums of chemicals lining the walls.

"Oh hell, don't pay that sign no mind. That's just for open flames," Dewayne said. "A cigarette don't hurt nothing 'cause it ain't a flame. Besides, I been smoking in here for years, so I figure if something was gonna blow up, it'a done it by now. See."

Holding the cigarette between his thumb and finger, he waved it around like a wand.

"Dewayne, do you know there's enough acetone in that drum you're sitting on to launch your ass the other side of the river levee?"

"I ain't trying to be disrespectful, boss, but you college guys think y'all know everything, but y'all really don't know nothin', except what you read in books. Did you know you can take a cigarette and drop it in the gas tank of a car, and it won't do nothin' but put it out?"

"Please tell me you haven't tried that," Jack said.

Jack looked around for Momo, but he'd disappeared.

"Sure as hell have," Dewayne said. "I showed a guy at the fillin' station one day, but he acted all goofy about it and took off even after it worked just fine. See, the gas just puts it out like water. Here, let me show you."

He jumped up and grabbed the cap on the acetone drum.

"No!" Jack screamed. "No," he said again, calmer now that Dewayne had paused. "Don't do that. Put the cigarette out, now, Dewayne, or I'm going to make an issue of this. You're not supposed to be smoking anywhere in the plant, except the designated areas."

"See, that's what I mean. You're getting all excited over nothing. That's why you know-it-alls cain't learn nothing 'cause you think you already got all the answers."

He ground the cigarette out on the top of the drum.

"Trust me on this one, Dewayne," Jack said. "If I catch you smoking again, I will take action."

Dewayne gave him a patronizing smile and shook his head. "Trust me—that's the same thing that fella at the car place said, but he stole the air scoop off my car. I found it in their dumpster, cut half-in-two."

"I thought they took off the old hood and put a new one on," Jack replied. "I heard they even repainted the entire car."

"Yeah, they painted right over my number '93' on the doors. Besides that, the air scoop cost me some big bucks, and I had to have it 'cause the motor was running hot."

Jack was certain that Dewayne's mind seldom hit on all eight cylinders, or in his case, what were probably four cylinders to begin with, but he tried to reason with him. "JT said they put a new water pump and thermostat on it, and that fixed the overheating. It hasn't been running hot since you got it back, has it?"

Dewayne got a faraway look in his eyes, as if he were concentrating on some emerging realization. "Uh, that's funny. Now that you mentioned it, I don't think it has."

"So, let's see," Jack said. "Your car has a brand new paint job, it's running better, and Miss April is happy now because she can see out the windshield. And you're not paying that three-fifty-a-month lease note on the Firebird, right?"

Dewayne absentmindedly lit another cigarette as he stared at the wall for several seconds. Jack pulled the cigarette from Dewayne's lips and ground it out on the floor, but as he turned to leave, Dewayne grunted and laughed. "You know, you must be one of them optimists," he said. "You just made me see the bright side of this whole thing."

Jack paused and turned, a safe distance outside the door—third-degree-burns-over-twenty-percent-of-his-body range, but a survivable distance if the whole damned shed went up like a Roman candle. This would be interesting, if for no reason other than it offered further insight into Dewayne's unique mind. He was grinning like a mule eating briars.

"What's that?" Jack asked.

"I can afford that bass boat I've been wantin' all these years."

The thought of Dewayne at the controls of a high-powered bass boat made Jack think about how Tuck had argued so adamantly against his coming here. Tuck said he'd forgotten the girl and all else when he was given a platoon of thirty draftees to lead in Nam. This wasn't Nam, but it was the first time in weeks Jack hadn't thought about Acey.

CHAPTER 5

BIG DOG'S BAR B Q SHACK

JACK SAT IN HIS OFFICE pondering the plight of his employees. If the gold-tinted windows of the Atlanta skyscrapers and the silver pyramid in Memphis represented the new South, the weathered gray shacks and house trailers around Tallahatchie represented remnants of the old. The town now existed mostly because it was where for eight hours each day the inhabitants of the county gathered in a homogeneous endeavor at the factory. They came to produce furniture that most of them couldn't afford even with their employee discounts. Yet they were looked down upon by Nickels and Grey.

Jack had come here to help Cici, but the employees at this factory needed him as well. While he was here, if there was one other thing he could do besides help Cici, Jack intended to save the factory and these people's jobs. He glanced up at the clock. It was nearly noon. The lunch bell rang, and when he went out to the production area, he found Clyde and Matt Oliver brushing the sawdust from their hair and washing their hands.

Most days they settled for the break room or the factory cafeteria, but occasionally they wanted something different, and there was only one restaurant in Tallahatchie. This was where Clyde and Matt Oliver were taking him today—Big Dog's Bar B Q Shack. "Not exactly a setting for corporate power luncheons," Matt Oliver explained, "but it has some pretty decent food."

Matt Oliver and Clyde had lunch at Big Dog's once or twice a month, dining on specialties that included fried fish, frog legs or a barbecued pork sandwich. The sandwich was laced with a hot sweet sauce *"that will make your tongue knock your brains out,"* they said. When the wind was right, the aroma of the simmering sauce drifted all the way to the factory a half mile down the road. The screen door popped shut behind them as Jack followed Clyde and Matt Oliver inside. A large black CD player with ghetto-blaster speakers sat on a shelf behind the cash register. It was pumping out enough Wilson Pickett to compete with the sizzling grease and clattering dishes.

A tall black man—Big Dog, no doubt—greeted them from behind a grill where he was turning burgers. He wore a white apron and a big white smile punctuated with a gold tooth. "Y'all come on in," he said. "I'll be with you in a minute."

Matt Oliver explained how Big Dog had started in a wooden shack with a 55-gallon drum cut and welded into a grill that sat beneath a shed roof. Things had improved since that humble beginning, and he now occupied one of the old store spaces on Main Street. Located in a section of the ancient redbrick building that ran the length of the block, the restaurant was between two vacant spaces with dusty plate glass windows. Although there were other tenants, Clyde said Big Dog's and the Laundromat were the only ones that stayed open all week, except of course on Sunday.

Lining the counter up front were several gallon jars with whole dill pickles the size of small submarines, pickled eggs appearing as white shadows in a purplish vinegar brine, and the one Matt Oliver said was his favorite, pickled pig's feet.

"There's something inherently sexy about pink pickled pig's feet, you know."

Jack laughed. "No doubt the sentiment of a truly sick mind," he said. He liked Matt Oliver's sense of humor, but it was his openness he liked most. He seemed like someone who could be trusted.

"During the week, Big Dog caters mostly to the people around town," Matt Oliver said, "but on the weekend they come from all over."

A few moments later Big Dog showed up at the table with a plate of appetizers: pickled okra, pig's feet, some pickled eggs, hot peppers, and a handful of saltines. "I see you brung somebody new," he said.

"This here is Mister Hartman," Clyde said. "He's our new Assistant Factory Manager."

Jack stood and extended his hand. "Pleased to meet you, sir."

"Likewise," Big Dog said.

After taking their orders, he quickly retreated to the grill, and it was only a matter of minutes before a young black man in a white apron returned with their lunch. While they ate, Jack looked about the room. Big Dog wasn't much on interior decorating, but he *was* original. Two tattered deer heads, their antlers dusty and strung with cobwebs, hung above the counter. The walls were graced with faded prints of ducks and geese in weathered wooden frames. And the centerpiece was a huge alligator gar, mounted on the back wall. It was every bit of eleven feet long, with a sagging belly and rows of needle-sharp teeth. Jack had seen gar before, but this was by far the biggest.

Matt Oliver chomped down on his catfish sandwich. Leastwise, according to him, it tasted like catfish, but he said if you didn't watch him, Big Dog would slip in a carp or drum from time to time.

"Don't matter none," Clyde said. "Big Dog is a fry-cook that's as good as they get. He can deep-fry an old shoe and make it taste good."

Clyde noticed Jack staring at the gar. "It come from the Tallahatchie River," he said, "out yonder by the bridge."

"No shit?" Jack said. "I didn't know there was anything that big in fresh water."

"Oh yeah," Clyde said. "They got that one right after a little colored boy, one of Odie Benjamin's kids, got his big toe bit off."

"He what?" Jack said.

"Yeah, him and a bunch of other kids was out there swimming under the bridge one Saturday afternoon. They said he went to screaming, and when he jumped out on the sandbar the end of his toe was bit plumb off. Big Dog took his deer rifle, and a bunch of the men from around town went out yonder, and they commenced to shootin' and snaggin' every gar they saw.

"'Course, that old river's so muddy, they couldn't tell much what they done, except that one there floated up later with a bullet hole plumb through the top of its head. Took four grown men to get him up to the road, and they carried him down to Grenada. Everybody wanted to buy him, but Big Dog paid a man two hundred and fifty dollars to mount him. Didn't know nobody around these parts had that kind of money. Yeah, Big Dog, he said he'd been saving up for a while, and he didn't exactly know what for, but he figured that was it. A newspaper man from Memphis come down and took a picture of it. He wrote an article, and people been coming to see it ever since."

While they finished their lunch, Clyde named several of the other employees from the factory who lived around Tallahatchie, but Dewayne was the only name Jack recognized. Clyde said Dewayne's trailer was on the road that ran between the gas station and the building that housed Big Dog's place. There was a hand-painted sign on the road just where it turned to gravel that said "Pigs 4 Sale."

"That's why everybody calls it Pigs 4 Sale Road," Clyde said.

After lunch Jack returned to his office where he continued studying the factory's production and inventory records, but it was difficult to maintain focus. He was here, close to Cici, but he was stumped for a way to approach her. And he kept seeing that roadside sign in the back of his mind, "Welcome to Tallahatchie, Home of Cici Cannon." It had struck him with an incontrovertible sense of futility, something he couldn't explain, but he was beginning to better understand the real Cici Cannon.

He'd been here for three days, yet the factory seemed to monopolize his every moment—or perhaps, he was allowing it. Perhaps Tuck was right when he said Jack was too much of an idealist trying to save people from situations that were of their own making. Just as he had talked Cici into coming to Orange Beach, he had now involved himself in the lives of the factory employees. His only hope was the outcome here would be better than it had been with Cici.

When she and Perry arrived that spring, Jack had found them adjoining apartments. The radio and newspaper advertisements were stirring interest and Cici was scheduled for several shows in the coming weeks. It looked like a huge win for both the club and Cici. Once they were moved in, Jack told them to take it easy the remainder of the day.

"So what do you have planned for tomorrow?" Cici asked.

"I want you guys to come down to the club, meet the band, maybe set up some practice sessions."

Perry nodded.

"I also want to show you around the area. My family has a boat over at one of the marinas near Perdido Key. We might take it out for a cruise."

"I don't get on no boats," Perry said.

"Why not?" Jack asked. "It's a big boat, and—"

"Perry can't swim," Cici said.

"Besides," Perry said, "I ain't fixin' to go out in no water where sharks stay."

"You don't have to get in the water," Jack said. "Besides, we—"

"Forget it," Perry said. "I ain't going on no boat."

Cici winked at Jack. "Looks like it'll be just me and you on the boat ride."

Jack smiled and nodded. It would take time with Perry, but Cici seemed ready to try anything.

Jack suddenly realizing he'd been daydreaming. As with the roadside sign outside of town, there was another constant reminder in the back of his mind. It was that he had missed the obvious with Cici. So, what was he missing here in the factory?

Having already observed most of the production processes, he began realizing the problem wasn't entirely systemic and that Nickels might be right. Perhaps it really *was* a "people" problem, but that was explainable, too. Nickels had given the employees every reason to believe they would get screwed, no matter how hard they worked. Even Henry and the two millwrights, Matt Oliver and JT, would say only so much before clamming up. Clyde was the same way. They trusted no one, but having lunch with them had been a big first step in gaining their trust.

Jack again joined the employees in the back breakroom for lunch that Friday. JT was bragging about his kid playing Little League baseball and invited everyone to come watch the boy play up in Batesville that afternoon. Jack was getting up early the next morning to go fishing with Clyde, but decided it was a good opportunity to get to know JT. He drove up to Batesville that afternoon to watch the game.

Multiple ballgames were underway when he arrived, and Jack found himself searching a sports complex with three baseball diamonds full of Little Leaguers. After wandering around the ball fields, he found JT sitting in some small bleachers, red-faced and sweating under the sweltering August sun. He was wearing another Dewey Hargrove T-shirt, this one with the infamous driver's face screenprinted across the front.

Jack climbed over the first rows of seats to where JT sat. Between ear-shattering shouts, he introduced his wife, Janine, and proudly pointed out his son. "That's my boy there," he said, "Little JT. He's the catcher. Oh, and back yonder," he pointed behind the bleachers, "that boy in the striped shirt is mine, too. His name is Donnie." Donnie was running around with a mob of kids throwing a miniature football and rolling in the dust. Everyone in the bleachers around them was screaming at the umpire as Jack took a seat.

JT Junior was taller and heavier than most of the other kids on the field, and he ruled home plate with the scowling confidence of a medieval executioner.

"Big boy," Jack said.

"Yeah," JT said. "We held him back in the fourth grade. Figured it would give him a chance to grow a little, you know? You hold them back a year, and when they get to high school they do a lot better, maybe even get a shot at the SEC."

"...a shot at the SEC?" Jack said.

"Yeah, you know, the Southeastern Conference."

JT gazed out across the playing field, nodding with confidence. "Yeah, that boy, he's good. And I ain't sayin' so just 'cause he's mine. Sit here and watch him. You'll see."

"He's played since he was big enough to walk," Janine said.

"That's right," JT said. "First time he ever played T-ball he hit the dang ball near 'bout all the way to the woods over yonder."

"Really?" Jack said.

JT lunged to his feet and screamed, "You're full of shit, Ump!"

All the parents in the stands were again screaming. They screamed at the umpire. And when the home-team parents across the way jeered them, they screamed at them, too. They screamed at the coaches, they even screamed at the kids on the field. Jack was certain a European-style soccer riot was about to break out as red-faced parents pounded the bleachers with their feet and hurled epithets at everyone in earshot.

The umpire, a teenager with acne, called time-out and walked around to the bleachers where they sat. He stared up at JT. "Sir," he said, "if you don't stop yelling ugly words that way, I'm going to have you ejected from the park."

"You little turd, you ain't ejecting nobody," JT screamed.

He threw his Dewy Hargrove hat at the boy and started down the bleachers, but Janine caught his shirt. Jack noticed the opposing team's coach sprinting across the field. One thing led to another as a shoving match ensued. As much as he didn't want to get involved, Jack knew he had no choice. He started down the bleachers, but as if by magic, a Batesville cop appeared and ran into the midst of the combatants.

Before it was over, Little JT was hanging his head in embarrassment, and Janine was begging the cop not to arrest JT. The cop finally relented, and after a stern warning allowed him to stay and watch the game. The young umpire was doing his best to keep the home team in the game as he made more bogus calls in their favor. JT was the epitome of a purple and red stroke about to occur as he fought to remain silent. He was successful until near the end of the game.

By the bottom of the last inning, the home team had crept to within a run. They trailed 10 to 9, but the score was not indicative of the absolute dominance Little JT's team had exercised over them. Only what Jack realized were intentionally bad calls by the young umpire had kept the home team in the game. Now, despite having two outs, the home team had the bases loaded. As the next kid came to bat, Jack glanced over at JT. If a pin nicked him, he'd explode. This was the first game of a double-elimination tournament in which Little JT's team was an overwhelming favorite to advance to the state finals in Biloxi, but things weren't going as planned.

The first pitch crossed the plate as the other team's little batter flailed wildly at it, catching nothing but air. The second pitch was the same. It looked good for Little JT's team as the pitcher wound up again. He let the ball rip toward home plate. The batter flailed wildly again, but this time he caught enough of it to send the ball sailing skyward, straight up above home plate.

Little JT threw off his face mask and walked forward. With his catcher's mitt dangling at his side, he took a step sideways and held his head back while watching the ball as it rocketed skyward. It seemed to enter the very edge of the stratosphere. Then ever so slowly, overcome by gravity, it stalled and plummeted earthward.

Little JT displayed the confidence of a professional baseball player as he popped his mitt with his fist and took one last step backward to adjust for the ball's trajectory.

That's when he stepped into his catcher's mask lying on the ground behind him. His cleat tangled in the wire mesh of the mask and he stumbled backward. The first kid from the home team crossed the plate as the ball hit the ground in a cloud of dust. Scrambling madly on his hands and knees, Little JT tried to recover the ball, only to knock it further away. It was too late. The second runner crossed home plate as well.

It was all over. The quiet that Casey heard that day so long ago in Mudville was nothing compared to the silence that now surrounded Jack. Parents stood in open-mouthed astonishment, unable to fully comprehend what had just happened. JT stomped down the bleachers to the edge of the field where Little JT stood with his head bowed. The home team was in a dusty pile of victorious ecstasy in front of their dugout, but everyone on the visitors' side seemed suspended in a horror beyond comprehension. Little JT shuffled toward the dugout, but JT blocked his progress.

"You missed it!" he screamed. "You missed it! I can't believe it! You choked!"

Little JT stood there, his head still hanging, while JT stared out across the diamond. There were shouts and cheers coming from the surrounding games, and a big truck was pulling away up the road, but there was only silence amongst his little group. The pitcher's dad walked down from the bleachers, staring at JT and Janine with the kind of look normally reserved for pedophiles. JT refused to meet his stare, but looked instead at his own son as if he were a dead snake. Tears streamed from Little JT's eyes, leaving shiny tracks down his dusty face.

"You let us down," JT said. "You let everybody in Tallahatchie down. I just can't believe it. You'll remember that missed catch the rest of your life. I just hope you can deal with it, 'cause I'm not sure me and your mama can."

"I thought it was a double-elimination tournament," Jack said.

JT jerked around to face him. "It is," he said. "But it's a matter of pride. You just don't go 'round losing to a bunch of humpties like these." With that he turned and stalked away.

When JT was out of earshot Jack patted the boy on the back. "Life has its ups and downs, son, but there'll be better times. Remember, it's just a game."

JT was already down near the end of the bleachers, but Jack had been betrayed by the surrounding silence. JT froze in mid-stride before slowly turning to face him. Knowing he had been overheard, Jack shrugged and smiled.

JT pointed a finger at him. "You may be one of the bosses at the factory, Mr. Jack, but I ain't toleratin' you saying stuff like that to no kid of mine. It ain't *just* a game. You hear me?"

"Sorry," Jack said. "I guess I was out of line."

JT stood his ground, staring at him in grim silence. Jack tried again. "I didn't mean to interfere."

Janine and Little JT both hung their heads, but said nothing. After a moment or two, JT motioned for his son to follow. "Let's go, son." With that he stomped away.

So much for building trust, Jack thought. Hopefully his fishing trip the next day with Clyde would go a little better. He could only wonder what other land mines awaited him.

CHAPTER 6

MOON LAKE

W ITH THE FIRST WEEK AT the factory behind him, Jack looked forward to the fishing trip with Clyde up at Moon Lake. The August air hung thick and warm in the predawn darkness as they loaded their gear. The anticipation reminded him of his bone fishing trips with Tuck down on the sand flats in South Florida. Not that Moon Lake was anything like the sand flats, but it was that same good feeling of anticipation. The lake was lined with towering cypress and home to some of the fattest bluegills in Mississippi. And according to Clyde, the old river-run wouldn't be near as crowded as the big reservoirs over at Enid or Grenada.

They stopped at the 61 Truck Plaza north of Clarksdale for country ham and eggs with biscuits, grits and coffee, then motored up the highway to the lake. Just after dawn Clyde held the tiller arm on the outboard motor as the little boat skipped across a fine ripple to a place he called his "honey hole." Gripping the gunwales of the jon boat,

Jack felt the tension of the week fading as the cool morning air streamed across his face. The promise of a quiet day was something he truly needed.

An orange sun rose in the east as the men baited their hooks with crickets and dropped them into the roots of a huge cypress. The first bream snatched Jack's cork under, and the line zipped through the water as he lifted back on his pole. Clyde laughed, slapping his knee. "Fight him, Jack. Bring that sapsucker in." Within seconds Clyde had one as well, and by midmorning they'd filled an ice chest with several dozen fish.

By late morning the action had slowed, and Clyde let the boat drift aimlessly in the shade of another cypress. Overhead the clouds were building into towering white columns, while a log of turtles baked out in the open sun. It was one of those lazy days when even the snake doctors seemed sluggish and the willows hung limp and unmoving. It was a quiet day and reminded Jack of how Cici talked about how much she loved it here and how she always wanted to go back. He would try to bring her here one day before the fall weather came.

It wasn't long after they met that Jack began to realize how Cici seemed to long for some indefinable fulfillment in her life, or perhaps it was a person or some unreconciled event from the past. Her second day in Orange Beach he had taken her on the family boat, out into the Gulf. He had called Acey and tried to get her to go, but she was tied up at work in Mobile and couldn't get away. They made plans to take Cici and Perry out to dinner later that evening. For now Jack wanted to show Cici a good time, and they cruised slowly along the beaches. She stood beside him at the helm as Jack turned the big fishing boat out to sea and pushed the throttle open.

He motioned to a small refrigerator below the console. "Why don't you open us a couple beers?"

Twisting the caps from the bottles, Cici handed one to Jack and turned hers up. Afterward, she pointed at the array of computer and radar screens on the console. "What's all that stuff?"

"There's everything there from weather radar, to a nav unit and a depth finder."

"What's a nav unit?"

"Nav is short for navigation. It utilizes GPS technology along with computerized mapping so we don't get lost when we get out of sight of land."

"GPS?"

"Yeah, Global Positioning System. It works off of satellites, same as your cell phone. You know?"

"How did you learn all this stuff?"

Jack laughed. "I never gave it much thought. I guess I've been around it since I was a kid. It's kind of like you and your singing."

When she downed her first beer in less than a minute, Jack began to realize nostalgic longings weren't Cici's only tendencies. She opened a second one, and after a few minutes excused herself. When she returned from the cabin below she was wearing the tiniest of bikinis.

"Does this boat have autopilot, or do you have to park it when you're, uh, busy?"

Jack had already begun steering back toward the mouth of Perdido Bay. He smiled. "No, no autopilot, and nowhere to park around here, either. We'll be approaching the main channel to the bay soon, and we don't want to get run over."

"Too bad," Cici said.

Standing beside him, she put her hand on his shoulder and gazed out through the windshield. Jack's first reaction was to pull away, but he didn't want to hurt her feelings.

"Here," he said, taking her hand, "you steer for a while."

He retrieved another beer from the refrigerator. "Can I have another one, too?" Cici asked.

It was her third, and by the time they approached the marina that afternoon Cici had downed five bottles of beer.

"You want another beer?" she asked.

"No. I'm good."

Cici frowned. "You're just no fun at all."

"Sorry. Someone has to drive this thing. Besides, Acey is meeting us with Perry, and we're going to a really good restaurant in Gulf Shores. You better go below and get dressed."

It wasn't something Jack would have described as outright alarming, but as he steered the boat into the marina later that afternoon, Cici remained in her bikini, holding her empty beer bottle and waving at Acey and Perry standing on the pier. Both wore looks of consternation, and Jack could only shrug and shake his head. Returning to port with a drunken, bikini-clad Cici wasn't the best of beginnings.

Suddenly realizing he had been lost in his thoughts, Jack glanced over at Clyde. Sitting at the front of the jon boat, the old man held his pole and concentrated on his red and white bobber. Despite the summer heat, he wore a pressed long-sleeved white shirt and denim overalls. His gray sideburns extended from beneath a green John Deere cap. Clyde wasn't the talkative type, but when he spoke it was usually about something with substance. Something about him drew Jack's respect.

Having spent much of the last few days at the factory with Clyde, Jack had learned more about the machinery from him than anyone. Henry and Matt Oliver had tried to help when they could, but the aging machinery kept them running continuously. Jack asked them why Clyde seemed so disinterested in moving up, but they changed the subject. When he asked Tommy Grey, he received a more direct answer. According to Grey, Nickels didn't like Clyde and "*sure as hell didn't want him fucking around with the company's machinery.*"

"Have you always worked at the factory?" Jack asked.

Clyde leaned forward and spit a stream of tobacco juice into the water. "Seems like it," he said. "But, to answer your question, no. Me and my younger brother, Son, first went to work for the Illinois Central Railroad back in the early sixties. We were on the track gang—gandy dancers they called us—made good money, too."

"What happened?"

"We quit."

He adjusted his cap, picked up his pole and dropped the baited hook beside another tree.

"We was working on a track up in Memphis at the South Yard when the switchmen, they accidentally kicked a boxcar down the track where we was working. It kill't one of our boys on the gang, Skinner Wilbanks. After it was all said and done, they toted his body off, and the trainmaster, he come down and said we had to get back to work. We told him we had to go see about Skinner's wife, but he wouldn't listen. That about done it. Me and Son and one other fella, we just walked off. We brought Skinner's body on back home to Tallahatchie. Son and I did a year at a seminary school, but we run out of money. I went to work at the factory, so he could finish school. I been there ever since."

"Why don't you want to move up and become a supervisor or a lead?" Jack asked.

Clyde grunted and laughed, then pulled a pouch of Redman from the pocket of his overalls.

"I'm serious," Jack said. "You know as much about the factory machinery and processes as anyone."

Clyde shook his head. "And you think those white bosses, Mister Nickels and Mister Grey, are gonna give me a job like that?"

"Why not?" Jack asked. "Times have changed. These are the 1990s. That racial crap doesn't float anymore."

"Yeah, that's what they say, and I ain't saying you're not meaning to be truthful, but it's business as usual for some people. You weren't here when Mister Nickels first showed up a few years ago."

"No, I suppose not. Why?"

"'Cause that was the last time I tried to do something more than sweeping the floors, and it got me nothing. You see, that's when Fernwood sent Nickels down from somewhere up north. He come in thrashing around like a little Adolf Hitler, said he was gonna fix everything or fire everybody. Got the employees all worked up, and that's when Henry had his heart attack.

"Anyway, Mr. Nickels, he went to looking for help after he darn near kill't his best man, and that was when somebody told him I could fix things. He come to me, making promises about job promotions and pay raises and all kinds of things."

The tone of Clyde's voice wasn't bitter or angry, nor did it carry the inflection of a whine that usually accompanies complaints of unfairness. It was with hard cynicism and irony that he laughed and explained what had happened.

"That man had me doing more tricks than a circus dog. I spent fifteen-sixteen hours a day up in there, lying under motors, climbing scaffolding up forty feet above the floor, and for what? When he was done with me, he hired Tommy Grey. That boy couldn't fix a broken hoe handle, but I needed my job, so I kept my mouth shut and went back to sweeping floors."

"What if I offered you that job? Would you take it?"

Clyde laughed. "Look-a-here, Mister Jack, I ain't trying to be disrespectful. I mean, you're a good fella and all, and I know you mean well, but can't you see the writing on the wall?"

"I'm telling you, Clyde, I can swing that job for you. I might have to work around Nickels, but I can do it."

"That ain't what I'm talking about," he said. "I believe what you say, but I'm gonna be a supervisor of what? That damned old factory is so decrepit it ain't gonna last much longer."

Clyde's words were the hot slap of confirmation that made Jack see what he had tried to ignore. There was little chance the factory could continue manufacturing profitably without a major overhaul, and that might cost more than it was worth. If only he could turn things around—it was a long shot, but not altogether impossible. The rhythmic buzz of the cicadas rolled through the trees as the two men drifted in silence for several minutes.

"So you think the factory can't make it much longer?" Jack asked.

Clyde slowly turned and stared at him with an amused grin. "Ain't no 'think' to it," he said. "There's just been too much bad management for too long."

His red and white bobber bounced once—twice, and he picked it up. The cricket was gone.

"Hook's empty," he said. "Picked clean, just like the factory."

He began re-baiting.

"The numbers show we're still turning some profit," Jack said.

Clyde nodded. "I don't doubt that, but it's because we ain't bought a new machine in twenty years. We're probably the only furniture factory in the country that doesn't specialize. Fernwood ain't never figured out what to do with us. We still make all our furniture parts, do our own assembly, all of it, but our machines, the building, everything is patched together with duct tape and bailing wire. You said it yourself when you first got here Monday. Remember? We were walking around, and you said it was one of the most— what'd you call it?"

"Antiquated," Jack said.

"Yeah, antiquated," Clyde said. "That's right. The whole cotton-pickin' factory—it's running on wishes and prayers. And the employees—Mister Nickels treats them terrible. They're working on promises that ain't never been kept, and Mr. Nickels, he goes out every day to play golf with big-shots and takes them out to eat at the company's expense. The first time something big breaks, we ain't gonna have the money to stay afloat."

"Things change," Jack said. "If we get the employees pulling in the same direction there's no telling what we could accomplish."

"Hmmph. There's some things you can't change, and you'd do good to see the factory is one of them."

"So what should we do," Jack asked, "roll over and play dead?"

Clyde shook his head and turned, looking directly at Jack. "Hell, I don't know, but you sure got some fire in you. I reckon we can try, but it's like you said: the only way it'll work is to get the employees behind you."

Clyde went back to staring at his bobber and Jack at his. In the distance there came the faint rumble of thunder as the billowing thunderheads matured with the day's heat. A flock of coots skittered from the buck-brush across the lake. It seemed a long time before Clyde spoke again, but his question caught Jack by surprise.

"Why'd you come up this way to work?" he asked.

Jack hesitated, trying to think of something besides the truth. "I don't know. Got tired of my family interfering with my personal life, I reckon. Why do you ask?"

"Just talk going around. You know how people are."

"What kind of talk?"

"They say you got plenty of money—don't really need the job. And Cleve Thomas says he seen you over yonder in Clarksdale at a juke joint, drinking alone and wearing dark glasses."

Jack didn't answer for several minutes as they floated in the sun-dappled shade of another big cypress. He played instead with his fishing line, adjusting the cork and bending the hook to just the right angle. After a while he ran out of things to fidget with, and stared out toward the bank where a stilt-legged blue heron waded in the shallows.

"Have you heard of Cici Cannon, the Blues singer?" Jack asked.

Clyde grunted and laughed. "I reckon so. Cici was one of the hottest things around these parts for a long time. Besides, her and her two kids live with her auntie in Clarksdale."

Jack was suddenly dumbstruck, and only after a moment or two did he find his voice. "Cici Cannon has kids?"

"Yeah, little twin girls, almost two years old now. They mostly stayed with their auntie while Cici was off up on Beale Street or down yonder on the coast. Yeah, that girl, she's good," Clyde said. "Good enough to go anywhere, but she went down to the Alabama Gulf Coast where she got all goo-goo-eyed over some white boy. They said he dumped her, and she went to drinkin'. Had a bad car wreck. Really messed her up something awful."

Jack remained silent, as Clyde pressed his lips together and shook his head. "That was a terrible thing. She's good—real good, best woman Blues singer I ever heard—could've gone to St. Louis, Chicago, anywhere, but that whole thing just messed her up bad."

Jack felt his face burning, but if Clyde noticed, he didn't let on.

"Where's the kids' daddy?"

"Boy brought a knife to a gun fight up there in Memphis. He was kill't before the babies was even born. Cici, po' girl, just can't catch a break. You know, her mama was married to a boy in the military. He was Cajun. They lived down south of New Orleans, and they was married for a long time. He done become a master sergeant, and been in the Army nearly twenty years, but he got kill't in Vietnam. That's when Cici's mama sent her up here to Tallahatchie to stay with her sister, Netta. Cici's mama somehow knew that little girl was full of talent, and she was afraid she'd end up singing on Bourbon Street, but sendin' her here didn't work either, 'cause Cici, when she got older, she went on up to Beale Street in Memphis."

After pausing a minute, Clyde looked over at Jack. "They say she's too pretty to be a Blues singer—girl looks like a little fashion model—maybe even prettier. Her daddy was a handsome man, too, a paratrooper with the Hundred and First Airborne. I think it was him getting kill't and her mama sendin' her up here that really done her in. Po' thing looks like a scarecrow now."

As they rode home from Moon Lake that afternoon, Jack found himself a poor companion for conversation. Clyde drove in silence as they passed through the intersection of Highways 61 and 49—"The Crossroads"—the place where Jimmy Johnson sold his soul to the devil. An urban, yet rustic, intersection with a traffic light and corner gas stations, it was no longer the rural crossing of two gravel roads, but remained the holy shrine of the Blues. The iconic Blues guitars mounted there on the pole struck Jack anew with a deep feeling of loss—a loss that he precipitated when he talked Cici into coming to Orange Beach.

Seeing those guitars reminded him of her voice and her music. He glanced over at Clyde. If the old man was aware of his involvement with Cici, he hid it well. Gripping the steering wheel, Clyde stared straight ahead as he drove down Forty-Nine toward Tallahatchie.

CHAPTER 7

DORIS ANN AND THE CANDLELIGHT VIGIL

MONDAY MORNING JACK COULDN'T ENGAGE. Sitting at his desk he scrolled through the various screens on the computer, never fully concentrating on one before going to the next. He worried about the employees—people like Dewayne and Momo—people with real problems—people who depended on the factory for their livelihood, and who now depended on him. Could he truly make a difference, or was his selfish pride going to make their lives even more miserable at the hands of Nickels? Was it, as Clyde said, too late? If the factory was doomed to failure, Tuck was right. He was a dreamer, a Don Quixote. Or maybe he was just a fighter.

It seemed he was on another road to folly, but what worried him most was Acey. He feared that he might have lost her forever. It was six years ago when she accompanied her father on a fishing trip with Jack and Tuck out in the Gulf. Acey's father and Jack's were business associates, and Jack's old man persuaded Tuck to take the father and daughter out on the family boat for a day of deep sea fishing. This was the first time he saw her.

Tanned and lithe, Acey wore white shorts and a blouse that day, but beneath them was the outline of a pink bikini. She hadn't taken off the shorts or the blouse the entire day. Even after her father nodded his approval when Jack offered the use of the foredeck to sunbathe in privacy, she avoided it. And when a gusty Gulf wind sent her straw hat sailing overboard, Jack dove in to retrieve it, feeling afterward like an overanxious teenager showing off for the new girl next door. He'd never met a woman so beautiful, yet so unassuming about her looks, and she loved to fish, too. Later Mr. Kimmons invited him and Tuck up to Georgia to deer hunt at his company's corporate lodge. Jack's guide was Acey Kimmons.

At first it was something that happened between two young people—total infatuation—but later it developed into a relationship that burned with blinding intensity. And when she came to work at Hartman Manufacturing, she stood with him in the all-consuming battle he was waging with his father over treatment of the employees. He and Acey had made a difference, and the factory became known as one of the better employers in the Mobile area.

Jack now faced some of the same obstacles at Fernwood. There were definite opportunities for increased productivity and profitability, but it required gaining the employees' trust and coaching them into giving something extra. If only he could keep Nichols at bay, that was the biggest problem. Monday morning disappeared into the haze of the past as the lunch bell sounded throughout the factory.

When Jack arrived at the breakroom, Arlis was reading his usual Bible passage aloud, while the others listened to JT telling how he'd gone by Dewayne's place on Saturday to check out the big barbecue. JT said his wife and Dewayne's old lady didn't get along, so she refused to go, but he felt obliged since Dewayne went to all the trouble.

"I didn't want to go alone," JT said, "so I called Matt Oliver, but—"

"Sorry," Matt Oliver said. "Like I said Saturday, I just don't care much for eating pigs that have been tortured to death."

JT's jaw flexed. "Didn't nobody miss you nohow. Besides, there wasn't no pig."

"What happened?" Henry asked.

JT dropped his head, shaking it slowly from side to side. "Oh, hell, you know Dewayne. He tried some new trick he heard about, where you wrap the pig in wet burlap and put it under a bed of coals. He dug a big hole in his backyard and burned some pallets he borrowed from out yonder on the truck dock. Then he put the pig in the coals Friday night. When I got there Saturday morning, he was out there in his pajamas with a shovel digging around in the ashes, but there weren't no sign of the pig nowhere—not even a tooth."

"Reckon what happened to it?" Doritoe asked.

JT shrugged. "It was just too much fire for that little pig. I reckon it burnt plum up."

"What'd he feed everybody?" Matt Oliver asked.

"Nobody else showed up 'cept me. I kinda felt sorry for him and April and the kids, so I took them up to Clarksdale for Kentucky Fried Chicken."

Jack glanced around the room. "Where's Dewayne now?"

"He laid off sick," JT said. "Said he was going up to Batesville to buy something."

"Buy something?" Jack said.

JT shrugged. "He wouldn't say what it was—just for us to be out on the truck dock before work in the morning 'cause he was gonna have a big surprise for everybody."

Jack turned to Henry. "Don't pay him a sick day unless he has a doctor's note."

Henry nodded, but JT's mouth dropped open. "I thought you were gonna be a nice guy—different from them other suits."

"How about I put you back there in the paint shed the rest of the day to replace Dewayne?" Jack asked. "Would that make you feel better about my decision?"

"I don't want to go back there."

"My point exactly," Jack said. "And being nice doesn't mean I have to give away the store. If I don't hold folks accountable for coming to work, everyone loses. And don't worry about Dewayne. If he has a legitimate explanation, he'll get paid."

During his observations the first week at the factory, Jack noticed production bottlenecks in several areas and asked Henry about them. Henry simply shrugged. "I've tried fixing them a hundred times," he said.

"What do you mean?" Jack asked.

"Nickels and Tommy Grey don't care for my suggestions. And when they don't like something, it doesn't happen. Ask Clyde about my last suggestion."

"What was that?"

"I tried to get them to make him supervisor over maintenance so I could concentrate on production, but I'm still wearing both hats, and he's still sweeping floors."

Jack shook his head. "I'm going to Nickels and—"

"I wouldn't bother," Henry said.

"Why?"

"You're wasting your time. Wait and watch a little longer before you decide what you want to do."

Jack nodded, and late that afternoon he was looking at future work orders on the computer when he heard footsteps outside his office. He looked up to find Nickels standing in the doorway staring at him. Like Henry suggested, it was probably better to simply observe for a while, but the more Jack thought about it, the more he was compelled to make one small suggestion. Nickels turned to walk away, but Jack called out to him. "Hey, Mister Nickels."

Nickels reappeared in the doorway, his eyebrows raised. Jack knew instantly it was a mistake, but he never backed away from something that needed fixing.

"You know, maybe we could have a 'family day' sometime for the employees—nothing expensive. We could have hamburgers and hotdogs. It'd be a good morale booster, and we might be surprised at what we learn—what do you think?"

Something between a grimace and a smile crossed Nickels's face as he ran his finger around inside his collar. He gazed up at the ceiling for a moment before locking his eyes on Jack.

"I don't need to learn *anything* from the employees," he said. "What I have to do is run this damned factory and make sure they do their jobs."

So much for "Theory Y" management, Jack thought. "Sorry, sir. It was only a suggestion."

"So you've been here a week, and you think you've got all our problems solved, huh?"

"No, sir. I just—"

"Make an appointment with my secretary, and we'll talk."

With that he stalked away in sullen silence. Make an appointment? What kind of crap was that? Jack found himself jabbing at the keyboard with a vengeance as he began shutting down the computer. He was pissed more at himself than at Nickels. He'd shown his hand too soon, and put the little prick on the defensive.

Later, after doing his final walk-around of the premises, Jack was about leave when he noticed a car still sitting in the employee parking lot. It was Arlis McCallister's old Lincoln. Arlis was nowhere to be seen, but there came a sound from the far end of the loading dock near the dumpster. Walking that way, Jack saw a discarded chair leg sail upward out of the dumpster and bounce off the metal wall of the building. The metallic clack echoed across the empty lot. Someone was in the dumpster, muttering and cursing.

Standing on the dock, Jack peered into the dumpster. Arlis was up to his waist in sawdust and wood scraps. The sawdust had stuck to his body, giving him the appearance of a fuzzy wooden monster. After a few moments, Arlis noticed him and stopped digging as he looked up. His lips and nostrils were red and wet—the only parts of him that resembled human flesh besides his eyes.

"What the hell are you doing down there, Arlis?"

"For God's sake! Do you know none of the stores around here rent girlie videos?"

"No, I didn't," Jack answered, "but you're not going to find any down there either."

"How come?" he asked. "Did somebody steal my videos?"

"Not that I know of, but the truck came out and swapped the dumpster last Friday."

Arlis stood panting, and for a moment his eyes began to moisten. He climbed out onto the loading dock.

"Where's the dump?" he asked.

"They say it's east toward Charleston, off Thirty-Two, but why don't you give it up? You're not going to find those tapes. They're long gone."

Arlis didn't answer. Turning instead, he hurried down the steps and out to his car. The tires scratched in the loose gravel as he sped out the gate.

The next morning the sun cast an orange glow on the cottonwood trees across the road as everyone waited for Dewayne to drive through the gate. JT had told them there was going to be a big surprise. Jack was standing with the little group out on the dock as Dewayne's red Toyota scraped over the speed bump at the guard shack. The car looked like an ant laboring with a giant banana as it towed a shiny new yellow bass and ski combo the size of an aircraft carrier.

"Sweet Jesus in heaven..." Clyde mumbled under his breath.

Waving at everyone on the dock, Dewayne wore a shit-faced grin as he drove around the parking lot. He circled down to the far end, still waving as he went. Jack was certain he would have done a few Dewey Hargrove victory-donuts had there been some grass and he wasn't pulling the boat. Instead, Dewayne turned and drove back, stopping at the dock. Throwing the car door open, he jumped out and danced a little jig, turning a full three-sixty beside the car while clapping his hands.

"Hey, hey, whatta you boys think about this baby?" he shouted.

"That addle-brained sonofabitch," Matt Oliver muttered.

"That boy just ain't right," Clyde said.

Jack turned and glanced at Clyde, who was shaking his head in disbelief. Momo was standing beside him with his hands buried deep in his pockets, but he said nothing.

"Dammit, boy," JT shouted. He was grinning and scratching his head. "She's a beaut. Where'd ya git 'er?"

"Got 'er up at Boat City in Batesville. Whatta ya think?"

"Sheeeiit," JT said. "She's big—real big. How fast you reckon she'll go?"

Dewayne shrugged as everyone walked out to see the new boat. A twenty-four-foot bass and ski Bayliner with a canary-yellow metal-flake hull and a walk-through windshield, it sported a Mercury Inboard/Outboard motor. Matt Oliver raised the deck lid above the engine and let out a long soft whistle.

"Damn. This thing has a 454 cubic-inch Mercruiser with a Rochester Quadrajet four-barrel carburetor," he said. "It'll run like a brokedick dog."

Jack stood with Henry and Clyde, taking it in like bystanders at an intersection with a failed traffic signal.

Dewayne and his new boat had the makings for an inevitable disaster.

"How fast you reckon it'll go, Mister Henry?" Clyde asked.

"Don't rightly know. Sixty-five—maybe seventy."

"Boy gonna kill hisself," Clyde muttered.

They moseyed around the boat, running their hands over the metal-flake finish.

"How in the hell are you gonna pay for this thing, Dewayne?" Matt Oliver asked.

Dewayne glanced at Matt Oliver and nodded with the knowing look of a man who had thought through every aspect of his plan.

"See, y'all think I'm stupid, but I got it all figured out right here," he said, jabbing a finger at his temple. "Old Dewayne ain't dumb as you think."

"This is gonna be good," Matt Oliver muttered as he kicked the back tires on the Toyota. They were nearly flat from the weight of the boat.

"Damned right, it's good," Dewayne answered. "See, think about it, I got this here big boat, so the next most natural thing is to make some money with it. Right?"

"How you gonna do that?" JT asked.

"I'm gonna be a professional bass fisherman—that's how." He nodded his head confidently.

"You're crazy, Dewayne," Matt Oliver said. "Have you ever been fishing before?"

"Hell, yes, Mister Know-it-all. I done been a bunch a times with my Uncle Selmer out at the bridge where

Opossum Bayou runs into the Tallahatchie. We caught some big cats down there, least he did, but I caught one, too, one time. It was so big I couldn't even get it in the boat till he shot it three times with his .22. Then I still had to hit it on the head with a paddle. Yeah, it was a damned big fish, so don't tell me I don't know nothing 'bout fishing."

"This thing's a barge," Matt Oliver said. "How come you didn't just get a regular bass boat?"

Dewayne rolled his eyes and looked off to one side as if he was totally put out with Matt Oliver's stupidity. "Man, don't you know nothing? What do you think I'm gonna do with it when I ain't fishing? See, you gotta think about the women-folk, too. April said if I was gonna buy a boat, she wanted one her and the kids could ski behind. So there you go."

"You ain't gonna be able to get back in the shallows where the bass are," Matt Oliver said. "I bet it draws three feet or better."

"You just don't have the head for this sort of thing," Dewayne said. "Me, I got it all planned out. Hell, I ain't really gotta catch no fish. I'm gonna put me some decals on it, you know—like STP and Strike King, and I'm gonna get me a bunch of patches for my coveralls, too. With this boat, there'll be people begging me to wear their patches, and I'll make all kinds of money."

He turned, lowering his voice, "In case you don't know, that's how them professional bass fishermen make their money. They call 'em sponsorships."

Matt Oliver turned toward the loading dock, but stopped to look over his shoulder at Dewayne. "It's a mighty nice boat, Dewayne. I just hope you don't go out and kill your fool self with it."

"When are we gonna try 'er out?" JT asked.

"I figure we can head over to Persimmon Hill at Enid Lake, Labor Day weekend, and have a big picnic," Dewayne said. "Whatta ya say?"

"Hail yeah," JT answered.

"I ain't fixin' to get in that boat with Dewayne behind the wheel," Henry said, "but I reckon a picnic at the lake might be okay."

JT turned to Jack. "Maybe it can be that company picnic you mentioned. What do you think?"

Despite the visceral jolt of adrenaline Jack felt, thinking about the liability of Dewayne and his boat at a company function, he did his best to remain poker-faced. "We can't give it an official company sanction. It's something you guys will need to do on your own, but I suppose I can join you for a little picnic."

"Hail, yeah," JT said. "Me and Dewayne can go out and catch some fish that morning. We'll invite everybody and have us a hellacious big fish fry with hush puppies and watermelon."

Dewayne clapped his hands together. "Hail yeah!"

Henry looked over at Clyde. "Have you got some fish fillets in your freezer?"

Clyde nodded. "Yeah, I reckon I can bring a few bags."

"Otherwise we might all starve," Henry said.

Dewayne and JT ignored them as they began making plans. Momo followed the crowd back inside, but he remained silent. The corners of his mouth were turned down, and he squinted as if some mysterious force was hurting his brain. Jack suspected it was the aura of brilliance surrounding Dewayne and JT.

Late that afternoon after everyone had gone home, Jack walked up the hallway past the administrative offices to check the doors. The building seemed all but abandoned until he heard someone sobbing quietly in one of the offices. Following the sounds, he found Doris Ann sitting at her desk with her face buried in her hands.

"Are you okay?" he asked.

She jumped with a start. "You scared me," she said, dabbing a lace handkerchief at her eyes.

"I'm sorry. I didn't know anyone was still here. Has there been a death in your family?"

"I wish," she said. "If it'd been that worthless old ex of mine or one of his hussy sisters, I'd be laughing instead of crying."

Jack paused, unsure what to say next.

"No, it's him," she said, pointing to the framed photo of Elvis on the credenza.

It was the eight-by-ten color glossy of "The King" in all his sequined glory, tossing sweaty scarves to swooning females at the foot of a stage in Vegas. Doris Ann walked over and picked up the photo, clutching it to her breast.

"Such a tragedy," she said.

"Didn't he die back in the seventies?" Jack asked.

"August the sixteenth, 1977," she said. "He went to take a nap that afternoon and got up later to go to the potty, and his little old heart just stopped."

She heaved a retching sob.

"Are you sure you're okay?"

Doris Ann set the photo back on the credenza, turned and threw her arms around Jack's neck.

"You're such a sweetheart for asking. Most men just wouldn't understand."

"I—uh, yeah," he said.

She let out another fitful sob as she buried her face against his neck. Jack made a pretense of patting her back as he glanced around to make sure no one was still around. After several more sobs, Doris Ann tapered it off to a few mild whimpers before suddenly raising her head and staring at him with a look of wonderment. With her make-up smudged into purple and black rings around her eyes, she looked like a psychotic raccoon.

"You could go to Graceland with me," she said. "We could have a really great time. Have you ever been there?"

Like a calf caught grazing too close to the forest edge, Jack realized he was staring into the eyes of a she-wolf.

"I've gone to every candle-light vigil since I can remember—every year except 1991," she said. "That was the year I split up with that worthless sleaze-bag, Logan Dancy. God, what a hunk. He was from Gadsden, Alabama, and he looked so much like—like..." She let out another agonizing whimper.

"I won't desecrate his name by mentioning it in the same sentence with that worthless Logan. He was an impersonator—the best one I ever saw. I swear. He could sing, too. I met him up in Memphis, you know—the year before, but he was so weird and all with his damned handcuffs and vibrators. I mean not at first, you know? I mean—when he had that wig on and those sunglasses, he was The King to me. You know? I mean—well—like I said, he was weird—kind of kinky—you know?"

Jack started to say he didn't but thought better of it. "Yeah. Yeah. Sure I do."

"No you don't," she said.

Jack shook his head. "Okay, maybe I don't."

"I mean, like when we were—you know—in bed—I mean—you know—making love. He'd always want me to—oh, I shouldn't say this—but he..."

To say Doris Ann took her celebrity deaths hard would have been an understatement. Matt Oliver said the previous August when Princess Di was killed in the car wreck in Europe, Doris Ann didn't come to work for a week. Then she placed a garland-laden photo of the princess on the credenza beside Elvis and lit a candle in front of it, until one afternoon when the drapes caught fire and nearly burnt the office down.

"So, anyway, the straw that broke the camel's back was when Logan invited me to his cousin's church in Alabama," Doris Ann said. "Hell, I got so excited I had chill bumps all over, just thinking he was gonna pop the big question, but turns out his cousin was a preacher with one of those weird snake-charming churches. You know, the ones who hold the snakes to prove they believe in God?

"Well, that was when I told him I wasn't going to no church where I gotta prove I believe in God by rasslin' with a damned rattlesnake.

"So, how about it? I really need somebody to go to Graceland with me, you know? Somebody who ain't weird like Logan was. What do you say? It won't cost you a whole lot, neither. You can get the Platinum Tour ticket for twenty-five dollars, and that includes everything, the two airplanes, the car museum, all of it. You should see the Lisa Marie. I never saw an airplane fixed up so gorgeous."

Overhead, a faulty ballast buzzed in one of the fluorescent lights. Jack felt himself sinking fast as he clawed viciously at the water for an excuse.

"Well, ugh, you know it really wouldn't be the best timing for me right now. I mean I just got here at the factory, and I need more time to adjust and all. Besides—"

"If it's the expenses you're worried about, I can take care of most of that," she said. "Besides, we can share a room, and who knows what might happen?"

She smiled and winked.

"Look," Jack said, "maybe when you get back from Graceland, we can do something."

As soon as he said it, he knew he had screwed up. He had stuck his foot in his mouth up to his knee, and her face lit up with the radiance of the Orpheum marquee in Memphis.

"Okay," she said.

She had sucked him in, and only now did he realize she had never really expected him to go to Graceland. She'd played him like a chess-master, all the way to checkmate. The outside door to the waiting room opened, and Henry walked in. He stopped and stared as Jack pushed Doris Ann away. It was too late, but Henry acted as if he'd seen nothing. Jack felt his face burning crimson.

"I thought everybody was gone home," Henry said. He glanced back toward Nickels's office. "Is Nickels still here?"

"He never came back from lunch today," Doris Ann said, pushing her hair in place.

"Well, I reckon I'll let you lock up," Henry said.

"No," Jack said almost too loudly. "It's your day to lock up. I'm going to run check the back dock, then meet you out front at the gate."

It was a bald-faced lie, but Henry grinned as he got Jack's drift.

"You lock up and show Doris Ann to her car, and I'll see you in a minute," Jack said.

He tried to appear casual as he backed toward the door. He was escaping this time, but he'd made a terrible tactical error, one certain to haunt him. Not that he was worried about having a tryst with Doris Ann, but he had left her believing there was the chance, a complication he didn't need at the moment.

He was determined to stick with it, but the longer Jack stayed at the furniture factory, the more it seemed coming here was a comically stupid idea.

CHAPTER 8

ACEY AND CICI

IN A WAY, BEING TOO busy to think about Acey was a blessing, but sometimes late in the evening when he was back at the old farm house, Jack would again find himself longing for her. He simply couldn't accept that she had walked out on him and wouldn't even give him a chance to explain. This thing with Cici had caused a rift he feared couldn't be closed. Acey had taken a leave of absence at Hartman Manufacturing and gone home to Georgia, leaving Jack's heart spinning like a leaf in the wind.

He thought back to that morning when they first talked about the issues with Cici, and Jack wondered if there was something he could have done differently. Propping himself on his elbow, he lay beside Acey in the bed. She had stayed the night at his place after another Saturday night show. The late morning sun cast clean golden shafts from the bedroom skylights, and he admired the outline of her breasts rising and falling beneath the sheet while she slept. He couldn't imagine being in love with any person more than he was with Allisson Catherine Kimmons, and it seemed she felt much the same.

Although their relationship wasn't exactly a well-kept secret, their executive positions with Hartman required her stay-overs be kept low-profile, but Jack intended to remedy that issue. Acey didn't have a clue, but he had purchased a ring, and later in the summer he was going to pop the question.

She sighed and opened her eyes.

"G'morning, sleeping beauty," Jack said.

Acey smiled. The gold of the morning sun reflected in her brown eyes. A natural brown-eyed blonde, she had stolen Jack's heart from the very beginning. Now, those eyes ruled him. He bent over and kissed her lips.

"How long have you been awake?" she asked.

"Long enough to shower and make coffee."

"Oh my. It's that surf out there," Acey said. "It makes me sleep like I'm drugged."

"And I thought it was my lovemaking—oh well."

She smiled and pinched his cheek. "That helps, too."

Jack's house was out at Point Clear, and the calls of the sea gulls were the only sounds other than the rhythm of the surf.

"The coffee smells heavenly," she said. "Are we going for a run this morning?"

Jack nodded and gazed out the big window at the sparkling waters stretching away toward the Gulf of Mexico.

"What are you thinking about?" Acey asked.

"Cici."

"Oh." Acey's lips flat-lined, and she too gazed out the window.

It was a strange departure from her normal self-confidence, but any mention of Cici seemed to bring out a different Acey of late.

After a few moments she turned back to Jack. "Maybe you need to cut off her free liquor."

"I already thought about that, but my dumb ass wrote free meals and free drinks into her contract."

"Well, you need to do something. She's been here a month now, done eight shows and hasn't finished one sober yet."

"I know. I know," Jack said. "I just don't want to piss her off. She has people standing in line to get in the club— been one of Tuck's best draws ever."

Acey fixed him with those brown eyes.

"Come on, Jack, you know she's dynamite with a short fuse. It's only a matter of time before something bad happens. Tell Tuck to let her go."

"No, it's my fault. I shouldn't have encouraged her to travel way down here. She's just being young and irresponsible. I'm going to sit her down and have a talk with her tomorrow."

"Where?"

"I don't know. Why does it matter?"

Acey sat up in the bed clutching the sheet against her breasts.

"You know why. That girl hangs all over you."

Jack grinned. "She *is* a little clingy."

Acey squinched up lips. "A *little* clingy?"

Jack gazed steadily into Acey's eyes. He had never seen a hint of jealousy in her, something he always assumed came from the unshakeable trust between them. "I think you're worried about something that won't happen, no matter what."

"I just wish she would keep her hands off you."

Jack pushed a wisp of her blond hair from her eyes and grinned. "It's a hard thing for a girl to do, isn't it?"

Acey's mouth dropped open. "Jack Hartman, I'm going to kick your smart ass!"

Jack rolled over and straddled her. Acey screamed as he pulled the sheet away and began tickling her ribs. Their lips met, and within seconds they were again making love.

The old farmhouse was a lonesome place at night. Jack looked over at the alarm clock beside his bed. It was nearly midnight and he had to be back at work before first light in the morning. He pulled the sheet up under his chin and closed his eyes, hoping to dream about Acey, but his mind wouldn't allow it. He back-tracked over his every action and how he had approached Cici about her drinking.

He arranged to meet her the Friday before her next performance at a coffee shop near her apartment. It was a place where she couldn't order anything with alcohol.

He was on his second cup of coffee that morning when she finally arrived and ordered a Coke. They sat in mutual silence for the first minute or two, before she finally spoke.

"So, is this our first official date?"

She gave him a coy smile.

"Cici, we need to talk."

"Well, here I am. Talk to me, pretty boy." She drew on the straw while looking up at him with wide-eyed innocence.

"Cici..." Jack had thought about what he wanted to say, but he paused. He had to get this right.

"Jack..." Her voice was quiet and calm, but she seemed to be mocking him.

"Look..." He paused again.

"Okay, let me help you out. You think I'm drinking too much, right?"

"What do you think?" Jack said.

"I think I do all my shows and finish them in style. The people seem to love me, and you said yourself I'm drawing some great crowds. So, I don't see the problem."

"You're going to hurt yourself. If that man hadn't caught you the other night when you fell off the stage, it might have killed you."

"That was part of the show. The men loved it."

She was lying. She had been drunk and lost her balance.

"This is a lot more serious than you seem to think. I want to take the free drinks out of your contract."

"So take them out. I don't care."

She stared back at him with defiant eyes. It wasn't the response he had hoped for, not even the hint of a mea culpa. He had no choice but to do what he and Tuck had discussed. Jack reached into his pocket and laid two business cards on the table. He pushed them across to Cici.

"What are those?"

"I spoke with two club owners. They want to talk with you about performing in their clubs. Both clubs are nice places and they're nearby. One is over in Pensacola, and the other is in Gulf Shores."

Cici lost her smirk. "What about our contract?"

"We'll honor it. You can finish out the remainder of your scheduled shows, but I don't think we're going to exercise the renewal option, at least not for now. Besides, performing in these other clubs will broaden your exposure."

Cici's green eyes grew moist. "Your girlfriend put you up to this, didn't she?"

"Acey had nothing to do with it. Tuck and I just think it will be a good move for both you and us."

A hot tear ran down her cheek. "Good move, my ass. You're dumping me."

Jack bowed his head. "You're wrong," he said. "I'll help you negotiate something with those new club owners."

Cici pushed her chair back and stood up. "No, Jack. *You're* wrong. You talked me into coming here, and now, when things get a little uncomfortable, you can't handle it. Don't worry about me. I've been dumped before, and I don't need your help. Tell your damned old uncle I'll keep my end of the contract, but when it's done, he can shove it up his ass." With that, she walked out.

When Jack arrived back at The Gulf Sunsetter that morning, Tuck met him at the door. "Have you spoken with Perry?"

"No, why?"

"He called and said she came back to her apartment a little while ago and started drinking again."

"Shit."

"I take it you had to tell her we weren't renewing the contract."

"Yeah, it didn't go well at all."

Tuck nodded, and put his hand on Jack's shoulder. "You did what you had to do, nephew."

"Maybe we can get her into rehab," Jack said.

Tuck shrugged. "You can try, but who's going to pay for it?"

"We can help."

Tuck shook his head. "She has to want to do it. Otherwise, you're wasting your time. I just hope she shows up tonight."

"I'll drive out there later," Jack said, "and try to sober her up."

Jack arrived back at the club that evening with a semi-sober Cici. Acey was already there, sitting at a table with Tuck.

Cici smiled and winked as Perry led her to the back. Jack sat down at the table.

"Have you been at her place all afternoon?" Acey asked.

"Yeah," Jack said, shaking his head. "She was pretty drunk."

"She looks okay now," Acey said.

"I know. Perry gave her an upper."

"I say we pay her and send her away," Tuck said.

He stared hard across the table at Jack.

"Let her finish the show tonight," Jack said. "I'll break it to her later."

Tuck nodded. "Yeah, that might be better. It'll give us a chance to get someone else in here for tomorrow night's show."

Jack stood.

"Where are you going?" Acey asked.

"I'm going to get a drink, and then I'm going back there to talk with Perry. He needs to know."

"You just got here."

"Chill, little sister," Tuck said. "Jack thinks he has to be everyone's babysitter."

Jack shrugged. "Just trying to help." He looked down at Acey. "Don't worry. She'll be gone soon."

Acey said nothing, but looked away instead. Jack understood her worries, but she should know better. Cici was a beautiful woman, but even with her aggressive behavior, she could never turn him away from Acey. Their three years together had grown into a relationship with an unbreakable bond of trust. Acey was his soulmate and a woman who had been willing to do almost anything as long as it was with him. Fearless, she went along as he took her on her first scuba diving trip out in the Gulf, then rock climbing in the Arkansas Ozarks and white water canoeing in North Georgia.

She balked at nothing, not even the skydiving adventure Jack talked her into trying. Yet he now detected a glimmer of fear in her. Fear was something he had coached her to respect, but to not allow it to control her actions, a lesson seemingly heeded until now.

Acey hardly spoke that night, as they watched Cici perform, and Jack was too distracted worrying how Cici might take the news. He decided it would be best to drive her back to her apartment first. That probably wouldn't go over well with Acey, but he could go by her place later and make amends. At least Cici wasn't drinking her signature "gin and juice" during tonight's show. She had only a glass of water, but after midnight the upper Perry had given her seemed to be wearing off. She was acting silly again, playing with the lyrics, teasing the customers and toasting the band with her glass of water.

Jack sprang to his feet. *Surely not*, he thought.

"What is it?" Acey asked.

Jack paused. He didn't want to make a scene in front of everyone in the club. He glanced at his watch. The show would be over in twenty minutes. He looked around for Tuck. He was nowhere in sight.

"What's wrong?" Acey asked.

"Nothing. I was just wondering where Tuck was."

What Jack wasn't, was an accomplished liar, and he saw it in Acey's eyes. She knew he wasn't telling the truth.

"I just need to talk with him, maybe go ahead and get the check for her, before I tell her she's fired."

It didn't work. Acey knew there was something more he wasn't telling her. Their eyes met, and there was that glimmer of fear and distrust. "Okay. It just dawned on me," Jack said. "I don't think that's water in her glass."

Acey glanced at the stage then back at Jack.

"I think it's gin," Jack said.

"What are you going to do?"

"I'm going to let her finish the show, then I'm going to drive her back to her apartment. I'll break it to her there."

"Why can't Tuck or Perry drive her?"

"Tuck has to close tonight. Besides, I'm the one who brought her down here. It's my job to tell her she has to go. I'm going backstage. See if you can find Tuck and get him to write her a check."

Jack spotted the empty gin bottle as soon as he walked into the dressing room. She had apparently polished off another three-quarters of a liter. The muffled sounds of applause came from outside. The show had ended. A few moments later, Cici walked through the door.

"What are you doing back here?" she asked.

"I want to drive you home, so we can talk."

"Really? You know if we keep meeting this way, your girlfriend is going to get suspicious."

"You ready?"

Cici walked over and locked arms with him. "Sure. Let's go."

Pulling his arm free, Jack opened the back door and showed her to his car. They were nearly back at the apartment when Jack realized he'd forgotten the check. No big deal, he figured, he'd take it to her later. The alcohol was apparently hitting her full force, as Cici slumped over, resting her head on his shoulder. When they arrived, she was barely conscious. He pulled her from the car, but she swayed on wobbly legs. Jack caught her in his arms and carried her toward the door.

The headlights of another vehicle reflected on the apartment windows as it turned into the lot. Hopefully, it was Perry. Jack didn't want to leave her alone in this condition.

"Where's your door key?"

Cici pointed inside her bra. The key was attached to a gold chain around her neck. Jack ran his finger between her breasts catching the chain and retrieving the key. Without warning Cici wrapped her arms around his neck and crushed her lips against his. It took several seconds before he could pull away. "Stop," he said.

"Wassa matter? You don't want a little brown sugar?"

Jack carried her into the apartment and laid her on the bed. After removing her heels, he tossed a blanket over her and went into the living room where he sat on the couch. Perry's apartment was next door, and Jack waited, hoping to catch him when he arrived. He glanced at his watch. It was two-thirty a.m. He closed his eyes and waited, listening for Perry's car outside the door.

It seemed only a few minutes passed before Jack opened his eyes. He glanced at his watch, sat up and looked at it again. It was six a.m. Cici was standing there in nothing but lace panties, looking down at him. She had an open envelope in one hand and held a check in the other, examining it carefully.

"What's this?" she asked.

"Where'd you get that?" Jack asked.

"Your girlfriend left it a few minutes ago."

Jack half stood as he glanced at the door.

"She's gone. I told her you were sleeping."

He ran to the door and threw it open. The sky was streaked with pre-dawn purple and orange clouds, and the air was heavy with the scent of an approaching rain.

"I ask you what this check is about," Cici said.

"Just what it says. It's payment for the remainder of your contract, plus some additional for relocation. We cancelled the rest of your shows. How long has she been gone?"

"You bastard."

Cici threw the check at him, walked back to her bedroom and slammed the door. Jack grabbed his phone from the couch. He always left it on silent mode while at the club's live shows. It showed a half-dozen missed calls—all from Acey.

He went to Cici's door and shouted through the closed door. "I'll talk with you later about this. Right now I'm going to find Acey."

There came only a muffled sob from inside.

His tires squealed as Jack turned out onto the highway. He dialed Acey's number repeatedly, but to no avail. She wasn't answering. He drove back to the club, but the lot there was empty. Frustration set in. He drove to her apartment near Fairhope, but her car wasn't there either. By now the morning sun had been blotted out by a light rain that was falling.

Perhaps she had gone to his house out at Point Clear. He was speeding back up the highway when his phone warbled. "Thank God," he muttered as he grabbed it, but it wasn't Acey. It was Perry.

"Mister Jack." Perry's voice was strained.

"What is it, Perry?"

"It's Cici."

"What happened?"

"She took the rental car. I couldn't stop her. She done gone and had a bad wreck."

"How bad is she hurt?"

"Real bad. She flipped the car and hit a pole. I don't think she's gonna make it. You gotta come quick. We're at the hospital in Fairhope."

"I'm on the way."

CHAPTER 9

THE SIGN

THE DAYS PASSED IN THE hazy void of too many remembered yesterdays as the factory and its employees monopolized Jack's time. Cici did survive, but her injuries kept her hospitalized for nearly a month. Now, as far as Jack could learn, she was improving, but still a long way from regaining her strength. Perry had brought her back home to stay with her Aunt Netta in Clarksdale.

After fighting the battles at the furniture factory each day Jack had little strength left, and he fell into bed at night still determined to help Cici, and still holding the vague hope of someday making amends with Acey. His next break came when he spotted a handbill tacked to a pole outside Big Dog's place. Cici was appearing Saturday night, back at Messenger's. It was her first performance since the aborted show earlier in the month. She was again receiving headline billing. How to approach her, that was the problem.

Sometime after ten Saturday evening Jack made his way up Fourth Street. Even after dark, the day's heat still radiated from the concrete sidewalk, but the humid night air was diluted with a mild breeze as crickets chirped, and moths fluttered beneath the streetlights. The muted vibrations of a bass guitar came from the club, while a nearby mockingbird sat on a wire singing as if it were midday. It seemed a celebration of sorts as the town slipped from the grip of another scorching summer day and basked in the tolerable shade of nightfall.

There was standing room only at the club, and the band was warming the crowd as Jack slipped inside. A waitress had brought him his first beer when a man stepped up to the microphone and announced Cici Cannon. The club erupted with a standing ovation, and Jack stood on tiptoes, looking out over the crowd. Cici came through the curtained door near the stage, walking slowly with a silver cane. A tomato-size lump stuck in his throat.

Cici made her way up on the stage, and when the lights hit her face, the lump became a cold pain in Jack's gut. The sparkle was gone from her eyes—the green in them faded like September leaves. Lines creased her face, and her skin was ashen. In her early thirties, she now looked more than twice that. Hooking her cane on the chair, she took the microphone and began clapping her hands with the beat. It was a forced smile, and though she tried to hide it, her pain was obvious as she began singing. It wasn't a Delta Blues piece, but one from the Carolinas.

Freight train, freight train, run so fast
Freight train, freight train, run so fast
Please don't tell what train I'm on
They won't know what route I'm going

Freight train, freight train, comin' round the bend
Freight train, freight train, gone again
One of these days turn that train around
Go back to my hometown.

It was that old Elizabeth Cotton song, but Jack didn't recognize the second verse. His gut ached as he realized Cici was singing about her own life. The haunting tune told him something, not about Cici, but why he'd come to Tallahatchie.

Despite her debilitated condition, Cici sang for nearly an hour while Jack drank. Only when she took a break did he notice a familiar face off to the side of the stage. It was Perry. That wouldn't have been disturbing except he was talking with Cleve and Doritoe, who were stealing furtive glances back his way. Jack didn't hesitate as he slipped along the wall and back out the door. Hurriedly he walked up the street to his pickup.

It simply wasn't going to work. And as he drove home that night he again passed the sign just outside of town, "Welcome to Tallahatchie, Home of Cici Cannon." Now more than ever he was beginning to understand the futility it represented. He had come here uninvited, resented by everyone and with only a vague idea of what he hoped to accomplish. Yet, it was if the town and the people owned him.

After falling into a restless sleep that night, he awoke Sunday morning to the phone ringing. It was Tuck. They exchanged the usual small talk, while Jack told him about his new boss and the problems at the factory. It was good to hear a familiar voice. Tuck agreed that he was taking the only practical course by trying to win over the employees, but summed up the situation as pretty much a "lose-lose" situation—something Jack wasn't yet ready to admit. Only when the conversation slowed did Tuck asked the inevitable question.

"So, have you seen Cici?"

Jack hesitated. "Well, yes and no."

"What's that mean?"

"I was at a Blues club up in Clarksdale last night and saw her perform, but I haven't actually spoken to her yet."

There was silence on the other end.

"You still there?" Jack asked.

"Yeah, I'm here. Why don't you just pick up the phone and call her?"

"Because it's not that easy."

"What is it you want, Jack?"

"What do you mean?"

"Why did you go up there?"

"I think that's why I'm stuck. I'm not sure. Other than getting away from my father, I think I just want to go see her and see if she needs my help."

"So, pick up the phone, call her and tell her that."

"I can't tell her that over the phone."

"So, get her on the phone and tell her the part about wanting to see her. Ask her to lunch."

"You make it sound easy, but—"

"I didn't say it was easy, but you're not accomplishing a damned thing sitting on your ass."

Tuck was right. Jack decided to call Cici that afternoon. At least that was his plan as he studied the phone and glanced at the clock. A telephone call seemed so superficial. There had to be a better way to meet her again for the first time, but Tuck was right—he had to get off his ass. Sometime after noon he made up his mind. He was driving back to Clarksdale.

He'd gotten Aunt Netta's address, and he drove down a street shaded by stately oaks, searching for the house number. The quiet Sunday afternoon made the neighborhood seem nearly deserted, and Jack slowed his pickup as he searched. The homes were large with wide porches and high gables—relics of a once more affluent citizenry. He spotted the number to Aunt Netta's house and rolled to a stop.

He was here, but he hadn't thought it through. Pulling his cap down low, he sat in the truck, eyeing the house. He wanted to see her, but as he hesitated the front door opened and an elderly woman stepped out onto the porch. Jack sank lower in the seat as she began walking down the driveway. She was looking his way. Hiding was useless. Pulling off his sunglasses and cap, he stepped out of the truck.

The woman stopped a few feet away. "Can I help you, sir?"

"I'm Jack Hartman." Jack's heart thumped in his throat, and the old woman's mouth fell open.

"I only came here to see Cici," he said, "and to talk with her if I can. That's all."

His words seemed pitifully inadequate as tears welled in the old woman's eyes.

"Mister Hartman, I been waiting for you to come. I thought, maybe you wouldn't, but you're here. Oh, my."

She put a hand over her mouth as if to hold back a sob.

"Please don't be upset," Jack said. "I don't want to cause trouble. It's just that—well—I moved here a month ago, and I wanted to come see Cici."

He glanced up at the house. The old woman stood at the center of the drive dabbing her eyes with a handkerchief.

"I swear, I mean no harm."

The woman nodded. "I know that. It's just that, her health is failing, and you know it's not you that really caused all this. It's just that she just never got over losing her daddy."

"You must be Aunt Netta," he said.

"That's what Cici calls me. Netta James is my name."

"It's good to meet you, Ms. James."

"You can call me Netta, if you like," she said.

"Perhaps I should come back another day," Jack said.

The old woman nodded. "I reckon that'd be best, and I can tell Cici you come by. It'll be easier that way."

"But will you do me one favor, please?"

"What's that?" she asked.

He went back to the truck and scribbled his telephone number on a scrap of paper.

"Give this to her. Tell her to call me if she wants. I live down in Tallahatchie now, and I'd like to come visit her."

"Yes, sir," she said. "I will. I sure will."

Jack returned to the truck, and started the engine. Quickly pulling away, he glanced into the rearview mirror. The old woman still stood at the end of the drive, clutching her handkerchief and shaking her head.

He drove home, and that evening as he sat looking out the kitchen window at the pecan grove, he thought about his encounter with Aunt Netta, and what Cici might do when her aunt told her of his visit. Would she call? He sipped his bourbon and hoped, but he had no idea how she might react. His thoughts were again interrupted by the telephone. It was too soon to be Cici. She would think about it first. He picked up the receiver. His hand was sweaty as he pressed the phone to his ear.

"Hello?"

"Hello, Jack?"

It was her.

"Cici?"

"Yes, it's me. I was wondering when you were going to get around to stopping by."

Her voice was weak.

"I moved up here to Tallahatchie," Jack said.

She gave a little laugh. "Yeah, I know—a month ago, wasn't it?"

"How did you know? I mean, how long have—"

"Snookey Harris, my lead guitarist, recognized you the first time you came into Messenger's. He remembered you from when we first met in Memphis. And some of the boys who work for you at the factory said they saw you again last night. I figured you'd come around when you got ready."

Jack felt like an idiot. She had known he was here all along.

"Cici, can we get together and talk? That's all. I just want to talk. I'm not here to complicate your life any more than I already have. I swear."

"Jack, you couldn't complicate my life more, no matter how much you tried."

"Then how about we meet next Saturday for lunch? Sound good?"

"Slow down, Jack. Give me a few days to think on it. I'll call you back next week, okay?"

"Yeah, sure," he said. "Whatever you say."

"I'm just too sick this week, but I should be better in a few days."

As Jack hung up he caught his reflection in the kitchen window. Was there anyone in Tallahatchie who didn't already know his business?

CHAPTER 10

THE REBEL RABBIT

JACK SAT IN HIS OFFICE that next afternoon, feeling somewhat vindicated. His primary purpose for coming to
Tallahatchie was finally about to be realized. Perhaps
he could help Cici with her medical bills, get her better
medical treatment, whatever it took to help her regain her
health. Then perhaps he could help her with her singing
career. He felt a surge of positive adrenaline. Anything
now seemed possible, perhaps even saving the furniture
factory.

Tuck had agreed with him. Building relationships with
the right employees was the key to winning the employees' trust—at least most of them. Winning Nickels, Grey,
and a few of their die-hard cronies was hopeless, but Henry
was the most important one, followed by Matt Oliver, both
affable, but still cautious in Jack's presence. Matt Oliver
was important because he was the group's informal leader.
Everyone except JT looked up to him. Of course Matt
Oliver wasn't perfect, and according to some, he was having a terrible time with his marriage.

When Jack thought about his own relationships, he could only laugh at the idea of judging someone else's. Every window in his glass house was already shattered, but this was one of the reasons he understood Matt Oliver so well. Pretty much a straight shooter, Matt Oliver was more honest than average and fairly intelligent to boot, but none of this seemed to help with his marital issues. According to the others, there was something about salon tans and glued-on fingernails that sent him into a hormonal overload, a weakness that had caused him to discover the underlying sinkhole in his wife's character only after the "I dos."

Jack heard a knock at the door. It was Matt Oliver. *Speak of the devil,* he thought. "Hey, I was just thinking about you. Come in."

Matt Oliver had done this previously—come by his office to sit and talk. Usually it had something to do with the factory, but this time it was to invite him to his house for dinner. Somewhat surprised by the invitation, Jack hesitated—something didn't seem quite right. Matt Oliver noticed and nodded with a grim countenance.

"Okay," he said. "It's like this. My wife put me up to it. I reckon Muff thinks having my boss over for dinner is some sort of big deal, you know?"

"No problem," Jack said. "I'll come by."

Matt Oliver still didn't seem satisfied as he stared down at the floor.

"Have you ever had woman troubles?" he asked. "I mean, you think you're doing everything right, but… I don't know. They can be so damned complicated."

Jack grunted and worked up a half-ass smile. "I could write a book about complicated relationships."

Matt Oliver fiddled with the miniature sailboat on the desk. Jack turned and stared out the window. High above the Delta a distant formation of geese reflected the orange glow of the late afternoon sun. Matt Oliver sat in silence, until Jack suddenly realized his mind had wandered. Their eyes met.

"I take it, you don't want to talk about yours right now," Matt Oliver said.

"Autopsies can be ugly," Jack said, "especially when there's nothing to explain things."

"That's kind of the way I feel about my marriage with Muff," he said. "Look, there's something else I need to tell you."

"What's that?"

Matt Oliver began telling Jack about his wife's scheme to hook him up with her younger sister, another Ole Miss sorority sister like herself, except seven years Jack's junior and badly in need of a breathing male with a decent income. Being one of a very limited number of white-collar bachelors in the area, Jack was now dead-center in the sights of Matt Oliver's wife and her baby sister.

"Look, you really don't have to do this," he said. "I can tell Muff you refused. I mean it really doesn't matter what I tell her, because she's still going to think I didn't try."

Matt Oliver seemed desperate.

"Give me a date and time," Jack said. "As much as you've helped me around here, I owe you this one."

Matt Oliver looked as if the doctor had just told him he didn't have cancer. "Jack, you just don't know how much I appreciate this."

The others had explained how Matt Oliver always set his sights too high by going after the hoity-toity sorority girls from Ole Miss. Henry was kinder with his remarks, but he did mention that drinking white wine and grilling bacon-wrapped fillets in The Grove on game day didn't come without its price. He said Matt Oliver was like a coyote that visited the same chicken coop once too often.

It was an Ole Miss tradition over at Oxford—partying in The Grove on game day. It was a tailgate party that sprawled across the entire campus with tents, barbecue grills, picnic tables and ice chests spread beneath the stately oak trees— and linen tablecloths with candles and wine weren't out of the ordinary. As JT explained it, "Matt Oliver met Muff tailgating in The Grove the year before, and got married faster than a cat could lick its ass." Muff had moved in with him at his old family home over in Charleston.

That Saturday afternoon when Jack arrived, he parked on the road out front. The house, much larger and nicer than most in the area, was an older one with ornate trim and an expansive front porch. Matt Oliver's family had apparently been well to do at some point. He had used his woodworking expertise to refinish much of the exterior trim and the molding around the front door. Jack rang the bell and watched through the leaded glass on the door as the fractured forms of Matt Oliver and his wife approached in the foyer.

"Come on in," Matt Oliver said. "This is Muff."

Matt Oliver was his usual easygoing self as he introduced Jack, but his wife was totally different. Coifed, clipped, and combed, with not so much as a thread or a hair out of place, she was tight with propriety as she extended her hand. Her manicure was flawless and her nail color matched her lipstick perfectly. God only knew what her real name was—but that was the tradition: give them cutesy nick-names to go with their richer-than-cow-manure, three-part names—the ones with the "tons" or "bys" suffixed to make them sound like future authors, attorneys or patrons of the arts. There were several like that in Jack's family.

Matt Oliver had an accent more attuned to Moon Pies and doublewides, but for whatever reason, he had chosen this sorority-sister-for-life from over at Oxford, and her accent came right off the set of *Gone With The Wind*. Doris Ann said Muff had all the "high-dollar" nail and tanning salons on speed-dial, and if something didn't have a logo on it, it wasn't worth wearing. She also said that Muff took Matt Oliver to Memphis to get twenty-five-dollar haircuts and tasseled loafers. And soon after they were married, she made him put his woodcarvings in boxes and store them out in his shop in the backyard so she could display her rabbit collection.

As Muff led the way down the hall, Jack became aware of the rabbits. Doris Ann was right. There were stuffed rabbits, ceramic rabbits, rabbits in suits, rabbits in dresses, rabbits holding umbrellas and rabbits reading books. There was even a rabbit dressed like the Ole Miss mascot, Colonel Reb—a rebel rabbit. They lined the walls and sat on tables, white rabbits, brown rabbits, rabbits with bows and rabbits with button noses. There were rabbits in every nook and cranny. Jack imagined there must even be rabbits hiding under the couch.

Matt Oliver glanced back at him in silence. Probably knowing what Jack was thinking, he raised his brows ever so slightly as Muff went on about how it was so nice of him to come by for dinner. She looked back, and Matt Oliver quickly turned to meet his wife's glance as she walked ahead of them down the hall.

Guiding them to the living room, she said, "Now, you two fellas just go right on in there and make yourselves comfortable while I fix us some dinner." A room with ivory-colored carpet and furniture so clean and perfect, it looked as if it hadn't been used since the preacher last visited.

Muff disappeared, and Matt Oliver grabbed the remote, punching up a ball game on the TV, but as if she'd pivoted mid-stride, she reappeared. Standing in the doorway, she stared in silence, eyeing Matt Oliver with steely gray eyes. He looked back at her, then slowly raised the remote and punched off the TV. This seemed to please her immensely as she gave him a tight-lipped smile.

"Now then, I'm sure Mr. Hartman didn't come all the way over here just to sit and watch TV. Why don't you show him our wedding album? That would be fun, now wouldn't it?"

"Sure," Matt Oliver said. "Why not?" And he almost made it sound like a great idea. Sitting on the edge of the couch, he began thumbing through a strategically placed copy of *Southern Living*. And only when there finally came the muted rattle of kitchen utensils, did he seem to relax.

"You want to look at the album?" he asked.

Jack shrugged.

"Muff's pissed at me," he said in a low voice.

Jack raised his eyebrows, while Matt Oliver shot a nervous glance at the doorway. The comforting sounds of activity still came from the kitchen.

"She insisted that we go all the way up to Memphis just to buy some clothes for me to wear today, but I wore the khaki pants fishing yesterday afternoon and forgot to tell her. When she found them in the dirty clothes hamper this morning, she went berserk."

"Nice shirt anyway," Jack said.

He looked down and thumbed the manufacturer's embroidered logo on the pocket.

"I hate labels," he said.

It was clear Matt Oliver was trapped, and now the trap was set for Jack with Muff's sister. The dinner was the bait, and he was the prize. It was all supposed to seem so happenstance and he'd played along to help out, but a sudden skittishness came over him. The front doorbell rang and he jerked his head around, staring toward the hallway. Matt Oliver, who remained seated, turned and gave him a knowing nod. The sister-in-law had arrived.

Jack waited, expecting that Muff would call for Matt Oliver to go answer the door, or at least she would answer the door herself. Instead, she showed up at the doorway to the living room with a big open-mouthed grin and her finger stuck in the side of her cheek.

"My, my," she said. "Now, whomever in the world could that be? I suppose I'll just have to go and see."

There was no doubt an A-plus on her transcript from eighth-grade drama class. She wiped her hands with a rabbit dishtowel and headed up the hallway to the front door. The setup was so bad, Jack would have figured it out even without Matt Oliver's warning, but he tried to act surprised anyway.

"She's really not bad-looking," Matt Oliver said.

"Oh hell, don't worry about it," Jack replied. "I've had blind dates before."

The front door creaked, and Muff cast her voice back down the hallway—loud enough for God and everyone south of Clarksdale to hear. "Well, I'll swanny—if it's not my baby sister, Sissy. What a pleasant surprise! Come on in, girl."

Jack heard the front door close, some furtive whispers and a few moments later they walked into the room.

"Look who's here, y'all!" You'd have thought her long lost sister had just returned from a ten-year missionary trip in the jungles of South America.

"Hey, Sis," Matt Oliver said, giving his sister-in-law a two-fingered salute.

Muff sat on the couch beside him, and jabbed Matt Oliver with her elbow.

"Oh! Oh yeah," he said. "Sissy, this is Jack. Yeah, uh, Jack Hartman. Jack, this is my sister-in-law, Sissy Mattox."

Jack stood, extending his hand. "Pleased to meet you, Ms. Mattox."

"Oh, I don't think we have to be so formal," Muff said. "You don't mind Jack just calling you Sissy, do you?"

"Of course not," Sissy said. "And it's a pleasure to meet you, Jack."

"This is such a wonderful coincidence," Muff said. "Can you possibly stay for supper? We'd love to have you."

"Sure," Sissy said.

They had their lines down perfectly, and Jack felt the jaws of the trap closing around him. Matt Oliver was right. She wasn't bad-looking—at least at first glance. There was, though, a certain cosmetic façade that could mislead the untrained eye. She wore the same out-of-place-in-daylight dangling earrings like Muff's, and was equally coifed, clipped, tanned, and combed. Not so much as a loose thread hung from a blouse that seemed somehow expanded by the unnatural effects of a pushup bra with extra padding.

The meal went fine, although the white linen and candles were a bit much for a Saturday afternoon dinner in Charleston. It fit the fare, though: Cornish game hens, asparagus spears in cream sauce and an array of cuisine the likes of which Jack hadn't seen since leaving Fairhope. The madam Ms. Muff was pulling out all the stops for her baby sister. He thought about asking if this became hamburger helper after the "I dos," but opted instead to play the game by raving about everything.

Matt Oliver didn't say more than a dozen words the entire time, and when they were finished, everyone adjourned back to the living room. When Jack sat on the couch again, he found Sissy strategically guided to his side. The room began to close in, and he nervously cast about for a distraction. There was a Grisham novel along with a stuffed rabbit in a basket beside the couch. He picked up the novel.

"Who reads Grisham?" Jack asked.

"That's mine," Matt Oliver said.

"Oh," Sissy said. "I just love literature, too. You know it was such a big thing at Ole Miss, Robert Faulkner and all, you know?"

"I can imagine," Jack said, opting to let her misnomer pass without comment. "Which of Faulkner's works do you like best?"

She placed her finger on her chin and looked off to the side. "Well, now, let me see. You know, I really liked the one about the men that went up to Memphis. Oh, what is it called?" she said. "You know—I saw a movie about it."

"*The Reivers?*" Jack said.

"Yeayus, that's it," Sissy said. "But now that I think about it, the one that was saddest was the story about the two men who worked on the farm. You remember? One liked mice and was retarded, and he accidentally killed that girl."

"Do you mean *Of Mice and Men?*" Jack asked.

"Yeayus, that's it," she said, "I simply *could not* recall the title. That was a wonderfully intriguing story, now wasn't it?"

Sissy, like Muff, talked with a lilt reeking of Scarlett O'Hara and antebellum mansions.

"I reckon so," Jack said, "but was it Faulkner who wrote it?"

Throwing her hand over her mouth, Sissy gave an over-animated look of dismay—the kind normally reserved for when trays of food are accidentally dumped in someone's lap.

"Well, you know, I'm really not sure. Silly me, have I gone and mixed my authors?"

"It was Steinbeck who wrote *Of Mice and Men*," Matt Oliver said.

Sissy's face turned as red as her lipstick, and Muff shot Matt Oliver a glance loaded with double-aught buck. He looked bewildered.

"What'd I do?" he asked.

"Nothing, Mister Know-it-all," Muff said. "Nothing at all. Besides, I've told you not to leave your old paperbacks lying around the house."

"What other interests do you have?" Jack asked.

This got Matt Oliver off the hook for the moment, but the rest of the evening was equally awkward. Muff made sure Jack got Sissy's phone number and planned a double-date at some unspecified time in the future. The guillotine had been hoisted, and as he escaped Matt Oliver's house that night, Jack did his best not to appear relieved. Still, he realized he had done it again. As with Doris Ann, he had left the door open, this time with Sissy Mattox.

Matt Oliver was normally Mr. Dependable when it came to his job, but Monday morning when he didn't show up, Henry came to Jack's office saying Matt Oliver had called, mumbling something about a fire.

"He said it was mostly out, but that's all I could get from him. Reckon his house caught fire?"

Jack shrugged. "What else could it have been?"

"You might want to send somebody over there to check on him," Henry said. "He sounded bad—like he was in shock or something."

Jack decided to drive to Charleston himself to see if he could lend a hand. Thirty minutes later he was driving up the tree-lined street of older homes, expecting to find fire trucks with hoses stretched up and down the road, but it was quiet. There was no one around as he parked in front of the house. Matt Oliver's pickup was sitting in the drive, but there was a light haze of what appeared to be smoke drifting over the wood fence from the backyard.

Jack got out and walked around to the side gate. Peeking through the wood slats, he spotted Matt Oliver standing with a garden hose. He was in front of a huge smoldering heap of ashes—the remains of what Jack quickly realized was his woodworking shop.

Matt Oliver had made a name for himself with his wood-carving. Although he hadn't made a big deal of it, he told Jack about his hobby and how he sold his work to several shops around the state and at craft fairs. Jack had a deep foreboding as he let himself through the gate. Walking across the backyard to where Matt Oliver was standing, he stopped beside him, but said nothing.

The shop was gone. Lathes and saws were reduced to blackened skeletons. Wisps of smoke still filtered from the ashes. Matt Oliver's entire collection of carvings, along with the exotic woods he had collected from all over the country—bois d'arc, maple, cherry, walnut, cypress—all were reduced to charcoal. He stood in silence, his eyes moist and reddened.

The water ran feebly from the garden hose, puddling at his feet. Several long minutes passed while Jack stood beside him in silence. Only when Matt Oliver finally glanced over at him did Jack speak. "What happened?"

Matt Oliver stared into the ashes as he talked. "Muff was already mad at me 'cause of the way I got my hair cut the other day. She said I didn't look like a professional, and when I said, 'a professional what, chair leg maker?' she went psycho on me."

"Women can be that way sometimes," Jack said.

"She hates it 'cause I work at the factory," Matt Oliver said. "She hates my friends. Hell, she hates everybody. She said I needed to find a job where I can wear a necktie or else be an artist and try to sell my carvings. I asked her if she'd ever heard the term 'starving artist,' but that made it worse. She accused me of sabotaging her trap to hook you up with Sissy. Said I purposely made baby sister look stupid because I left my book out. I said some stupid things back at her, and one thing led to another, until she came out here, doused everything with gasoline and set it on fire. She singed hell out of her hair—blamed me for that, too."

Everything was gone—all his carvings, his tools, everything destroyed out of sheer meanness. And no amount of words could make a difference. Jack stood in silence for the next hour while Matt Oliver sprayed the remaining hotspots. When the fire was out, Jack called Henry and told him not to expect either of them that day. Matt Oliver took a shower, and they drove over to a little place on the county line and got drunk together.

By late afternoon they had played every Vince Gill song on the jukebox a dozen times and drank enough beer to float Dewayne's bass boat. The after-work crowd came in, took over the jukebox and began shooting pool. From the back room came their voices and the rattle of balls on the pool table. Jack was fighting to stay on his barstool when Matt Oliver turned to him with bloodshot eyes, but he said nothing.

"What?" Jack said.

"I've been wanting to ask you something."

"All right."

Matt Oliver paused and looked straight ahead. Their eyes met in the mirror behind the bar. "It's kind of personal—no, it's *real* personal," he said.

"You want to know why I've been going to those joints over in Clarksdale—right?"

Matt Oliver shook his head. "No, we know that. I mean, the gossip is it has to do with that girl, Cici Cannon. I mean we know something happened between y'all, but we don't know the real truth—just talk going 'round."

"Who is 'we'?" Jack asked.

"Me, Clyde and Henry," he said. "Cleve and Doritoe have been running their mouths, but Clyde shut them up by telling them they'd get fired."

"What were they saying?"

"That you were the one who dumped her before she had the car wreck."

The noise from the jukebox was growing unbearable.

"What do you think?" Jack asked.

"I don't know," Matt Oliver said. "It's just gossip, and I don't put a lot of stock in it."

"Okay, so what would you think if I said I *did* know Cici Cannon, but it was only a business relationship?"

Matt Oliver shrugged. "What does it matter what I think?"

"It matters because I have a lot of respect for you. What do you want to know?"

Matt Oliver tipped up his beer and finished it, then shook his head. "Nothing, right now. Let's wait till we're both sober."

When they approached Matt Oliver's house that evening, there was a U-Haul Truck backed into the drive. Jack stopped up the street, and the two men gazed in silence for several long seconds before Matt Oliver began shaking his head.

"You want to stay at my place tonight?" Jack asked.

"If you don't mind," he said. "I'll come back in the morning and see what's left."

"You don't think she'll burn the house down, do you?"

Matt Oliver shrugged. "I don't know, but it ain't worth going in there and tangling with her. She's crazy. I'll let you know tomorrow if I have a house. Let's just go."

CHAPTER 11

LABOR DAY AT THE LAKE

S INCE JACK COULDN'T GIVE HIS official blessing to the gather-ing at the lake, the Labor Day picnic was reduced to a mini-reunion of mostly the employees from the back break-room. Just the same, JT and Dewayne made it clear that Jack was expected to attend, and they gathered around a concrete picnic table near the boat ramp at Enid Lake. It was 10:00 a.m. and already hotter than hell, but the shade under the pines and a mild breeze coming off the lake made it tolerable. The drone of outboard motors out on the water and the shrieks of kids playing down near the water drifted up through the trees as they sipped cold beer and waited. Dewayne hadn't arrived, and they'd begun to worry.

"Dumb-ass probably got lost," Matt Oliver said.

"Nah," JT said. "He told me he was going to the grocery store in Batesville and fill all three live wells on the boat with beer and ice. He's just running a little late's all."

Everyone relaxed and continued drinking their beer—everyone except Momo. He was drinking a Mountain Dew, but no one else noticed until JT spoke up. "You don't drink beer, do you?"

It was obviously something JT had been contemplating, but it caught Momo and the others by surprise.

"N-n-nnnno-no, no-not to-today," Momo replied.

He spoke with the conviction of one who had overdone it a time or two.

"Good thing," JT said. "I hear you Indians get kinda crazy when you drink."

Jack winced, but Momo remained poker-faced. Matt Oliver stopped his conversation with Henry and stared at JT. With his pending divorce, Matt Oliver had been relatively quiet for the last week or so, but he leaned toward JT and smiled. "At least he has to drink to get that way," he said.

JT got persimmon-faced, but said nothing.

"Okay, guys," Jack said, "why don't we cool it awhile."

Turning up his beer, JT killed it and crushed the flimsy can on the table. With that, he got up and walked out to the parking lot where he scanned the horizon for some sign of Dewayne. The tension at the table quickly melted away as friendlier conversations resumed, but a few minutes later JT shouted. He was pointing at something off in the distance.

Dewayne's little Toyota, dwarfed by the yellow Bayliner, was crawling across the top of the dam. A line of cars trailed behind him for a quarter mile, unable to pass. A little while later he pulled into the parking lot and circled to where JT was standing. April and the kids were hanging out the windows, grinning and waving like participants in a parade.

"I'll be damned," Matt Oliver said. "Reckon that sonofabitch could have gotten any more shit in that boat?"

Dewayne had yards of kite string spread like a spiderweb over a mound of inflated rubber rafts, lawn chairs, balls, fishing rods and God only knew what else piled in the boat. As he rolled to a stop, he shouted out the window, "Yee-haa. It's *par-tee-time!*"

"I believe his car is overheating," Jack said.

After towing the gargantuan boat, the little Toyota was smoking and rattling like a Model-T, but a lesser machine would have no doubt ended up abandoned somewhere in a roadside ditch.

"Mommy, Mommy," the oldest girl cried, "are there sharks out there?"

April whipped her head around, furrowing her red brows, and stared out at the expanse of Grenada Lake. Jack sensed her protective maternal instincts kicking into high gear as she searched the distant haze for signs of a telltale fin. April had thin pale lips, a high rounded forehead and wispy red hair, "kind of like her daddy and big sister might have been her parents," Matt Oliver once said.

She turned back to Dewayne. "There ain't no sharks in lakes, is it?"

He scratched his head. "I don't reckon."

April whipped her head back around and squinted at the far horizon where a lone white sail shone peacefully through the haze.

"Better not be," she said.

"Damned," Matt Oliver whispered. "She may be dumber'n he is."

"That's not possible," Henry said.

JT helped Dewayne as they rummaged about, tossing coolers, chairs and other paraphernalia out onto the parking lot. April busied herself putting life jackets on the kids, while Jack helped Henry and Clyde carry the coolers and other things down to the picnic area. When they finished, Jack sat with the others back at the table, watching while JT helped Dewayne prepare the boat for launch. When all was ready, April and the kids climbed on board, and JT began making circular motions with his arms.

"Bring'er on back," he yelled.

Dewayne put the Toyota in reverse and began backing down the ramp. April and the kids stood in the boat, waving again as if they were in a parade.

"Easy!" JT shouted, but Dewayne didn't seem to hear.

"Dumb-ass better slow down," Matt Oliver said. "He ain't even unhooked the boat from the trailer yet."

The car and boat picked up speed on the steep incline of the ramp, but Dewayne was still grinning as he gazed into the rearview mirror. Everyone at the picnic table stood in unison, watching the scene out on the ramp, and Jack wondered if his presence would in some way liable the company.

"Damned!" Matt Oliver said. "He's gonna back right into the lake."

JT, by now, was jumping up and down, waving his arms. "Whoa," he screamed.

Dewayne locked the wheels on the Toyota, but it was too late. The boat's stern crashed into the water. Like wide-eyed refugees, April and the kids white-knuckled the side rails. A huge wave broke over the back of the boat as people everywhere stopped what they were doing and watched the unfolding drama. For a moment it seemed the boat and car hesitated at the water's edge. Jack and those at the table held their breath, but it was as if some inexorable force overcame the entire rig—car, boat, and trailer—as it slid majestically into the lake.

"That stupid sonofabitch," Matt Oliver muttered.

Jack scrambled with the others to help as the car sank nose-down on the ramp. The front of the boat, still locked to the trailer, dipped precariously, but not so much that it took on more water. April and the kids were busy abandoning ship. Holding the baby in one arm and her nose with the other, she launched herself unceremoniously over the side. JT was chest deep in the water, struggling with the car door while Dewayne crawled out through an open window on the opposite side.

Everyone dove into the water, fighting to keep the Toyota from drifting farther out into the lake. April and the kids drifted off to the side in their little orange life jackets and yellow water wings. Matt Oliver climbed into the boat, which, thanks to its size, was still floating—trailer and all. Finding a ski rope, he tossed it to Jack, who tied it to the front bumper of the Toyota. Everyone lined up and began pulling with desperation, until several bystanders joined in.

Within minutes the car was partially back on the ramp, and everyone stopped for a breather. April and the kids made their way ashore, and a park ranger showed up and called for a wrecker. The car was waterlogged, and the wrecker towed it away, but the boat and trailer came out none the worse for wear. Henry hooked his truck to the rig and parked it nearby.

Jack's muscles ached from the strain, as he wiped the sweat from his face and finished his beer. He sat back at the picnic table, hoping they would call off the boating for the day, but the thought had no sooner occurred than JT and Dewayne showed up, saying they still planned to launch the boat. Jack could only shake his head as Matt Oliver and the others tried to convince Dewayne and JT to at least wait till after lunch.

Still giddy from the near disaster, they agreed and began soothing their nerves with Bud tall-boys while Jack helped Henry begin frying the fish. The others sat around the table replaying the attempted boat launch, and when they grew tired of that, they began making fun of the sunbathers down on the beach—not the least of which was

JT's old lady. Janine was wearing a blaze-orange two-piece swimsuit—not quite a bikini, but close enough that it was catching everyone's attention.

"I told her she was too fat to wear that skimpy thing," JT said, "but you know how women are when they make up their minds."

"Janine has definitely put on a few pounds since high school," Matt Oliver said, "but she doesn't look fat at all."

JT gave him his usual open-mouth look with furrowed brows—like he wasn't certain how Matt Oliver knew what she looked like wearing a bikini in high school.

"That damned bikini would be tight on one of them anorexic show girls," JT said.

"You mean 'fashion models'?" Matt Oliver asked.

"Whatever," JT replied. "I don't need you commenting about my wife."

He got up from the table and walked down to the beach. Matt Oliver shrugged. "Didn't mean to piss him off."

"I think there's something else bothering him," Henry said.

"Mr. Henry's right," Dewayne said in a furtive voice. "JT and Janine ain't exactly speaking right now."

"How come?" Matt Oliver asked.

"She left him to babysit their boys last night and went up to the casino with Doris Ann. They got drunk and put all JT's rent money in the slot machines. That's why Doris Ann didn't come today. She's too embarrassed—that and she's still bad hung over."

"JT ought to know 'fiscally-responsible' is an oxymoron when it comes to Janine and Doris Ann," Matt Oliver said.

"It's a what?" Dewayne asked.

"Nothing," Matt Oliver said. "Just a joke."

A little while later JT came back up the footpath from the beach, looking bluer than ever.

"It ain't even noon yet, and that woman is already half-drunk and blistered all to hell," he said, "but she won't come up here. She thinks y'all know we're fighting, and she's embarrassed."

JT and his two boys stood watching while Jack set up the homemade ice cream maker he'd bought at Walmart. Little JT and Donnie had been eating potato chips, honey buns, and anything else they could get their hands on all morning. Their appetites seemed insatiable as they gnawed Slim-Jims while watching Jack pour a mix of blackberries and cream into the ice cream maker. After sprinkling salt on the ice, he began turning the crank.

Jack noticed the conversation around the table suddenly ceased. JT and his boys, along with Dewayne and April, were fixated on him. Matt Oliver had gone to help Henry fry the fish, but the others seemed caught in a hypnotic trance as their eyes followed the ice cream maker's crank around and around.

Jack grinned and shrugged. "Don't worry. It won't be long, but you guys have to eat the fish first."

"What are you gonna do with that ice cream?" JT asked.

"I'm making it for dessert," Jack said.

"Who's gonna eat it?" JT said.

Jack paused. "What do you mean?"

JT was grim-faced. "Don't you know eatin' ice cream after eating fish will kill you graveyard dead?" The others at the table nodded in agreement.

"Never heard of such a thing," Jack said.

"Well, it will. It killed hell outta my great-granddaddy. He was 86 and healthy as a horse. Ate some fried fish then had a bowl of ice cream—died right there in his rocking chair on the front porch."

Jack had heard a lot of urban tales, but this was a new one. He glanced at Clyde. "You ever heard of such a thing?"

Clyde shrugged, and Momo wasn't paying attention. Henry and Matt Oliver were still frying the fish on the other table. Dewayne and April continued nodding in earnest agreement. Jack had intended for the ice cream to be his special treat for the group, but it seemed some evil spirit was throwing every obstacle possible in his path toward gaining the employees' trust.

"Oh well," he said, "I suppose I'll just have to eat it myself."

Their eyes widened, but a moment later Henry called for everyone to get in line. Paper plates piled high with hot fried fish, french fries, slaw, and hush puppies made for a lakeside feast, and when they were finished, they sat in lawn chairs and at the table, drowsy with contentment. Jack checked the ice cream. It was frozen to perfection.

"Who's ready for dessert?" he asked, scooping the first dollops into a bowl.

No one answered, but JT, Dewayne, and April sat up, their faces drawn and tense. Jack glanced back at them as he raised the first spoonful to his lips. Bug-eyed, April threw her hand over her mouth.

Jack paused, looking over at Clyde. "You want some?"

"Ain't no colored folks I ever knew of died from eating homemade ice cream," Clyde said. "'Sides, if it's my time, ice cream with fresh blackberries, cain't be a half-bad way to go."

"Give me some too," Matt Oliver said.

Jack scooped servings for Momo and Clyde's wife as well.

"I don't believe that stuff neither, Daddy," Little JT said. "Can I have some?"

"Hell no," JT said. "You ain't committing suicide on my watch. Your mama'd kill me."

"You know, it really don't seem to be hurting them none," Dewayne said. "I might just try me a little."

He reached for the ice cream bucket, but April slapped his hand.

"I don't need no dead husband," she said.

They watched the ice cream eaters as if they would begin dropping dead at any moment. Several minutes later Jack gave a slight cough as he lit a cigarette. April sat upright, and JT stopped talking with Dewayne as they all stared expectantly. Jack smiled and shrugged, and only after another half-hour had passed did their paranoia begin to wane. That's when JT began explaining how Jack and the others were lucky, because it had to be the blackberries countering the lethal effects of ice cream and fish.

After lunch, Henry used his truck to launch Dewayne and family in their new boat. When they were safely afloat and motoring away, everyone breathed a sigh of relief. Walking back over the hill, they lined the beach in the cove, and waited as Dewayne sped up the lake from the boat ramp and made a wide circle. Standing in the hot sand, they watched as the big Bayliner returned, roaring into the cove at full throttle. April and the kids were clinging to the side rails and squinting against the wind. Dewayne made a few reckless dipsy-dos near the beach, sending a two-foot wake breaking onshore. After a few more passes, he eased the boat to a stop and slowly backed it into the shallows near the beach. The big Merc-Cruiser rumbled, even at an idle.

"Here, hold my beer," JT said, handing the near-empty can to Momo.

JT laid out the skis on the sand ten feet from the water's edge and waded out to the boat. April tossed him the end of the ski rope, and he carried it back to the beach where he coiled the slack neatly in front of the skis. The powerful Mercury gurgled ominously just offshore, its smoky exhaust drifting away in the breeze while JT adjusted the skis on his feet.

"You ever skied before?" Henry asked.

JT looked back over his shoulder at Henry. "No, but there can't be much to it. Look out yonder at those little girls. I know damn well, if they can do it, I can."

Two little pixies in pink swimsuits were slashing the water back and forth behind their daddy's ski boat.

Henry walked back to where Clyde and his wife were standing in the shade with Jack.

"Boy's gonna kill his fool self," Clyde mumbled.

"I believe you're right," Henry said.

Janine came running down the hill from the picnic area in her teenincy orange swim suit. She was swinging like a Guernsey cow as she hot-footed it across the sand. She and JT hadn't spoken since earlier in the day, but with a worried look on her face she now stared pensively as JT strapped on a red and yellow Dewey Hargrove signature life vest. It had a big number 93 across the back.

Jack looked around for little JT and Donnie, but they were nowhere in sight. Probably still up at the picnic table, like a couple of park bears scrubbing the crumbs from every pan, foil wrapper, and Tupperware bowl they could find. But this was a good thing—no sense in them witnessing their dad trying to ski drunk.

After tightening the last strap on his life vest, JT straightened up and looked out at the boat. Dewayne was sitting cocked and ready, looking back at the shore with his hand on the throttle.

"Don't you reckon you ought to get a little closer to the water first?" Matt Oliver called out.

"Man, I'm a skiing fool. I know what I'm doing. You just watch and see."

JT extended his fist over his head and shouted, "Put 'er in orbit, ski daddy."

Dewayne turned, and without looking back, shoved the throttle all the way forward. April and the kids tumbled into a heap at the back of the boat as the exhausts on the big Mercury roared and the Bayliner lunged up and out into the lake. JT grasped the handle firmly with both hands. A split-second later the slack snapped from the rope.

Jack had seen skiers at Sea World do some amazing things, but he was pretty sure there was no way this was going to end well. One moment JT was standing perfectly still, and the next it seemed some law of physics had been terribly violated. One might think he would have been dragged in the skis across the sand to the water's edge, perhaps leaving skid marks or something of that sort, but that wasn't the case. The skis never moved. They didn't so much as budge as the line snapped taut and JT was snatched cleanly from them.

It seemed his arms should have been pulled from their sockets, but JT held tenaciously to the ski rope, his chin hitting the sand at the water's edge. Still he held on, and the next time he made contact was when he skipped on the water about thirty feet from shore. When he finally found the presence of mind to let go of the rope, he was bobbing listlessly forty yards from the beach.

"Jaaaay Teeeee!" Janine wailed.

"That stupid sonofabitch," Matt Oliver muttered.

Dewayne made a high speed turn out in the lake, leaning the Bayliner on its side as April and the kids hung on for their lives. It was something Jack sensed: Dewayne saw his friend in trouble, and he was heading back for the rescue. Making a beeline, the boat hurtled toward the beach, a rooster tail of white water spouting from behind the roaring Mercury. The crowd on the beach stood in pre-stampede mode as the boat bore down on them.

Dewayne had the throttle wide open and was standing on the seat, looking over the windshield, his long blonde hair whipping in the wind. Janine, who by now had waded waist-deep in the water, was suddenly screaming at the top of her lungs. She'd realized it first: Dewayne was heading straight for JT.

"No. No. Stooooop!"

"Man, he's ballin' the jack," Clyde said.

"He's got'er plumb skin't back," Henry added.

"That stupid sonofabitch is gonna run smack over him," Matt Oliver shouted.

At the last possible moment Dewayne seemed to realize what was happening. Snatching the throttle back, he steered the boat into a sharp turn, but it was too late. JT, who by this time had come to and was flailing wildly, disappeared beneath the skidding Bayliner. Janine sagged in the water, resigned that her husband was probably dead.

"Dumb sonofabitch done run plumb over him," Henry said.

About that time, JT bobbed to the surface as he fought the foamy three-foot wake. Bloodied but still kicking, he flailed the water as he fought his way toward the idling boat.

"You better git," Matt Oliver yelled at Dewayne. "I think he's gonna kill you."

Dewayne shut off the engine instead and went back to help JT over the transom. JT crawled over the back of the boat and tackled Dewayne right there amongst the water wings and fishing tackle. April and the kids cowered in one corner as the two men groped at one another. Everyone lined the water's edge, watching, and Jack was certain he was witnessing his first homicide. They'd probably have to call the rescue squad to pry JT's hands from Dewayne's throat. Everyone shouted for JT to stop, but only when Dewayne finally went limp did he let go.

Jack and Matt Oliver waded out and pulled the boat back to the beach. Afterward, they bandaged a big cut on JT's head, while the others put ice on the thumb marks around Dewayne's throat. A few minutes later JT and Dewayne were together again, drinking beer as if nothing had happened, and it occurred to Jack that they were acting as if this were all normal. He was here with these people—the people from his culture that Cici had known as a child, and he was lost in their surreal world of the inane.

By the time dusk settled everyone was pretty much shit-faced, sitting around the picnic table, slapping mosquitoes, and dreading work the next day. Jack had begun cleaning up when he noticed the rest of the blackberry ice cream was gone. Picking up the empty bucket, he turned to the others and commented how *someone* must have liked it. JT sat up like he'd found a bug in his drink and began looking around.

"Junior—Donnie!" he shouted, almost desperately. "Where y'all at?"

The boys came skulking out of the shadows. They'd been listening the entire time, and looked as if they'd been caught stealing watermelons.

"Where you boys been?" JT asked.

"Over yonder," Little JT said, pointing to some vague spot in the darkness.

JT seemed satisfied with that explanation as he began a new line of questioning. "Di'ju boys eat the rest of Mister Jack's ice cream?"

They both wagged their heads with wide-eyed innocence.

"Tell the truth, now," he said. "Don't lie. I ain't gonna whup you. I just gotta know. Did y'all eat the rest of Mister Jack's ice cream?"

Donnie nodded first, and Junior rolled his eyes at his wimpy little brother, then turned and nodded too.

"Your mama is gonna be madder than hell if y'all get sick. And if one of y'all was to die—well hell, she's just liable to kill me, too."

It was about then that Jack realized Janine hadn't been around for the last several hours. JT, too, seemed struck by the realization, but almost as if on cue there came a yelp and a scream from down near the beach. Up through the pines she came running, butt naked and slapping at her body with the remnants of the orange swimsuit. She had passed out on the beach and the fire ants had eaten her up. By the time JT got them all off and wrapped her in a sandy towel, everyone had seen more female anatomy than any titty bar in Memphis ever thought about showing.

Jack suggested a stop at Tallahatchie General in Charleston that evening, where JT got twelve stitches in his forehead. The doctor also assured him that Little JT and Donnie didn't need their stomachs pumped, and the only problem they had from eating the ice cream and fried fish was a virulent case of obesity. Poor Janine, who was bloated like a sunburned blimp, got a shot of Benadryl, some steroids, and some pain pills. Other than that, Matt Oliver said it was pretty much an average weekend at the lake—nobody killed, divorced, or too severely maimed.

CHAPTER 12

THE DATE AT BIG DOG'S

TWO WEEKS HAD PASSED SINCE Labor Day, and despite two phone calls Jack hadn't yet spoken with Cici. He poured his Evan Williams over ice and picked up the phone again. Outside the farmhouse window another orange sunset had the Delta sky aglow with its last somber light. Like the two times before, her phone rang several times, and he was about to hang up when she answered. Her voice was still weak. Trying to sound like he wasn't desperate, Jack went for a little humor.

"You famous singer types are hard to reach. When are we going to do lunch?"

Half-expecting another excuse, he waited through a silent pause.

"Where do you want to go?" she asked.

"You name it," Jack said, knowing his enthusiasm was instantly unmasked. He tried to temper his voice. "I mean you're the one who grew up here."

"You're the one wanting a date. Now, choose the restaurant, big boy."

His first thought was Kathryn's up at Moon Lake—a special place. It would be perfect, and Cici would love it—a restaurant that was quiet and friendly.

"How about Kathryn's on Moon Lake?" he said.

"No. I want to go somewhere a little bit closer in case I get to feeling bad."

Unfamiliar with the restaurants in Clarksdale and fairly certain she wouldn't go to just anywhere, Jack was at a loss. An idea came to him, but he wasn't sure she would go for it. "What about Big Dog's down here in Tallahatchie?"

There was a dreadful silence, and for a moment he thought the phone had gone dead until she finally laughed.

"What?" Jack said.

"Big Dog's?" she said. "Where we gonna sit—on the curb?"

Jack realized Cici hadn't been back to Tallahatchie in years.

"Big Dog has moved up in the world," he said. "He's on the main drag now."

"Really?" she said.

"Yeah. It's not a fancy place, but it's actually pretty good. Why don't I come by and pick you up?"

They made it a date, and Saturday after picking her up in Clarksdale, Jack drove back to Tallahatchie. Cici was wearing a slate gray dress, with sunglasses and a wide-brimmed hat. The dress was an old woman's dress, and she looked frail.

"Are the shades and hat for old times' sake?" he asked.

She smiled, but said nothing.

He was feeling like a mega-dork, but he had to re-establish some kind of dialog.

"There you go again with the silent treatment."

Cici bent forward and looked up through the windshield at the sky above.

"It's a beautiful day, isn't it?"

It was sunny, and the distant V-formations of ducks and geese dotted the sky. The highway ran through miles of Delta lowlands.

"Yes, it is," Jack said.

He turned on the radio, and as they approached Tallahatchie the sign came into view. "Welcome to Tallahatchie, Home of Cici Cannon."

As they passed, Cici turned and looked back. "I can't believe that old sign is still out here. I hate that thing. I'm going to tell Perry to come tear it down one day."

For some reason, Jack found himself angry, but he wasn't sure why. A couple minutes later they pulled up in front of Big Dog's. The aroma of fried catfish hung in the air. Cici nodded her approval, and Jack walked around to help her out of the car.

"I'm a decrepit wreck," she said as she stepped up on the curb.

He wanted to tell her she wasn't. He wanted to tell her she was still beautiful. He wanted to tell anything that might make her feel better, but it was useless. Her cynicism wouldn't allow it. He held the door as she walked into the restaurant.

The dusty black ceiling fans rotated slowly, and the naked light bulbs high in the ceiling threw a kind of afterglow over the room. It was an ambiance achievable only in the Mississippi Delta. Big Dog glanced up from the grill, then did a double-take. He stood open-mouthed, watching while Jack helped Cici with her chair. The burgers on the grill began smoking, but after a few seconds Big Dog regained his wits and quickly motioned for one of his helpers to take over. Scrambling to the jars on the counter, he threw together a plate of "hors de oeuvres," and walked over to the table, barely masking his excitement.

"Mr. Jack, Miss Cici, how y'all doing today?"

Big Dog seemed nearly breathless.

"Best as can be expected," Cici said.

"I brung y'all some appetizers," he said. Big Dog set a plate of pickled okra, peppers, cheese, and crackers on the table. His signature smile was wider than ever.

"Don't reckon you been around here in years, Miss Cici. Sure is good to see you again."

Cici gave him a half-grin. "The last time I was here, you were selling shoulder sandwiches out of a 55-gallon drum over on High Street."

Big Dog laughed. "Yes m'am. It's been a long time. Sure has. So what can I fix y'all? The barbecue is good as ever."

Jack glanced at Cici, and she looked up at Big Dog. "Give me a glass of ice and milk mixed with a couple shots of whatever you got under the counter," she said.

Big Dog's smile evaporated instantly. "Oh, Miss Cici, I ain't got no license to sell hard liquor, but I can get you a beer."

"Don't bullshit me. Bring me some of that stuff from under the counter."

Big Dog glanced around to see if anyone was listening. "I can't sell it," he said, "but being's it's you, I don't reckon there'd be no harm if I just give you some."

He looked at Jack. "You want a glass too, Mister Jack?"

"Make mine a double," Jack said. "But no milk—just ice."

As Big Dog walked away, Cici nibbled tentatively at a saltine.

"What do you want for lunch?" Jack asked.

She glanced up at him. "I'm not hungry. Go ahead and get yourself something to eat."

"You need to eat," Jack said.

"How do you know what I need? Besides, I had some broth before you picked me up. If I can hold that and this cracker down, I'll be doing good."

Big Dog came back with two tea glasses—one full of bourbon over ice, the other with bourbon and milk over ice.

"Y'all decided what you want for lunch?" he asked.

"I'm afraid we're not going to eat," Jack said.

"Bring him a plate of something," Cici said. "He's just trying to be polite."

"I don't want to sit here and eat in front of you," Jack said.

"Bring him a plate," she said.

Big Dog cast a glance at Jack.

"Don't look at him," Cici said. "I said bring him a plate, and it don't matter what it is."

"Yes, Ma'am, Miss Cici," Big Dog left for the kitchen.

She looked across the table at Jack. Her eyes appeared incredibly tired.

"What are the doctors telling you?" Jack asked. "Are you getting better?"

"I want to know exactly what you're doing here," Cici said.

"What do you mean?"

"Why did you come here, Jack, and where is your girlfriend? Why isn't she here?"

She waited several seconds while he stopped to take a breath.

"Look, Cici, let's just relax and talk about some things. I don't have any hidden agenda. Hell, I'm here because I haven't slept one good night in months, and all I think about is you."

For a moment, he saw the tiniest chink in her armor as she blinked, but she quickly looked away. He waited, as she took her sunglasses from her purse and put them back on.

"I just don't understand you," she said. "You got money, looks, and a beautiful woman, but you just don't get it—do you?"

"Why do you have to be so sarcastic?" he asked.

"Jack, you and me, we come from different backgrounds, and you really don't know anything about where I'm from. Just because you came off up here doesn't mean shit to me."

Jack found himself fighting to remain calm.

"You know, I made up my mind before I picked you up today, that no matter what you said, I wouldn't let you make me angry, but you've just about done it."

Her face softened. "I didn't mean to make you mad, but don't you understand—people don't make money singing the Blues? Hell, the Blues are dying, just like me and this old town. Who cares anymore?"

"What do you mean you're dying?"

A tear trickled from under her sunglasses, and she swiped at it with a paper napkin.

"Oh, nothing. It's just the way I feel."

"So, you really aren't dying, right?"

"It was just an expression," she said.

"Look, Cici, I care. I know I can't change what's happened, or the way you feel about me or life or anything else, but I want to make sure you are taken care of."

"I do just fine living with Aunt Netta. It ain't home, never will be, but it's good enough."

It was something he'd come to realize about Cici—this deep attachment to her home in Louisiana.

"Have you ever gone back down to Louisiana to see your mother?"

"A time or two, years ago, but after daddy got killed in the war, she just up and sold the restaurant. She went home and died after that."

Jack sat in silence.

"I remember helping her cook when I was a little bitty thing. At least she let me think I was helping. You know her restaurant was called Mama Cici's Place. She had a live band, and people came in from all around to eat and dance."

They stared at one another across the table.

"I guess it's all gone 'cause she lost Daddy."

"I can't change the past, Cici, but let me help you. I can take care of your medical bills, and maybe take you up to Memphis to see some specialists."

"Look, why don't we take this a step at a time," she said.

Jack was ready for another glass of bourbon.

"At least let me visit from time to time and help you get back on your feet. That's all I'm asking."

Cici removed her sunglasses again, and stared across the table at him for several long seconds. Jack gazed into her teary eyes until she turned and looked out the front window for what seemed forever. He waited, and the ceiling fan woofed quietly above. Finally she turned and spoke.

"I done been to a specialist up in Memphis. I—I mean Aunt Netta and me, we could use some help with the doctor bills, but you're wasting your time with anything else."

He sat frozen like a stone, hearing only the ringing in his ears.

After sipping her bourbon and milk, she set it aside. "What happened between you and Acey?"

"She walked out on me. She thought you and I were having an affair."

"And you're just going to let her go without even—"

"I already tried, but she's shut me out. She won't listen."

Cici picked up her glass and took another drink.

"Call her again. I know. She really wants you to call."

"What makes you so sure?"

"I'm a woman. I know."

"I suppose I will at some point. It's just that right now I have so much else happening."

"Don't wait."

Jack said nothing as he thought about how he might approach Acey.

"Look, I have an idea," Cici said. "Why don't you take me and my little girls up to Moon Lake for a picnic one Saturday?"

Jack reached across the table to touch her hand, but she drew it back.

"No need to rush," she said, "but we probably need to go before the weather turns cold."

Big Dog brought out a plate of fried catfish with hush puppies and slaw, but Jack had no appetite.

After a few minutes he motioned to Big Dog. "If you don't mind, could you put this in a box? I'll eat it later."

Cici said she was tired and ready to go. Jack paid Big Dog and gave him an extra twenty bucks for the whiskey and appetizers, then drove Cici back to Clarksdale. At her insistence, he let her out in front of the house. She used her cane to limp up the drive, and when Aunt Netta stepped out on the front porch, he waved and drove away.

The veil was slipping away, and more than ever he now understood how she sang the Blues so well. It was because they came from her heart. The trip to Moon Lake would be good for them both. In the meantime he had to turn his attention back to the furniture factory.

CHAPTER 13

RETURN TO MOON LAKE

T HE CLOSER JACK GREW TO his employees, the more he wanted to save their jobs. People like Henry and Clyde had invested their lives in the factory. They deserved more than a "Sorry, we mismanaged the business, your job, and your livelihood." And there were others, like Matt Oliver, one of those Jack respected most. His woodcarvings weren't the mass-produced junk found on every flea market table between Memphis and New Orleans. Matt Oliver could take a piece of wood and turn out a work that even the untrained eye could tell was something of rare beauty and value. And it was income from his job at the factory that enabled him to do this.

He gave Muff an uncontested divorce, and the old family home survived her wrath. After replacing some of the tools he lost in the fire, Matt Oliver gave several employees his sculptures as gifts. He never said much and avoided fanfare, but Matt Oliver was sometimes hard to figure— like the day he came in with one of his works wrapped in brown paper.

Never had Jack imagined Matt Oliver would actually give Dewayne Pritchert one of his prized works. There were a few times when he was certain Matt Oliver might carve Dewayne, but never did he imagine he would carve a sculpture for him. Matt Oliver had sculpted a life-size largemouth bass, scale by scale, fin by fin, down to the tiniest detail, and put it in Dewayne's hands.

It was beautiful, and the natural grains and patterns in the birdseye maple were exquisite. The proportions were exacting and the work so unrelentingly detailed that had the thing begun flopping to life there on the table Jack would have been no more impressed. It said more to him about Matt Oliver's heart and soul than words could ever express. It also ran counter to Matt Oliver's dour façade and commentary.

Of course Dewayne took it home and spray-painted it OD green. Yeah, Matt Oliver said he was a stupid sonofa-bitch, but other than that, he took it in stride, saying it was Dewayne's, and he reckoned he could do with it as he pleased. That was on Wednesday, but it was now the end of the week, and when Jack walked to the back breakroom, another conversation was already in progress.

"So, how's your professional bass fishing career going, Dewayne?" Matt Oliver asked.

It was nearly October, and Dewayne hadn't mentioned his bass fishing ambitions since Labor Day. Henry and Clyde acknowledged Jack with nods as he walked in and took a seat at the end of the table. Arlis was reading his usual Bible passage aloud, while everyone else awaited Dewayne's reply. JT answered instead.

"It's going just fine. Ain't it, Dewayne—tell him?"

Dewayne nodded and gave everyone his usual shit-faced grin, which, as Matt Oliver explained, was the only one he ever wore, because he'd been naturally shit-faced since birth. Other than the grin and nod, Dewayne said nothing as he unwrapped his peanut butter and jelly sandwich.

"Tell 'em about your new TV satellite dish," JT said, but he didn't give Dewayne a chance to answer. "Man, he went out and got the deluxe platinum-plus package with over three hundred channels. He gets HBO, Cinemax, ESPN One and Two—all of 'em. He even gets the ones from down in South America with the naked women. Tell 'em, Dewayne."

It struck Jack that JT found as much purpose in Dewayne's life as he did in his own. Whether it was empathy, sympathy, or jealousy was difficult to tell.

Dewayne smiled. "Yeah, but I don't need but one channel," he said. Nodding confidently, he pressed his lips together with the satisfied grin of the all-knowing.

"Which one's that?" Matt Oliver asked.

"The one that gets the Bass Masters Show on Saturday mornings," Dewayne said.

"That's right," JT said. "Where do y'all think ol' Dewayne's been every Saturday morning for the last month?"

Dewayne nodded, "Been watching TV."

"You been doing any fishing?" Henry asked.

"Tell 'em, Dewayne," JT said. "Him and Percy Williams went over to Enid and caught a shit-load of bass last week. Go on. Tell 'em how you done it."

"Well, we got a bunch," Dewayne said, "but there wasn't much to it." For some reason Dewayne's air of confidence quickly gave way to one more like that of a dog caught killing chickens.

"Percy Williams?" Matt Oliver said. "I thought they kicked his ass out of the bass club down at Grenada for cheating."

Dewayne's cheeks turned as red as the new paint job on his Toyota.

"Yeah," Henry said. "The game warden caught him with a shocker."

JT's lips formed a circle as he furrowed his brows and stared suspiciously at Dewayne. "That electric fish finder you said y'all been using—the one with the hand crank—you said it was the secret. That thing ain't illegal, is it?"

Dewayne continued eating his sandwich, ignoring him.

"Dewayne, have you and Percy been shocking up fish?" Matt Oliver asked.

"Damned, boy," Henry said. "Don't you know the game warden will throw your ass *under* the jail for that shit?"

Dewayne looked like a wild-eyed animal caught in a trap. "Percy said it wasn't really nothing wrong with it, long as we didn't keep more than the limit."

"Then how come you're all of a sudden looking like an egg-sucking dog?" Matt Oliver asked.

"I just didn't know."

"Why don't you take up deer hunting?" JT asked.

Dewayne raised his eyebrows. "Do they have professional deer hunting tournaments, too?"

"No," JT answered, "but all you need is a gun and some bullets—maybe a truck."

Jack couldn't understand why anyone would suggest that Dewayne Pritchert purchase a gun, but then JT wasn't exactly a MENSA candidate himself. It seemed at times that JT was Dewayne's only link to reality, a concept that was frightening in its own right.

JT turned to Henry, "Are we still going hunting out at Clyde's place opening day?"

The room fell suddenly silent, and everyone looked at Dewayne, who remained oblivious while stuffing the last of the peanut butter and jelly sandwich into his mouth. Henry stared back at JT without responding.

"Well?" JT said.

Henry's eyes became lasers focusing on JT.

"What?" JT said.

No one said anything, and a moment later the five-minute bell rang. A visible relief came over Henry as everyone began filing out of the breakroom.

Matt Oliver muttered to Henry under his breath, "Saved by the bell."

"Thank God it's still almost two months till deer season," Henry said.

"I'll try to talk to JT," Matt Oliver said.

The spark had been thrown, and Jack worried. No one in his right mind would want to be in the same county with Dewayne Pritchert carrying a loaded gun. Someone would probably get shot if they allowed him to go.

When the little group reached the dock, Matt Oliver pulled JT to the side to explain matters. "You need to think before you suggest to Dewayne he buy a gun."

"Goddamit, if we go huntin' and leave him behind," JT said, "it's gonna hurt his feelings."

"The only way I'll go along with it," Matt Oliver said, "is if he stays with you—understood? And he doesn't load his gun till he's in the woods, you hear? First, though, the others have to say it's okay."

JT and Matt Oliver turned to look at Jack. He shrugged. There was no way he was getting sucked into this one. Besides, anything he said would probably be wrong. He turned to Henry, but the old foreman shook his head slowly from side to side.

"It just wouldn't be right," JT said. "Besides, Dewayne ain't gonna hurt nobody."

Jack couldn't help but glance at the scar on JT's forehead.

"I can't go, anyway," Jack said. "I have an important meeting with a vendor that Saturday. Besides, it's Clyde's place. Shouldn't he decide?"

Everyone turned to Clyde, but he shrugged. "I don't know. I've got family lives around there."

Only when JT swore he would keep Dewayne with him the entire day did Clyde finally agree. Momo never said anything, and Jack was happy to escape what was certain to be another venture into the rabbit hole.

Jack's long-awaited meeting with Nickels was scheduled after lunch that day, and it seemed it might actually occur this time because Doris Ann called just before lunch to remind him. The others were still arguing about Dewayne going on the deer hunt when Jack left for Nickels's office. With the last-minute cancellations of three previous meetings, it was still doubtful that Nickels would show for this one.

Doris Ann greeted him with a smile when Jack tapped on her door. "Come on in," she said. "He's still out to lunch, but he called, and I reminded him about your appointment."

Jack took a seat beside the credenza with the Elvis and Princess Di memorial and waited. Doris Ann blushed and pretended to work on her computer. Forty minutes after the appointed meeting time Nickels hurried in. Without a word of acknowledgment to either of them, he walked in and closed his office door. A few moments later the phone beeped on Doris Ann's desk.

"Yes, sir. He's here for your meeting. Yes, sir. It was at one o'clock. I did remind you! Well, I did. Okay. Yes, sir."

"Mr. Nickels will be with you in a few minutes," she said, then curled her lip in disgust and whispered, "Prick."

After another ten minutes the phone beeped again. "Yes, sir," she said and hung up.

"Mister Nickels will see you now, Mr. Hartman," she said in a sing-song voice loud enough for Nickels to hear through his closed door.

Nickels feigned preoccupation with the computer on his desk and didn't look up as he held his hand over his head and pointed toward a chair. "Sit down," he said.

Another couple minutes passed before he looked up. "Okay, Jack, what can I do for you today?"

"Mr. Nickels, there are a number of things we need to discuss concerning the employees, the equipment, and our manufacturing processes, but thirty minutes isn't enough time."

"So, do I have to teach you basic time management? Why don't you just hit the high points for now, and we'll focus on what's most important?"

"I'm concerned with employee morale as well as the condition of our—"

"One thing at time. You *should* be worried about employee morale. That's your job—you and the supervisors. Why are you telling me about it? If I have to fix it, why do I need you?"

Jack drew a deep breath. This long-awaited meeting was already looking hopeless.

"What's your next problem?" Nickels asked.

"Well, sir, the condition of the machinery. It's all so old—"

"—that you want to replace it with that fancy computerized machinery you sold before you came here, right?"

"No, sir, that's not—"

"Look, Jack. When I came down here years ago, it was because I was forced to. My father's factory was bought out by Fernwood the same time they bought this place. Do you know why most of Fernwood's plants are in the South?" He didn't give Jack a chance to answer. "Because labor is cheap. People up north refuse to work for peanuts like they do down here. In other words, it's cheaper to throw more labor in the mix than it is to purchase those new whiz-bang machines."

"I believe you're mistaken, sir. I can provide you with figures that verify—"

"So you're going to come in here after barely two months on the job and tell me how to run my plant—one I've run successfully for years. Is that it?"

"No, sir. That's not it at all."

"You know, Jack, we can all learn by listening to the people around us. It's called good leadership. You should try it. What I suggest you do is get out there and talk to some of the old-heads like your buddy Freeman or Henry Smith. Learn how they keep that machinery running. If you continue coming in here whining, instead of finding solutions, people are going to lose respect for you. I don't need negative people on my team. I need people who can think outside the box and make things happen.

"Now, you said you have three things—what's the third one?"

There was no sense stopping now. An OSHA inspection could shut the plant down indefinitely, and Jack had to make Nickels realize the risk.

"As you know, I moved Dewayne Pritchert and Arlis McCallister out of the paint shop. I've also replaced some of our solvent-based coatings with water-based ones and begun a documentation process, but we still fall short of EPA and OSHA requirements. If their inspectors show up—"

"Trust me on this one, Jack. I have us covered. I take the OSHA man to play golf at the Tallahatchie Country Club in Charleston any time he comes in town. Is there anything else you want to talk about?"

The futility of the situation left Jack wagging his head. The whole mess was bigger than his ability to address it. It was the same feeling he'd had with Cici, and now the factory seemed no less of a salvage operation.

"No, sir, Mr. Nickels. I just want to say thanks for meeting with me and letting me share my thoughts."

"No problem, Jack. Just think about the things I've said. We need team players, but there's only one quarterback, and that's me. I am the Bart Starr of this operation, and I say what we change and when. Now, I'm still confident you have what it takes, so let's see what you can do."

Nickels stood, hitched up his trousers and shoved his hand across the desk at Jack.

"Oh, and one more thing." Nickels had lowered his voice to a near whisper. "There's a hell of a lot more niggers around here than rednecks, and there's a rumor going around that you're dating a black woman. If brown sugar is your thing, then so be it, but you need to remember you're still a member of management at this factory. You need to keep a lid on it. I don't need the niggers getting all riled up. And remember the rednecks have to respect you, too."

Jack had never been hot-tempered, but he bent forward across the desk, fighting the impulse to physically drag Nickels across the desk, to push his face into the floor and put a foot on the back of his neck and ask him if he was sure he meant what he had said. Instead, he bent forward and placed his hands flat on the desk, not so much to brace himself as to keep from throttling the little bastard.

"Mr. Nickels, my personal life is my business. And I suggest you stop participating in the rumor mill and get your facts straight. As for the rest of your remarks, calling people niggers and rednecks, I'm going to pretend I didn't hear them. And, by the way, your quarterbacking sucks, because this damned factory is failing."

He stood over Nickels, who was staring up at him in wide-eyed fear, and Jack knew instantly he was the loser—he'd blown everything. Apparently, though, his boss had enough sense to remain silent, while his eyes flickered between the authoritarian Factory Manager and a man who faced imminent annihilation. After several seconds Jack stood upright and walked out.

He understood now why Henry and the others kept their mouths shut. Nickels could turn a nun into a homicidal maniac. Walking into his office, Jack slammed the door. It wasn't the first time he'd thought about returning home to Fairhope, but it now seemed prudent to make arrangements—especially since he was probably fired anyway.

Jack had come to the Delta knowing he might accomplish nothing, but here he was, on his way to Moon Lake with Cici and her two little girls. It was a sunny fall morning, and the yellow leaves fluttered from the cottonwood trees as he turned off Highway 61 and drove down the narrow road toward the lake. Once there, he unloaded the picnic gear and walked with Cici and the toddlers out to the pier. A mild breeze barely rippled the water, and Cici had left her cane behind. She walked with care as she led the kids by the hand. Jack carried lawn chairs and unfolded them at the end of the pier then helped Cici as she sat down.

The day was perfect, and he bided his time waiting for her to begin the conversation, but she seemed to purposely avoid it. After a while he realized if there was going to be a conversation it was up to him.

"Have you given any more thought to what we talked about the other day at Big Dog's?"

She gave a wry laugh. "Just about every day since."

"And?"

"I don't know. I guess I need more time."

"Look, I'm not trying to push you. I can be whatever you want me to be—a friend, whatever."

"Have you called your girlfriend yet?"

She had that mischievous spark in her eyes—the one she always got when she intentionally jerked his chain.

"I will," he said.

He reached over and put his hand on top of hers. She let him.

"You said you were going back to the doctor. What did he say?"

"Nothing good. I've got too much scar tissue on my liver, and the one kidney I have left is failing. Other than that, I'm a wreck."

"I'm sorry I did this to you," Jack said.

Cici turned and looked directly into his eyes. Her lips were parted slightly as the color rose in her cheeks. "You *what?*"

"I'm sorry that I talked you into leaving here and coming to Orange Beach."

Cici shook her head, "No, Jack. I can't believe you're even saying that. You didn't do this to me."

"I understand what you're saying, but—"

"Shut up, Jack. Just shut up. You don't understand at all."

Jack fought to keep a cool head.

"I understand that I've screwed up your entire life."

She pushed his hand away. "Like I said, shut up. You don't understand shi..." She paused and glanced down at the kids. "You don't understand anything. I did this to myself. You didn't do anything wrong, and what happened was my fault."

"If I hadn't encouraged you to go to Alabama, none of this would have happened."

"Oh for God's sake, Jack, let's not argue, please? What happened, happened, and the only person who could have stopped it was me. I was drinking gin by the gallon before I ever knew you. And it was you that almost got me out of the habit. Hell, I drank less in those few weeks down there than I have my entire adult life. It was gonna happen with or without you."

The sun slowly sank into the trees on the other side of the island, and the wind calmed as the lake took on the slick appearance of gray marble. They sat in silence for several minutes.

"So, how are things going at the factory?" she asked.

"I probably won't have a job when I get back Monday."

Her eyes showed a start of concern. "What happened?"

"My boss is an assh...." He caught himself as the little girls sat staring up at him.

"Did you tell him that?"

"In so many words."

"Why?"

"Hell, I don't know. The factory is failing because of mismanagement, and he's the one responsible, but he won't listen to anything I say. A lot of people are going to lose their jobs if that place closes down, but it seems hopeless."

"Have you tried going over his head?" she asked.

"No. There's just too much—I mean the machines in the factory are all relics, and there are so many other issues, it just seems like a lost cause."

Cici smiled. "You're a sucker for lost causes, aren't you?"

"Maybe so," Jack said.

This day wasn't going the way he had hoped. Never had he imagined it would be so difficult to rein in his emotions.

"I shouldn't have said that," she said. "I owe you an apology."

"No, you don't. You don't owe me anything."

"You know, Jack, there are some things you just can't fix."

From somewhere up toward the Yazoo Pass a barred owl howled. Its spooky call echoed down the lake as another owl answered in the distance.

"Are you talking about the factory or you?" he asked.

"Both."

"Maybe you're right, but if there's a chance in hell I can make a difference, I'm going to keep trying."

It was Cici this time who reached over and took his hand in hers.

"You are too much of an idealist, but I do appreciate your help."

He squeezed her hand gently, and the timing seemed right to press her for an answer on her health. "Do you trust me?" he asked.

She turned to face him, her forehead wrinkled with perplexity. "I think you're the most honest man I've ever known."

"Then why don't you tell me the truth?"

She turned away and looked out across the lake. "The truth about what?"

"About your health."

Far up the lake a string of light bulbs came to life on another pier, their reflection stabbing out across the water into the gathering darkness. Music echoed so faint and distant that only an occasional note could be heard as it drifted down the lake.

Cici nodded. "I haven't been up front with you."

"Okay, and?"

It was something he pretty much knew, but having her say it would probably help her as much as it would him. At least it would give them a starting point.

"Are you...?" He paused again. The kids were sitting on the dock playing, seemingly uninterested in the adults' conversation.

A tear trickled down Cici's cheek, and she gave a slight nod. "Yes. The doctor says my internal organs are failing. He said it was a miracle I ever left the hospital, and...." Her voice trailed off into silence, and Jack put his arm around her, pulling her close.

"I will be here for you, and when you're gone, I'll make sure Aunt Netta and your little girls are okay. You have my word."

She wrapped her arms around him, and they embraced as the glow of the evening sky faded into nightfall.

CHAPTER 14

DORIS ANN SPRINGS HER TRAP

I T WAS NOVEMBER AND WITH Christmas only weeks away,
Jack decided to do some early shopping. Cici had invited
him to visit her and the kids during the holidays, and this
meant gifts to buy. He was on his way to the only place he
knew was close, Walmart in Clarksdale. Walking out to the
factory parking lot, he spotted Doris Ann. She had parked
her car beside his pickup.

"What'cha got planned this evening?" she asked.

The woman was relentless, having stalked him like
a hungry panther ever since that day in August when he
barely escaped her Graceland trip. Jack had done everything possible to avoid her, but she never gave up, and she
did little to hide her intentions. It wasn't that Doris Ann
was unlikable—she could be disarmingly sweet at times,
but his heart belonged to Acey. Besides, Doris Ann was
not a woman with whom he could even imagine having an
affair—not to mention the possible complications created
by doing so with an employee.

Jack did not want to hurt her feelings, but it was inevitable. He had to tell her, and it wasn't going to be pleasant, especially since Doris Ann had spread it around the factory that theirs was a relationship of destiny.

"I have plans, tonight. Maybe another time."

He winced as the words escaped his lips. He'd done it again.

A buxom bleach-blonde that JT swore was Marilyn Monroe reincarnated, Doris Ann had tested the tensile strength of every halter top Walmart sold. Of course, JT's perceptions were somewhat skewed. His eyes probably carried special filters that made Godzilla look like someone's pet lizard—which was not to say that Doris Ann was necessarily unattractive, but Jack was determined. It simply wasn't going to happen with her.

"Can't you put your plans on hold? I'm going up to the Horseshoe later and was kind of hoping you might go along. We might just win the big one, you know?"

Telling her *"hell no, not now, not ever"* passed through his mind, but Jack couldn't bring himself to hurt her feelings. "I really appreciate the offer, Doris Ann, but I have something I need to do."

Climbing into his truck he waved her good-bye and drove from the parking lot. Eventually there'd come a time when he would stop this masquerade and tell her once and for all there was no chance in hell of them having a relationship.

After several stress-relief drinks at a place in Clarksdale, Jack drove over to Walmart. Mellowed by the bourbon, he relaxed and wandered up and down the aisles. A rack of shirts gained his interest, and he was studying them when something else caught his eye—almost a subliminal flash. He swore he had just seen Doris Ann walking across the end of the aisle. Blinking, Jack shook his head. The paranoia was catching up with him. But he turned and look again. It wasn't paranoia.

Doris Ann's head was bobbing down the adjacent aisle. She was chewing gum, probably in perfect rhythm with her step, and she was on her game—already painted up and ready for a night at the casino. Maraschino cherries couldn't compete with her lipstick, a version with the appearance of wet gloss enamel. Rumor was her lipstick smudges were hell to get off a shirt. Matt Oliver said the guys at the factory called them red badges of courage, because wearing a shirt home with one could lead to death or dismemberment.

Jack turned his head and tried to melt into the background as she passed. It worked. She turned up another aisle and disappeared—a good time for a strategic retreat. He headed for the exit. The Christmas shopping could wait.

Trying not to appear like the store was on fire, Jack left the men's clothes and started through the women's lingerie as he attempted to make good his escape. A quick glance over his shoulder confirmed Doris Ann was nowhere in sight. Freedom was only yards away, just beyond the cash registers. He had only to make it past the checkout counters and out the door. Another glance back had him feeling the exhilaration of a coyote escaping a chicken coop.

He was almost home free—or so it seemed, until he turned and collided head-on with her beside a rack of colored bras. Jack didn't know which hit him first: Doris Ann's ample bosom or the odor of her perfume, but the collision and the drinks left him off-balance and desperately clinging to her to avoid falling. They stumbled together, their bodies pressed close as Jack fought to regain his balance.

Her perfume, an overpowering floral eau de funeral home, made Jack's eyes water, but not so much that he didn't see her sequined halter top was askew and her massive breasts bulging precariously close to freedom. *Who the hell except Doris Ann would wear a halter top in November?* She had somehow made a one-eighty turn around the store and gotten in front of him, a feat that defied the same laws of physics her breasts were now fighting. She was looking amazingly composed for such a chance collision. When Jack finally regained his balance, he released her and picked up the red bra knocked from the rack.

"You know, stepping into aisle-ways without looking can be dangerous," she said.

"Uh, yeah," he mumbled.

She smiled and said, "You're lucky I have good brakes."

Jack, still tipsy from the drinks, let his thoughts become words before he realized it. "Yeah, but it was those airbags that saved us," he blurted.

It seemed a slap across the face would have been more appropriate or even a mild blush, but Doris Ann's eyes virtually sparkled as she straightened her halter top, pulled her jacket together and checked her black tights. She was wearing open-toe, spike heels and a string of fake pearls surrounded by nothing but pure cleavage.

"So, mister crash test dummy, I thought you had big plans. What are you doing at Walmart on a Friday evening?"

"Just doing a little Christmas shopping," he said.

"Christmas shopping? You've got to be kidding. I sure would hate to be the poor girl you're buying that bra for."

Jack glanced down at the red bra still in his hand. "It fell off the rack. I was putting it back."

"You need to go to the factory outlet stores over in Batesville. There's a bunch of nice gift shops there," she said.

Jack shrugged. "Maybe tomorrow. It's too far to drive tonight. Besides, I was looking for something for my uncle, and Walmart usually has most anything he needs."

"Hey!" she said. "I have an idea. Have you ever been to the outlet stores up at Tunica?"

Jack wagged his head as he fought for an excuse, anything besides an uncontested surrender, but Doris Ann had the initiative. His bourbon-dulled mind left him unable to react as his mental wheels skidded toward the roadside ditch of catastrophe.

"Come on," she said. "You can ride with me. And after we finish shopping, I'm gonna take you over to the Horseshoe. You ain't been to a casino till you been to the Horseshoe, and I'll show you a good time like you ain't never had."

"Really, I can't drive that far. I've had several drinks, and—"

"No problem," she said. "I'm driving."

Matt Oliver had warned him, saying that calling Doris Ann aggressive was the equivalent of calling a barracuda a guppy. But she was much more than that. She was a Great White cruising the casinos in search of a hapless male blissfully surfing the dollar slots, but tonight she was bringing her own meal, and Jack was it.

He had overheard her telling another female employee, "I don't waste my time around the quarter slot machines. I go for the dollar slots. That's where the men with money hang out, but I do keep my eyes on the fifty-cent machines, too. You can pick up an occasional bargain there when things are slow."

Before he knew it, she had him in her red Mustang, hitting nothing but the high spots on Highway 61. Supposedly they were on their way to the factory outlet stores in Tunica. Of course, Jack saw through that ploy as he tried to come up with a graceful exit, but for the moment, Doris Ann had him in her charmingly psychotic clutches. It seemed inevitable that he would soon be tossing his hard-earned dollars on a craps table somewhere in Tunica.

Regardless of this temporary setback, Jack had no intention of total capitulation. He could stand a little drinking and gambling, but the line would be drawn there. And the bright side of this little tryst was that they would at least be incognito at the Horseshoe. After all, it was a pretty long drive from Tallahatchie. But as he walked in with Doris hanging on his arm, Jack felt the full impact of her checkmate as she guided him to a craps table where several of the factory employees were already gathered. Matt Oliver, Dewayne, Momo, JT, and Arlis were all leaning over the table, placing their bets.

Making a break for the door crossed his mind, but it was too late. Doris Ann shouted her greeting. "Hey y'all, look who's here."

As they looked up, their faces said it all. Doris Ann held Jack with one hand and grabbed a passing waitress with the other. "Hon, can you bring me a White Russian, please?"

She turned quickly to Jack. "What do you want, baby?"

His blood pressure soared as he told the waitress to bring him a glass of bourbon over ice. He needed something to kill the pain.

By one a.m. Doris Ann had ordered him so many bourbons Jack was a borderline vegetable, steadily tossing his hard-earned money down on the craps table. Matt Oliver, who had been eyeing him all night, was no doubt wondering how in hell he had hooked up with her, but he remained self-consciously silent. Doris Ann plopped the dice into Jack's hand. It was his turn to roll, and he no longer gave a shit when JT began chanting some mumbo-jumbo about how "ol' Jack was set, to cover my bet, with a good throw, to steal the show."

Doris Ann glanced over at JT, then back at Jack, tweaking his cheek. "Don't y'all worry, none. My baby has you covered."

This sudden ownership didn't escape Matt Oliver's or JT's attention as they cut their eyes over at Jack. Helpless in her clutches and damned near too drunk to care, Jack refused to meet their stares as he rolled the dice. He was a stricken swimmer in the jaws of a man-eating shark, and the more she said, the more bloodstained the water became. He matched his seven.

JT pumped his fist in the air, shouting, "You're the man, Jack," and raked in his winnings.

"Y'all stick with me'n Jack," Doris Ann said. "We'll make you rich."

As if he'd suddenly awakened, Dewayne stared first at Jack then at Doris Ann. It was in his eyes—the light bulb had finally come on. Doris Ann and Jack were an "item" or possibly engaged, maybe even secretly married, but somehow he'd missed it all. Dewayne continued staring at Doris Ann until she noticed. She stared back at him with a look that could wilt kudzu.

"You got a problem?" she said in her patented eat-shit-and-die tone of voice.

Dewayne's mouth dropped open. He slowly shook his head and looked away. Doris Ann turned to Jack, wrinkling her nose as she gave him a squinty-eyed smile.

Later that night Jack recalled some vague reference to him being too drunk to drive, and she was right. He was feeling as if he were drugged, and somewhere along the way he must have passed out. When he awoke, Jack realized he'd been dreaming of Acey, or was it a dream. He felt her hair on his belly and his penis was rigid as she stroked it. He felt her take him into her mouth, and the room spun as he came with a passion.

"That's my boy. That's my big boy."

It was not Acey's voice. He forced open his eyes. In the dim light he realized he was lying on a couch in a strange room, cramped and unfamiliar. Still in a nether world of drunken passion, he looked down to see Doris Ann kneeling beside him, smiling.

Jack tried to move, but his body was unresponsive. He closed his eyes, only to realize he was being pulled into her bedroom. And never had he experienced anything like the ever-wear erection he now had, something of which Doris Ann was taking full advantage. Somewhere in the other room Elvis was singing on the stereo.

The flames are now licking my body
Won't you help me
I feel like I'm slipping away

Through the drunken haze, Jack continually crossed paths with a red and black butterfly tattooed on Doris Ann's butt.

A black widow would have been more appropriate, because surely his life was over after this.

When he finally awoke Saturday afternoon, Jack was alone on the couch and his head was pounding as he lay perfectly still. On the wall above him was a huge three-by-four-foot velveteen print of Elvis in all his rhinestone-studded regalia, framed in tiny blue lights. Years ago Jack had stopped swearing off liquor during a hang-over because the memories always faded with time. But this was certain to scar him for life. There would always be the BD and the AD years—Before Doris and After Doris.

His ever-wear erection had finally disappeared, but his penis was raw, and every muscle in his body ached as he picked up his boxers from the floor. He squinted with his one open eye against a single laser-ray of sunlight penetrating a moth-hole in the front curtains. His entire body was in revolt—or was it retreat—a panic-stricken slide down a rope from a sinking ship? Half stumbling, half crawling, he made his way down a narrow hallway to the bathroom, where he clung to the sink and dug through Doris Ann's medicine cabinet in search of some aspirin.

The first thing he found was a half-empty bottle of Viagra. There was another bottle sitting open on the back of the toilet. He picked it up and peered at the label. It was something called Rohypnol.

"I see you found my little secret," she said.

Startled, he looked over his shoulder. She said something else, but the last thing he remembered before passing out again was when he stubbed his toe on a door jamb. Doris Ann had said it wasn't considered a "damned trailer" since it was a doublewide.

By the time Jack returned to work that Monday it was common knowledge. Doris Ann had reversed the male-macho role of bragging about sexual conquests, spreading it all over the factory and half of Tallahatchie County how she and Jack were damned near engaged. And to hear JT tell it, Jack was to be revered for having bedded such a fine woman, even admitting he would have done the same if it weren't for the instant death and dismemberment Janine promised him if he did. Jack avoided the breakroom that day, opting to drive down to Jake's E-Z Stop where he bought a Goody's Headache Powder and a Diet Dr. Pepper.

All his work gaining the employees' trust had gone awry. Some had already tried and convicted him of being a lecherous bastard, out for a one-night stand with poor Doris Ann. And since he wasn't returning her calls, she was telling them how she was considering a sexual harassment suit—a plan that fizzled when she let it slip that she had worked long and hard before finally cornering Jack at Walmart.

The more Jack heard, the more he realized he had totally underestimated his adversary. She'd trapped him and laced his drink with doses of Rohypnol and Viagra, but to hear her tell it, he'd committed rape and gotten away with it. Henry said he thought Jack had more sense than that, and Matt Oliver simply broke into fits of laughter whenever the subject came up. Momo and Clyde were the only ones who didn't have anything to say about it.

CHAPTER 15

THE NINETY-EIGHT DOLLAR MULE

JACK HOPED TO AVOID THE deer hunt, but his alibi fell through when Doris Ann let it be known there were no vendors coming to the factory that Saturday. He was cornered again, and the opening day deer hunt at Clyde's place was on. No more excuses—JT and the others made it clear that he was expected to be there. Jack resigned himself to whatever fate awaited him, and given the potentially lethal mix of guns, JT and Dewayne, it couldn't be good. Actually, after his debacle with Doris Ann, he figured death might come as a relief.

Clyde and his family owned several hundred acres over on the bluff near Tallaha Road. This was beyond the eastern edge of the Delta where it gave way to the red clay hills. Mostly clear-cut, some pines, briar patches, and bean fields, it held a decent number of deer. Clyde had a pack of "full-blooded Mississippi deer dogs" as he called them— a group of mutts ranging from mixed-blooded beagles to an ancient black and tan that looked like an old rug stretched over a dog's skeleton. Jack was relieved when it began raining that Friday night, and he went to bed hoping the hunt was cancelled, but the phone rang at four the next morning. It was Henry. The hunt was on.

Driving over to Charleston, Jack picked up Matt Oliver and Momo and headed out to a gravel crossroads near Clyde's house. Clyde and Henry were already there, sitting in Henry's truck on the opposite side of the road. Jack pulled his pickup off the road and sat with Matt Oliver and Momo, sipping coffee from Styrofoam cups. As usual, they were waiting on Dewayne and JT.

It was warm and wet, and the eastern sky had just begun graying up. Jack wiped the moisture from the inside of the windshield as he tried to look out. A wet fog hung across the road, shrouding the adjacent fields and woods. Only the black skeletons of the trees protruded from the foggy mist.

"It might be a pretty good day, after all," he said.

"I don't reckon I've ever been what you'd call a serious deer hunter," Matt Oliver said.

"You haven't hunted much?" Jack said.

"I've killed a few deer, but there's a lot to be said for sitting at home in the easy-chair and drinking coffee when it's nasty out."

Matt Oliver's Marlin thirty-thirty was propped between his knees. The rifle had scarcely a scratch on it.

"Yeah, I know what you mean," Jack said. "I'm pretty much a social hunter myself. I did some hunting with my Uncle Tuck up in central Alabama and Georgia after he got back from Nam, but this is the first time I've been in years. How about you, Momo?"

Momo cradled his coffee cup in his hands as he took a deep breath and began working his lips in silence. After a moment or two it came out: "Wu-wu-we hu-hunt ffo-for fffoo-food."

Momo's ancient single-shot twelve-gauge was propped against the seat between him and Matt Oliver. With most of the bluing worn off and electrician's tape wrapped around the stock, it looked as if it had been handed down through several generations. No doubt, Momo's old shotgun had taken more deer and small game than Jack's and Matt Oliver's rifles combined.

Dawn broke gray and overcast before the headlights of JT's truck finally pierced the fog as it came up the hill. Excited about the coming hunt, the dogs were yelping and bawling in the back of Clyde's truck. Jack got out and stretched in the middle of the road. Despite the fog, the morning air was warm. Matt Oliver and Momo stepped out on the other side, as JT pulled up in the middle of the crossroads and rolled down his window.

"Y'all ready to kick some serious deer ass?" he asked.

Jack and Matt Oliver exchanged glances, but said nothing. JT pulled off the road and got out. He was decked out from head to toe in a National Guard outfit that included camouflaged fatigues, a pistol belt, canteen, compass, and a bayonet. He also showed them his two ammo pouches stuffed with bags of pork skins and Moon Pies. And as if that wasn't enough, he'd smeared his face with green camo-paint.

His unshaven face appeared as eyes and a mouth hidden in a mask of green moss. Reaching inside his truck, he came out with a World War II vintage .30 caliber carbine. It had a huge banana clip, one that probably held thirty rounds or more. Matt Oliver raised his eyebrows, but said nothing.

"Y'all sure are a sleepy-headed bunch," JT said. "How come ain't nobody saying good morning?"

"Good morning, JT," Matt Oliver said. "Where'd you get the army stuff?"

"My brother's in the guard down at Grenada."

Dewayne, who'd gotten out on the other side, walked around the front of the truck. The headlights reflected off his head-to-toe blaze-orange hunting outfit.

"Damned, Dewayne," Matt Oliver said. "Reckon you got enough orange on?"

Dewayne was dressed in shining new blaze-orange coveralls—glow in the dark, sure enough blaze-orange. His hat and gloves were orange, too. His freaking underwear may have been orange, but Jack decided not to ask. No doubt, once the sun was up, his reflection would interfere with satellite cameras far above the earth.

"Don't want no dumb-ass shooting me," Dewayne said.

"And what are you going to do with that?" Matt Oliver asked, pointing to a huge K-bar strapped to Dewayne's leg. The knife stretched from his ankle up to his knee.

"Whatta ya mean? It's my deer skinning knife."

"I've seen swords weren't that big," Matt Oliver said. "You could gut an elephant with that thing."

Dewayne simply shrugged as Henry began planning the hunt.

"Clyde's gonna turn the dogs out over yonder behind the old dump. JT, you and Dewayne drive around to that catch-pen above Clyde's house and watch them hollows coming up that way. Matt Oliver, you and Jack, y'all need to go back down yonder about a mile or so and cover the creek bottom. You can drop Momo off about halfway between here and there. I'll just stick with Clyde and try to cut the dogs off whichever way they go. We'll all meet back here at noon."

Jack unsheathed his rifle, and JT walked over to size it up. A Ruger single-shot .308, the rifle was one Tuck had described as a true marksman's weapon. Jack broke it open and checked the chamber.

"That thing don't hold but one bullet?" JT asked.

Jack nodded.

"Shiiiutt," JT said. He grinned and looked around at the others. "Y'all come over here and look at what Mr. Jack is huntin' with. I ain't believin' this shit."

He shook his head as Jack handed him the rifle. "You're gonna lose a lot of deer with this thing," he said. "But I reckon it's good you're at least trying, anyway. I mean, I figured a guy who hangs around Blues clubs wouldn't even want to hunt. You know?"

"You'll have to excuse JT," Matt Oliver said. "He thinks if you aren't humming *Free Bird* and packing a Thompson sub-machine gun, you're not qualified."

"Kiss my ass," JT said.

"I would," Matt Oliver said, "but you have green camo paint all over it."

Dewayne pulled his rifle from JT's truck, and everyone ducked as he swung past them and pointed at a nearby fence post.

"This here's a real deer rifle," he said. "I got it at trade day up in Batesville. It's a genuine Chinese SKS."

He handed it to Jack, and while Dewayne and JT looked over Jack's Ruger, Matt Oliver and Jack examined Dewayne's military surplus rifle. The little SKS still had the military bayonet folded under the barrel and splotches of rust on the receiver, no doubt the result of an Asian monsoon.

"What are you gonna do with the bayonet?" Matt Oliver asked. "Finish 'em off?"

"If I have to," Dewayne answered. His jaw was set firm, and there was no doubt he was dead serious.

"Have you shot this thing?" Jack asked.

Dewayne shrugged. "Sure, out behind my trailer yesterday after work. I got the scope at the dollar store in Charleston and put it on, then shot it at an old drum. I shot it three times and hit the drum twice at forty yards. That ain't too bad, now, is it?"

"Maybe the bayonet *will* come in handy," Matt Oliver said.

JT caught his sarcasm. "At least he's got more than one bullet."

Jack smiled. The idea of killing a deer with a single-shot was a foreign concept to JT, who by now had turned his attention to Momo's single-shot twelve-gauge.

"I figured you'd be hunting with a bow and arrow, Momo. That shotgun's a step up for you, ain't it?"

"F-fu-fuck you, Ju-ju-Jay Ttt-Tee."

"Y'all better quit jawin' and git," Henry said. "It's gonna be full light soon."

With that everyone piled into the trucks and headed for their designated stands. Jack dropped Momo off near a scope of woods a half-mile down the road, then drove on to the creek bottom where he and Matt Oliver walked up the edge of a bean field. They decided to sit against a big white oak and talk, until the dogs jumped. They'd been there only a few minutes when they heard something, but it wasn't the dogs.

There were gunshots echoing in the distance—many shots, but they were all coming from the same weapon. A constant pop, pop, pop, pop, that eventually petered out to a single shot, then one more, then silence.

"Reckon he got him?" Matt Oliver asked.

"If he didn't, he's a mighty poor shot," Jack replied. "How many shots was that?"

"Hell, I don't know—twenty, thirty, maybe. It was a bunch. Who do you think it was?"

"Sounded like JT's carbine," Jack said.

"Reckon we ought to go see?" Matt Oliver asked.

"Let's wait. Let his adrenaline settle. Know what I mean?"

Matt Oliver grinned. "Yeah, you're right. No sense getting our asses shot."

After a few minutes watching some squirrels in a nearby hickory, Matt Oliver laid his rifle aside and leaned back against the tree. Folding his hands behind his head, he closed his eyes.

"Wake me up if you decide to shoot at something," he said. "I don't want the shit scared out of me."

"I was thinking of joining you," Jack said. "I'm sleepy too."

Matt Oliver opened his eyes for a moment, then closed them again. "You really don't want to be out here, do you, Jack?"

"What do you mean? I enjoy being—"

"Jack..." Matt Oliver paused a moment. "You don't have to lie. I just think it's important that you know how the people at the factory appreciate the time you spend with them. It means a lot to us, even idiots like Dewayne and JT. They trust you. We all trust you."

They sat in silence while the sun burned away the morning fog. By nine a.m. there hadn't been so much as a yelp from the dogs—at least, none they'd heard. A half-dozen does crossed the field just down from where they sat, but Matt Oliver refused to shoot, saying an old buck might come along behind them. Jack agreed, but no more deer appeared, and by nine-thirty their appetites overcame them. Matt Oliver suggested they drive into Charleston for coffee and a late breakfast. It was noon when they returned to the crossroads near Clyde's place.

Clyde and Henry were sitting in Henry's truck drinking coffee when Jack pulled up behind them. He got out with Matt Oliver and walked up as Henry rolled down his window.

"Where's Moe and Larry?" Matt Oliver asked.

"Well," Henry said with a tired voice, "JT's gone off looking for Dewayne over-"

"Was that JT shootin' this morning?" Matt Oliver asked.

"Yeah," Henry said. "He shot a little four-pointer over behind Clyde's house."

"Shot it so many times till it looks like a sieve," Clyde said.

Henry nodded. "Every time it kicked, that damned fool put another bullet in it."

"Deer ain't fittin' to eat, now," Clyde said. "Gut-shot all to hell."

Henry shook his head and pulled his glasses off as he began wiping them with a handkerchief. "He's right. The damned deer is not only gut-shot all to hell," he said, "he even shot one of the horns off."

"You say he went looking for Dewayne?" Matt Oliver said.

Henry had a strained look on his face. He put his glasses back on and blinked his eyes. "Yeah, Dewayne went off running with the dogs."

Matt Oliver cocked his head to one side. "Running with the dogs?"

Henry nodded as Clyde leaned forward on his side of the truck. "He's not kiddin' you. Dewayne came up after we threw what was left of JT's deer in the back of the truck. We were fixing to turn the dogs out again, and he asked if we didn't mind, could he run with them."

"Run with the dogs?" Matt Oliver said again.

Clyde nodded. "That's right. I told him to have at it if he thought he could keep up with 'em."

"You mean, he actually went running out through the woods trying to keep up with the dogs?"

Henry and Clyde both nodded. Matt Oliver shook his head in disbelief. "That dumb-ass. I can't believe.... You know, we're liable to be looking for him till dark."

"I know," Henry said. "Especially if he gets out in that creek bottom."

"Anybody seen Momo?" Jack asked.

"I saw him back yonder on a ridge for just a second," Clyde said, "but that was 'round ten-thirty, and before I knew it, he just disappeared like a ghost."

"He'll be all right," Matt Oliver said. "Momo knows his way around the woods. It's that dumb-ass Dewayne I'm worried about."

After more discussion, they decided to split up and ride the roads to see if anyone could spot Dewayne or hear the dogs. Circling the county roads, Jack drove for several hours, stopping every few minutes to listen, but the dogs had disappeared. Other than the squawks of crows and the occasional distant bark of a housedog, he and Matt Oliver heard nothing all afternoon. It was as if Dewayne and Clyde's pack of hounds had dropped off the face of the earth.

They continued searching, the truck tires crunching slowly down miles of gravel roads. Stopping occasionally, they shut off the engine and stood in the bed of the truck to scan the distant fields and woods. They cupped their hands around their mouths and called for Dewayne, then quickly switched to cup them behind their ears to listen. There was nothing—nothing but the sound of knobby tires rolling along somewhere out on the blacktop, or an owl hooting down some distant bottom. To Jack, it seemed deathly silent, and he began to worry as the search extended toward evening with no sign of Dewayne or Momo.

The sun dropped down on the horizon, a dull orange ball dissected by the stark silhouettes of trees, as he and Matt Oliver rolled slowly down a long stretch of county gravel road. They tried to penetrate the gathering dusk with their eyes, and Jack had about decided that both Dewayne and Momo were destined to spend the night in the woods when Matt Oliver grunted and pointed at something up ahead.

A distant, solitary figure stood motionless on the side of the road. Jack sped up, and as the truck drew near, he saw a man. He was standing, unmoving, a lone sentinel with his gun slung across his back and his arms folded. It was Momo, staring intently at something in the roadside ditch. They rolled to a stop beside him, and Matt Oliver rolled down his window.

"Wassup?"

Momo slowly turned his head and looked back.

"Have you seen Dewayne?" Jack asked.

Momo gave the slightest hint of a shrug and turned, motioning with his head toward the weeds on the shoulder of the road. That's when they saw him. It was Dewayne. They were near Ebenezer Church, over four and a half miles as the crow flies from where Clyde and Henry had last seen him when he took out after the dogs. Sitting with his back to the road, Dewayne rested his chin on his knees, hugging them as he rocked to and fro.

After pulling the pickup to the side of the road, Jack and Matt Oliver got out and walked back. It wasn't long before JT drove up and stopped, too. Dewayne appeared shell-shocked with his new blaze-orange coveralls in shreds, muddy, and covered top to bottom with beggar's lice and cockleburs. His hat and one of his gloves were missing, too. Momo only had a little mud on his boots, looking like he'd been for a stroll in the park. He stood staring down at Dewayne—stern, tight-lipped, and half-ass poker-faced. Something was wrong—bad wrong.

JT bent over beside Dewayne. "Dewayne?" he whispered.

Dewayne stopped rocking and looked up at JT. His face was sullen and covered with scratches and dried blood. It was pretty obvious that he'd been through several briar patches and a few barbed wire fences that afternoon.

"I kill't a horse," he said.

He turned his head, dropping it between his knees and went back to rocking.

"You what!?" JT said. "Where?"

Without raising his head, Dewayne pointed out across a barbed-wire fence.

"I don't see anything," Matt Oliver said.

"Me neither," JT added.

About that time another vehicle came up the road from the opposite direction. It was Henry and Clyde, in Clyde's truck. Jack picked up Dewayne's little SKS and cleared it. The scope was covered with mud, and a piece of kudzu vine hung from the sling. He handed it to Momo.

"Damned, Dewayne," Matt Oliver said. "You sure covered some country today."

"How am I gonna pay for a horse?" Dewayne asked, his voice cracking and tears streaking his dirty face.

Clyde pulled his pickup to the side of the road and walked with Henry up to the men surrounding Dewayne. Jack wondered if it could get any crazier than this.

"Dewayne kill't somebody's horse," JT said.

"He didn't kill no horse," Henry replied, glancing back at Clyde.

"I reckon it was him kill't my cousin Nate's mule," Clyde said.

"His mule?" Matt Oliver said.

"Yup, kill't it graveyard dead right over yonder 'bout a quarter-mile 'cross that pasture." He pointed out across the barbed wire fence. "It's layin' between that corn patch and some okra growing on the other side."

"How in the hell did you manage to shoot a damned mule, Dewayne?" Matt Oliver asked.

Dewayne looked up at Clyde. "How much does a mule cost?"

"I don't reckon they run too bad. You can get a young one that ain't broke most anytime for a couple hundred dollars."

Dewayne perked up. "Just two hundred, that's all?"

"Well, that and you got to figure out how you're gonna get him back over here, dependin' on where you buy him," Clyde said. "I mean, you got to have a livestock trailer, you know?"

Dewayne stood up and tried to knock some of the mud off his coveralls. "Well hell, that ain't so bad," he said. "I could buy a mule and just ride it over here if I have to."

"Dewayne, you dumb-ass," Matt Oliver said. "You can't ride a mule on a state highway."

Dewayne looked at Momo. "You could ride him over here for me, couldn't you? Indians ride horses good, don't they?"

"Nnno-no. Th-th-that's cow-cowboys. I-I-Indians rrr-ride po-po-ponies." Momo turned and winked at Jack.

Of course, Dewayne missed it entirely as he cursed and kicked the gravel. It was well after dark by the time they drove around to Clyde's cousin Nate's house. A paintless wood shanty, weathered gray, it didn't look a day under seventy-five years old—and neither did Nate.

He walked down the steps to meet the little hunting party. His wife, a woman of generous girth, sat on the porch under a single light bulb, fanning the bugs away with a dishrag. It was still warm out, even though it was late November—El Niño, Matt Oliver said, was screwing up the weather something terrible. Mother Nature didn't know if she was having hot flashes or running a fever.

"We come to settle up for the mule," Clyde said. "How much you reckon we owe you?"

Nate hitched up his overalls and spit a stream of tobacco juice in a mud puddle beside the porch. "That old mule was on its last leg. 'Sides, it ain't done nothing but tromp down my corn lately."

Nate's wife grunted to her feet and waddled to the edge of the porch. "Just a dog-gone minute now, old man. Don't you go short-changing us." The big woman stood with one fist on her hip and her head bobbing while she talked. "It ain't gonna be that easy. No suh, sho ain't."

She held the dishrag in the same hand she was using to wag her finger at him.

"We done fed that old mule all these years, and it wasn't that bad off, and it'd a fetched three or four hundred dollars if'n we was to sell it. 'Course we can't now it's shot dead."

"She's a few biscuits past a full load," Matt Oliver muttered under his breath.

"Sshh," Henry said.

Dewayne's shoulders slumped as his fortunes changed.

Nate turned to the group and shrugged. "Well, I reckon she's right."

Jack was beginning to understand why eighty percent of mankind was doomed to live in poverty, and he was destined to be one of them. He could already feel his wallet getting lighter. The others stared at one another for several seconds before Henry stepped back and motioned everyone together. Clyde continued talking with his cousin Nate, while the others huddled. Henry lowered his voice to just above a whisper.

"That cotton-picking mule wouldn't bring ten dollars at a glue factory, but I don't want to mess up our chances of deer hunting up here again. How about we take up a collection? Reckon we got a hundred dollars amongst us?"

The inevitable had occurred—something Jack had sensed more than visualized the moment they had begun talking about the deer hunt. He pulled his wallet from his coat pocket, fishing out thirty-two dollars and handful of change. Matt Oliver did the same and came up with a twenty, three ones and some change. JT had six ones and four-fifty in quarters left over from the casino. Dewayne had a dollar-twenty-three. Henry came up with thirty-one-fifty, and Momo was flat broke. They ended up with ninety-eight dollars and twenty-three cents. Henry motioned for Clyde to come over.

"We've got ninety-eight-twenty-three. Think they'll take it?"

Clyde turned to his cousin Nate. "We got ninety-eight dollars and twenty-three cents. We'll give it all to you right now if that'll settle things free and clear."

Nate turned to his wife who had again sat down in her rocker. After swiping the dishrag at the sweat on her forehead, she nodded. Nate turned back to the men clustered at the bottom of the steps. "Sho sounds good to me," he said, rubbing his hands on the sides of his overalls.

The old man was grinning bigger than his dead mule as Henry handed him the wad of cash, and that settled it, except they had to talk Dewayne out of trying to skin the mule before he left. He was dead-set on getting a dollar-twenty-three worth of steaks out of it, and said everyone else should do the same for their shares. Only after JT threatened to leave him behind did he relent.

According to Matt Oliver's assessment, except for Dewayne's mule, it turned out to be a pretty average deer hunt—nobody got killed, and they got one deer, albeit well tenderized. As for Jack, he'd made up his mind this was his last junket with employees outside of work.

"You ain't gotta go gettin' all harelipped over it," JT said. "I mean, it ain't like he shot it on purpose."

It was the Monday after the big hunt, and the lunch-time conversation was getting heated as Dewayne sat in embarrassed silence—the accused listening while the attorneys argued his case.

"No, but look-a-here what I got," Matt Oliver said.

He slapped a quarter down hard on the breakroom table.

"What's that for?" JT asked.

"It's my spending money for the next week," Matt Oliver said.

"Crack open that door a little bit," Henry said to one of the others. "It's getting hot in here."

Doritoe jumped up and opened the door.

"What makes you so special?" JT asked. "We all had to pitch in. I lost my money too."

"I wasn't the one who shot the damned mule," Matt Oliver said.

"No-no," JT said. "Don't go trying to play that game. We was all there. Dewayne may be the one pulled the trigger, but it could have been any of us."

"Damned if that's so," Matt Oliver said. "I ain't never shot nothing I didn't mean to shoot." He turned to Dewayne. "How in the hell did you mistake a damned mule for a deer anyway?"

The breakroom grew suddenly silent as everyone turned and looked at Dewayne. It was time for the defendant to take the stand.

"I still don't know why everybody's so all-fired mad at me," Dewayne said. "It was an honest mistake."

Not a word was said as he looked around the room for someone to bail him out. Even JT remained silent this time. Everyone waited for what had to be a good story—or at least a unique one, considering Dewayne's perspective on things.

"I mean, I was turned around everywhichaway when I come up out of the woods, and I didn't know where I was, and I sure didn't know I was near nobody's house. The dogs done run through there chasing a deer, but they got out of hearing real quick, and I was 'bout give out. That's when I jumped over a fence, and all of a sudden, this thing bolted right out of the corn patch in front of me. I saw it had big ears so I shot. I knowed I messed up soon as I pulled the trigger, but it fell dead right off, just like it'd been struck by lightning."

"You mean you kill't it with one shot?" JT asked.

"Hit him right behind the eye," Dewayne said, pointing his finger at the side of his head. "And it just made a itty-bitty little ol' hole too."

"Damn," JT replied. "Just a lucky shot, I reckon."

"Lucky?" Jack said.

Dewayne gave him a slack-jawed nod.

"Well, your luck has me broke for the rest of the week," Matt Oliver said. "And right here before Thanksgiving. I'll probably have Vienna sausages and crackers for Thanksgiving dinner."

Jack tried to avoid involving himself in their conversations, but it was time for a little relief. "How about a little good news?" he said.

Everyone turned and looked at him.

"I've talked the home office into cutting everyone a twenty-dollar check as a bonus to buy a Thanksgiving turkey."

"No shit?" JT said.

"No shit," Jack said.

"Nothing but a token," Arlis said.

The entire room went suddenly silent as everyone turned toward Arlis. They had been ignoring him while he read his usual Bible verse, but this sudden response had caught everyone by surprise.

"What'd you say?" JT asked.

"I said, it's nothing but a token—a crumb tossed out to appease the masses."

Dewayne had his usual lost-in-space look, but JT turned to Henry, "What the hell's he talking about?"

Henry started to reply, but Arlis interrupted, "I'm saying you have mortgaged your souls. The moneychangers own you. All you do is work to make the rich men richer. You're all trapped like rats, running through a maze—to where? For what?"

"Oh hell, Arlis," Matt Oliver said, "lighten up. It ain't like anybody around here really gives a shit, long as they have TV rasslin' and stock-car racing on the weekend. You know?"

JT missed Matt Oliver's sarcasm as he joined in. "And don't leave out SEC football and my Bulldogs."

JT was a big Mississippi State fan.

"Yeah," Dewayne said. "And bass fishing, too."

Matt Oliver turned back to Arlis, "See what I mean?"

Arlis was already gone. Eyes glazed, he had returned to his tortured inner world of Bible-belt guilt.

"You muthufuckas is all crazy," Doritoe said.

CHAPTER 16

WALKING IN MEMPHIS

I
T WAS A SUNNY SATURDAY afternoon in December when Jack and Cici left Clarksdale and headed north up Highway 61. He was taking her to a surprise location for supper.

"So, how are things going at the furniture factory?" she asked.

Jack grunted and laughed. "Between my crazy boss and some of my crazy employees I'm having a wonderful time."

Cici laughed. "You're funny."

"I laugh, because otherwise I'd go crazy."

"So, why didn't your boss fire you?"

Jack shrugged. "The only thing I can figure is he thinks I know too much about his shortcuts, and that I'll go over his head."

"My Uncle Clyde told Aunt Netta you're the best boss they've had down there in years."

Jack felt the blood running from his head. "Clyde Freeman is your uncle?"

Cici nodded. "Yes. He's Aunt Netta's younger brother."

"Really?"

"Yeah. He likes you. Said you might actually get things running better for once."

Jack was again blindsided. He was the one in the spotlight, and everyone knew all there was to know about him. Yet, he was learning something new almost every day. This time it was about Clyde.

"Well, that's good news. At least I have one supporter."

"Oh, you got more than one. Uncle Clyde said most everybody feels that way."

They rode for several minutes as Jack wondered what more he had missed. And he wondered how much Clyde knew about his relationship with Cici. Before long they passed a sign that said "Tunica 18 Miles, Memphis 55 Miles."

"Are we going to one of the casinos?" Cici asked.

Jack smiled. "Maybe, maybe not."

"Well, I hear rumors that you have a bad reputation with some of the casino goers. You sure that's where you want to go?"

"I don't know what rumors you've heard, but most of them are bullshit. It was all a set-up."

"Oh, really?" Cici raised her eyebrows in anticipation.

"That devious bitch slipped some drugs and a Viagra into my drink, then drove me to her place."

Cici let out a whoop and turned facing him with an open mouth smile. "She didn't?"

"Yes, she *did*."

Cici began laughing harder than Jack had ever seen her laugh. "You mean to tell me she date-raped you?"

"Well, I don't know if you could call it—"

"She date-raped you!" Cici crossed her arms putting her palms against her chest, laughing until she had to come up for air. She paused, then fell into another fit of laughter.

"Have your fun, baby sister. She all but ruined my chances for ever getting back with Acey."

Cici momentarily choked back her laughter. "Acey doesn't need to know. Besides, it wasn't your fault."

Jack shook his head. "No, I have to tell her. Put yourself in her position. Wouldn't you want to know?"

Cici began coughing.

"Do you want to stop and get a Coke or something?" Jack asked.

"No, I'll be okay." She gasped, caught her breath then continued, "You're just too damned honest, even when it's better not to be." She giggled again. "I can't believe that bitch date-raped you. That's the funniest thing I ever heard."

"I suppose it *is* kind of crazy, I mean a woman doing it to a man." he said.

"So, not meaning to get too personal, but how does a woman date-rape a man—I mean, other than spiking his drink with drugs and Viagra?"

"The first time I woke up, she had me on the couch giving me oral sex."

Cici threw her hand over her mouth. "Oh, my God!"

"The second time I woke up, she had me pinned to her bed with my face pulled up between her breasts, and she was hiking herself up and down on an erection I didn't even know I had."

Cici laughed, coughed several times then let out another giggle. "I have to stop laughing. I can't stand it anymore."

They eventually passed Tunica and the casinos.

"So, I see we aren't going to the casinos. Are we going to Memphis?"

"I thought it would be a nice evening if we visited Beale Street again."

"We're going back where we started, huh?"

"I thought you might like seeing it again."

She drew a shivering breath. "It has been a while."

Neither of them said anything more, and the sun had set by the time they crossed over the Illinois Central railyards. Catching the interstate, Jack drove around to Riverside Drive, where the Memphis skyline came into view. The big "M" bridge over the Mississippi was lit up, its lights casting wavering amber reflections down the river, while the last orange afterglow of the sun faded on the Arkansas horizon.

"You know," Cici said, "there's something about knowing you're going to die soon that sets you free. You see things in a totally different way, and your mind isn't cluttered with the stupid stuff most people always worry about."

Jack turned under the railroad overpass onto Beale and drove up to Front Street where he parked the car. After he helped Cici to her feet, they walked down to BB's. A crowd waited outside the door.

"My legs are hurting," she said.

"You want to try somewhere else?" he asked.

Cici bowed her head.

"What is it?" Jack asked.

"I really wouldn't mind just going back home."

"You sure?"

"We can stop somewhere along the way," she said. "I promise. I'm just not ready for the memories here."

"I understand."

As they drove back down Riverside Drive, Cici gazed out at the lights along the river. They departed downtown Memphis, driving in silence for a long while before the highway dropped off into the Delta again. In the distance the Gold Strike Hotel rose up, its golden lights gleaming against the night sky. The highway was awash with headlights and the glittering casino billboards tempted travelers with free meals and entertainment. The traffic moved swiftly, and Jack found himself having to focus on his driving. When Cici finally broke the silence, her voice was husky with emotion.

"You know, the bright lights can really blind you to what's real," she said. "I always wanted to stay close to what was real—never turn it loose. Maybe that's why we never.... I mean...."

Her tears reflected in the dim light from the dash, and Jack found himself lost in a jumble of emotion and half-thoughts.

"Are you going to run that light?" she asked.

Slamming on the brakes, Jack barely got stopped in time.

"Sorry," he said.

She looked over at him and smiled through the tears. "Hell, who am I to complain about someone's driving?"

The tension suddenly abated as he smiled back at her. "You have a sick sense of humor."

"Just keeping it real, my man, just keeping it real."

They were again silent as they passed through Tunica and drove into the night toward Clarksdale. After they'd passed Dundee and Lula she began talking again.

"You know, my daddy was Cajun. He was mostly white, and Mama, she was mulatto, but she was mostly black. I don't think they ever did live together—I mean, Daddy was never there—not that he was a bad man. He was in the Army. He'd come home at Christmas, and during the summer he'd take us on a little vacation somewhere like Grand Isle or New Orleans. Mama said he left her pregnant every time, but he always sent most of his money back home."

Jack thought about the many times he and Tuck had talked about the war, and the buddies his uncle had lost. Yet Tuck was one of the lucky ones who seemed to have survived with his psyche mostly intact.

"Uncle Tuck says that damned war messed up this country. He says it affected all of us in some way, and some folks are still paying the price."

"I reckon so," Cici said. "It's been almost thirty years ago Daddy died, and I was maybe four, but I remember it like it was yesterday."

It was clear that Cici had deep emotional scars from when she lost her family and her father. For the first time Jack fully understood why he had come here. Despite all the trouble she had been, and her own hell-bent self-destruction, she deserved someone's care and support.

"I'm sorry our dinner date didn't work out," he said.

Cici turned and looked at him with sympathetic eyes. "Oh, but it did. I mean, we didn't eat, but I wasn't hungry anyway. What's important is we spent some time together. I don't know too many men who would put up with my crap, and keep coming back."

"You've been dealt some bad hands in your life. I only want to make a difference."

Cici shook her head slowly. "Oh, Perry, Perry, Perry, that boy. I'm worried about him."

"Why is that?"

"You know he's had a crush on me for years, and I never done nothing for him. I just don't know what he's gonna do when I'm gone."

Cici turned to Jack. "Maybe you can do me a really important favor."

"What's that?"

"Look after Perry. Give him a job—I mean if he wants one down there. He's going to need something to keep him going. He actually plays a really good Blues guitar, but he had to take bass 'cause I already had Snookey. Actually Perry is a lot better than Snookey ever was. That's why they never got along. Snookey and the rest of the boys resented

Perry 'cause he was so talented, and they worried that me and Perry might get hitched someday."

Jack promised and Cici smiled. "There's one more thing."

Jack glanced over at her then back at the road while Cici explained. It was something she had thought long and hard on, and was now certain it was the right decision. Of all her final wishes, it was the most important, and when she finished explaining, Jack pulled to the side of the highway and took her hand.

"You have my word," he said.

When they arrived back at Aunt Netta's house, he helped Cici from the car and walked her to the door. Later, when he got back to the farmhouse that night, Jack poured himself a glass of bourbon and sat on the couch in the darkness. For the first time in months, he felt he had done something that turned out well.

And it was if Cici was reminding him, because from somewhere in the night there came the distant sound of an Illinois Central freight train blowing for a road crossing. He sat into the wee hours of the morning sipping his drink, and his mind wandered back to someone else to whom he owed so much. He wondered about Acey and where she might be.

CHAPTER 17

JACK TAKES OVER

THE DORIS ANN AFFAIR FINALLY blew over after New Year's, and Jack breathed easier as he walked across the factory floor that morning. Doris had drawn her sights on one of the long-haul truck drivers who made pickups at the factory, and with this new distraction, she seemed willing to forgive and forget. Jack was finally able to focus his attention on more important matters. He wanted another meeting with Nickels, but there had to be a better way of approaching him. Henry could probably help, and Jack went out to the production area where he found him, hands on his hips, staring at the rows of storage bins lining the walls.

"Look at those things," Henry said, making a sweeping gesture toward the south wall. "We don't have room left to store any more inventory."

The storage bins were filled with spindles, chair legs, and various other furniture parts manufactured for future orders. Jack nodded. Already aware of the problem, it was part of what he planned to bring to Nickels.

"I'm going to talk with Nickels about it."

Henry turned to face him. "I've tried for years. He's not going to listen."

"We've got to do something," Jack said. "If we don't get busy, this place is going to go belly up."

"You're probably right," Henry said.

"So, you think talking to Nickels is a waste of time?"

"Look, I don't want to discourage you, but this factory needs a boss with better business-sense, and who knows how to treat people."

After discussing it with Henry, Jack decided to avoid Nickels's appointment gauntlet. Instead, he walked into the office unannounced and told Doris Ann he needed to see him. She picked up the phone and announced his presence, and after a moment or two she lowered her voice while Jack looked the other way and pretended not to hear. "I don't know," she said. "No. No, he doesn't seem to be. Yes, sir. Yes, sir. Okay. I'll tell him."

She hung up the phone. "Mr. Nickels said he'll see you when he can. Just have a seat."

Another light on the telephone came on. Nickels was, no doubt, calling Henry out at the floor office. After a minute or two the light went out, and Doris Ann's phone warbled again. She answered and said, "Yes, sir," then hung up.

"Mr. Nickels can't see you right now. He said to come back in an hour."

Jack glanced at his watch. It was 10:00 a.m. After giving Doris Ann a nod, he turned and walked out. At 11:00 a.m. sharp he returned. Doris Ann looked up at him from her desk, but said nothing.

"Can you tell Mr. Nickels I am here for our meeting?"

"I suppose I could if he was still here," Doris Ann said.

"What do you mean?"

"I mean he left around 10:15. Said he had a lunch and golf date with the OSHA man."

Jack felt his blood pressure rising.

"Where are they meeting?"

"The Ajax Diner over in Oxford, why?"

Jack turned and walked out. Trotting out to the parking lot, he jumped in his truck and sped toward Oxford. Normally an hour-and-twenty-minute drive, this one would take much less. He pushed the accelerator to the floor, streaking across the Delta on Highway 32. By the time Jack walked into the Ajax Diner on the square in Oxford it was 12:15, and he had calmed considerably. He spotted Nickels who had already spotted him. Jack walked his way.

As Jack approached the table, Nickels jumped to his feet. His face was instantly flushed, but he grinned broadly.

"Jack!" He grabbed Jack's hand, shaking it vigorously while patting him on the arm with the other hand. "Come sit down and join us. Man, I just remembered you stopped by the office earlier. I am so sorry."

Nickels turned to the other man seated at the table. "Buddy, this is Jack, uh, Jack Hartman, my new helper down at the factory."

The man remained seated as he extended his hand. "Buddy Walters."

"Buddy is our OSHA rep out of Atlanta," Nickels said.

"Pleased to meet you," Jack said.

Walters' demeanor was one of calm control, and his remaining seated spoke volumes. He was the man with the power and authority here.

"We were just having a drink before lunch," Nickels said. "Why don't you join us?"

He turned to the OSHA man. "Jack here is my right-hand man, and he's begun putting all those reports together you requested a while back. As a matter of fact, he'll probably be mailing them to you in a few weeks. Isn't that right, Jack?"

It crossed Jack's mind to simply tell the truth, to describe the disarray in the paint shop and the near total absence of documentation, but he thought better of it. If OSHA hit the factory with steep fines, or worse, closed the factory, the jobs he hoped to save for his employees would go with it. He smiled weakly and nodded.

"Yes, so won't you have a seat and let me buy you a drink?" Nickels said.

Jack was now feeling nearly as flustered as Nickels appeared when he first walked in. The schizophrenic bastard had turned the tables on him.

"I'm going to have to beg off this time," he said. "Can we meet first thing in the morning, say around nine?"

"Sure! Sure!" Nickels said.

His enthusiasm was sickening, and Jack forced another weak smile.

"I'll meet with you first thing, nine a.m. That's perfect."

"Pleased to meet you, Mr. Hartman," Walters said.

"Likewise."

At nine a.m. sharp the next morning Jack walked past Doris Ann without stopping as he entered Nickels's office. Nickels ignored him as he stared at his computer. After two or three minutes standing in silence, Jack was rewarded with a comment. "Stock price dropped again."

A few seconds later Nickels looked up. "Sit down, Jack. So, what kind of problem did you bring me today? Henry tells me you want to discuss some inventory issue."

Nickels acted as if Jack had been in his office complaining day after day, instead of once in six months. *Careful,* Jack thought. *Don't get baited into an argument. Just stick to the point.*

"Mr. Nickels, we have a lot of excess inventory out there, and most of it will become obsolete before we can use it. That needs to be addressed, but it's only part of the issue. There are several other problems costing us money, and we need to discuss them, but first I want to—"

"Keen observation, Jack. That's what management is about: dealing with problems, and I've done quite well dealing with ours for a number of years now."

"Yes, sir," Jack said, "but don't you think we should try to do some things differently?"

"Absolutely. I look to make changes every day, but there are certain factors that will never change, like the rising cost of labor. People down here in Mississippi are finally catching on. They want the same wages we pay in factories up north. Solve that one.

"As for your supposed inventory issue: Milling parts takes less time than assembly, painting, and upholstering. This means while the assembly is going on, the machine operators make parts for future orders. We can't allow people to sit around on the clock, so we keep them productive. And that's where the excess inventory you're so worried about comes from."

Jack shook his head. "Yes, and most of it is becoming outdated. We need to stop adding to the problem."

With a smirk, Nickels spun his chair around and stared up at the framed print of Vince Lombardi hanging on the wall behind him. After a moment or two, he slowly turned back toward Jack.

"You know something, Jack? I started like that man behind me on the wall. I started in this business when I was a kid. Yeah, I worked in my pop's factory, and I learned what it took to run one of these monsters, and by the way, I'm damned good at it. When Fernwood bought us out ten years ago, I came down to this shit-hole factory, and I've turned some pretty decent numbers. Now you come in here, a hotshot machine salesman with a degree in industrial something-or-other and think you can reinvent the wheel.

"Don't think I haven't been watching you. You've been trying to be everyone's friend, and you tolerate people who argue with you, but that makes you weak. If an employee argues with me, I put his ass out the door. So, consider yourself lucky."

Nickels paused, staring as if he thought Jack should be intimidated.

"Mister Nickels, the people who argue with me may not always be right, but at least they feel free to speak their mind. And they not only tell us what's wrong, they often tell us how to fix it as well."

"And that's why you will never be a top-notch manager," Nickels said. "You're the one who should know how to fix things, not some ten-buck-an-hour machine operator. You tolerate whiners. You tolerate people who aren't team players—people who settle for second place. There's only one winner, and you can't be one if you let negativism run your business. That entire bunch you eat lunch with every day is nothing but a leper colony, a bunch of misfits.

"I'll tell you what," Nickels said. "You want to prove something? Go out there and reduce that inventory, but you better keep those machine operators busy. I'm not paying them to sit on their asses. Hell, you want to tell me how to run my factory? You have my permission. Show me how it's done, but you fuck up and I'm finding me a new—what do they call you?"

"Assistant General Manager," Jack said.

"Yeah—I'm finding one who knows how to follow my directives. You understand?"

Refusing to be baited again, Jack simply nodded and walked out, ready to prove the little prick wrong. Saving the factory was now an obsession, but it was a mountainous task. Short-term changes would help, but he needed buy-in from the employees more than ever.

Jack's voice echoed like a preacher's promising salvation, and he hoped he wasn't making undeliverable promises. The employees were gathered in the big lunchroom at the front of the factory that morning as he explained the situation. The factory was no longer turning a profit, but it wasn't a lost cause. He promised the employees more respect from management and that their ideas and suggestions would be heard. Making sure they understood there were no guarantees, he said their extra efforts were voluntary, but failure was certain if they didn't do something to turn things around.

He appealed to them to help the company, but more importantly, to help themselves. When he finished his speech they cheered and applauded. Almost everyone committed to working overtime the next few weeks to catch up on the backlog of orders. They also agreed to work across job lines and to take extra care with the quality of their work.

There was a rebirth of excitement as people suddenly found motivation beyond a paycheck. Jack took Nickels's invitation to fix things as carte blanche and contacted the other factories. What inventory that wasn't already outdated, was shipped to other factories for immediate use, with reciprocal agreements for other parts and some idle machinery. Employees agreed to cross-train, so they could help in other departments. This would improve his ability to replace key absentees, and maintain the quality of the furniture.

By the end of six weeks, productivity had climbed to record levels. Problem was this led to further opportunities—which as Matt Oliver put it, was corporate-speak for more problems. The regional office, recognizing the sudden increase in productivity, sent more orders, and the office staff had to do something besides play solitaire on their computers all day. Jack also needed additional labor in the packing and shipping department.

All of these should have been positive signs, but Doris Ann said Nickels wasn't particularly happy about his disgruntled office staff, and he absolutely refused to increase his labor costs by adding help in the shipping department. Jack also received an e-mail from Nickels saying he was creating unrest with an un-named production supervisor and his employees. No doubt, Tommy Grey had been to his office complaining. Another meeting with Nickels was unavoidable. Jack needed Grey to support his efforts or get the hell out of the way.

It came a deluge that day—one of those early February thunderstorms. Hail was thundering down on the metal roof of the factory until it created such a din that people were shouting to be heard. Nickels had come out on the floor the day before and demanded that the complaining employees in Grey's area be moved to easier jobs. Despite Jack's protests, Nickels insisted, and production bottlenecks resulted. Tommy Grey and his whiners had put things in disarray.

The entire operation was working on a large order from a new customer, and it was already behind schedule. Newly motivated employees were waiting impatiently for materials stuck in the bottlenecks, when the sudden crack-pop of lightning reverberated from a transformer across the road. The lights browned down, and circuit breakers began tripping. Within seconds the entire building was without power. Other than the rain still pelting the roof, a strange silence gripped the factory as all the machines, ventilators, everything went down, and the emergency floodlights pierced the spooky darkness. The air became suddenly stagnant.

If the transformer wasn't damaged, it would take several minutes to bring the systems back up, and most people were hurrying to restock their workstations. Henry and

Jack began discussing how they could realign the work-flow when someone began yelling and cursing over in the upholstery department—Tommy Grey's department. Their eyes met, and they both hurried across the floor in that direction.

"The damned lights go out and you people think you can just sit on your asses."

It was Nickels. His voice reverberated in the silence, as he pitched a world-class hissy-fit. Jumping about like a mad Munchkin, he had Arlis and Dewayne standing in front of him. Dewayne had his head down, but Arlis stared hard while Nickels waved his arms and jabbed his finger up in his face.

"Don't just stand there," he shouted. "Get your asses in gear. Go find a goddamned broom and start sweeping. Do something! I want to see some activity around here."

Dewayne began nosing around as if he might find a broom under a roll of material, but Arlis stood unmoving, staring with fire in his eyes. Only then did Nickels seem aware of Arlis's anger. He took a step back.

"What's the problem, Mr. Nickels?" Jack asked as he approached. Henry was close behind him.

Nickels spun around. "Why are these people sitting on their asses, when we're behind on our orders?"

"I don't know, sir," Jack said, "but I'll see if Tommy can find them something to do."

Jack spotted Grey slinking away toward the back of the department, but Nickels jabbed his finger in Jack's face.

"Tommy is probably busy trying to fix this mess, unlike the two of you, who are just standing around doing nothing. Instead of getting him, why don't you pitch in here? Try to help out."

Seemingly satisfied, he whirled and strutted back toward the offices. Jack glanced at Henry, who pursed his lips and shrugged. There wasn't much anyone could say, especially to the employees who had witnessed it. A few moments later the lights came back on, and everyone began restarting their machines. Arlis remained in the same spot, staring at nothing in particular.

"Don't let it bother you, Arlis," Henry said. "He was just letting off a little steam."

Arlis slowly turned his head. His eyes had that look again—the one that could burn holes through sheet metal. Henry glanced at Jack.

"Forget it, Arlis," Jack said. "Let's go back to work."

Arlis stared across the factory floor toward the doorway leading to the offices. Henry shook his head and walked away.

Jack patted Arlis on the back. "Let it go, okay?"

Arlis turned and walked back to his workstation. Dewayne and several other employees watched him as if they'd just witnessed a rape. And it had been—a verbal rape. In less than five minutes Nickels had effectively killed whatever renewed spirits Jack had nurtured with the employees. It would take days to regain their confidence— if he could at all.

CHAPTER 18

DEWEY HARGROVE'S WAKE

MATT OLIVER AND HENRY WERE the scheduled early-starters that morning, and Jack arrived a little before seven, expecting an otherwise normal day. He hoped to continue rebuilding what Nickels had wrecked a few days before, but as he pulled through the gate it struck him that something was amiss. At least a third of the employee parking lot was empty. He glanced at his watch. What the hell? Even the guard shack was vacant.

He ran up the front steps and hurried inside. The door to Nickels's office was closed—of course. Hurrying down the hall to his office, Jack found Matt Oliver sitting in the chair beside the desk, playing with the sailboat.

"Where the hell is everybody?" Jack asked.

"I take it you haven't heard."

"Heard what?

"I figured you'd be upset. You might as well sit down a minute and chill out, while I explain."

"Explain what? Is it a sick-out because of Nickels?"

"No, nothing like that," Matt Oliver said. "It's something as old as the South itself—the same kind of thing that happened when The Bear died back in 1983."

"Bear Bryant?"

"Yeah."

Matt Oliver went on to explain how half the state of Alabama and a good many others south of the Mason-Dixon went into mourning the day the legendary Paul "Bear" Bryant passed away.

"The Crimson Tide faithful flew the flags in Tuscaloosa at half mast and wore black for a month. And I'm not meaning to be disrespectful, but I wanted you to understand just how serious people in the South are about their football. You see, it's damned near a religion, second on most people's lists by a gnat's breath to Jesus and the twelve apostles."

"So, did some football coach die?" Jack asked.

"No. Worse," Matt Oliver said. "You see, I told you that so you would understand this: SEC football isn't the only show in town. Now there's NASCAR."

"Please, tell me what the hell is happening?" Jack said.

"I take it you didn't hear about Dewey Hargrove getting killed Saturday."

Suddenly, it all made sense. NASCAR had its own high priests—the drivers, and everyone had their favorites, but far and away the leading fan idol was Dewey Hargrove in his red, black, and yellow number "93" Chevy. Dewey, a beady-eyed pretty boy with an Errol Flynn mustache, was known as the Red Marauder. Half the people in the factory, including JT and Dewayne, were obsessed with him. They all wore Dewey Hargrove T-shirts.

It promised to be another interesting day, and later that morning Jack made the dreaded walk to Nickels's office. He was certain this would somehow become his fault. Nickels had just arrived when Jack tapped on the door, and walked in past Doris Ann's empty chair. The little Factory Manager appeared startled, but his surprise turned to anger when Jack explained the situation.

Nickels, who at first thought NASCAR had something to do with the space program, began foaming at the mouth when he learned production was being reduced because a race car driver had died. Pushing past Jack, he stormed out onto the production floor, demanding that everyone who'd called in be fired. Only when Henry convinced him this would shut down the factory completely did Nickels finally stomp away, cursing and threatening reprisals as he went.

It was up to Jack to make things work, and it was true, they were short-handed, but most everyone in Henry's shop had shown up that morning. He met with Henry, closed down a couple of areas and scattered the men throughout the other departments. The morning wasn't a total loss, and everyone remained busy trying to keep up. It wasn't until lunchtime that they were together again in the back breakroom.

Jack, Henry, Clyde, and Matt Oliver discussed plans for the afternoon operations, while Arlis read from his Bible, but Dewayne and JT sat in solemn silence. After nearly ten minutes the group came up with a plan, but that's when Matt Oliver finally noticed that neither Dewayne nor JT had said a word the entire time. JT's eyes were blood-shot and reddened.

"What's wrong with you two?" Matt Oliver asked.

JT glared back at him in silence, but Dewayne responded in a near whisper. "Didn't you hear the news about Dewey Hargrove?"

"Well, duh! What the hell do you think we've been talking about all morning?"

"Well, it's a damned shame," Dewayne said.

"Yeah, it is a shame," Matt Oliver said. "He was a damned good driver." Matt Oliver took a ravenous bite from his sandwich, talking while he chewed. "But it's also a damned shame this factory is about to go belly-up and there ain't nobody at work today."

JT's eyes widened as he stared at Matt Oliver. "A shame?" he said.

"Yeah," Matt Oliver replied. He tipped up his Coke and took a quick swallow. "A shame—you know? I mean I really hate the poor guy got killed, but I think our damned jobs are a little more important."

"Our damned jobs ain't shit," JT said. His voice ratcheted up several notches. "Dewey Hargrove was the greatest man to ever drive a race car. It's, it's... hell, don't you know what that means—him getting killed?"

A tear trickled from JT's eye.

"Damned, JT," Matt Oliver said, "you don't have to go getting all upset. What'd you want me to say?" Matt Oliver shook his head and took another bite from his sandwich.

"You could show a little goddam respect," JT said.

Matt Oliver swallowed. "You're crazy, JT. I didn't say anything disrespectful. Besides, it's not like your brother died or something."

"You're right," JT said. "It wasn't my brother died. It was the greatest stock-car driver that ever lived, and you ought to be showing a little damned respect."

"How in hell am I not showing respect, JT? Tell me."

"It's 'a shame' 'cause ain't nobody at work, you say? Why it's a goddam tragedy that Dewey got killed—worse than anything I've ever seen. That man was a national hero, and you're just sitting here eating your sandwich and worried 'cause a few people didn't show up for work."

Matt Oliver remained calm—chewing and talking at the same time, but his face began to redden.

"JT, I hope you will excuse the hell out of me for caring about my job. Besides, you're really stretching it with that 'hero' crap. The man wasn't a war veteran or nothing. He was a race car driver—not the President or even somebody who helped people, like a doctor maybe."

"You don't know shit," JT said.

"I know you're acting like an idiot, moping around here, and getting mad 'cause I ain't slobbering all over myself like you and Dewayne."

JT slammed his fist down on the table. "You're just an asshole, Matt Oliver."

Jack cast a quick glance at Henry.

"Okay," Henry said. "Why don't you two let it go for now?"

Everyone in the room stared at Matt Oliver, awaiting his response. "Okay, JT. I'm sorry. I didn't mean to sound like an asshole. You know something. I admired the hell out of old Dewey myself, but really, don't you think you're making way more of this than you should?"

"That's your opinion, and it ain't worth shit in my book," JT said.

"Try to put it in perspective," Matt Oliver said. "Maybe you won't be so upset. Look at it this way: Do you think two hundred years from now anybody in the universe will know who Dewey Hargrove was?"

"Hell, yeah they will," JT screamed. "Dewey Hargrove will *always* be famous."

"Damn it, JT, quit yelling." Matt Oliver stuck a couple of Cheetos in his mouth, crunching on them as he talked. "Besides, you're wrong. People probably won't even remember the names of all the presidents in two hundred more years. And who knows? They might not even remember exactly what states were in the United States by then."

JT glared back at him. "You know what, Matt Oliver? You just like to talk all that crazy shit to make yourself sound important, but you don't know shit about nothing.

You think you're some kind of big philosopher, but you're stupider than my kids' goddam pet goat."

Dewayne chimed in, "Yeah. I'm gonna write a letter to Dewey's pit crew and tell them about you. They'll come over here from Alabama and whip your ass. That's what they'll do."

Matt Oliver turned slowly toward Dewayne. "You know, Dewayne, I didn't even know you could write, but I sure as hell don't want my ass whipped. You ain't really gonna write them, are you?"

Dewayne gave him a sideways look. "You ain't being cute again, are you?"

"Hell, yes, he is," JT said. "He's being the same old smart-ass he always is."

"You're right, JT, and I'm a damned fool for sitting here arguing with you."

Dewayne nodded. "Well, there you go. See? You're finally starting to understand, but don't worry none. I wasn't really gonna tell Dewey's pit crew about you."

"Goddamit, Dewayne, just shut the fuck up," JT said. "You're dumber'n a sack of rocks."

Dewayne looked suddenly hurt and confused as he stared open-mouthed at JT.

Jack could take it no longer. "I've heard enough!"

The room was suddenly still.

"Let's focus on how we're going to hold this thing together for the next few days."

There were nods of agreement around the table, but the next day JT and Dewayne joined the rest of the Dewey Hargrove fans and called in sick. Jack struggled to maintain production, but he was certain of one thing—if the South was going to rise again, Dewey's untimely demise had given the uprising a severe economic setback. The factory's revival was also in jeopardy—Nickels was talking about taking back control of operations.

Jack wasn't sure what they finally decided to call it, but later that week JT described it as a get-together in memory of Dewey Hargrove. Cleve Thomas said it was a redneck wake, but Dewayne said it was more than that, except he wasn't exactly sure what to call it either. Momo said nothing, while Arlis said he would take his guidance from God as to whether or not to attend. Doris Ann, who'd left them high and dry as well, wasn't there to give her opinion, but Matt Oliver said it didn't matter what they called it as long as the beer was free.

Jack would rather have avoided it altogether, but everyone insisted, and it was an opportunity to regroup his wounded troops—something that, even given the venue, was desperately needed. He drove to JT's house late Friday afternoon. Misty and dreary, the weather lent itself to the occasion. When he arrived the street was lined with cars and pickups, and more were parked on the front lawn.

Beer cans littered the yard, but the mood was solemn as Jack passed several knots of people talking quietly. JT's house was a typical two-bedroom on a slab, nothing fancy, but enough to raise a couple boys and get by.

As Jack walked up the driveway Dewayne and April drove by, leaving a trail of smoky exhaust hanging along the rows of parked cars. They'd draped the red Toyota with black crepe, and a new decal emblazoned the door with the number 93. Jack rang the front doorbell, and Janine appeared wearing a black sweater with black slacks. She cracked a nervous smile, seemingly taking matters as seriously as her husband. The only thing she lacked was a black veil.

"JT's in the back," Janine said. "He's so upset, he's been drinking all day. Maybe you can make him feel better."

The tone of reverence in her voice reminded Jack of the way people talked at funeral homes. He nodded and tried to embrace the mood. The house was packed with people, shoulder to shoulder, but it was eerily quiet with only subdued murmuring coming from the surrounding rooms. As he worked his way to the cramped den in back, he heard someone reading the Twenty-third Psalm—it was Arlis. JT sat on the couch beside him, wearing a black suit with a white shirt and a red and yellow tie. He looked as if his mother had just passed away. On the coffee table in front of him was a nearly empty Jim Beam bottle.

JT stood and threw his arm around Jack's neck. "Damned, it's good to see you, boss. Come on in and sit down."

The rings around his eyes and his grim countenance left no doubt. He and Janine were serious about this wake, official or not, for the great Dewey Hargrove. Jack glanced around the room, nodding at familiar faces. The only one who didn't acknowledge him was Arlis. He was sitting on the couch between JT and Doris Ann, still reading aloud from his dog-eared Bible—by now having begun reading something about angels in chariots of fire.

On the den walls were photos of several drivers and their cars, including one draped with black cloth. It was the infamous number 93 and his red, black, and yellow Chevy. There was another photo of JT standing in the back of a pickup truck wearing a Mississippi State ball cap and holding a dead deer by its antlers. Jack sat down, but no sooner had he gotten comfortable than there came a commotion from the front room. Someone was pounding on the door.

"It's the law," someone said.

JT jumped up and pushed his way through the crowd. For whatever reason, Jack felt a degree of responsibility and followed him, along with Henry and Arlis.

One of JT's guests pulled the curtain aside and peeked out the front window. "Looks like the SWAT team," he said. "They got everything but their assault rifles."

JT opened the door. Standing on the porch were two uniformed men with white-wall haircuts and spit-shined black leather boots. Looking past them, Jack saw a white van parked out front in the middle of the road with flashing strobes and blue lights reflecting off the parked cars.

The two men on the porch stood rigid, wearing starched black military fatigue pants and black leather belts loaded with an assortment of pepper spray, side arms, ammo pouches, radios and God only knows what else. Stone-faced, they eyeballed JT and his guests as if attempting to determine the threat level they represented.

"James Stoker?" one of them said.

"Yeah," JT answered. "I reckon that'd be me."

"We're from the county animal control unit. We received a complaint from your neighbor about your dog."

JT scratched his head. "Are you saying you're dog catchers?"

"Ain't nothing but a couple of dog catchers," someone behind Jack said.

A chorus of subdued snickers came from down the hall, and the two men on the porch seemed momentarily taken aback. JT picked up on it.

"If you're here to talk to me about a complaint, what's with the SWAT-team get-ups and all the goddam flashing lights?"

The two stone-faces turned red.

"It's because this is a serious matter, Mr. Stoker," one of them said.

"So, just what the hell is the complaint?" JT asked.

"Looka here now, Mr. Stoker, if you're gonna act this way, we'll have to call for back-up."

"Act what way?" JT said, his voice growing louder with each exchange. "You come out here with your damned blue lights flashing and pound on my door like we're common criminals or something, and—"

Arlis put his hand on JT's shoulder. "Patience," he said.

"Patience my ass," JT said, throwing his arm away. "Let me handle this."

"Look, Mr. Stoker, your neighbor says your dog has been howling and moaning every night, and she can't get any sleep. If you don't do something about it—"

"I know the dog's been moaning. He's dying, for Chris' sakes. So how come somebody didn't just pick up the damned phone and call me? And can't you see we're having a wake here?"

The two dogcatchers looked around as if they'd suddenly realized this wasn't just another weekend block party.

"We're sorry, Mr. Stoker. We didn't know. Please, just see if you can keep the dog quiet."

Henry pulled JT back inside the door.

"Give our sympathies to the family of the deceased," one of the men said.

When they'd gone, JT pushed his way through the crowd back to the den.

"Nothing but goddam dogcatchers," he mumbled. "Can you believe that shit?"

It took several minutes for things to calm down, but they were no sooner settled on the couch again than Matt Oliver arrived. JT greeted him with a handshake, but everyone in the room traded furtive glances while the two men stared at one another. The animosity between them was no secret, and no one breathed, until JT spoke.

"I figured we could just sit a while," he said. "You know? Then, maybe we'll show some of Dewey's racing tapes later."

"Cool," Matt Oliver replied.

JT looked like he'd been slapped across the face with a wet washrag.

"Cool?" he said. "What do you mean by that?"

JT's lips always formed an open circle when he got angry, like he'd had too much Louisiana hot sauce. His eyes narrowed and he stared back at Matt Oliver.

Matt Oliver smiled. "Oh, hell, JT, calm down. I came to your party, didn't I? I'm here trying to cheer you up, but you're just spoiling for a fight."

The solemnity of the moment went out the window.

"You what?" JT yelled. "Party? Cheer us up? Dammit, ain't you got no respect? This ain't no party, and we don't want to be cheered up. Don't you get it? This ain't about being happy. It's a goddam tragedy. That wasn't just some nobody that got killed. It was Dewey Hargrove, man. Dewey for Chris' sakes. Dewey is dead."

"Yes, I—"

"Like hell you do. You come over here while we're trying to pay our respects to the man, and—shit, I just don't know anymore."

"Okay, okay," Matt Oliver said, "just calm down. I swear I wasn't trying to be disrespectful."

"You're just crazy, Matt Oliver. You know that? Hell, everybody's crazy now days. Nobody shows respect anymore. Things in this world are just going to hell."

"Aw, hell, JT, they ain't that bad," Matt Oliver said.

"Like hell they ain't," JT said. "My poor dog's so damned old he cain't even get around no more, and the goddam dogcatchers come out here like they was gonna surround the place, and Dewey gets killed, and you say things ain't bad?"

The entire house had grown silent as JT's trembling voice carried into the other rooms.

"Dewey's dead, and Boomer's dying. And how come? What'd they ever do to anybody? Hell, it ain't gonna be worth going hunting next fall without Boomer, and I'll never go to another race again without Dewey there. Shit, this has already been one fucked up year, and it ain't even spring yet. I just can't take it any…." His voice choked with emotion, and he turned away to hide his tears.

Doris Ann, who'd been sitting on the couch whimpering since Jack's arrival, suddenly broke into mournful sobs. April, Dewayne, and several of the women rushed to her aid as she swooned into Arlis's lap. Arlis carefully pulled the black veil away from her face, giving Jack an instant flashback to that day when she'd cornered him in her office. With her make-up smudged and running, her face reminded him of a Salvador Dali painting.

Matt Oliver muttered to Jack in a low voice, "This is too much for me. I'm going out front and smoke a cigarette."

That seemed like a good move, and Jack followed as they pushed their way to the front door. They lit their cigarettes and stood under the front stoop, staring out through the misty evening twilight. After a minute or two Matt Oliver seemed to focus on something across the street. A neighbor had painted a big number 93 with angel's wings and halo on the front door. In the front yard there was a sign that said, "Dewey, we'll never forget U, Luv, The Harrisons."

A few minutes later they returned to the den, and JT came back as well. Dry-eyed but grim, he walked in and sat on the couch. His presence killed the conversation as everyone sat in nervous silence, watching while he rubbed the top of his legs, staring at the far wall as if he had x-ray vision. If a pregnant silence incubates conversation, Jack was certain this one was destined for stillbirth, because JT definitely wasn't going to start it, and everyone else in the room was too much on edge to say anything.

The verbal impasse lasted nearly a minute until JT startled everyone by jumping up again and stalking out. Little JT nearly bowled his mother over as he ran to her side and hugged her arm. Janine could stand it no longer as she hollered after her husband. "Dammit, JT, quit actin' so cotton-pickin' weird. You're scarin' the kids."

He ignored her and disappeared into the back of the house.

"Y'all just relax," Janine said. "I'll fix us some cake."

A few minutes later she walked in with a large single-layer cake. The candles burning on top lit her face with an orange glow as she set it on the coffee table and stepped back.

"I thought they only put candles on birthday cakes," Matt Oliver whispered.

"Sshh," Henry said.

"Just consider them like those little candles the Catholics use," Janine said.

Matt Oliver turned red and stared at the floor.

"We might as well enjoy this," she said. "I drove all the way to Baskin Robbins in Memphis just to buy it. It's an official Dewey Hargrove Memorial ice-cream cake. What do you think?"

It had a little number 93 race car on it, along with the words: In Memory of Dewey Hargrove.

"Great," Henry said.

"Yeah, real nice," Matt Oliver added.

"Looks good," Jack said.

"I hope it's good," Janine said. "It cost me twenty-nine-ninety-nine and a tank of gas."

Everyone joined in to blow out the candles, and she began cutting the cake, until there came a loud noise from the kitchen. The back door slammed shut, followed by the slap of the screen door.

"What was that?" Janine said.

Dewayne peeked out the window into the backyard.

"Is it JT?" Henry asked.

Dewayne nodded as he pried the venetian blinds further apart.

"What's he doing?" Matt Oliver asked.

Dewayne shrugged and squinted as the setting sun appeared on the cloud-shrouded horizon.

"Looks like he's going out toward that storage shed," he said. "Only, I'm waiting to see what he's gonna do with the gun."

"The what?" Matt Oliver said.

"Yeah," Dewayne said, "He's got a big pistol, except he went behind the shed now, and I can't see him."

"Shit," Matt Oliver said.

Everyone started for the back door at once, but there came a loud pop from behind the shed. Janine let out a scream that rattled the windows and lunged toward the door, knocking little JT on his ass.

"JT's done shot hisself," she yelled.

Henry and Arlis restrained her.

"Wait, Ms. Janine," Henry said. "You better not go out there right now."

Janine made a couple of half-hearted attempts to get away as Matt Oliver and Jack slipped past her. They trotted across the backyard to the utility shed where Jack carefully peeked around the corner. Expecting the worst, he stood momentarily puzzled but relieved when he saw JT standing with his hand hanging at his side, still holding the gun. He had his back to Jack and his head down.

Not wanting to startle him, Jack softly called his name. JT didn't move. Again, Jack called his name, but nothing happened, except this time he heard a sob. Easing carefully around the corner, he walked up behind JT. Lying there on the ground was the dog, dead as a hammer, a widening pool of blood surrounding its head. Jack carefully put his hand on JT's shoulder, but he started.

"Easy," Jack said. "Why don't you just give me the gun and go on back inside? I'll get a shovel from the shed, and me and Matt Oliver will bury the dog."

Without a word, JT handed over the pistol and turned toward Matt Oliver. Throwing his arms around Matt Oliver's neck, he buried his face against his shoulder and began sobbing.

"I love you, man. I really love you," JT said.

Matt Oliver gazed at Jack and shrugged while rubbing JT's back.

"It's okay, buddy. Now, go on back in the house. Me and Mister Jack will take care of old Boomer for you."

Without raising his head, JT turned away and walked toward the house.

As Jack dug the hole, Henry and Arlis came out and joined them. Matt Oliver hadn't said a word since JT went back inside. He stood staring down at the dead dog, its pathetic corpse the next thing to a skeleton.

"Do you think I made him do this?" Matt Oliver asked.

"Hell, no," Henry answered. "You know that boy ain't right."

"Well, I sure didn't mean to make him freak out."

The sun had set, and nightfall was rapidly approaching.

"Like I said, it ain't your fault. If it hadn't been you, it'd a been somebody or something else that set him off."

"JT told me to ask you to wrap Boomer in this," Arlis said.

He held out JT's red, black, and yellow Dewey Hargrove jacket.

"He wants me to say a prayer, too," Arlis added, thumbing through the pages of his Bible.

"You mean you're gonna pray over the dog?" Henry asked.

"That was his request," Arlis said. "I have to respect JT for his convictions."

Jack was now numb to the events occurring around him. After wrapping the dog's corpse in the jacket, the men buried it and stood back. Henry removed his ball cap, but Arlis continued thumbing through his Bible. After a while he stopped and seemed to give up as he closed the book.

"I guess I'm so upset, I just can't find the right verse," he said. "Besides, it's getting too dark to see, so I'll just wing it."

He bent over and picked up a handful of dirt.

"Anyway: From dust to dust and dirt to dirt, we all will leave this earth, and we ask you, Lord, to let this fine hunting dog lay down in the green grass and walk beside the still waters of your kingdom. Please give our brother, JT, the strength to bear this loss and forgive this fine hunting dog, Boomer, his trespasses, 'cause you know dogs can't read posted signs."

He sprinkled the dirt over the grave and resumed talking nonstop for the next five minutes, but as soon as he paused to catch his breath, Henry interjected a quick "Amen."

Arlis looked up, startled by the interruption.

"Amen," Matt Oliver repeated.

"Amen," Jack added.

Arlis looked around and shrugged. "Uh, okay then. Amen."

Jack joined the others as they formed a little procession, walking single-file back to the house. He thought about Tuck and the people back home. If only they saw him now—they'd probably have him committed. Inside, the crowd had thinned considerably, and JT had gone to bed. Jack handed Janine the revolver, and she thanked everyone as they said their good-byes, leaving a teary-eyed Dewayne on the couch, still trying to comfort April and Doris Ann.

CHAPTER 19

THE TRAIN DERAILS

S EVERAL WEEKS HAD PASSED SINCE Dewey Hargrove's death, and things were back to normal—at least what qualified as "normal" at the factory. Jack simply hoped for a few days of peace. JT was getting past his grief, and despite occasional interference from Nickels, the employees did whatever Jack asked of them. Arlis, though, was one who continued to trouble him. He was sinking further into his own little weird world, and Jack planned to discuss it with Henry, as soon as he found the time.

Arriving at dawn that Friday morning, he joined with Henry as they brought up the computers, lights, and ventilation system. It would be another thirty minutes before the first employees arrived. When he was done, Jack returned to his office, while Henry went to unlock the doors. It was March, but wintry weather had returned frozen and overcast.

Jack was thinking about his trip with Cici to the doctor the previous week. He had taken her up to Memphis for blood tests and an exam. The doctor had been upbeat, but a few days later they called with her test results. Her liver and kidney functions had worsened. Given her already debilitated condition, it wasn't good news.

Jack sipped his coffee, while printing the day's work orders and hoping for a better day, but there came the slap of shoes on the tile floor. Someone was running up the hallway. Henry, breathless, poked his head inside the office door. His face was ashen.

"Come quick," he said. "We've got a problem."

Turning, He ran toward the front office, talking over his shoulder as he went. "Arlis is out in the parking lot holding a gun on Nickels."

The two men stopped at the front window and peeked through the dusty venetian blind. Nickels was on his knees beside his huge white Escalade, and Arlis was standing over him with a long-barrel revolver. Laid open across his other hand was his Bible, from which Arlis was reading aloud. Jack reached for the door, but Henry grabbed his arm.

"Wait a minute," he said. "I already called 911. Wait till the deputies get here."

Jack paused. It could be ten minutes or more before they arrived. He had to distract Arlis—perhaps stall him.

"I'm going out there and try to talk to him," Jack said.

He pulled the door open slowly, but Henry pulled him back. "Wait. Let me ease up behind him and grab the gun."

Before Jack could object, Henry pushed him back and stepped through the door. Regaining his balance, Jack followed the old foreman. Arlis had his back to them, but Nickels saw them coming and began babbling. "Do something. Talk to him."

Any chance of sneaking up on Arlis was quickly shot to hell as he turned around. "Stay back, Henry, you too, Mister Jack. This ain't none of y'alls' affair."

"What are you doing, Arlis?" Jack said.

Arlis took a deep breath and stood erect. "I am an extension of the will of our Lord, Jesus Christ, and I am acting on his behalf to fulfill the word as it is written right here in the Holy Bible."

He held the book on his extended fingertips as if to offer it symbolically to heaven.

"Where does it say you can kill a man?" Henry asked.

"Damn it! Stop talking and do something," Nickels shouted. He had suddenly become the authoritative Plant Manager again. "Don't just stand there like idiots. One of you call 911."

Arlis hammered back the big revolver and shoved it against Nickels's face. "Silence, Satan!"

"I suggest you shut the hell up, Mister Nickels, and let us try to talk to Arlis," Jack said.

"Who?" Nickels said. "What's his name?"

"Arlis," Henry said. "He's worked here for almost a year now. He's one of the people you—uh—were yelling at when the power went out last month."

"Sure, sure. I mean, uh, I know his face."

"Never mind," Henry replied. "Just be quiet a minute." He looked at Arlis. "He didn't mean you any harm. He doesn't even know your name."

"That's right. That's right," Nickels said, his voice cracking and shrill. "It wasn't anything personal."

"Mister Nickels, sir," Henry said, "please, I need you to be quiet and let me talk to Arlis."

Arlis turned and pointed the big gun at Henry. "Mister Henry, you're interfering with the work of the Lord, and if you don't step back, I am going to be forced to act in his behalf."

Henry threw his hands up and backed away. Despite the bitter cold, sweat poured from his face.

"Don't do this, Arlis," Jack said. "God doesn't want you killing people."

Ignoring them both, Arlis turned and aimed the gun at Nickels as he again began reading from the Bible. "It is written, he said to them, my house will be called a house of prayer, but you are making it a den of robbers."

"Stop this, Arlis," Jack said. "No one robbed anybody."

Arlis paused and glanced back at Jack. The icy breeze blew beneath a foggy gray sky sending the pages of his Bible fluttering. Arlis seemed unfazed as he turned and began reading from a different passage: "I am not possessed by a demon, said Jesus."

He stopped reading again and looked down at Nickels. "Are you saved?" His voice boomed and echoed across the lot. Nickels by this time had soaked his pin-striped suit with sweat and could barely speak. "Saved?" he said.

The distant sound of approaching sirens gave Jack a sudden sense of relief. The cops, no doubt, would talk some sense into Arlis. He was probably frustrated and a little over the edge, but now that he'd made his statement, perhaps they could calm him. The sound of the sirens drew closer, and Jack spotted the first squad car as it turned onto the access road from the highway.

The powerful .357 magnum bucked upward, its report echoing like a cannon down the side of the metal building and out across the fields to the distant tree line. Henry ducked behind the Escalade, but Jack stood stunned by the horror of what he was witnessing. Nickels's eyes bulged and his head swelled as he fell backward. Arlis lowered the pistol and went back to reading from the Bible. Jack stared down at Nickels, lying there, a smoking hole in his face and the dark gray stain of urine spreading on his pants.

The squad cars squealed into the parking lot, but Jack remained frozen in shock, as the deputies trained their shotguns and pistols on Arlis, who still stood over the body. He turned and handed the pistol to Jack, then continued reading from his Bible. Jack dropped the big revolver to the pavement and stood staring at the widening pool of blood beneath Nickels's head. The deputies shouted at them to get down, but Jack stood in shock, unable to move. A young cop ran forward in a combat crouch, holding his pistol with both hands as he trained it on Jack's chest.

Henry came around the front of the Escalade and yelled at the deputy. "Stop. He didn't do anything."

Arlis bowed his head as another deputy pulled his arms behind his back and cuffed his wrists.

Several minutes later, Jack, still dazed, became aware of the squad cars parked all around with their lights flashing, blocking the main entrance to the factory. It was a circus of the macabre as the employees arrived outside the gate to see the paramedics placing a sheet over Nickels's body. Yellow tape was stretched around the scene. A cluster of deputies and other men in suits stood together while the employees watched from outside the gate, staring grimly at the spectacle. With their fingers locked in the chain-link fence, they peered across the lot at center-ring, but the ringmaster was dead, and somehow it occurred to Jack at that moment—that so it was with the factory as well.

Jack was sickened when the county coroner pulled the sheet back and a white vapor rose from the body, escaping into the cold morning air. Deputies and paramedics stood around talking, making notes on clipboards, but they ignored the employees standing outside the fence. The chief deputy and another investigator took notes as they questioned Henry. Everyone was getting attention except for the employees. Jack turned and slowly walked across the parking lot to the fence.

Matt Oliver, Momo, JT, Clyde, and Dewayne were standing together near the main gate. Behind them stood Dorito, Cleve, Doris Ann and dozens more.

"Goddam, Jack. You look like shit," Matt Oliver said. "What the hell happened?"

"It was Arlis," Jack said, pointing to the squad car where Arlis sat handcuffed in the back seat. Jack knew he should have acted sooner, because Nickels never understood just how deeply loathed he was by his employees. Now it was too late. The shrinks would come and tell everyone that everything was going to be okay, but it wasn't.

"How'd he do it?" JT asked.

"He just blew his brains out," Jack said, surprised by the callousness of his own words.

"Crazy bastard," Matt Oliver muttered.

Dewayne hung his head, staring at the ground with unfocused eyes. "I never figured Arlis to be that way, I mean with his Bible studying and all."

Everyone turned to look at Dewayne.

"Don't be a dumb-ass," JT said.

Had Matt Oliver called him a dumb-ass, Dewayne would have pouted, but when JT did, it didn't seem to bother him. It must have had something to do with Dewayne believing he was in some way JT's intellectual equal, something not entirely beyond reason.

"I ain't being a dumb-ass," Dewayne said. "He was gonna be godfather to my kids."

"Nickels?" JT asked.

"No. Arlis," Dewayne said. "I figured with his religion and all, he'd make a good one, but I reckon I'm gonna have to find somebody else now. You interested?"

JT's eyes widened, but before he could respond, Henry walked up. The rest of the employees had already moved down the fence and begun gathering behind JT and the others.

"We ain't working today, people," Henry shouted, "Plan on being back at work Monday."

"How come he shot him?" someone asked.

"Cause he's a crazy sumbitch, that's why," someone else answered.

"The sheriff deputy told me to tell y'all to clear out now," Henry said. "Just come back in at the regular time Monday morning."

"Who's gonna run the factory now?" someone asked.

"Hey, maybe Mister Jack can run it," another person said.

Jack held up his hand to silence them. "That's something the home office will have to decide. Just go on back home for now, and we'll see you all Monday."

One of the deputies, Steve Gentry, strutted up to the fence. He was the one who had trained his weapon on Jack's chest. Now he carried a black nightstick. Gentry wore a military style haircut and had more trinkets on his gun belt than a high-rise maintenance man. He stepped up to the fence.

"You heard the man," he boomed. "Clear out! Now!"

JT still had his fingers interlocked in the fence as he seemed lost in thought, staring at Nickels's body. Gentry rapped the fenced with his nightstick, hitting JT's fingers.

"Shit!" JT screamed. "You almost broke my finger, you stupid bastard."

"I'll break more than that if you don't watch your mouth."

JT walked away cradling his injured hand, while Jack walked over to Gentry.

"You got a problem?" Gentry asked.

"You're the one with the problem," Jack said. "You didn't need to hit that man's hand that way." With that he turned to walk back to the office.

Later when most of the investigators had gone and the blood was mostly cleaned from the asphalt, Jack and Henry sat down to discuss what to do next. It was around noon when they decided to lock up, and as they walked down the front steps Jack noticed a deputy still on the lot. It was Gentry, and he was standing behind Jack's truck, with a ticket book. When he finished, he ripped a ticket from the book, and walked up to within inches of Jack's face, staring intently at him.

"What's the problem?" Jack asked.

"I was trying to disperse the crowd, but you seemed to have a problem with that, so, when I came back here—"

Henry walked up. "What the hell do—"

"Wait a minute, Henry," Jack said. He turned back to Gentry. "What's your problem? How come you're harassing everybody today?"

Gentry turned and pointed at the license plate on Jack's truck.

"No harassment, just doing my job. The sticker on your tag is improperly displayed. It's upside-down."

Jack glanced at the tag. "Okay, Barney, looks like I'm busted."

"You've got a smart mouth," Gentry said.

Jack turned and opened his truck door. "We're getting ready to lock the front gate. You might want to move your vehicle outside the fence. Let's go, Henry."

Jack and Henry pulled their vehicles through the gate and waited until Gentry drove past before securing the big chain and lock.

"I'm going to call the Sheriff about that little turd," Henry said.

"Today was probably more than the asshole could handle," Jack said.

"Give me that ticket," Henry said. "My son, Clayton, is a deputy. He'll take care of it."

After stuffing the ticket in his shirt pocket, Henry paused and looked at Jack. "Are you going to be okay?"

Jack shook his head. "Hell, I don't know. Just when I think it can't get any crazier around here...." He paused, at a loss for words.

"Let's go get a drink somewhere," Henry said.

That night Jack called Uncle Tuck, and when he told him about Arlis killing Nickels, Tuck's voice tightened noticeably.

"Jack, you need to cut bait and get the hell out of there, before one of those crazy bastards shoots you."

"I can't. I've got to see this thing through. Besides, Cici needs me now more than ever."

There were several seconds of silence before Tuck finally spoke. "Sounds like you could use a little company."

"Are you thinking about coming up for a visit?"

"Actually, I was planning to make the offer before you called. How about next week?"

"I'd like you to hold off for a while. Things are really crazy around here right now."

"You sure?"

"Yeah. Just give me some time. I'll call you, maybe in a few weeks."

"Well, hey, Acey called me the other day."

"Really?"

"Yeah, she asked about you."

"Well, I'm afraid with some of what's happened up here, it's really over between us now."

"What happened?"

Jack began relating his weekend adventure with Doris Ann, and the more he said, the more uncontrollable Tuck's laughter became.

"I got the same reaction from Cici when I told her," Jack said. "She called it reverse date-rape."

"You gotta admit, she *did* take being a cougar to a new level."

"Yeah, and maybe, if I weren't the butt of the joke, I might laugh too."

It had become more important than ever for Jack to stay close to the employees, and there was no better venue than the breakroom at lunchtime. He was running late that day as he hurried across the factory floor. Subsequent to Nickels's death, plant productivity had grown. The employees were smiling again, and it seemed the oppression of a thousand years of slavery had been lifted from their shoulders. Without the intimidation he had wielded like a sledgehammer, the unhealthy competition between departments ended and people once again cared about their jobs.

They simply pulled together and fixed the problems. According to Matt Oliver, working at the furniture factory was almost fun again. Jack saw the faintest glimmer of hope rising from the ashes of the past, but the factory was still a long way from redemption—if that was even possible. Nickels's murder had made the front page of the *Tallahatchie County Tribune* several days running, and for the first time, a columnist made reference to the future of the factory. It probably would have gone unnoticed except there was a photo of Dewayne's and Percy Williams's smiling faces on the same page.

They had won the first big bass fishing tournament of the year, the Lake Washington Freeze-fest down at Greenville—so named because of the blustery cold weather that usually occurred during the competition. Nickels's murder notwithstanding, this was major news in Tallahatchie County, and the paper covered it with the front-page photo, as well as a lengthy article in the sports section.

It was a pick-your-partner tournament, in which Dewayne and Percy surprised the local favorites, catching what was described as a tournament record. Sitting between them in the photo was a huge trophy and a large facsimile of a check for five thousand dollars. Of course Dewayne had shown up at work with the trophy, putting it in the middle of the breakroom table. When Jack arrived the conversation was already in progress.

Dewayne stood and pointed at the trophy. "You see that, Mr. Jack? I told you I was gonna be a professional bass fisherman."

Jack nodded as he took a seat. "That's good," he said. The trophy was nearly three feet tall.

"You and Percy are fixing to be professional jailbirds if they catch y'all," Matt Oliver said.

"What'd they do?" Jack asked.

"They ain't done nothin'," JT said. He turned to Matt Oliver. "And you cain't prove nothing either."

"I won't have to, if the game warden catches him."

"If I was Dewayne I'd kick your ass for trying to ruin his professional bass fisherman career," JT said.

"Okay," Matt Oliver said, turning to Dewayne, "just look me in the eyes and tell me you caught all those bass fair and square."

JT smiled. "Go ahead, Dewayne, tell him."

Dewayne stared down at the table. "Well, I reckon you could say that."

"What do you mean, 'you reckon'?" Henry asked.

Dewayne took a bite from his sandwich and stared straight ahead.

"Percy's taking your dumb ass right down the primrose path to jail," Matt Oliver said. "If those folks down at Greenville find out y'all cheated, they'll probably lynch you both."

Matt Oliver explained how Percy had been booted out of another bass fishing club a few years back. They doused his boat with gasoline and set it on fire in his front yard, after spray-painting the word "Cheater" on his house trailer.

Jack and the others turned to Dewayne, but he was still chewing his sandwich, probably too simple-minded to understand the seriousness of the situation.

With the increased productivity at the factory there came another set of problems. Nickels had not spent a dime on capital improvements. What wasn't repaired was replaced the cheapest way possible. The ventilation systems were clogged and all the machinery was running on borrowed time. To make matters worse, the Tupelo office ignored Jack's recommendations. Instead, they hired a consulting firm to come in and suggest solutions.

The consultants ignored most of what Jack and Henry suggested. Instead they interviewed only certain employees. Word was Tommy Grey had traveled to Tupelo and filled them in on who could be trusted. It was evident that Jack, Henry, Clyde and Matt Oliver weren't included. And the one they consulted with most was Grey. Nickels's legacy clung to the factory like the stench of a road-killed skunk.

Packaging their report in a slick binder, the consultants presented the home office with everything Tommy Grey had already told them was the problem. The home office ordered an immediate flurry of changes—changes that were at best convoluted attempts to stave off what now had become the inevitable. The factory was going under. Refusing to give up, Jack tried to make his voice heard, but he was met with indifference.

CHAPTER 20

SONNY T TAKES CONTROL

THE FIRST THING THE HOME office did after receiving the consultant's report was hire Sonny T. Wilborn out of Memphis as the new Human Resources Manager. The home office said they would do all future hiring, firing and promotions based on Sony T's recommendations. This edict gave the new Human Resources Manager unprecedented power. Complicating matters worse was Sonny T's reputation for controversy in Memphis, something the home office had overlooked. His activities were well documented in the Memphis newspaper. His two jobs, one as an employee rights advocate in the city Human Resources department and the other as a Memphis City Councilman, were considered a conflict of interest by most—except in Memphis.

Sonny T, a middle-aged native Memphian, wore the best Lansky Brothers three-piece suits and more gold chains and diamond rings than a Pinch District pimp. He had also been convicted—as he was quoted in the newspaper "on a phony charge of temporary reallocation of public funds," got it overturned on a technicality, then got busted again when a crack pipe was found in his Lexus. The judge—a fraternity brother of Sonny T's—tossed that one out, too, saying the Memphis cops conspired to frame him.

Only after a gun-waving incident where Sonny T threatened a cab driver for racial profiling, was he forced to shop around for something else to do. Jack figured some idiot at the home office had not bothered to check Sonny T's references, and he was now wreaking havoc at the factory.

According to Sonny T, the factory didn't have enough minorities in the skilled positions. When Jack showed him that the overall demographics matched those of the county, he blew it off, saying Jack was using numbers like smoke and mirrors. Jack suggested that Sonny T recruit minorities from the college down at Cleveland, and establish training programs for the nearly illiterate laborers, but Sonny T's solution was to move them up anyway. At Sonny T's suggestion, the home office moved Shamika, Cleolanda and Sharon from the janitorial staff to clerical positions in the office. Sonny T told Jack to give them on the job training then caught a plane at the company's expense to a jobs conference in Atlanta.

Jack found them agreeable. Shamika could actually read and write at an eighth-grade level, which was a big plus, but mostly she and her fellow office assistants sharpened pencils, made copies, and talked on the phone with their boyfriends down at Parchman Prison. Jack tried coaching them, but the cultural and generational differences were a chasm he couldn't bridge.

When he returned from Atlanta, Sonny T was pleased and promoted several more employees to machinist positions. He also told the clerical staff to beware of Jack and the other "company" people, because they were out to get them. Later he informed Jack that Tommy Grey was resigning and the home office was hiring a new supervisor. Jack recommended Clyde, but again the unpredictable Sonny T refused his suggestion, saying Clyde was an Uncle Tom, and he wanted his "own man watching the store."

His next strangest move came when he promoted Dewayne to a machinist's position. Jack and Henry decided to confront Sonny T and explain how they had recently moved Dewayne from the paint shop and given him a broom. They even allowed him to keep the same hourly pay. He was now in a job where he couldn't hurt himself or anyone else—no chemicals, sharp edges or moving parts.

Jack walked with Henry up the hallway to Sonny T's office. The plan was for Dewayne to begin training on a band saw the next day. They had to convince Sonny T to rethink this one. They arrived to find the hallway cluttered with office furniture. Henry and Jack traded questioning looks while studying the new gold nameplate on the door. It was engraved in old English script with Sonny T's name. Jack tapped lightly on the door.

"It's open," came a voice from inside.

Opening the door, they were met with the odor of fresh paint and new carpet. The office had been completely remodeled—plush ivory carpet, sunset gold paint and framed oil paintings on every wall. Lush tropical plants filled the corners, complementing a huge mahogany desk and a leather couch the likes of which had never been produced at Fernwood. Sonny T sat in a high-back leather chair with his feet propped on the desk, staring at them with raised eyebrows.

"We came to discuss Dewayne Pritchert's promotion," Jack said.

"Discuss?"

"Yes, we want to talk with you about it," Jack said, "so you might reconsider."

Sonny T put his hands behind his head and smiled. "You don't get it, do you, Mister Manager?"

Jack said nothing.

"My decisions are not up for negotiation, and the first person that interferes is gonna get a pink slip."

"Can't we just move Dewayne to something a little safer," Henry said, "like a maintenance position, maybe?"

"Looka here," Sonny T said, dropping the smile from his face and his feet from the desk. "I'm gonna invite you two out of my office *nicely* this time. Y'all just need to understand it's my job to recommend and approve them, but the main office actually does the hiring. All y'all got to do is train them. Have a nice day, now, and close my door on your way out."

Jack pulled at a red-faced Henry's shirtsleeve. "Let's go," he said.

Henry followed him up the hall.

"That fool's new labor force is already causing more delays and rework than we can afford," Henry said. "And God only knows what he paid for that office furniture."

Productivity plummeted and internal strife grew along with Sonny T's influence. Morale sank to a new low. No one was happy except for Dewayne. He had gotten his title as Machine Operator, and Jack held his breath, hoping he could be trained, but a few days later the emergency alarm went off. Trained as a first-responder, Jack scrambled from his office with the first aid kit in hand.

Matt Oliver came sprinting up the hall with Momo. He hollered into the front office, "Call 911!"

Cleolanda looked up, "Don't you yell at me, white boy!"

About that time Doris Ann came out of the restroom.

"Call 911," Matt Oliver said again. "Transfer them out to the floor office."

"What's going on?" Jack asked.

Momo tried to tell him, "D-d-dddddu-du—!"

"JT said the dumb bastard cut his hand off," Matt Oliver said.

"Dewayne?" Jack asked, already knowing the answer.

"That's what JT said, but I haven't seen him yet."

As soon as he stepped out the door into the plant, Jack heard Dewayne's ungodly screams. It was as if his balls were in a vice, a half-crank away from bursting. Jack sprinted with Matt Oliver and Momo across the floor to the crowd of people surrounding Dewayne's workstation. As he pushed his way through, Jack's first impression was that Matt Oliver was right, Dewayne had cut his hand off. There was blood everywhere, and JT was sitting straddle of him, holding him down.

Jack fell to his knees as he attempted to assess the situation. JT and Dewayne were both covered with blood, and JT had a piece of wire wrapped around Dewayne's arm just above the elbow. He had twisted the wire with a screwdriver until the arm looked as if it were about to be cut in two.

"He's cutting my goddam arm off," Dewayne screamed.

"Shut up, Dewayne," Jack yelled.

He went down to a whimper then a low moan while Jack grabbed the screwdriver and began unwinding the wire.

"What the hell are you trying to do?" he asked.

JT shrugged. "It's a tourniquet, man. Don't you know?"

There was somewhat of an amputation to Dewayne's right thumb, but it wasn't as serious as first described. The tip had been severed—sliced through above the base of the nail. Grabbing it, Jack applied pressure around the thumb with his hand.

He looked up at Matt Oliver. "Go to the phone in the floor office," he said. "Tell them we have an amputation injury near the tip of the right thumb. It's not life-threatening, but we'll need to transport him to the emergency room in Charleston."

Jack turned to JT, "Where's the tip of his thumb?"

"It might be up there on the table," he said, motioning toward the saw.

"See if you can find it."

When the ambulance and paramedics arrived, Jack turned Dewayne's treatment over to them while JT, Momo, and Matt Oliver assisted in the search for the tip of the thumb. They looked everywhere, including the vacuum bins, inside the machine, and in the scrap bin, but it was nowhere to be found.

"I really feel bad about ol' Dewayne," JT said.

"Wasn't your fault," Jack said.

"Yeah, I know. I sure didn't know he had his thumb up there when I slapped him on the back."

"You slapped him on the back?" Matt Oliver said.

"Well, not hard or anything," JT answered. "I was just letting him know it was lunchtime. I didn't know he was checking to see if the saw was sharp."

Jack was throwing wood cuttings back into the scrap bin, but stopped. "How was he checking to see if the saw was sharp?"

JT shrugged, "Like I showed him, I reckon."

"And how's that?"

"Well, you barely push the callused part of your thumb up to the edge of the saw while it's running. If it's dull it'll just vibrate against your skin a little. If it's sharp, it puts a itty-bitty cut on it—but it's a callus, so it don't hurt nothin'."

"You're kidding, right?"

JT stared back at him, and Jack turned away before he lost his temper, but Matt Oliver was incensed. "JT, you are one dumb sonofabitch, you know that?"

JT lunged at him, and it took Clyde, Henry and Momo to keep them apart. It was a fitting end to the morning. The worst of it, though, was the realization that this was only the first manifestation of Sonny T's administration.

Dewayne stayed in the hospital for a week—not that it was necessary, but when Honey Lips Baker, an attorney out of Oxford, got wind of the accident, he rushed to Tallahatchie General. The ER doctor was about to release Dewayne with a few stitches and some antibiotics when Honey Lips arrived and got his new client's name on the dotted line. After a hurried consultation, Dewayne convinced the doctors he needed further tests and observation. By late April, he was still off work, and according to JT suffering from post-traumatic stress. Seems the thumb injury had put his future as a professional bass fisherman in jeopardy.

As the last week of April began, Jack hoped the controversy over Dewayne's injury had passed, but he realized more trouble was brewing when he saw Henry walk into Sonny T's office. He wasn't overly concerned because Henry usually remained calm in even the worst situations, but he hurried down the hall, stopping to listen outside Sonny T's door.

"So you second-guessing my decision, huh?" Sonny T said.

"Ain't no second-guessing to it," Henry replied. "We told you he would get hurt, but you wouldn't listen."

"You knew it wasn't gonna work," Sonny T said, "'cause you and that dumb-ass factory manager didn't train the boy right."

"Mr. Jack isn't a dumb-ass, and we did everything possible," Henry replied, "but that boy isn't trainable. Hell, his IQ isn't much higher than yours."

"Say what?"

Jack pushed the door open.

"I don't reckon I stuttered, did I?" Henry said.

Sonny T looked past Henry to Jack standing in the door. "You heard him," he shouted. "He was being insubordinate."

"Us dumb-ass factory managers are hard of hearing," Jack replied, grabbing Henry by the arm. "Come on."

"Yeah, old man, take your tired ass on outta here. I'm calling the home office, and you'll have your termination letter in a hot minute."

"Termination letter?" Henry said. "Man, you're crazy."

"You gonna think crazy if you don't get your mutha-fuckin' ass out of my office. Now, git."

"Come on," Jack said again.

Henry turned to walk out, mumbling as he went: "Dumb sonofabitch ain't gotta clue."

By now Doris Ann, Cleolonda, Sharon, and several others were peeking down the hall toward Sonny T's office.

"And if you're really serious about getting him fired, I hope you can find someone with his knowledge and experience as a replacement."

"You better believe I'm serious, and I already got his replacement. Mr. Grey's replacement is supposed to start tomorrow."

Jack turned and walked away, confident the home office wouldn't allow Henry to leave.

Sonny T's new man started the next day, and to make matters worse, the home office had created a special position for him, General Floor Manager. At Sonny T's suggestion, they had made him boss over everyone but Jack. Mort Kingman was no doubt supposed to make the "old school" types like Henry toe the line.

A retiree from Illinois, Kingman had moved down to live near the casinos. Rumor was that after a year and a half he had lost most of his 401K playing poker, and found himself back in the employment line. Henry's wife, a teller at the bank in Clarksdale, said Mort bragged openly about being a "professional poker player." She also said he claimed all the casino managers knew him by first name, but respectfully called him Mr. Kingman.

That morning when Jack passed the work orders to Henry, the old foreman simply handed them back and pointed to Mort. "That's your new assistant in there."

Mort was on the phone inside the glass-walled floor office. Standing beside the desk, he laughed and waved his hand in the air, probably talking with a bookie or a gambling buddy. Jack went inside, and tried to hand him the stack of work orders, but the new Floor Manager rolled his eyes, making it obvious he didn't appreciate the interruption. Jack shrugged and tossed them on the desk. He was about to walk out when Mort stopped talking and put his hand over the phone.

"What are those?" he asked.

Jack picked up the stack of papers from the desk and began explaining how they had to be prioritized and assigned to each department, but Mort cut him off in mid-sentence. "That's enough, sport. Just leave them there on the desk, and close the door on your way out."

Jack paused. Mort must have assumed he was one of the office staff. It was better to explain things than to let the new man screw up even worse. Mort again motioned him toward the door with the back of his hand as he resumed his telephone conversation, but Jack shook his head.

"I haven't given you all—"

Mort screwed up his face and slapped his hand over the phone. "Can't you see I'm talking on the phone?"

Mort stood glaring at him.

Jack shrugged. "Okay, call me if you have any questions."

With that he turned and walked out. By lunchtime, the factory was in turmoil with production behind in every department. After Mort had rebuffed him several times, Henry resigned himself to silence and went to find Jack. They decided to wait and see just how bad it would get before Mort asked for help. The gregarious bastard was an expert on everything, and if anyone doubted it, all they had to do was make a suggestion. Word was Sonny T had warned him how the present supervisors would try to undermine his efforts, and the paranoid Mort was doing the opposite of anything they suggested.

At lunchtime Jack followed Henry toward the breakroom. There'd been production bottlenecks, pissed-off employees, and downtime waiting on supplies all morning. Everyone was in a sullen mood.

"How long are you going to let this go on?" Henry asked.

Jack shrugged. "This guy will have to learn the hard way."

Henry nodded, but coughed and cleared his throat as he motioned with his head. Jack looked back to see Mort approaching.

"I figured he'd go to lunch with Sonny T," Henry said, "or at least eat in the big lunchroom with the office people."

"Sonny T probably hasn't shown him around," Jack said. "Hell, he hasn't even introduced him to anyone."

Mort walked in, and Jack began introducing him. "Guys, this is the new General Floor Manager, Mort Kingman."

Matt Oliver, JT, Clyde, all of them, took turns shaking his hand until it came around to Momo. Momo seemed nervous as he eyed Mort's gold rings and fancy retirement watch. He stood and extended his hand. "M-m-mo-mo-moore-m-m-an Bu-bu-Beaver."

"Damned Momo," JT said. "You ain't gotta tell him your name but once."

"Fu-fu-fuck y-y-you, Ju-Ju-Jay Tu-tu-Tee."

"You Indian?" Mort asked.

"Cha-Cha-Choctaw," Momo answered.

"Yeah," JT said. "He was a real stud back on the reservation. That's why they call him Momo Beaver—get it: More Beaver?"

Mort let out a laugh, but Momo grew silent—not that he wasn't that way most of the time. Jack was certain Momo had never met a conversation he couldn't kill with an onslaught of silence, but he'd learned to read him, and this time it was different. It was the calm before the storm—something that could get ugly if he didn't calm the tension.

"Damned, JT. Did you think of that all by yourself?"

Since Jack seldom inserted himself into their petty arguments, JT seemed taken aback. "I reckon," he said. "I mean it just came to me. You know? I mean it's obvious, ain't it?"

"What's obvious," Matt Oliver said, "is that you're trashing the man's name. So why don't you show him some respect and shut the fuck up?"

"Jeesus," Mort said, "What a fun-loving bunch of guys."

Mort looked over at Jack. "So what's your job around here, partner?"

"Name's Jack Hartman. I'm the Acting Plant Manager."

Mort's eyebrows narrowed.

"Yeah," Henry added. "He gives us the work orders each day."

Jack walked over to the coffee maker and started a new pot while everyone else began opening lunch boxes and unwrapping sandwiches. Mort turned a couple shades of sheep's wool white.

"Why didn't you tell me who you were this morning?"

Jack flicked the switch on the coffee maker and turned toward him. "Because you never gave me the chance. From here on out, I suggest you listen to what that man tells you," he said, pointing at Henry.

Saying nothing more, Mort turned and walked over to the vending machines. After scanning them through wire-rimmed bifocals, he dropped several quarters into the carousel sandwich machine.

"Sometimes, that shit ain't fit to eat," Matt Oliver said. "Check the date."

Matt Oliver was right. The sandwiches were often left for weeks at a time.

"Yes," Mort said. "Thank you, but I've had a vending-machine sandwich or two in my day."

Mort's sarcastic response was the same he'd been giving Henry all morning. Jack shook his head in resignation. His advice to Mort had been wasted. Matt Oliver's face reddened, but he said nothing as Mort put his "Big Red" sausage hoagie into the microwave and punched the buttons. When it was heated, Mort sat down at the table and unwrapped the sandwich.

"Not bad," he said, after taking the first bite.

"You ain't gonna catch me eating one of those things," Matt Oliver said.

Mort rolled his eyes. "Okay, sure, whatever, and I suppose I'm supposed to ask why you *ain't* going to eat one, right?"

He swallowed and took another big bite from the sandwich as he cast a sideways glare at Matt Oliver.

"You must not read the paper," Matt Oliver said.

"Which one?" Mort asked, talking with his mouth full.

"The *Tallahatchie County Tribune*," Matt Oliver said. "They did a big write-up on the company down in Cleveland that makes those things."

"I subscribe to the Memphis paper," Mort said.

He raised the sandwich for another bite, but this time barely nibbled at the bread.

"One of the employees at the sandwich company called the health department and told them they were using the meat from an old milk-cow that died in some farmer's barn. The county couldn't prove it, but they found a deer carcass hanging when they went to investigate. The owner claimed it was for his own personal use, but it wasn't even deer season. The owner said it was road-kill."

Mort turned to Henry. "Are you aware of what he's talking about?"

Henry nodded, and Mort spit the half-chewed sausage and bread into the wrapper. The only thing that would have made it better was if it were actually true. Mort had been at the factory half a day, and already alienated everyone there.

"So, where are you from?" Henry asked.

"Illinois," Mort answered, wiping his mouth.

"Oh?" Henry said. "What did you do up there?"

Jack and Henry had both seen Mort's résumé claiming he was "Supervisor of Fiduciary Operations" for the city where he had lived, but when Jack called to check his references, Mort's old boss said he was an accounting clerk who supervised two cashiers. It was nothing to be ashamed of, but Mort had done the same thing for twenty-five years, and none of it related to running a factory. He had fooled Sonny T and the home office with his fancy talk, and now the factory was stuck with him.

Mort looked straight-faced at Henry and said, "I was in charge of fiduciary accounts."

"Fiduciary accounts?" Henry said. "Is that the person who counts the money?"

Mort rolled his eyes. That seemed to be his favorite way of showing disdain.

"I suppose that's correct in its most elementary sense. Actually, I was responsible for city tax receipts."

Henry cut a quick glance over at Jack, who remained poker-faced.

"So what do you fellows do for entertainment around here?" Mort asked.

It was obvious—he wanted to change the subject.

"A little hunting, a little fishing, and we play a hand or two of poker now and then," Henry said.

Mort's eyes widened ever-so-slightly at the mention of poker. Henry's plan became immediately evident. It was the classic battlefield tactic, sound the bugles and beat the drums while feinting a frontal assault—Henry's inquiry about Mort's previous job—and while they prepare for the frontal attack, send a slashing attack in from the flank, devastating your foe. With the mention of "poker," Henry had drawn Mort all the way in.

"So you guys are poker players, are you?" Mort said.

"Like I said," Henry replied, "We play a hand now and then."

"Where do you play?" Mort asked.

The five-minute bell rang, and everyone began filing out to the dock to catch a smoke. Clyde, Doritoe, and several others were already outside enjoying the spring sunshine.

"I have a little cabin up at Moon Lake," Henry said. "Maybe you'd like to go with us some weekend?"

Mort began running his own con game as he feigned reluctance. "I don't know. I play a little poker now and then, but it'd be foolish to play with a bunch of Mississippi gamblers like you guys."

"That's fine," Henry said. "I was just trying to be sociable."

"Well, heck, I don't want to seem unsociable."

This was the first time Mort had said anything that sounded even mildly humble.

"When are you playing again?" he asked.

Henry set the hook. "Probably sometime in early May."

"That's nearly two weeks away," Mort said. "Why so long?"

"Oh, we go fishing, too. We'll put trotlines out Friday evening. We play cards a while, then go back out and run the lines toward morning. I understand why you wouldn't want to go, since you don't fish."

"Who said I didn't fish?" Mort said. "I've wrestled a Muskie or two in my time. What kind of fish do you catch?"

Mort was completely hooked when Henry told him he could name the stakes. Of course, Mort whined that he didn't want to risk too much, but he didn't want be a poor sport either, so he would make it open stakes with no limit.

After lunch, Matt Oliver caught up with Jack as he walked back toward the floor office. "That guy really pissed me off back there."

"I know," Jack said. "He's too proud to listen to anyone."

"Well, between him and Sonny T, they're gonna ruin this factory if we don't do something."

Jack stopped at the door to the floor office and turned to face Matt Oliver. "I believe it's too late. Nickels already did that."

With matters at the factory worsening and largely beyond his control, Jack turned his attention to Cici. Her health was worsening, and she had become a recluse, refusing to see him, and seldom returning his calls. As he drove into Clarksdale that afternoon, he was determined to see her. Parking on the street, he noticed a car full of medical supplies, and a woman sitting inside making notes on a clipboard. The car pulled away as Aunt Netta answered the door. Greeting her, Jack pointed to the car as it rounded the corner a block away.

"Who was that?"

"That's the hospice nurse. She's been coming twice a week now for the last month. Come on in. Let me see if Cici will let you come back."

Aunt Netta, who was in her eighties, walked slowly down the hallway, and Jack looked around. The house was dark and a medicinal odor hung in the stagnant air. In an adjoining room, Cici's twins sat on a couch watching TV. The two-year-olds were watching an afternoon soap opera. Ten minutes passed before Aunt Netta returned.

"Cici says she'll come out for just a minute. Me and the nurse just gave her a bath, and I'm going back to help her dress."

A few minutes later, Aunt Netta pushed Cici into the room in a wheelchair. She was emaciated and her skin yellowed. The look on Jack's face must have betrayed him.

"Oh, don't look so damned tore up," Cici said. "It's just a wheelchair."

"Yeah, but—"

"I can walk. It's just easier, 'cause I don't have much strength right now."

"Have you been back to the doctor?"

"I don't need you asking me forty-million questions. The last time I went, the doctor said he was getting me that nurse, and it really wasn't much use coming back every week."

"There are some good internal specialists up in Memphis. Why don't you—"

"Jack!"

He paused.

"I know you are here for me if I need you. I know if I pick up the phone and call you will come. That's all I need. From now on I don't want company until I get better. When that happens, you and me and the babies can all go up to Moon Lake again, okay?"

He gave her a reluctant nod. Cici, as always, dominated the conversation with a stubborn finality. If only there was something he could say—but he was lost. An uncomfortable silence gripped the room, and after a few moments Cici announced she was returning to bed. She bid him good-bye.

CHAPTER 21

POKER AT MOON LAKE

S UMMER IN THE DELTA HAD arrived—not officially by the
calendar, because that was well over a month away, but
according to the bank sign in Clarksdale it was a ninety-
one-degree, sweat-dripping-off-the-end-of-your-nose kind
of hot Friday afternoon. Jack had Momo and Matt Oliver
with him and they stopped at Walmart for bait, beer, and
ice. They were on their way to Henry's cabin at Moon Lake
for a little poker playing and catfishing.

Clyde had opted out, saying he had other plans—something that disappointed Jack, but he understood. Clyde
probably realized the promise of more drama with a weekend that included JT and Dewayne—and now Mort. Henry
was picking up Mort at his place, while JT went by to get
Dewayne. They all planned to meet at the 61 Truck Plaza
for supper. Leaving Clarksdale, Jack headed up Highway 61.
With sunset approaching, he had just turned on the headlights when a pickup truck blasted by pulling a small boat.
It was JT's flame red Dodge with its V-8 Hemi and dual

glass-packed exhausts. Jack glanced at his speedometer. He was doing sixty-five. JT had to be running close to ninety.

"He's in one hell of a hurry," Jack said.

As the red pickup grew more distant up the highway, JT held his beer can out the window, over the top of his truck. Jack sighed. It was a salute for God, the Highway Patrol, and everyone else on the road to see.

"Dumb-ass," Matt Oliver muttered. "He's probably already drunk."

"I hope the damned fool doesn't kill someone," Jack said.

"At least they're pulling JT's jon boat instead of the Bayliner," Matt Oliver replied. "Maybe we'll get lucky and they'll just kill themselves."

Several minutes later Jack pulled into the truck stop. JT's truck was parked in a row of eighteen wheelers, and he and Dewayne were already sitting at a table in front of a large plate-glass window. A few moments later Henry and Mort arrived, and everyone went inside.

As they walked through the crowded restaurant, Jack noticed how sorely out of place Mort seemed in his bright green slacks and yellow golf shirt. Most everyone else wore blue jeans and baseball caps, but Mort seemed oblivious. He strode toward the table with the confidence of a man crossing the green after making a forty-foot putt.

"What took y'all so long?" JT said.

"Hey, dumb-ass," Matt Oliver replied, "we actually drive the speed limit when someone's had a beer or two."

"Fuck you," JT said. "You wasn't driving. Jack was, and he wasn't drinking."

Matt Oliver rolled his eyes at JT's logic, but let it drop as they pulled their chairs up to the table. A waitress wearing a too-tight, stained white uniform, stood with pad in hand ready to take their orders.

"You bring the Maalox?" Henry asked.

"Outside in the cooler," Jack said.

Matt Oliver laughed. "Manager's elixir, I assume?"

Ignoring him, Henry placed his order. "Give me a hamburger and fries, and a cup of coffee, black."

"The same for me," Jack said, "except make my drink sweet tea."

Dewayne and JT ordered the all-you-can-eat steak dinner special, and began arguing about who could eat the most, while Momo struggled to order a burger and fries. When he finally got it out, the waitress turned to Mort. He was still studying the menu. She stood at least fifteen seconds before clearing her throat. Mort seemed oblivious.

"You gonna order, partner?" she asked.

Mort raised his head and stared straight ahead as he made a show of regally folding his menu and setting aside. With just enough hesitation to put her in her place, he looked toward the waitress. "I believe I'll have the twelve-ounce sirloin, medium rare, and a baked potato with sour cream and chives, a Caesar salad, and...." He glanced at Jack. "I'll have tea like him, except simply add a wedge of lemon to mine."

Since Mort spoke with impeccable grammar, he was immediately suspect. The middle-aged waitress cut her eyes around the table. Jack turned and looked out the front window. She was sizing up the group and trying to determine if this was some kind of practical joke. After a moment or two she turned back to Mort.

"This ain't Western Sizzler, partner. The potatoes are gonna be fried or mashed. What's it gonna be?"

Mort seemed taken aback and started to pick up the menu again but apparently thought better of it. "Oh, just bring me the creamed potatoes," he said.

"What kind of dressing on your salad?" she asked.

Mort rolled his eyes and looked around the table.

"I say something wrong?" the waitress asked.

She reached down and straightened her nametag—Billie Sue. Perhaps she wanted him to know exactly who he was messing with.

"Anyone who knows anything about salads," he said, "knows Caesar salad is normally served with its own Caesar dressing."

"Well, spank my butt, your highness," she said. "All we got is regular old salad, but I'll see what I can come up with."

She stroked the order pad with a vengeance, shoved the pencil into her hair and strode away.

"Man, you got some kind of balls," JT said.

"Oh?" Mort replied. "How's that?"

"You just don't mess with waitresses that way."

"Especially a truck stop waitress," Matt Oliver added.

Mort pursed his lips and shook his head with disdain. "You fellows can accept shoddy service if you wish, but I'll not allow it."

Billie Sue returned, and the discussion quickly faded into nervous silence as she expertly placed each person's drink on the table. She was about to leave when Mort set his glass down hard.

"This tea has sugar in it," he said.

His voice had the tone of a cement mixer, and instead of looking at her, he faced straight ahead. She stopped and stared at him for several seconds before replying. "I beg your pardon, but you ordered iced tea, just like his." She pointed at Jack. "He ordered sweet tea."

There was an edge in her voice that made chalk sliding on a chalkboard sound pleasant, and Mort somehow found enough sense to keep his mouth shut. She walked away, and a few minutes later brought the food along with a new glass of unsweetened tea for Mort. While everyone else began doctoring the food with heavy doses of salt, pepper, and Tabasco, Mort busied himself arranging his utensils. He tucked his napkin into his shirt and rearranged the food on his plate. When he was done, he picked up the fork and steak knife and began carefully sawing on his steak. It was about what you'd expect from a truck stop steak, a half-inch thick chunk of range-reared beef.

JT and Dewayne knew better as they broke out razor-sharp pocketknives and prepared to devour their all-you-can-eat steak specials—and special they were—platters piled high with mystery cuts of beef. Flank steak appeared to be the predominant cut, but there was some round steak on JT's plate. The meat's color ranged from a vein-riddled purple to a rainbow-slick gray, and it was well marbled—with gristle. On a lean day, a "B" rated restaurant might have used some of it in the stew pot, but the quality of their steak didn't seem to faze them.

Barely chewing, they wolfed it down while Mort continued sawing at his with the restaurant knife. He was making little headway. Eventually he came up with a moderate-size chunk, forced it into his mouth and began chewing. Dewayne and JT were making short work of their platters, but Mort was still chewing his first bite when he finally grunted, tossed his utensils down and spit the wad of chewed meat into his napkin.

"This steak isn't fit to eat," he said.

He threw his hand into the air, trying to get Billie Sue's attention, but she was having none of it. Ignoring him, she crossed the room with the coffeepot, refilling cups.

"Waitress," he called. "Oh, waitress!"

Mort held his index finger high overhead, and only after he all but stood in his chair did she finally walk over to the table.

With the empty coffeepot dangling from her finger, she put her other hand on her hip. "What's the problem now?"

"It's this steak," Mort said. "It's atrocious. It's so tough I can't even cut it."

"Atrocious, huh?"

"That's right," Mort answered. "I'm not paying for it."

"This *is* a truck stop, partner. Just exactly what did you expect, a bacon-wrapped fillet of corn-fed Angus?"

"I'll eat yours if you don't want it," Dewayne said.

He and JT had already worked their platters down to a few pieces of gristle and some bones.

She turned to Dewayne. "I don't care what y'all do," she said, "but Clovis ain't about to let him leave without paying for his meal."

Mort stood up. "I've had just about enough of your rudeness, young lady. Where is this Clovis?"

Billie Sue threw her thumb over her shoulder. "Over there at the cash register."

Clovis, who was only slightly smaller than a Volkswagen bus, was wearing a T-shirt that had probably been white at the beginning of the week. He punched the keys on the register with the same hand that held a fat cigar stub. He was running the fingers of his other hand through his greasy hair. Mort paused.

"Go tell him I would like to speak with him," he said to the waitress.

Billie Sue ignored him as she totaled his ticket, tore it from the pad and laid it in his plate. "Why don't you take your ticket up there and talk to him. I'm sure he'll be eager to hear your complaint."

"Maybe I'll do just that," Mort snapped.

After Dewayne and JT gnawed the last speck of gristle from the bones on their platters, they split Mort's steak between them, then sat back and belched with satisfaction.

"Are you boys ready to hit the road?" Henry asked.

"Man, yeah," JT said. "One more bite and I'll pop wide open."

When he got to the register, Mort dutifully paid big Clovis without a word of complaint.

It was dark by the time Jack's headlights lit up the front of Henry's cabin, and they launched the boats using lanterns and a Q-beam. Cranking the outboard, Jack followed Henry and JT in their boats up the lake to Henry's favorite catfish hole near the Yazoo Pass. After stretching and baiting a couple of trotlines, they motored back down to Alcorn Island and put out two more near some old pilings. When they were done baiting the hooks, they killed the lights, and let the boats drift quietly a few yards apart. Dewayne was with JT in his boat. Mort was with Henry in his, and Matt Oliver and Momo were with Jack. He had borrowed Clyde's boat.

A huge yellow moon rose behind the cypress trees, while off to the south, silver and orange lightning flickered silently in a distant thunderhead. There wasn't a hint of a breeze and the water was flat as a layer of slate. From somewhere back across the lake came the barely discernible sound of a radio playing on one of the piers and people laughing and talking. Henry lit a cigarette and propped up his feet as they drifted in silence, enjoying the beauty of the night.

Jack leaned back, closed his eyes, and listened to the distant music. The stress drained from his body, and he felt peace.

"Hey, y'all," JT called out, "is that not the purdiest goddam moon you ever saw?"

Jack's eyes flew open.

"I sure wish Janine and the boys was here to see it."

"Well, that pretty much wrecked the moment," Matt Oliver muttered.

He turned and called out to JT, "You've got such a poetic way with words, maybe you should tell them yourself, when you get home, just how *goddam purdy* it was."

Already half-tanked, JT popped the top on another beer as he sat up and looked across at Matt Oliver. "What the hell is that supposed to mean?"

Matt Oliver ignored him as Henry sat up and hit the switch on his forty-horse Merc. It was poker-playing time. Back at the cabin they tied up to the pier and made their way up the rickety wooden steps to the back porch.

Henry's cabin was weathered gray cypress with a large screened-in porch, lit by a single yellow bulb. The boards creaked beneath their feet as they crossed the porch and went inside where a wooden dinette table sat in the center of a combination dining room/kitchen. It was the perfect poker-playing, fishing lodge: rustic enough to keep the women away, but comfortable enough for drinking and card playing.

As they pulled out their money, Momo tore the plastic wrapper from a deck of cards, discarded the jokers and counted the rest out on the table. He wasn't a poker player, but at Jack's request, he had agreed to deal. Knowing Mort's reputation, Jack figured a neutral dealer might preclude any arguments. Matt Oliver began counting out the chips while Momo shuffled the deck. He shuffled frontward then backward, and the cards danced through his hands in a virtual choreography of card handling magic. It held everyone momentarily spellbound.

Momo explained how his brother, a black-jack dealer at the Silver Star, had taught him to shuffle cards when he was a kid, but Mort, despite doing his best to act like one of the boys, eyed Momo with snake-eyed intensity. Jack suddenly realized the mistake of using Momo as a neutral dealer. Not wanting to hurt Momo's feelings by telling him he couldn't deal, he decided to wait and see how things went. Hopefully, it would work out.

"How many chips you want?" Matt Oliver asked.

"Give me a hundred dollars' worth," Jack said.

"Same here," Henry said.

"Gimme fifty," JT said.

"I'm taking a hundred for myself," Matt Oliver said.

After dropping the money into the cigar box, Matt Oliver looked across the table at Mort. He was still fumbling around in his wallet. Although it was technically open stakes, Henry and the others always kept the games friendly by voluntarily limiting their bets. Even with a bad run of luck, someone could usually play the entire weekend with a hundred bucks.

"What'll you take?" Matt Oliver asked.

With a confident sideways tilt of his head, Mort thumbed a C-note from his wallet and tossed it on the table.

Expecting as much, Matt Oliver shoved a hundred-dollar stack of chips toward him and reached for the hundred, but Mort quickly slapped his hand down on the bill. The table shook and the beer bottles swayed as everyone grabbed for them.

"Not so fast," Mort said.

Matt Oliver pulled his hand back in surprise while Mort reached for his glass of bourbon—something Jack was certain he was drinking for show, because bourbon just didn't fit his personality. Mort was more of a rum and Coke kind of guy, but he'd brought bottle of Jack Daniels. Probably wanted to show he could be one of the boys, except everyone here drank Jim Beam or Evan Williams.

Mort set his glass down slowly, and reached back into his wallet, thumbing out another hundred-dollar bill, then another, continuing until he'd laid five one-hundred-dollar bills on the table.

"I don't think you'll need that much," Henry said.

"I thought we were playing open stakes?" Mort replied.

"Yeah, but—"

"Then I believe I can determine how many chips I need. You can't bet with what you don't have."

Henry's jaw rippled with tension, and his face reddened, but he said nothing as he cut his eyes toward Jack. Jack simply raised one brow.

The first hands began with everyone betting cautiously. After his truck stop supper, Dewayne didn't have but a dollar and a half left in his pocket, so he pulled his chair up beside JT and watched. Momo, who was nipping at a long-neck bottle of Wild Turkey, dealt the cards like a professional. It was the first time Jack had seen him drink, but Momo seemed in perfect control. He dealt a hand, which Mort won, then another that Henry eked out over Jack with a higher pair.

Things seemed to have settled down, when Mort suddenly spoke. "You fellows must think I'm some kind of sucker."

Everyone stared at him, but Jack already knew what was coming next.

"You have this shill dealing, and you think I'll simply sit here and give you my money, right?"

Jack had never heard any of them accuse another of cheating, but here it was. Mort was saying that Momo's dealing was a set-up. Momo's face hardened almost imperceptibly, much as it had that first day in the breakroom when Doritoe wanted to fight with him.

"Are y-you sa-saying, I-I-I'm chu-chu-cheating?"

"I'm not saying anything, except that in games like this the deal is usually rotated."

Momo had the deceptive calmness of a cougar about to spring.

"It's my fault," Jack said. "I thought Momo could be a neutral dealer, but we can do whatever Mort wants."

Momo stood and tossed the deck to the center of the table. Saying nothing, he moved to a barstool on the wall where he continued sipping from his bottle of Wild Turkey. The tension in the room remained shrouded in silence as JT began shuffling the cards, and it seemed Mort felt obliged to offer some sort of an apology.

"Sorry, but poker is a game of variables, and it takes a great deal of concentration and attention to detail," he said. "I didn't mean to upset you fellows, but I hadn't planned on him dealing. You understand, don't you?"

"Sounds good to me," JT said. "Besides, I like calling my own games."

He began dealing the cards. "Seven card stud, boys, Doctor Pepper on the wild cards, with a one-dollar ante."

Mort swore and threw the two cards he'd been dealt to the center of the table.

"What now?" Matt Oliver asked.

"I don't play that silly shit," he said. "Deal me out."

"Oh, for God's sake, Mort, lighten up," Matt Oliver said. "It's just a fucking game."

"Too damned many wild cards," Mort said. "I'm passing."

"Talk like that makes me think you're a professional poker player or something," Henry said.

Mort grew suddenly red-faced. "What makes you say that?"

"Just that talk about variables," Henry said.

"Yeah," JT added, "and all that crap about concentration or whatever." He looked over at Jack. "You still want me to deal or not?"

Jack smiled, but Henry answered instead. "Deal," he said as he stared at Mort.

Mort turned and looked at Momo who by now was about a third of the way down into his long-necked bottle of Wild Turkey. "What's with that rebel flag on your hat?"

The room went silent again. JT stopped dealing and looked at Jack. It was bad enough that Mort had pissed off everyone over the card game, but now he was starting on Momo again. Jack wanted to intervene, but this was Henry's cabin. He remained silent, watching as Momo slowly pulled the baseball cap from his head. He looked at it as if to verify there was in fact a Confederate flag there. Seemingly satisfied, Momo put the hat back on his head, adjusted it low over his eyes and stared across the table at Mort.

"My great-great grandfather was a scout for Nathan Bedford Forrest," he said.

It was downright eerie. Momo didn't bat an eye, and his words came without the first hint of a stutter. He stared at Mort with cold-eyed confidence.

"Who's that?" Mort asked.

"Damned," JT said, "Don't you know who Nathan Bedford Forrest was? He was only one of the greatest military generals in history."

"Well, I got news for you fellows. The Civil War is over, and our side won, so what does it matter? Besides, it puzzles me why an Indian would wear a rebel flag."

Jack glanced at Henry, hoping he would say something, but Henry simply smiled. Momo's jaw flexed, as he slowly pushed the cork back into the bottle of Wild Turkey and set it on the floor. "So, you believe I should wear the American flag, instead?"

Again he had spoken without the hint of a stutter.

"You're damned right, I do," Mort replied.

"You mean the same American flag that Custer and Sheridan and the other Yankee generals carried when they rode through our villages, killing our women and children? The same American flag that represents a government that broke every treaty they ever made with us?"

"That's all past history," Mort said. "The way I see it, this is America now, and you can love it or leave it."

Matt Oliver bent toward Mort, "*They* were here first, Mort."

Mort looked around. "Who was?"

"The Indians."

Mort gave him a sour look and waved him off with the back of his hand. He looked back at Momo. "I'm sure we took care of your boy, Nathan-what's-his-name, and you need—"

Mort was cut off mid-sentence when, with a flash of his hand, Momo sent a long stiletto flying past his ear. It stuck in the wall with a loud "thunk." Mort's face turned white, but Henry sipped his drink casually as if nothing had happened. Dewayne dove under the table. Jack sprang to his feet, but he froze, his heart pounding in his chest.

"Finish dealing the cards," Henry said to JT. He turned to Jack. "Sit down, boss."

Mort turned and stared at the knife sticking in the wall behind his head, then looked back at Momo.

"I don't reckon I'd bad-mouth General Forrest anymore if I was you," Henry said.

Momo gazed steadily at Mort.

"Yup," JT said. "I reckon you done let that alligator mouth overload your bunny rabbit ass."

"Sorry," Mort said. "I didn't mean to make him angry."

"Angry?" Matt Oliver said. "Hell, you ain't made him angry, yet. Otherwise that knife'd had a piece of your scalp on it when it hit the wall."

"You best keep your opinions about our kinfolk to yourself," Henry said, "especially Momo's."

Jack slowly sat down, while Momo walked around the table and snatched the knife from the wall. Mort watched nervously as Momo slid the knife back under his belt. Pausing, Momo stared at the still quaking Mort. "I apologize, sir, for losing my temper. Liquor sometimes does that to me." He started back around the table, but paused again and looked back at Mort. "Mister Henry gave you advice that may serve you well, Mr. Kingman. You should learn the wisdom of silence when it comes to your opinions on people's ancestors."

With that, he returned to his stool on the wall. It was only after several more hands that everyone began to relax again. Mort managed to win a couple of pots, and his confidence was growing when the deal came around to Jack. He called five card stud with the last card down—a game that when the cards fell right could test a player's mettle. By the time he'd dealt everyone four cards the pot had grown to over sixty dollars—the biggest of the night, thanks to Mort—who was doubling everyone's bet. Jack dealt the fifth card down.

Matt Oliver and Henry folded. JT was showing two jacks, a ten, and a nine. Mort had the other three tens and a jack showing. Jack had a four card straight, eight high. If he drew the fifth card to his straight, he had them both beat, unless Mort got the remaining jack. Jack peeled up the corner of his hole card and glanced at it. It was the last jack—no go on his straight, JT's three of a kind or Mort's full house. Mort though, still held the winning hand with the three tens showing.

"Three tens bets," Jack said.

"Three tens bets fifty," Mort said.

"Shiiut," JT said. "That's too rich for me." He tossed his cards to the center of the table.

Dewayne, who by now had crawled back into his chair, reached for JT's discards, but Henry grabbed his arm.

"Leave them there," he said.

Mort's fifty-dollar bet was higher than any bet Jack had ever seen anyone in their little group make. Their card games had always been friendly affairs, meant to kill time and have a little fun. Mort's hardball tactic rankled him, and before he thought better of it, he decided to see if Mort had the one asset a real poker player needed— brass balls.

"I'll see your fifty," Jack said, "and raise you a hundred."

"Whoooeee," JT said. "Somebody's done made their straight."

Mort thumbed his cards, then looked down at his chips. After a second or two he looked over at Jack, who did his best to exude unbounded confidence.

"I suppose I'll let you buy this one," Mort said, tossing his cards on the table.

Jack tossed his cards toward the pile and pulled the pot, but as he did, Dewayne's hand shot out and flipped his cards.

"Look at that shit!" JT said. He looked at Jack then back at the cards. "He bluffed us."

Matt Oliver turned to Dewayne. "You dumb-ass! You're never supposed to turn another man's cards."

Jack wanted to be angry, but realizing it would be wasted on Dewayne, he let it go. Across the table, Mort was growing red-faced and looking a little homicidal as he stared first at the cards then at Jack. He'd just been bluffed out of the biggest pot of the night. After stewing in silence for a few moments he simply nodded. He didn't speak, but his message was clear. Before the night was over, he was going to make Jack pay.

Matt Oliver told Dewayne to move his chair over against the wall beside Momo as play continued. Momo moved only occasionally to sip from his bottle or to pour some of his Wild Turkey into Dewayne's Coke. After a while Dewayne began telling him how it was impossible to cast with his rod and reel since the end of his thumb had been cut off. He had been forced to give up his professional bass fishing career.

"But it's going to be okay," Dewayne said. "Mr. Baker said he could get me enough money so I won't never have to work again."

Dewayne babbled on about his lawyer, Honey Lips Baker, and anything else that came to mind, until Matt Oliver finally turned to him. "Why don't you give it a rest?"

Dewayne squinted back at him. "Give what a rest?"

"He means, shut the hell up," JT said.

Dewayne shrugged and crawled off his stool, curling up on the floor next to the wall, where he fell asleep. By three a.m. the ashtrays were overflowing with cigarette butts, and everyone was pretty much shit-faced. They were silently studying their cards when Momo toppled over, hitting the floor with a thud. Passed out cold, he lay atop Dewayne, who hadn't budged. Jack reached down and righted the almost empty bottle of Wild Turkey.

The most anyone had ever lost in a night was around ninety bucks, but Mort's brand of cutthroat poker had backfired on him. He sat in stone-faced silence, three hundred and fifty dollars in the hole. Henry and Jack had most of it. JT was broke and sitting out, and Matt Oliver couldn't stop yawning. Everyone agreed to one more hand before going out to run the trotlines.

Mort began dealing seven card stud and betting like crazy on every card. With six cards dealt, two down and four up, he had two pairs showing, aces and eights. Henry had a possible flush and Matt Oliver had two nines with an ace high. Jack felt like a snake sitting under a log with two kings in the hole and one showing. Problem was the rest of his cards were garbage. If Mort had a full house—and Jack was pretty certain he did—he had everyone beat.

"Two pair bets fifty dollars," Mort said.

"Too rich for my blood," Matt Oliver said.

He folded, but Henry matched the bet. Jack had to stay in the game if he wanted to see his last card. If he got the fourth king, nothing Mort could make would beat him. He met the fifty-dollar bet, and Mort dealt the last card down to each of them.

Jack raised the corner of his card and carefully peeked at it. It was the fourth king. He looked up to find Mort staring hard at him. Jack batted his eyes, scratched his head and faked a nervous twitch at the corner of his mouth. A big grin crossed Mort's face as he tossed another fifty dollars' worth of chips to the center of the table. Henry folded.

"Your bet," Mort said.

Jack hesitated, then placed his bet. "I'll see your fifty and raise you fifty more," he said.

Mort stopped, eyed him for a moment then grinned even more. He was out of chips but went to his wallet and thumbed out the fifty and then a hundred more, pushing it to the center of the table. "I'll see your fifty and raise you a hundred," he said.

Jack counted out his money, shoved it to the center of the table and called him.

"This is going to cost you, Mister Mississippi Gambler," Mort said. "I wasn't about to let you buy this one."

He spread his cards on the table. "Read 'em and weep. Full house, aces and eights."

Still wearing the same leering smile, he reached to pull the pot. "You gave yourself away," he said. "I knew you didn't have anything because you did the same thing the last time you bluffed: you didn't bet until the very end."

"I didn't need to," Jack said. "You were doing all the betting for me."

Mort stopped with his arms still cradling the pile of money at the center of the table. His brows came together with the quizzical look Damocles might have had if the hair holding the king's sword had snapped. Jack flipped the three kings in the hole and laid them atop the one that was showing.

"Four kings," he said.

"Devastated" somehow seemed inadequate to describe Mort at that moment. And despite a brief moment of remorse, Jack stood and pulled the pot while Mort walked around and picked up Momo's bottle from the floor. There was little more than a spider left, but he tipped it up, running his tongue into the neck of the bottle. Henry handed him his bottle. Mort grabbed it and chug-a-lugged the remaining half-pint. A few minutes later the bourbon hammered him as he passed out on the couch. They left him there, along with Momo and Dewayne still passed out on the floor, when they went to run the lines.

It was daylight when the party returned with two ice-chests full of Moon Lake catfish, but they were too exhausted to dress them.

"Let's go up to the cabin," Henry said. "We'll get a nap and clean the fish later."

Trudging slowly up the wooden steps, they entered the screened porch, but when Jack opened the cabin door, Mort was standing there over Momo, holding a butcher knife. Momo stared up at him as he sat on the floor beside a still snoring Dewayne. As Henry and the others stepped into the room, Mort wheeled about with the knife, slashing the air in their direction.

"Whoa," Henry said.

Mort swayed back and forth, brandishing the knife and looking like he might collapse at any moment. After a moment or two, he turned his attention back to Momo.

"Sshhtinking In-Indian stole my money. Nu-now I'm going to give him a do-dose of his own medicine."

Matt Oliver pushed up between Henry and Jack. "Let me—"

"No," Jack said. He pulled Matt Oliver back. "I've dealt with drunks like this before."

"He's all yours," Henry said. "Arlis gave me enough excitement for a lifetime. Just don't let him hurt you."

Jack held up his hand to silence the others as he stepped forward. Mort turned again, pointing the knife at him. Momo dropped his hand to his waist, but Jack glanced at him and shook his head. Momo paused.

"Oh, ish you," Mort said. "Misher Bluffer." His eyes were crossed, and he swayed like he was standing on the deck of a storm-tossed ship.

"You just stay back till I get—get my money from this thief."

He turned and pointed the knife at Momo, while holding his other hand out at Jack. Jack took another step toward him.

"I to-told you to sshhtay ba-back."

"Easy, Mort," Jack said. "Listen to what I have to say. Okay?"

Jack shuffled even closer.

"What?" he said.

He was nearly within reach. Watching Mort's eyes jerking back and forth between Momo and himself, Jack waited for the right moment.

"If he took your money and hid it, you'll never find it if you kill him."

He bent closer to Momo. "Wha-where'd you hi-hide my money, Indian?"

Jack had to hurry. When Momo decided to move, Mort's throat would be slashed before he knew what hit him. He took one last step and focused every ounce of energy he could muster into his right shoulder as he came with a hard overhand right. It landed flush on Mort's jaw, and the blow sent him sprawling on the floor. His eyes fluttered and rolled back in his head.

"Su-su-some people ju-just can't ho-hold their liquor," Momo said as he slipped his knife back under his belt. He must have gone for the knife the same moment Jack hit Mort. Thank God Mort had gone down with one punch.

Henry started a fresh pot of coffee while Matt Oliver held a bag of ice on the jaw of a still comatose Mort. Ended up, Henry took him back to Clarksdale to get x-rayed. When he returned to the cabin late that afternoon, Henry said the x-rays came back negative, and he'd taken Mort home. Henry had also made a deal with Mort: No one, particularly Mort's wife, would hear about his poker losses as long as nothing else was said about what happened at the cabin. Mort told Henry that he didn't remember much of anything. Despite his sore hand, Jack was glad it didn't turn out any worse.

CHAPTER 22

FREIGHT TRAIN BLUES

B Y LATE SATURDAY NIGHT, JACK was back home and exhausted from his night of fishing and playing poker. After turning down the telephone, he fell across the bed and succumbed to an instant and deep sleep. Only when the Sunday morning sun flooded into his bedroom did he realize he was still in the world. Groggy but rested, he stumbled into the kitchen and began fumbling with the coffee maker, but a blinking light on the telephone worried his eye until he could no longer stand it. Punching the play button, he listened. Several messages had been left during the night.

The first two calls were hang-ups with no messages, but the third was from Clyde. Clyde almost never called except when he wanted to go fishing, so it was somewhat of a surprise to hear his voice—one that seemed strained. Jack stopped and listened. Clyde's message said simply to call him as soon as possible. After pouring the water into the coffee maker he picked up the phone and dialed the number. As he did, he walked out on the front porch. Clyde picked up on the second ring.

"Clyde, this is Jack. I got your message. What's up?"

"I've been trying to call all night. Everybody's been trying."

"What for?"

"My sister Netta called. It's Cici, Jack. I think you better get on over there."

When Jack arrived that Sunday morning, there was a familiar car parked in front of the house. It belonged to the hospice nurse. He hurried up the drive, and Aunt Netta met him at the door.

"She's been going in and out of a coma since yesterday afternoon. She's been asking for you."

He followed her back to the bedroom. The tired-eyed nurse was sitting in a chair beside the bed. Cici was deathly still. A fine sweat covered her face.

"You must be Jack," the nurse said.

He nodded.

"She's been asking for you all night."

"Is she..." He couldn't say the words.

"I don't think it will be long," the nurse said.

The room was dark and stuffy, the only light coming from the vanilla glow of a bedside lamp. Jack walked to the window and pulled back the shades. The morning sun was shining brightly through the trees. He tried to open the window but it was stuck—painted shut.

"Is he here yet?"

He turned at the sound of her voice. Her eyes were still closed.

"I'm here, Cici."

He walked over and sat beside her on the bed.

"I told you I would call when I needed you," she said, her voice barely above a whisper.

"Well, I'm here."

Jack put his hand on her forehead, then caressed her hair. Cici opened her eyes, barely cracking them.

"Who opened the shade?"

"I did," Jack said. "Do you want me to close it?"

"No."

She ran her tongue over her lips, while taking quick shallow breaths.

"I couldn't get the window open."

"Is it a pretty day?" she asked.

"Yes."

"Take me out to the front porch swing, Jack, will you?"

He looked at the nurse. She shrugged and stood up motioning him toward the door.

"Just a minute, baby. I have to talk with the nurse."

They stood in the hall just outside the bedroom. "It doesn't matter. If you want to carry her out there go ahead, but she might—"

"I know," Jack said. "Please stay with Aunt Netta."

Jack went back into the bedroom and wrapped Cici in a blanket before picking her up in his arms. She seemed almost weightless as he held her and made his way through the front room and out onto the front porch. Sitting on the swing, he held her close. He held her there for several minutes. Her eyes were closed, and she was barely breathing.

"I hear a red bird singing," she said.

Jack had scarcely noticed, but she was right. A fat red cardinal was up in one of the big oaks, singing his heart out.

"It is a beautiful day," she said. "What day is it?"

"It's Sunday."

She gave a hint of a smile.

"That's a good day."

Cici opened her eyes again, pale shadows of the sparkling jewels they once were. Jack felt a tear running down his cheek, but quickly wiped it away.

"It feels good—you holding me this way."

He finally found his voice. "Yes, me too."

"Don't worry...." She didn't finish as she drew a quivering breath and closed her eyes. Only after a while did she speak again. "I did you wrong. I'm sorry for what I put you through."

"Just rest," Jack said.

She closed her eyes and slept, or perhaps it was the coma, Jack didn't know, but he was lost in thought for several minutes when she suddenly spoke again. "I'm gonna have plenty of time to rest, but I need to ask you something."

"Did you call Acey?"

"I promise. I will."

"Jack, please don't let them bury me in one of them fancy metal caskets. I want a simple wood box. You hear?"

He looked down at her. She was smiling and her green eyes had a spark of life—dim and wavering but real.

"You got it," he said.

She continued smiling. "And one more thing."

"Name it."

"Promise me. I want you to put me on the train and ride back home with me. I want to be buried beside my mama down in Louisiana."

"I promise," Jack said.

It may have been another hour—or two hours. Jack wasn't sure. They sat on the porch swing, and he held Cici close. He held her, and he didn't want to let her go, but later, as the morning sun rose above the trees, he realized he had to. She was terribly still, and the lyrics to that old Elizabeth Cotton song kept going through his mind.

> Freight train, freight train, run so fast
> Freight train, freight train, run so fast
> Please don't tell what train I'm on
> They won't know what route I'm going
>
> Freight train, freight train, comin' round the bend
> Freight train, freight train, gone again
> One of these days turn that train around
> Go back to my hometown.

His tears flowed freely, and after a while the nurse and Aunt Netta came out on the porch.

"Let's carry her back to the bed," the nurse said. "I'll call the coroner."

Jack held her head against his chest, and carried her to the bedroom. Laying her on the bed, he smoothed her hair, pulled her eyes closed and kissed her forehead. Echoing somewhere in the back of his mind was her voice humming that same old blues riff. He turned and walked out.

Jack walked off the porch and up the drive, and for a while he heard nothing. The whole world had gone silent. The road in front of the house seemed to stretch endlessly, beyond eternity out past the Sunflower River, into the Delta and across to a place where weary souls found reprieve. He lost track of time until he heard Clyde's voice somewhere in the distance. "Mister Jack? You okay?"

Through a blur of tears, he turned to see Clyde standing there beside him.

"Jack?"

Jack tried to say something, but his throat was knotted.

"Come on, boy, let me carry you back home," Clyde said.

After a couple days Jack sobered up and drove to Greenwood where he was meeting Perry, Clyde, and Aunt

Netta to catch the train to New Orleans. Across a distant field, sunlight glinted from the windows of a green John Deere tractor, and the smell of fresh-turned earth drifted inside his truck as Jack drove down Highway 49 past Swan Lake, Sunnyside, and on into Greenwood. Summer was coming, and the roadside ditches and distant tree lines sprouted new greenery, saw grass, honeysuckle, and kudzu. It should have been a feeling of regeneration, but it wasn't.

Clyde, Aunt Netta, and Perry were standing beside a white hearse backed up beside the old depot when he arrived in Greenwood. Amtrak had agreed to the special arrangements, and a small crowd gathered awaiting the train most referred to as "The City." The City of New Orleans was due to arrive within the hour. Perry and Clyde walked out to meet him as he got out of the truck.

"Where's Aunt Netta?" Jack asked.

Perry motioned with his head. "She's around yonder with some friends."

"Oh, good," Jack said. "I was worried we wouldn't have enough pallbearers."

Perry gave him a sad smile. "You ain't gotta worry about pallbearers, Mister Jack. Snookey Harris called and told me B.B. King and Ruby Wilson are already on the train— took it outta Memphis. And there's a lot more folks comin', too. Snookey said Al Green might come down, and Maurice White, too. Gonna be a whole fleet of limousines meetin' us in New Orleans."

"Really?"

"Gonna be more Blues royalty than you can shake a stick at," Perry said.

Clyde took Jack's arm. "Jack, I hope you don't mind, but I had Perry call your uncle in Orange Beach. He's meetin' us at the station in New Orleans. I figured you could use some family right about now."

Jack put his arm across Clyde's shoulders. "I appreciate you thinking about me. It'll be good to see him."

The train arrived in New Orleans by mid-afternoon, and Jack hurried ahead of the others into the station. Tuck's visit was a lifeline for him, something he needed badly, and when he walked into Union Station he spotted the wiry, blue-eyed veteran gazing pensively his way. They embraced, slapping one another's backs. A few moments later Clyde and Aunt Netta arrived, but after brief introductions, Tuck begged their pardons and pulled Jack to one side.

"I brought someone with me," he said.

Jack glanced around. "Carol?"

"Acey."

Jack looked over Tuck's shoulder. "But—"

"Don't worry. I've told her everything, and she's okay with it."

Jack felt his face burning. "You mean you told her about—"

"Doris Ann, all of it, and I did a much better job explaining it than you ever could. She actually thought it was kind of bizarre and felt sorry for you. And Perry told her how nothing ever happened between you and Cici."

"Where is she?"

"Right behind you."

Jack whirled around, but froze as he faced a teary-eyed Acey.

"I'm sorry, Jack. I should never have mistrusted you."

Jack felt his insides trembling as he extended his hand. Acey took it and pulled herself into his arms. "Please forgive me. I promise. I'll never—"

He put his finger across her lips. "It's okay."

"I told Tuck we should tell you I was coming, but—"

"It's okay," Jack said. "I'll kill him later."

Tuck slapped him on the back. "Before you kill me, why don't you grab one of her bags and carry it outside?"

Jack didn't respond because he was sharing one of the most passionate kisses of his life with Acey.

Driving out Highway 90 from New Orleans, the motorcade arrived at a little church south of Houma late that afternoon. The narrow blacktop road was lined with vehicles for a quarter-mile on either side of the church, and a field beside the church cemetery was crowded with at least fifty more cars. Jack helped Aunt Netta and Acey from the limo and they walked with Tuck, Clyde, and Perry toward the church where the hearse was already parked.

Breaking into an almost instant sweat, Jack removed his suit coat as they made their way through the crowd. There was no way the little church could accommodate all the mourners, and with the summer sun still above the trees, women held umbrellas for shade and fanned themselves with church bulletins. The men simply held their coats over one arm and sweated.

From inside the church came the sounds of an organ and a choir singing. Outside, rows of new sugar cane came in from the horizon, running up to the very edge of the churchyard and the wrought iron fence of the little cemetery. The distant tree line was hazy from the shimmering heat rising from the field. Jack stood sober, but comforted by Acey's as they watched the coffin being removed from the hearse.

He spotted familiar faces everywhere in the crowd. B. B. King stood nearby beside Ruby Wilson, and Acey whispered in Jack's ear pointing out B J Parker, an aging rock star from the seventies, and a former pro football player named Curtis Teague. Perry and the other band members were the pallbearers. They carried the wooden coffin to a tent in the cemetery beside the church. Jack and Acey followed behind Clyde and Aunt Netta.

Prayers were said, and at the end of the funeral service a big man with a throaty baritone voice began singing "Swing Low, Sweet Chariot." Accompanied by a small brass band, his booming voice quickly evaporated into the vast openness of the Louisiana bayou country, and when they were done, the sound of the brass horns echoed across the distant fields as they too faded into silence.

The funeral ended, and Jack led Acey by the hand as they walked back up the road, but someone tapped him on the shoulder. It was Perry. Perry had pulled several roses from the spray on the coffin, giving them to Aunt Netta and Clyde. "I got this one for you," he said. He held up the rose. "I knowed Cici would've wanted you to have it."

Jack took the flower, but he didn't know what to say. From somewhere far down in the Mandalay came the spooky call of a barred owl. Perry turned toward the sound, and looked out beyond the horizon. He seemed to be watching something, and after several seconds turned to Jack. "That girl just never could stop looking back," he said. "A bunch of us tried, Jack—a bunch of us, but you gotta know, it wasn't nothin' you did. Cici was on this train long before you come along.

"It all come from when her daddy got killed in Vietnam. They said it broke her mama's heart, 'cause Cici was her baby and her favorite, but she wanted to protect her, so she sent her up to stay with Aunt Netta. Mama Cici didn't really have no choice. She didn't have enough money. Did you see Curtis Teague and B J Parker over yonder at the church?"

Jack nodded, "Yeah, I did."

"Well, they was friends of Mama Cici's. She knowed lots of famous people. That's how come they came here to show their respect. You see, B J's husband, his name was Sergeant Coker, and him and Curtis Teague was in Vietnam together. They was paratroopers like Mama Cici's husband, and they looked after her when he got kill't over yonder. Them old people, like B J Parker's husband and Curtis Teague, they experienced that war first hand, but people like Cici, you and me, we kind of getting it later, you know?"

By sunset only a few scattered vehicles remained around the church. Jack sat alone with Acey on a bench beneath an ancient live oak.

"Will you come home, now?" she asked. "Please."

Her brown eyes were as hypnotic to his soul as they had ever been, and Jack had to fight the impulse to hug her and agree.

"I want to. You don't know how much I do, but I need to stay a while longer. I have to help the people at the factory."

Acey looked back at him with those wide brown eyes. "From the stories Tuck has been telling me, most of them are beyond being helped."

Jack looked down at the ground and shook his head. "I can't argue with that, but I can still make a big difference for some."

After a long pause, she put her head on his shoulder, and wrapped her arm around his waist. "I'll be waiting for you," she said.

Late the next day, Jack returned to Greenwood to get his pickup and drove back to Tallahatchie. He was lost in thought until something jumped out at him—the sign at the town limit. "Welcome to Tallahatchie, Mississippi, Home of Cici Cannon." Hitting the brakes he swerved to the side of the road and stopped.

Like the sign on the north end of town, this one was faded and peeling. Baby-blue letters scrolled over a white background with musical notes dancing across the top. Cici had said she hated the sign—perhaps because in her heart Tallahatchie could never be her home. Down a steep slope several feet off the road, the sign stood in weeds that had worn away the paint on the bottom edge, leaving nothing but weathered gray wood. Getting out of his truck, Jack walked down the slope.

He stood in front of the sign and touched its surface, carefully running his fingertips over her name, but his heart began pounding. His mind became a jumble of emotion bouncing around inside of him like a hand grenade tossed into an empty room—until it exploded. He slammed his fist into the sign, and the rotted boards burst apart.

Cars whizzed by above on Highway 49, but he scarcely noticed as he hit the sign again and again, breaking boards, ripping at them and flinging them into the roadside ditch below. He flailed at the sign until his fists bled and his arms bristled with splinters. When he could no longer use his fists, he threw his body against the posts, knocking them askew and finally breaking them off at the ground.

After several minutes he paused to catch his breath, as he threw the broken wood into the scum-laden water of the ditch below. With tears and sweat running into his eyes, he didn't see the first deputy's squad car until it skidded to a stop in a shower of dust and gravel, its lights flashing and radio blaring. A deputy jumped from the vehicle. It was Steve Gentry.

"What the hell are you doing?" he shouted.

"Urban renewal," Jack yelled.

Another squad car skidded to a stop as Gentry charged down the slope. Jack was standing stationary while Gentry came down the slope with a full head of steam. Realizing Gentry was about to plow into him with a flying tackle, Jack stepped aside, and the deputy's momentum carried him headfirst into the ditch below. Thrashing about in a froth of muddy water and floating beer cans, Gentry fought to regain his balance. Jack heard another voice and looked up to see Henry's son, Clayton, walking down the slope.

"Mr. Jack, what the hell is going on?" he said. "We got a call, saying someone was tearing this sign down."

Gentry scratched his way through the cattails and back up the slope. Pulling a can of pepper spray from his belt, he again charged at Jack, but Clayton stiff-armed him back down the slope.

"Put that shit away. Go get in your car, and get the hell out of here," he said.

"You can't let him get away with this," Gentry panted.

"Get away with what?" Clayton asked.

"Goddamn it, didn't you see what he did?"

"Stevie, you did that to your own dumb-ass self. I saw you. Now, get your ass out of here before I report you to Chief Brown."

As Gentry drove away, Henry's boy looked back at Jack and shook his head. "I reckon we better get our story straight before that prick starts running his mouth."

Jack shrugged. "There's not much to say. I did it, so I suppose I'll have to pay the price."

"I thought you said you were removing the old sign and replacing it with a new one. Isn't that right?"

Jack glanced up at him, but the young deputy turned and squinted toward the late afternoon sun. A lone tractor still droned in a field beyond the far tree line, and the mourning doves cooed from their evening roosts.

"I'll get with the sign people and have a new one made. When it's done, I'll send you the bill. Is that okay?"

Jack nodded. "I appreciate your help."

"My daddy thinks a hell of a lot of you, Mister Jack, and he doesn't warm easy to many people. Come on up here to the car. I've got a first aid kit with some tweezers to get those splinters out, and we can put some alcohol on the cuts so they don't get infected."

Henry's boy didn't say much, and he spared Jack the embarrassment of having to explain why he'd destroyed the sign. After escorting him back to the house, he assured Jack that everything would be taken care of. Later that evening, Henry showed up with Clyde, Matt Oliver and a bottle of Evan Williams. They played poker and watched TV until after midnight.

Jack would have gladly given it all up and gone home to Fairhope, but to walk out on the people who had put so much trust in him wasn't something he could do. He returned to the factory, if for no other reason than to stand with his employees and take what might come next. Although it was still unofficial, most everyone had accepted it as inevitable—the factory was closing. Nothing Jack or anyone else could do now would save it. Having all but given up the fight, he joined Henry, Clyde, and Matt Oliver maintaining a low profile and watching as Sonny T created so much strife the factory became a debilitated mule collapsing under the whip. Dewayne's lawsuit would only accelerate the process.

CHAPTER 23

HONEY LIPS BAKER AND THE BIG TRIAL

J ACK'S FOOTSTEPS ECHOED ON THE marble floors and the giant oak doors creaked with age as he slipped into the courtroom that morning. Honey Lips, fearing jealousy from the locals, requested and received a change of venue. The trial was being held at the DeSoto County courthouse in Hernando. An ancient building, its rotunda was decorated with murals of antebellum homes, Native Americans and Spanish Conquistadors, surrounded by live oaks and draped with Spanish moss. Somewhere in the bowels of the building the plumbing vibrated, and voices carried from far down the hallway, echoing against high ceilings and hard plaster walls. Dewayne's attorney had subpoenaed Jack along with several others from the factory, but the rest were there as spectators packing the courtroom.

The trial was scheduled to begin at 9:00 a.m., and the company's defense was weak at best. Jack had met with the lawyers and learned that Dewayne was suing for one-point-five million dollars in damages, but the biggest problem wasn't the quality of his case. It was his attorney, Jeramiah "Honey Lips" Baker. Honey Lips had a Jesse James kind of notoriety, and he was known statewide as the labor lawyer to have on your side when you went to court. Some folks called him Jerry, but most called him Honey Lips.

Some said he was shrewd, while others said he was a shyster, but it was common knowledge that Honey Lips Baker could talk a treed wildcat down into a pack of howling dogs. And when it came to jury selection, he began the process with one requirement in mind. The potential juror had to have a dull glaze over his eyes—something that might indicate he wasn't given to simultaneous thought processes. Matt Oliver described it best saying when given such a fertile field of malleable gray matter, Honey Lips took the level playing field, turned it on end and coated it with his snake-oil rhetoric. He was known to confuse even judges from time to time.

Having all but chased Dewayne's ambulance to Tallahatchie General in Charleston that day, he nursed him with legal advice during the following months. The company attorneys tried to get him to take a five-hundred-thousand-dollar out-of-court settlement, but Honey Lips was confident he could do better in front of a jury.

Jack was called first, then Henry. Together they remained on the stand for nearly forty minutes. Despite a grilling, they held their own, but both left the witness stand looking as if they'd been in a steam bath. Honey Lips was dancing on the periphery of something, but exactly what, Jack wasn't sure. Like a shrewd boxer, the old lawyer was biding his time. The real damage would come when Dewayne took the stand—that is if he could be coaxed into saying the right things. They swore him in, and Dewayne sat down, grinning and waving to everyone in the gallery.

The judge peered over the top of his spectacles, shook his head and rapped the gavel. Dewayne turned and glanced up at him, but the judge turned to Honey Lips. "You may begin your questioning, counselor."

Honey Lips left his suit coat on the back of his chair and locked his thumbs in his vest pockets. With the persona of a sad-eyed southern gentleman, he strode ceremoniously to the front of the courtroom. He had sandy gray hair and was dressed in a tan suit with red suspenders. Little wisdom-glasses were propped on the end of his nose, and he made it all seem as natural as drinking sweet tea. Jack was certain Honey Lips had watched one too many John Grisham movies.

There were the usual preliminary questions, after which Honey Lips began working his magic. "Mr. Pritchert, did you ever apply for or ask one of the supervisors about a promotion to a machine operator's position?"

"Yes, sir."

"Who did you ask, and what was their response?"

"I asked Mr. Henry."

"And?"

"And what?" Dewayne said.

"And what was his response?"

"Oh, oh, yeah, he said I couldn't be one, 'cause I'd hurt myself on a machine."

"Did he also tell you that you were already making the same amount of money per hour as the machine operators, therefore there was nothing for you to gain by being promoted?"

"Yes, sir."

"So, there was really nothing for you to gain by changing jobs and incurring the risk that came with a much more dangerous one?"

"Objection, Your Honor! Counsel is leading the witness."

"Sustained. Re-phrase your question, Mr. Baker."

"Yes, Your Honor." Honey Lips turned back to Dewayne. "Did the shop foreman tell you what you would gain by being promoted?"

Dewayne turned to the judge. "Does this mean I wasn't supposed to tell anybody that I was already making the same pay as the machine operators?"

"No it doesn't," the judge said. "Just answer the question."

Honey Lips quickly interjected, "So, you're saying you were already making the same amount of money as the machine operators, and the danger level was the only difference between the two positions?"

Dewayne huffed with exasperation. "I done said that once already—yes."

"If you were making the same amount of money, why did you complain to Mr. Wilborn about not being promoted?"

"Mr. Wilborn?"

Dewayne looked as if he'd never heard the name.

"Sonny T," Honey Lips said. He turned and pointed at Sonny T. "That guy over there. Why did you complain to him?"

"Oh, Sonny T, yeah! Well, I didn't really. I just talked to him because he came to me one day while I was cleaning a ventilation duct and wanted to know why I wasn't a machine operator."

"And what did you tell him?"

"I said 'cause Mr. Henry and the other bosses said I'd get hurt."

"What was Mr. Wilborn's reply?"

"He asked me if I wanted to be one, and I told him I guess so, you know? I mean, I told him it didn't really matter since I was already making the same amount of money."

"What did Mr. Wilborn say then?"

"Sonny T said I was gonna be his token white boy, and I asked him what kind of work a token boy done, but he said not to worry. He said 'cause none of the bosses wanted me on a machine, he was gonna make sure I was, so it'd look like he was being fair."

The two company attorneys glanced at one another. They'd been blind-sided.

"Did Mr. Wilborn explain to you the reason the supervisors didn't want you operating machinery?"

"Yes, sir. He did."

Dewayne blinked and sat there.

"And, what was that reason, Mr. Pritchert?"

"He said it was 'cause they wasn't treating me equal and fair."

"Did he mention their concern about the possibility of you getting hurt?"

"No, sir, but I *did*. I told him."

"What did he say when you brought the safety issue to his attention?"

"He said a dirty word—you know, the 'F' word, and said they were just making excuses."

"So in spite of you telling him about these managers' concern for your personal safety, and the fact that you were already making the same amount of money, Mr. Wilborn made you a machine operator just to spite them. Is that correct?"

"I reckon so," Dewayne said. "I mean, if I had my druthers, I'd—"

"Objection, Your Honor. Counsel is leading the witness."

"Sustained," the judge said. "Rephrase your question, Mr. Baker."

He did and received the answer he wanted, but Honey Lips had only begun as he took the questioning toward the condition of Dewayne's thumb. Having been coached masterfully, Dewayne explained how he could no longer cast with his bass rod because of the injury. Honey Lips went on to establish how Dewayne's promising professional bass fishing career had been cut short in its prime, and how this up-and-coming star of the professional bass fishing circuit had been viciously abused by corporate malfeasance.

When he was done, Honey Lips turned to the judge. "Your Honor, I would like to introduce two items into evidence concerning Mr. Pritchert's former career as a professional bass fisherman."

The judge nodded, and Honey Lips signaled toward the back of the courtroom. The two oaken doors swung open and a young woman wearing a full-length purple evening dress, spike heels, and diamond earrings, pushed a cart down the aisle. The cart bearing Dewayne's three-foot-tall trophy from the Lake Washington Open was draped with royal-purple linen and trimmed in gold. Leaning against the trophy was an eleven by fourteen photo of Dewayne holding the five-thousand-dollar first-place check. His partner, Percy Williams, had been conveniently cropped from the picture.

The company's case quickly collapsed when Sonny T put the coup de grace on the entire affair by getting argumentative with the judge. The judge was about to have the bailiffs haul him from the courtroom when the company attorney finally calmed him. A recess was called, and Honey Lips played his hand like an artist. Recognizing the uncertainty of the jury, he took the company's final offer of seven hundred fifty thousand plus expenses and hit the door.

Matt Oliver caught Jack as he walked from the court house. "I'm not believing that Dewayne just got more money than he could have made in the next fourteen years."

"If he handles it right," Jack said, "he might never have to work again."

Matt Oliver stopped and gave Jack one of the looks he usually reserved for Dewayne or JT. "If bullfrogs had wings they wouldn't bump their asses either. You watch and see. He won't have a nickel left inside of six months—I'll bet you ten bucks."

"What makes you so certain?" Jack asked. "Maybe we can help him manage his money."

"You'd just as soon pan for gold in the Tallahatchie, Jack. It ain't in Dewayne's genes. I'm telling you."

JT had arranged post-trial festivities with Dewayne's credit down at Big Dog's that evening, and a crowd was already gathered when Jack and Matt Oliver arrived. People spilled out the door, standing out front on the sidewalk and in the street. JT's truck and Dewayne's Toyota were parked at the front door.

Parking down the street, Jack and Matt Oliver walked back to the restaurant, making their way through the crowd. They stepped inside to see Big Dog wearing his white apron and carrying a platter of barbecued ribs to a table at the center of the restaurant. Dewayne, April, Doris Ann, JT,

Janine, and several others were gathered there with beer bottles in hand, celebrating the big payoff.

JT spotted Jack and Matt Oliver and shouted, "Hey, y'all come on over here. Everything's on the house this afternoon. Dewayne's got it all covered. Bring these fellas a beer, Big Dog."

Matt Oliver grinned and tapped Dewayne on the shoulder. "You're not going to spend all your money at once, are you?"

Dewayne gave him his usual dull-witted smile.

"Hell," JT said, "this ain't nothing. Dewayne's gonna buy a brand new place, and we're gonna have a real party—maybe early as next week. Big Dog's gonna cater it, and we're gonna float a couple kegs before we're done."

"Here's to hoping," Jack said.

"Here's to lost causes," Matt Oliver countered.

They clinked their bottles together.

Sonny T's performance during the trial put an end to his tenure as Human Resources Manager. He was given his walking papers the next day, but two days after his dismissal he showed up at the front gate passing out union cards as the employees arrived for work. With him were Shamika, Cleolonda and Sharon, all carrying signs and marching up and down the road, singing "We Shall Overcome." As long as they stayed on public property and didn't harass the employees, there wasn't much could be said, but later that morning Jack's office phone rang.

It was Henry, asking him to come talk with Sonny T. Seemed he'd gotten brave and walked past the guard at the front gate. When they found him, another Sonny T-style fracas had ensued. The guard was standing in the door at the foyer, preventing him from entering the office area, and Sonny T was shouting and cursing.

"I tried to tell him he was trespassing," the guard said, "but he tried to push by me, and he keeps yelling and screaming."

Sonny T tried again to rush past, but the guard quickly put his arm across the doorway, and Sonny T flipped backward like a wide receiver clothes-lined by a linebacker. A lesser man would have stayed down, but Sonny T sprang to his feet.

"Touch me again and I'll own this muthafuckin' place," he said. "Go ahead. Lay another hand on me. I dare you."

The guard, who was no little man, had the narrow doorway blocked as he looked back at Jack and shrugged. Sonny T readjusted his wire-rimmed glasses and smoothed his rumpled suit.

"There's no need for this kind of silliness," Jack said.

"Silliness?" Sonny T said. "You call me trying to talk to my people 'silliness'? The law says you can't stop a union if they want one."

"Maybe not," Jack said, "but the law also says you can't come on this property without permission. You need to leave."

The guard stepped to the side and Sonny T pushed by him. He stood toe-to-toe with Jack, jabbing his finger in his face. "What are you going to do if I don't? Huh? You want to call the law? Go ahead. I've already called the TV stations in Memphis. They got people coming down here with cameras. You hear me? We gonna be on every TV in the country."

Jack stepped back and whispered in Henry's ear, "Go call the sheriff."

Sonny T continued shouting and arguing until Henry's son, Clayton, arrived with several more deputies and put him in cuffs. He kicked at them and shouted as they pulled him down the hallway, but they stopped when they reached the doorway. Sonny T had wedged his legs on either side of the door, and refused to budge. It was as if they were trying to flush a wildcat down a toilet.

That was when Dewayne showed up to pick up his last check. Glancing first at Sonny T, then at the sheriff's deputies, Dewayne seemed unable to comprehend what was happening.

"How come y'all doing Mr. Sonny T that way?"

Sonny T answered for the deputies. "You cracker-ass muthafucka, you the one got me in this fix."

"Step aside," one of the deputies said.

Like a puppy dumped in a roadside ditch, Dewayne cocked his head to one side as he watched the deputies put Sonny T into the back of the squad car.

Jack was certain the Memphis news programs had often featured Sonny T, but thankfully, the squad cars and Sonny T were long gone when the vans arrived with their satellite dishes. Shamika, Cleolonda and Sharon had thrown their signs into a roadside ditch and gone back to work. Jack gave a "no comment" to the news people, but later that afternoon there came a call from the home office.

"We appreciate all you've done," they said, "but we have some bad news."

It was official. The factory would close for the Fourth of July holiday, and it wouldn't reopen.

The news came almost as a relief, and Jack exhaled. There was still a lot to get done, and he hoped to help the employees with out-placement. It was over, and as with Cici, he now had the duty of making final arrangements.

It had been a week since Jack announced the factory's closing, and the group in the back breakroom was already growing smaller. By the third week of June, it was down to Henry, JT, Momo, Clyde, and Matt Oliver. Jack sat with them discussing Dewayne's settlement, part of which included resignation of his employment. His leaving hadn't been without fanfare. JT announced that he had told Dewayne that as a member of the landed gentry it was his duty to meet certain social obligations, not the least of which was throwing parties and such. They had a big one planned.

Dewayne had gone out and purchased a double-wide and ten acres of land over near Tallaha Road. "Too damned close for comfort," Clyde said about his new neighbor. Dewayne had the entire ten acres bulldozed flat as a pool table, then poured gravel for a drive all the way back to his new trailer. It was surrounded by a desolate plain of mud, which was why JT talked Dewayne into having the party at the casino.

"I damned near buried my four-wheel drive out there the other day," JT said.

"That old mud gets mighty slick when it rains," Clyde said. "I don't know why he went and dozed off all the cover."

"It's just pure-dee hell when the riffraff moves in, ain't it?" Matt Oliver said.

"Ain't much we can do about it, except lock our doors at night and hope he don't go to shooting his gun across the pasture."

"Better lock up your livestock, too," Matt Oliver said. "I hear he's got a liking for young pigs."

"He's hell on the mules, too," Henry added.

Clyde turned to Jack, shrugged, and gave him a flat smile.

"Y'all are just jealous," JT said. "Dewayne made it big, and y'all didn't's all."

Matt Oliver pointed a finger at JT. "You know, maybe you're right. Maybe we're fooling ourselves. Maybe ol' Dewayne really *is* smarter than all of us. At least he's got something to show for the time he spent here."

"Damned right!" JT said, "And he's showing his appreciation by throwing a big party this Friday night at the Gold Strike Casino. Everybody's invited. It's gonna be a going-away party like nobody around here has ever seen."

He went on to explain how Dewayne was treating everyone to the all-you-can-eat dinner buffet, after which they were invited to his private suite for a party with a live band, more food, and an open bar.

Later, Henry and Momo said they had declined the invitation, but Matt Oliver said he was having mixed feelings. He didn't want to take advantage of Dewayne's misguided generosity, but he didn't want to hurt his feelings either. He turned to Jack. "Bad as I don't want to drive up there, maybe you can go with me, and we can just stop in for a little while. It'll make Dewayne and JT feel better, especially if nobody else shows up."

Jack smiled. Matt Oliver was doing the same thing he had done—thinking with his heart instead of his mind.

"You sure?"

"I think we should," Matt Oliver said.

Jack had agreed to go with Matt Oliver, and as they drove up Highway 61 that Friday evening, a deep orange sun was sinking amongst the thunderheads in the west. Matt Oliver was unusually quiet, and when he finally spoke, he said something about the weather moving in—nothing about the factory closing or the future. After that he was quiet again. Jack let the silence run its course.

When they arrived at the casino, they went directly to the buffet and asked about Dewayne. The workers there grew suddenly sullen, watching Jack and Matt Oliver as if they were accomplices in something that had already occurred.

"Mr. Pritchert's group has already gone," a tight-lipped hostess said.

Jack turned to Matt Oliver. "Looks like Dewayne and company made an impression on these folks."

They walked back out onto the casino floor.

"Yeah, that woman looked like she wanted to kill somebody," Matt Oliver said.

"You still up to this?" Jack asked. "They're probably all drunk as hell by now."

"I know," Matt Oliver said. "I mean, I know this was probably a bad idea, but I just wanted them to know that—well..."

"...that you really don't begrudge Dewayne's good luck?"

"Maybe that's it," Matt Oliver said. "I mean, I can't much stand either one of them, but I don't want them to think I don't care about them as people."

The din of the slot machines seemed a magical draw on his subconscious, as Jack smiled and nodded. "I understand. We'll pay them a quick visit then head back to Tallahatchie."

They walked to the front desk where the clerk gave them Dewayne's room number. Catching an elevator to the top floor, they heard the racket before the elevator door opened. Scores of people with plastic cups of beer lined the hallway as Jack and Matt Oliver slipped through the mob into the room. Only a handful of the guests were recognizable, but the band was from a little bar near Tutwiler. They were banging out a blend of Heavy Metal, Blues and Country.

At the center of the room was a champagne fountain—except there was a little guy in a red jacket with brass buttons and white gloves pouring Bud tall-boys into it. The beer was foaming over the sides, and no one seemed to notice, including the guy filling the fountain.

"Hey y'all, look who's here."

It was JT yelling loud enough to be heard over the band. Holding his glass high, he saluted Jack and Matt Oliver from across the room. JT was at a table with Dewayne and April. It was set with a buffet spread of hors d'oeuvres, but Dewayne, April, and several of their friends had made it a banquet table. Pulling chairs up, they had piled their plates high with food.

"Hey y'all," Dewayne said. "Come on over here and sit down. Fix you a plate. You ever seen so much food?"

They were all there: Janine, decked out in a sequined evening dress, Doris Ann, wearing a sequined spandex body suit, and April in what was no doubt the best dress Walmart sold. Over in the corner Jack spotted Honey Lips Baker carrying on a conversation with a young woman half his age—probably one he'd brought with him. Doritoe was sitting near the window wearing dark glasses and a full-length mink coat. He was talking on a cell phone. JT walked up with two plastic cups of foamy beer.

"Here you go," he said. "Man, we're all just about too full to eat anything else, but y'all get you some of this stuff."

The table was overflowing with high-dollar hors d'oeuvres.

"It's all pretty good," JT said, "except stay away from that black shit in that bowl yonder. I got hol'ta some a minute ago and liked to kill't myself getting somewhere to spit it out. It's caviar, you know?

"It's fish eggs," Dewayne shouted.

"It's yuck," April added.

"Yeah, it's some pretty nasty shit," JT said. "But everything else is pretty good."

Jack noticed April had a sandwich piled high with enough ham and Swiss to feed four or five people. She had it wrapped in a napkin and was slipping it into her purse. She saw that he noticed and explained. "This here is for the kids when we get home. I don't reckon the casino people will mind me taking it."

Jack nodded and smiled.

"Did y'all order up any chitterlin's?" Matt Oliver asked.

"We tried," Dewayne said. "They wasn't sure how to fix them, but there's plenty of other stuff. Try them fried oysters over there, and them boiled crawdads. They ain't bad."

Matt Oliver smiled as he slurped from his foam-filled cup.

"Hey, Jack," JT said. "Have you seen me and Dewayne's new tattoos?"

Jack shook his head, and they began unbuttoning their sleeves. It was a race to see who could show his first, as they jerked up their sleeves and simultaneously displayed identical red, black, and yellow Dewey Hargrove number 93 tattoos on their arms.

"What do you think?" JT said.

"They look great," Jack said.

He turned to see Matt Oliver's reaction, but he had walked away—no doubt, a move for the better.

"Be sure to get your bucket of coins, when you leave," JT said. He pointed to a line of plastic coin cups at the end of the table.

"Dewayne's got one for each of us, and there's a hundred dollars' worth of gold tokens in each one."

"And if that ain't enough, I got all this too," Dewayne said. He pulled a plaid jacket from the back of his chair and reached into one of the pockets. Jack nearly lost his breath when Dewayne came out with several bundles of twenty and fifty-dollar bills still in the bank wrappers.

"We're gonna do some gambling tonight," he said.

JT apparently noticed the look on Jack's face. "Don't worry," he said. "There's plenty more where that come from."

"I hope so," Jack said.

"You need to come out and see my new place," Dewayne said. "I got a doublewide with a deck and a gazebo on ten acres."

"A doublewide?" Jack said.

"Yeah, I figured it was time to splurge a little."

"Why didn't you just build a house?"

"Didn't need one," he said. "A doublewide's got more room than we'll ever need. Besides, if we decide to move again, we can take it apart and take it with us."

Jack nodded, knowing there was a lesson somewhere amongst the insanity.

"Tell him about your new bass boat," JT said.

Jack turned back to Dewayne.

"Yes sirree, buddy. Got a brand new seventeen-foot Skeeter with a two-hundred-horse Black Max outboard."

"It won't do nothing but shit and git," JT said.

"What did you do with the Bayliner?" Jack asked.

"Oh, I'm keeping it, too," Dewayne said, "in case April and the kids want to go skiing sometime."

"And you ought to see the truck he bought," JT said.

When Jack and Matt Oliver left the casino that night, it was pouring rain, punctuated by claps of thunder and flashing lightning, but Matt Oliver stared into the night and kept mumbling the phrase "a fool and his money." Jack glanced down at the five cups of tokens sitting on the seat between them. Dewayne had insisted that they take cups for Henry, Clyde and Momo.

"I think we should try to talk some sense into Dewayne," Jack said. "Maybe make some suggestions on how to manage his money. What do you think?"

"I think it'd be like pissing on a forest fire," Matt Oliver said.

He was probably right, but Jack still figured on cashing in his tokens and sending the money back to Dewayne. At the rate he was spending his settlement, a few bucks might look good in a month or two.

The Monday before the Fourth of July turned out to be busier than Jack expected. With almost no office staff remaining and the labor force dwindling rapidly, everyone pitched in to get out the last orders. It was a grim group, speaking only when necessary. Later they cleaned out desks and lockers. Cardboard boxes filled with memorabilia, photos, and keepsakes lined the hallway as people saved mementos from the years they'd spent at the factory.

Jack found it difficult to look into the eyes of people who'd spent their entire lives here. He was little more than a caretaker trying to comfort a bereaved family he hardly knew. When they finished loading the remaining inventory on trucks bound for Tupelo, it would be all over. They would lock the gates before the Fourth of July weekend and the factory would close forever.

CHAPTER 24

WHERE THE MUSIC'S PLAYING

I T WAS HOT THAT DAY, but not as hectic as the previous day. With the last truck-load ready to go, the end was near. The heat shimmered off the pavement while the driver went to the office for his manifest. A heavy-set man in a white T-shirt, George Letts was one of the regulars out of Oklahoma City. George was a regular kind of guy, always smiled and spoke to everyone. Jack stood with the few remaining employees on the dock, smoking and talking while everyone waited to bid George a final good-bye.

They were all resigned to moving on—all except for Clyde. Jack had told him there was a position waiting with Hartman Manufacturing in Mobile if he wanted it, but Clyde declined. He was retiring—said he'd worked enough for one lifetime. Clyde invited him for another bream fishing trip the next day up at Moon Lake, and Jack accepted. After that he figured on packing up and heading home to Alabama, where Tuck had assured him his father was more than ready to have him back at Hartman Manufacturing.

Henry was old enough to retire, but his son—the one with the Sheriff's department—got him on as a part-time security guard at one of the casinos. When he was off, he said he'd try to catch whatever fish Clyde missed.

Clyde held up his thumb and index finger and squinted with one eye between them. "I'll leave you the little ones."

They laughed, but it was a nervous laughter spawned by the impending good-byes. Jack watched them, feeling the pain they were experiencing. They fought to maintain straight faces, but no one could look a fellow worker in the eyes for very long without realizing the overwhelming finality they faced.

"What are you going to do, JT?" Matt Oliver asked.

Considering JT's usual reaction to things, Jack took a deep breath and prepared for a diatribe. He had called the home office and tried to arrange jobs at the Tupelo factory for JT and several other employees, but he hadn't yet heard anything on the results.

"I reckon people just know talent when they see it. The factory in Tupelo called, and I got me a job lined up there. Yeah, they just called out of the blue. Me and Janine are going over yonder tomorrow and drive around—see if maybe we can find a trailer or a house to rent."

"It's too bad you have to move," Matt Oliver said, "but at least you'll have a job."

"It's better than you think," JT said. "Tupelo has better Little League Baseball, and it's a lot closer to Talladega."

"I thought you gave up on racing after Dewey Hargrove got killed," Henry said.

JT grinned sheepishly and glanced around to see if anyone else was listening. He lowered his voice to near a whisper. "You know, I wouldn't tell just anybody this, but you guys are my friends."

He paused, almost as if for dramatic effect. Taking a long pull on his cigarette, he squinted across the parking lot, toward the distant cotton fields. After exhaling, he began talking. "When Dewey got killed, and then I had to put old Boomer down—well, it got to me, you know? I couldn't hardly crawl my ass out of bed, but Janine, she made me go to the doctor, and he gave me some pills. Hell, what can I say? They just make everything all right, you know? Since I started taking them, I've been watching racing again, and I'm thinking about getting' me another dog when I get to Tupelo."

"Whatever works," Matt Oliver said.

JT's eyes moistened, and he turned to Matt Oliver. "I don't know exactly how to say this, old buddy, but I reckon I owe you an apology. I mean…" He wrapped his arm around Matt Oliver's neck and pulled him close. Matt Oliver turned red and cut his eyes over at Jack. A tear ran down JT's cheek. "Even the doctor said you were right, buddy. I reckon you were just trying to help all along. You know, when Dewey got killed?"

Matt Oliver's neck bent under JT's grasp, as he tried to nod. "No problem."

Jack turned to Momo. "What are your plans?"

Momo glanced over at Matt Oliver, just freed from JT's passionate embrace. He was rubbing his neck. Matt Oliver shrugged and seemed embarrassed as his face grew red again, but Momo maintain his stare.

"Okay," Matt Oliver said, "I reckon I'll explain. You know that big piece I carved of the Indian Hunter?"

He had shown the sculpture to Jack a few weeks back, a four-foot-high statue of a Choctaw holding a couple of rabbits along with a bow and arrow. He'd carved it from cherry, and it was one of his finest. He'd given it to Momo as a going away present.

"Well, it was still sitting in my girlfriend's antique shop up in Memphis when some guy from Oklahoma came in and wanted to buy it. She told him it wasn't for sale, but he insisted on calling me about it. I told him the same thing, but he said he wanted it, so he could donate it to the Cowboy Hall of Fame in Oklahoma City. I told him it was Momo's, and he'd have to talk to him, so I drove Momo up there to meet with the guy."

Matt Oliver stopped and lit another cigarette. "So, anyway, this guy starts making offers, but you know how Mister Talkative here is." He motioned with his head toward Momo. "He just kept scratching his head and didn't say anything, so I reckon the guy thought he was holding out for more each time. He kept upping the bid, until he got to twelve thousand."

"Dollars?" JT said.

Matt Oliver cast a sidelong glance at JT, but resisted the temptation. He simply nodded and said, "Ended up, the guy wrote him a check for fifteen thousand dollars."

"Dad gum! Fifteen thousand dollars for a wooden Indian?" JT said.

Momo turned toward JT with a scowl on his face.

"If that don't beat all," JT said. "Damned fella must have been rich. So, what are you going to do with the money, Momo?"

"L-L-Leeeaarnn to t-t-talk."

"He's moving to Memphis for speech therapy," Matt Oliver said. "My girlfriend—her name's Maria—well, she's really my fiancée, now, because we're getting married later this year, but right now we're helping Momo get a lease on an apartment."

"I wo-wo-won't nu-nu-need whi-whiskey to t-t-talk r-right," Momo said.

"You and Maria getting hitched?" Jack asked.

"First of August," Matt Oliver said. "And you're invited. I'm taking my tools up to her antique shop. Maria wants me to live with her and work on my carving for a while."

A metal door slammed shut down near the end of the dock, and Doris Ann came walking their way. Behind her was the truck driver, George Letts, huffing and sweating in the July sun as he carried a cardboard box piled high with Doris Ann's Princess Di and Elvis memorabilia. She stopped in front of the little group, fist on her hip and chewing her trademark wad of pink bubblegum. George, who was wearing Doris Ann's Elvis sunglasses, had a box resting atop his potbelly as he eased down the steps toward his truck.

"I'll be out there in a minute, baby," she said.

He nodded without looking back, and she turned toward Jack and the others. "Well, fellas, I reckon this is it—the big adios."

She looked them up and down with a sideways grin. "It's been a real interesting few years here with you boys— more interesting with some than others." She gave Jack a wink.

"Where you going?" JT asked.

"Me and Georgie are headed to my place to load my things, and I'm going out to Oklahoma with him. He hates big weddings, so we're gonna get married as soon as we find a JP."

"No shit?" JT said.

"No shit," Doris Ann replied.

JT looked wistfully to where George had disappeared behind the truck. "Lucky bastard."

Doris Ann planted a red smudge of lipstick on JT's cheek, then swiped at it with her finger and wiped it on his shirt. She turned toward Jack, "At least someone around here is a good judge of girls."

Jack and Henry shut the power down in the factory that evening, and pulled a heavy steel chain through the gates. That was it. Jack gazed back at the building, but he saw only the vision in his mind of the people he'd been with for the last year—scattering to the wind.

The Monday after the Fourth, Jack was staring out the kitchen window at the squirrels in the pecan grove when his phone rang. Most of his belongings were packed, and he was looking forward to leaving later in the week. He answered the phone. It was JT, and he wanted Jack to go to the casino with him and Dewayne for a final fling.

"Kind of a special going away thing, just for you," JT said.

"Dewayne still has money left?"

"Bunches of it. More than he knows what to do with," JT said.

The math didn't add up, and Jack tried to make an excuse, but JT wouldn't allow it. Surely, the doublewide on ten acres, the new boat, new truck, and the casino party the previous weekend had put a sizeable dent in Dewayne's bank account. It seemed he would want to save what remained, but Jack was certain logic and reason were paradigms into which Dewayne and JT seldom ventured.

"Okay," he said, "but I'll have to drive up later and meet you guys. How about we meet around seven-thirty?"

They agreed on a late supper, and it was a little before eight that evening when Jack arrived. Making his way through the maze of burbling slot machines, he spotted

JT and Dewayne leaving the restroom. Both were red-eyed and well on their way to world-class hangovers. JT jabbered excitedly about how Dewayne had just won fourteen hundred bucks on the roulette wheel, and they were now headed to the craps table.

"I thought we were going to eat," Jack said.

"Man," JT said, wagging his head with a grim countenance, "I'm really sorry, Jack. Maybe we can catch the meal later, but right now we can't stop. We've got to go with this thing. You know? I mean, Dewayne's hot—really hot. He just won big on the roulette wheel, but we've still got a lot of lost ground to make up. We've been losing all afternoon, but we're going for the big bundle right now."

"Whatever," Jack said. He was about to ask how much the "lost ground" amounted to, but thought better of it.

JT continued shaking his head. "I'm sorry. You understand, don't you, Jack? I mean, we ain't just putting you off. This is something we've got to do right now. It's a matter of timing. You know?"

"No problem," Jack said. "I'll go over to the restaurant, grab a bite to eat and come back in a little while."

JT slapped him on the back and turned, all but running as he left, weaving his way through banks of slot machines toward the craps table. Jack managed to kill an hour or so before returning to find JT and Dewayne still there. Dewayne had the dice in his hands, rubbing them between his palms as he stared at the back wall of the table. JT was at his side, studying him intently.

"Well," Jack said. "How are you boys doing?"

JT didn't look up as he held his hand up for silence. "Ssshhh," he said.

He continued staring at Dewayne. "Come on, baby. Come on, baby. Don't say maybe. You can do it. You can do it."

JT was chanting a prayer to lady luck, who was no doubt lying in repose upon Dewayne's shoulder. A considerable crowd had gathered to watch these two high-rollers, and Jack noticed several huge stacks of chips on the table. Thousands of dollars were there, all wagered for this one big roll. Jack poked JT and pointed at the chips.

"Dewayne's?" he asked.

"Yeah, yeah," JT said. "Now, be quiet."

Dewayne blew into his fist and tossed the dice. It was as if they tumbled into a world of slow motion as the two little cubes bounced toward the back of the table. Rolling forever past the huge stacks of chips, they were about to decide if Dewayne's money remained his.

When they finally stopped, a moan went up from the crowd and JT slammed his fist on the table. The pit boss shot him a hard look, but JT wheeled and stomped away. Dewayne stood dumbfounded as his chips were raked away. Jack pulled him away from the table, and they caught up with JT.

"I ain't believing that shit," JT said.

He grabbed a beer from the tray of a passing hostess, and she was about to object when he tossed a wadded five-dollar bill on the tray. He took a long swallow from the bottle then looked over at Jack.

"Do you know how much money was out there on that table?"

"Looked like thousands," Jack said.

"That's right, around fifty thousand—give or take a few thousand, and you can't just walk up and start talking like that when somebody has that kind of money on the line. They got to be able to concentrate. You know?"

Jack glanced at Dewayne, who blinked stupidly as he stared at the butt of a passing hostess.

"Let's go buy some more chips and start over," JT said.

"You guys are going to blow Dewayne's last cent if you don't give it a rest."

"Jack, we know what we're doing," JT said. "We've got it under control."

Dewayne nodded stupidly.

"I'll tell you what," Jack said. "Why don't you guys do your thing for a while, and I'll head over to the poker room and see if I can get a seat? What do you say?"

"We ain't trying to run you off," JT said.

"I know, but poker suits me better. I'll check back with you guys in a few hours. Or maybe you want to join me?"

"Na," JT said. "Me and Dewayne don't get into card games much—too complicated when you're dealing with lots of money. You go ahead."

Jack played poker for several hours, actually winning a couple hundred dollars before a state of pre-drool exhaustion overcame him. He'd heard nothing from JT and

Dewayne, and after cashing out his chips, he searched the casino. They were pumping the dollar-slot machines.

"You guys doing any good?" he asked.

"We were," JT said, "but we just can't quite get out of the hole before we slide back again."

It was nearly five a.m.

"Man, I can't take much more," Jack said.

"Go help Dewayne with the money machine," JT said. "All we need is a couple thousand more. The way I got it figured, that's all it'll take to turn this thing around. I'm gonna run piss while you guys get the money. Okay?"

He disappeared, and Jack walked with Dewayne over to the automated teller machine. Peeking covertly at a scrap of paper from his wallet, Dewayne seemed hesitant as he punched in the numbers. He held the paper close to his chest, glancing nervously at Jack. Jack shoved his hands into his pockets, turned and gazed out across the casino.

"These are my private codes for my bank account," Dewayne said.

Jack nodded without looking back, but after a minute or two he glanced around. With furrowed brows, Dewayne was punching the buttons again, this time more forcefully.

"What's wrong?" Jack asked.

"I don't know," Dewayne said. "It just keeps spitting out little slips of paper."

Jack picked up one of the receipts. "It says here you have only thirteen dollars and forty-three cents in your account."

Dewayne looked up, his mouth hanging half-open and his brows hanging low. "That can't be. I got my whole settlement check in there."

"Well, read it yourself." Jack handed him the slip of paper. "It looks like you and JT spent it all. You're broke."

Tears welled in Dewayne's eyes. "I can't be broke." His voice was loud, and people began looking around. "JT said it would take years to spend that much money."

A couple of security guards walked over to where they were standing.

"What do you think I've been trying to tell you? You *can* spend that much money and you *did*. You're flat busted."

Tears ran from his eyes as Dewayne blubbered about how it wasn't fair and how it had to be a mistake, but he knew. In spite of his intellectual shortcomings, he knew he'd done it. He'd killed his golden goose. He'd gambled away the remainder of his settlement and had nothing to show for it but a hangover. Jack draped his arm across Dewayne's shoulders and told the security guards he would take care of him.

"Come on, man. Let's go home."

Red-eyed and sniffling, Dewayne followed him toward the big glass doors at the front of the casino. As they approached, Jack could see the morning sun, a huge orange sphere, creeping slowly out of the warm Delta mist. The casino was a climate-controlled island of magical sounds, smells, and lights that made one forget he was in the Mississippi Delta. Only yards away were scum-filled bayous, sticky buckshot mud, mosquitoes, and a Monday morning job with little more promise than putting hotdogs and pork-n-beans on the table most nights. It was this illusion and the hope for riches that drew people like Dewayne into its magical web of deceit.

JT hadn't returned—probably still draining off some of the buckets of beer he'd consumed that night. Dewayne began lagging behind, stopping to look back.

"We gotta wait on JT," he said.

"Dewayne, I know JT is your buddy, and I'm not saying he's a bad person, but you need to consider finding a new friend."

Dewayne looked back across the banks of chirping slot machines. "Why? What happened to him?"

"Nothing *happened* to him," Jack said. "It's what's happened to *you*. Can't you see he's a bad influence? Whose idea was it to have that big party? JT's. Whose idea was it to come back and try to win some of your money back? JT's. I'm telling you, you need to find someone a little more settled who can guide you to make better decisions."

Dewayne nodded, and for a moment Jack thought he'd gotten through to him.

"Hey! Hey, y'all!" It was JT calling as he came their way. "You're not quitting, are you? We gotta make this thing happen."

"Dewayne's broke," Jack said.

"Broke? Well, hell, didn't y'all go to the money machine like I told you?"

"He did," Jack said. "And the receipt shows he's got thirteen dollars left in his account."

"Thirteen dollars? That's bullshit. That machine done made some kind of mistake."

"It's not a mistake. You guys spent damned near every cent of Dewayne's money."

JT threw his arm across Dewayne's shoulder, but Dewayne shrugged it off. "I'm going home," he said.

"You ain't mad at me, are you?" JT asked.

Dewayne turned his head away.

"Hey, what gives? You blaming me?"

"He's not blaming anyone," Jack said. "Why don't we just head back home for now? You can talk about it later."

This seemed to put him at ease, and they walked toward the door, but just before reaching the main entrance JT stopped to stare at an unusually large slot machine. It was the one they called The Lightning Strike because it had only one progressive pay-off, and the chances of getting struck by lightning were greater than the possibility of winning it.

The big blue and silver marquee above the machine indicated the potential winnings had grown to over five hundred thousand dollars. Jack paused with Dewayne while JT put his last gold token into the machine and pulled the handle. It came up a mixture of clouds and smiley sun shines, but no lightning bolts.

"Got any tokens left?" he asked Dewayne.

Dewayne fished around in his pocket and came up with two one-dollar tokens.

"Might as well try them," JT said.

Dewayne looked at Jack.

"Why the hell not?" Jack said.

Dewayne hurried back to the machine, and dropped his first dollar token into the slot. He pulled the handle, and after several seconds it came up all clouds. He shrugged and quickly dropped his last token into the machine, pulled the handle and turned to walk away. JT stood watching it, while Dewayne walked up beside Jack.

The machine rumbled.

"The first one's a lightning bolt," JT shouted.

He bent closer to the machine. It rumbled again.

"Damn, he got another one," he said.

He held his fists clenched in front of him as he waited. A brilliant flash shot from the strobe light overhead and the machine rumbled and cracked with a rumble of thunder that challenged the real thing. More lights began flashing. Casino managers, guards, and bystanders came running as JT screamed like a banshee.

"You did it! You did it! You lucky sonofabitch, you did it!"

Wednesday morning after the Fourth of July, Jack got into his pickup and drove down to Big Dog's for breakfast. On the way, one of those unexplainable feelings of nostalgia made him drive out to the factory. The temperature was already in the mid-eighties, and it promised to be another scorching hot day. The blacktop shimmered with mirages and the roadside grass was parched brown. This was one thing about Tallahatchie he wouldn't miss. The Gulf Coast was hot, but there was at least the relief of an ocean breeze.

When he turned down the road toward the factory, he saw two men standing outside the gate. Slowing, he pulled over. They hadn't seen him. After a moment or two he recognized them. It was Clyde and Henry standing together, staring through the chained gate at the empty building. It was a stark and lonely sight as the two men stood side-by-side gazing at the remnants of what had been their lives for the last forty years.

Everything was dark inside—not a hint of activity or even a wisp of smoke anywhere. It was dead. The wind blew a loose piece of metal siding, causing it to bang against a beam on the side of the building, and for the first time, Jack noticed how rust had formed on some of the outside walls. There were also several potholes on the empty parking lot that he hadn't noticed before, and it suddenly seemed the factory was older than he ever realized.

Henry and Clyde had been at the furniture factory longer than anyone—nearly forty years. Jack was about to drive down to the gate when they turned to face one another. He paused, watching as Clyde extended his hand and Henry shook it, then he pulled Clyde closer as the two men embraced. It was one of those embarrassingly private moments, and Jack would have left, except Clyde noticed him sitting up the road in his truck. After driving down to the gate where the two men stood, Jack got out.

On the truck seat were the two cups of gold tokens Dewayne had sent them. Jack picked them up. When he turned their way he noticed a tear in Henry's eye, and Clyde's eyes were moist as well. Henry pulled his sleeve across his face as Jack walked over to where the men stood.

"I've got something here that might brighten your day a little," he said.

He gave them the plastic cups, each filled with a hundred dollars in tokens.

"What's this?" Henry asked.

"A going-away present from Dewayne."

Henry glanced down at his cup then back at Jack. "I figured he'd be damn near broke by now."

"I take it you didn't hear the news," Jack said.

"What news?"

"You won't believe it, but he blew just about every last cent he had, until—"

"I figured he'd do that," Henry said.

"That's not the best part," Jack said.

"Oh?"

"Yeah, him and JT invited me up to the casino again the other night. While we were there Dewayne found his checking account was damned near empty. He broke down and cried. Anyway, I was feeling sorry for him, and—"

"Poor bastard," Henry said.

"Wait," Jack said. "That's not all there is to it. When we were walking out he found a couple tokens in his pocket. JT talked him into putting them in that Lightning Strike machine. You know—the big one near the door?"

"Don't tell me he hit the progressive?" Henry said.

Jack nodded.

"You're messin' with us now," Clyde said.

"I'm not kidding. It's the gospel truth. The crazy bastard hit a progressive jackpot for over five hundred grand. I swear."

"You're right," Henry said. "I don't believe you. Come on. Tell me you're pulling my leg. What are the odds of that happening?"

"I'm not lying," Jack said. "I tried to talk him into putting the money in the bank, but the casino gave him and JT complimentary suites and meals for the weekend. I did my best to convince them to leave, but JT called last night, telling me they were going shopping up in Memphis this morning."

"Shopping for what?" Clyde said.

Jack hooked his fingers in the chain-link fence and stared at the factory while he talked. "He said they were both getting another tattoo, then going to the Harley-Davidson dealership to buy a pair of hogs. I called Matt Oliver to see if he wanted to go with me to try to talk some sense into Dewayne."

"What did Matt Oliver say?" Henry asked.

"He said it was a waste of time, because there aren't a half-dozen good brain cells between them."

"I reckon he's right," Clyde said.

Henry laughed.

"I reckon this is it," Jack said, extending his hand to Henry.

They shook, and Henry wished him luck.

Jack turned to Clyde. "I want to thank you for all you've done. I wouldn't have lasted a month without your help."

They shook hands, and Jack walked back to his truck. When he reached the door he stopped and looked back at the two older men standing with the backdrop of the rusted furniture factory.

"Don't either of you ever go wanting for anything. You have my number. I'll be only a phone call away."

Jack drove back to the farmhouse to finish packing, but as he drove up the drive there was a car parked out front. He had sold or given away most anything he couldn't carry with him and figured it was someone looking for a last minute bargain. Parking the pickup, he got out. Whoever it was, had let themselves inside. He pushed the door open.

"Hello?"

There was a familiar scent in the air. She stepped from his bedroom. It was Acey.

The next morning Jack and Acey left the pickup at Clyde's, telling him it was his, then drove up to Clarksdale to Aunt Netta's house. It was nearly noon when they departed Clarksdale that day and took Highway 49 south toward the Gulf Coast. Jack sipped coffee while Acey curled in the seat beside him sleeping with her head on his shoulder. Neither had slept much the night before, but it had been worth it, and with the way matters were playing out, it might have been their last fun fling for a while.

Jack glanced into the review mirror. In the back seat were twin toddler car seats where Charise and Caroline slept peacefully. It had been one of Cici's last requests, one he was more than happy to fulfill, and with Acey's immediate buy-in he had agreed to take his soon to be officially adopted daughters back home to live in Fairhope, Alabama.

Within a few hours the earthy smell of the Delta gave way to the fresh salty odor of the Gulf as they caught Interstate 10 and headed east. The pines grew thick on either side of the highway, and it wasn't until they reached Mobile Bay that he caught a glimpse of the Gulf off in the distance.

He took the Fairhope exit, and it was late evening when they arrived home. They put the kids to bed, and walked out on the deck. Back in the distance across the bay thunderheads sparkled and blinked in the nighttime sky. Taking Acey by the hand, he looked into her eyes as they stood listening to the waves lapping gently ashore. Except for an occasional call from a sea gull it was extraordinarily quiet.

"It's good to be back at Point Clear," she said.

Jack had wanted to wait. He had planned to do it in some exotic location, Trinidad or perhaps Hawaii, but for some reason, now seemed like the right time. He reached into his pocket and retrieved the small white box.

"I want you stay here with me forever," he said. He opened the box and took out the diamond solitaire. "Will you marry me?"

Acey's eyes grew moist in the ambient light from the bay.

"Spending the rest of my life here with you and raising a house full of kids is all I ever wanted."

She held out her hand, and Jack slid the ring on her finger. In the distance, an array of lightning spider-webbed across the nighttime sky, stretching from the lights of the high-rises in Mobile all the way down to the Gulf of Mexico.

Acey took a deep breath. "I believe we just got Divine approval."

An on-shore breeze blew her hair in her eyes, and Jack pushed it away.

"Yeah, I've had the feeling all along that someone was looking out for me."

Their lips met in a passionate kiss, and when they separated, Acey took him by the hand. "Let's go inside. I think with that level of approval, we should get started making the rest of those kids.

The End

Thank you for sharing your time with me. If you enjoyed this story, please write your review and post it on Amazon. com and Goodreads.com. This increases readers' awareness of my work and frankly, it helps me get sales on occasion. Those sales help me afford to publish more of my books. Your support is deeply appreciated. Learn more about Rick DeStefanis and his books at: The Word Hunter, www.rickdestefanis.com.

Following are readers' reviews and the first chapter of another novel by Rick DeStefanis, *Raeford's MVP.* It is a story about love and redemption as a young veteran fights his way past Post Traumatic Stress after Vietnam and finds the love of his life.

READER REVIEWS OF RAEFORD'S MVP

*5.0 out of 5 stars*A Reslient Soldier Overcome PTS Post-Traumatic Stress - A MUST READ by everyone in the VA

★★★★★ By Robert Enzenauer on March 15, 2016
Format: Paperback Verified Purchase

I have now read ALL THREE of Rick DeStefanis's novels, and I love them all. They are ALL excellent Vietnam-era fiction. But, this new book is very different. After a brief "end of tour" combat action fiction, the main character, Billy Coker, is severely wounded and "shipped home." This book should probably be read by every person working in our own Veterans' Administration, because it eloquently described the journey from combat injury to "waking up" in a military hospital, and vividly describes the further journey through PTS Post Traumatic Stress and eventual recovery. This book definitely stands on its own, but it is also worth reading EITHER of DeStefanis' earlier novels before picking up RAEFORD'S MVP. It is definitely a good love story. But it is an incredible story of the resiliency of an individual soldier. And every combat veteran has known at least ONE combat veteran struggling like Sergeant Coker. It is truly a blessing that the author decided to become a writer. Because I suspect that DeStefanis is writing his own version of personal history in the form of historical fiction.

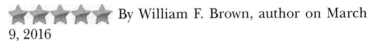 By William F. Brown, author on March 9, 2016
Format: Kindle Edition

I reviewed and liked Rick DeStefanis's two earlier novels, "Melody Hill" and "The Gomorrah Principle." They are good Vietnam War mystery suspense novels. Like "The 13th Valley," "Fields of Fire," and "A Rumor of War," they are written by a guy who was there. This new book is very different. It is a very personal story about the 18 and 20 year olds who went through hell over there and came home as damaged goods. Like the author, his main protagonist, Billy Coker, is in the 82nd Airborne Division, fighting for nameless hilltops, patches of jungle, and trails in the Central Highlands, with flashbacks to Raeford High School and how Billy got where he is. One huge difference between serving in Vietnam and Iraq or Afghanistan, is that we went there as individuals to be plugged into one random unit or another. We didn't go with friends as part of long-standing reserve units, which made it a very lonely experience, and we went there for a full 365 days, not short "deployments." That's why every grunt's most prized possession was his 'short-timer calendar,' and he knew exactly how many days he had left. That was one of the issues bothering Billy Coker. He was "less than 30," and everyone knew the cruelest of all fates was to be a "short-timer" and get killed. By that time, the daily physical and emotional beating guys went through in line infantry companies ground everyone into the dirt. In "Raeford's MVP," when Billy gets wounded and shipped home, the PTSD which overcomes him is all the worse, forcing him to fall back on old friends and old loves. A touch of "A Farewell to Arms?" Perhaps. That aspect of the story could just as easily be about an Iraq or Afghanistan War veteran, or a lot of earlier ones. However, in truth, 'PTSD' is much more of a recognized disease of these more recent wars. It took a long time to be recognized, as it took a long time for Agent Orange disabilities to be recognized for Vietnam Vets. That is one reason why "Raeford's MVP" should be read. We may not have called it PTSD back then, but that war hangs over a generation. Get a copy if you want to understand at least a piece of it.

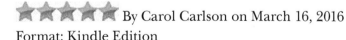 By Carol Carlson on March 16, 2016
Format: Kindle Edition

Rick DeStefanis is perhaps one of the greatest "undiscovered" writers of our time, with a special knack for telling a story in a way that transports the reader to the scene and allows you to see, hear, and feel the action around you. In Raeford's MVP, his third published novel, he does not disappoint. Like his first two books, The Gomorrah Principle and Melody Hill: A Vietnam Thriller about Love and War (The Gomorrah Principle Book 1), most of the intense action takes place in Vietnam, circa 1970. But from there, Raeford's MVP deviates, following our young war hero, Billy Coker, back stateside, where he faces a life very different than the one he left a year ago. The demons of that war, and for Billy, those from his days at Raeford High School as well, threaten to overwhelm him as he struggles to put the war and all it cost him firmly in the past. Then there's the girl; the girl he can't quite purge from his mind, or his heart. This is a love story, no doubt about it, but one that has to fight to survive and find its place, much like Billy himself.

Raeford's MVP examines the destruction of war on a soldier's psyche as well as his body. Today we know this emotional turmoil as PTSD. I've seen it personally, in friends and family returning from Iraq or Afghanistan. This story shows us that war, regardless of its time or location, takes a toll on those with boots on the ground, as well as those back home, taking us through the struggle to find peace again.

Well written and sure to capture any audience, with a perfect blend of the intensity of battle, the turmoil of recovery, and the gentleness of love, Raeford's MVP is now my 3rd reason why Rick DeStefanis stands as my favorite author writing today.

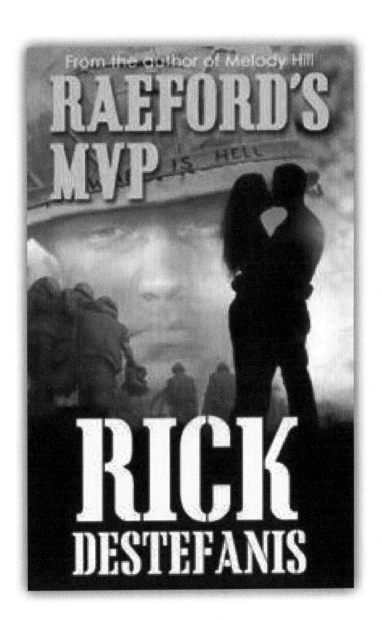

CHAPTER 1

PUT A CANDLE IN THE WINDOW

CENTRAL HIGHLANDS, REPUBLIC OF VIETNAM, 1970

BILLY COKER SAT ON A sandbag, smoking a cigarette and staring out at the fog-shrouded mountains of Vietnam. It was another dripping wet afternoon—quiet, except for the muffled voices of his men, playing cards in the bunker below. The rain had passed, and somewhere on the firebase behind him a radio played Credence Clearwater Revival. John Fogerty's plaintive voice came from the outside world, "Put a candle in the window." It was Billy's invitation to become human again, because in less than thirty days the freedom bird was taking him home. He'd have a real bath, sleep in a real bed and no longer worry about dying or watching others die. He was happy to be leaving Vietnam alive and unscathed, but without a clue as to why. It was as if somewhere along the way his life had ended, and he didn't even know when it happened.

He dropped the cigarette into a puddle, and fished another from the pack in his pocket. Other than escaping his current predicament, a total lack of anticipation had him teetering on the finest edge between happiness and despair. Those years in high school when he thought he was on top of the world now came back to haunt him with guilt and regret. And the strangest part of it all—he wasn't even thinking about the last eleven months in Nam. His thoughts weren't about the futility of the war or any of the recent events that should have culminated as the defining experiences of his life. He wasn't thinking about the man he'd become, or the men he'd seen die in the mud and rain—men like Butch and Danny, men closer to him than his own brother.

He absentmindedly rubbed his thumb over the Saint Sebastian medal hanging around his neck. He rubbed it as he had a thousand times in the last eleven months. He had clung to the silly medal like a raft in a storm. It was a gift from Bonnie Jo Parker. He smiled at the thought.

Where she given the chance, Bonnie Jo probably could have charmed the pants off of most men, but she wasn't that kind of girl. She was one of the fat girls at Raeford High who wore glasses and laughed too much. She laughed, not because she was silly, but because she was happy. Billy had spent time talking to her when he could—just to be nice—but Bonnie Jo wasn't his type. Perhaps, this was why he thought about her so much. Seems the fat girls never got a break, and he sure as hell never gave Bonnie Jo one.

Of course, they hadn't been *close* friends—only buddies of a sort—but he'd seen her almost every day. He ran cross-country track, and he was good at it. Back then he was skinny as a rail, and he liked the running. It was a way to clear his mind, not that there was much to clear. But cross-country track was the only thing he did well, besides chasing girls. Billy lit another cigarette as he thought about his after school runs. Crossing the pasture behind the school, he took the same course every day, down the hill to the creek and up through the woods. Skirting the back of town, he went behind the drive-in and around the old gravel pits, making a six-mile circuit. And Bonnie Jo was almost always there sitting at the tables behind the Dairy Queen with a couple other girls. When he passed on the trail in the woods, they waved, but he seldom did more than raise a finger in acknowledgment.

They had been in school together since their freshman year. He'd passed her in the halls almost every day, but the first time they spoke more than two words was at the beginning of their senior year. It was a Saturday in September when she walked out of the dollar store in Raeford. Billy was staring at the sale sign in the window, "Women's Summer Clothes 50% Off", thinking of—what else?—a girl with half her clothes off.

"Hey, Billy."

Bonnie Jo stopped and smiled, but he was daydreaming his way into Sissy Conroy's pants, and several seconds passed before he realized she had spoken. She started to turn away, but he snapped out of his trance.

"Oh, hey, Bonnie Jo."

She turned back. "What's up?"

He cast another glance back at the sale sign and lingered a moment before giving up on his daydream.

"Oh, nothing. Just trying to figure out how I'm gonna pass natural science this year. I failed the first test."

Billy began walking toward his truck. It was parked down by the Laundromat. Bonnie Jo tagged along.

"The way the football players talk, I thought you helped them with their studies."

"I only help those assholes with English," he said. "Grammar and comp are easy, but I'm not worth a crap with math and science. I missed all the test questions on population statistics."

"Why do you call them assholes?"

" 'Cause they are—and so are most of the cheerleaders and the rest of their cliquey friends."

"Hmmm," she said. "I thought you were part of their group."

"Not really. I just run cross-country and try to survive in their world. All I want to do is graduate and get the hell out of here."

"I can probably help you if you want."

"You think?"

"Sure."

Climbing in, he cranked the truck and rolled down the window.

"Need a ride?"

"You don't mind?"

He glanced over his shoulder to see if anyone was around. Giving a fat girl a ride in Raeford, Mississippi got you permanently stigmatized by the Lizards. The name was his personal invention—one he was proud of. They all wore shirts with little Alligators on them—but he figured they were more like lizards.

"Get in," he said.

"My house is out that way, off the highway." She pointed up the street then glanced down at the schoolbooks on the seat. "So, let's start with what you know."

She picked up the science book and opened it.

"That won't be hard. I don't know shit about natural science."

Bonnie Jo giggled but stared straight ahead down the road.

"What's so funny?" he asked.

"Nothing," she said, "except that's not what I've heard."

"Huh?"

"Never mind. I was just kidding."

It finally dawned on him what she was implying.

"You can't believe the crap you hear," he said.

It was better to lie than to be like the jocks who bragged about their sexual conquests, most of which Billy was pretty sure were with their hands and not with the girls they claimed. He continued driving past the traffic light, and headed east out the highway. The roadway narrowed just outside of town passing a pasture ripe with the odor of cattle manure. White cattle egrets roosted on the backs of Black Angus that grazed in scattered groups all the way to a distant tree line.

"Oh, well, I'm glad it's not true," she said.

The tone of her voice was patronizing, but he let it pass as she thumbed through the first chapter.

"So, tell me," she said. "What do you consider the best relationship for humans to have with their environment?"

"What the hell does that have to do with anything?" he asked.

"It's the first chapter, dummy—Humans and Their Relationship with the Environment."

"You mean like what's my idea of a perfect world?"

"Okay, what's your idea of a perfect world?"

"Are you sure you want to know?"

"Sure," she said. "Tell me about your Utopia."

It was time to give goody-two-shoes a dose of reality— show her what really matters.

"Okay," he said. "In a perfect world there's a high school called Beaver Valley High, and all the girls have perfect bodies and wear cheerleader outfits year round. And on weekends they're barrel riders in the local rodeo, crouching low on their quarter-horses with their perfect little butts bouncing high in the air as they whip around the barrels with auburn, blond and chestnut hair flowing from beneath their lady Stetsons."

She laughed. "Like I said, I've heard this about you, Coker."

"Heard what?"

"That you have a one-track mind."

She seemed so self-assured. It was time to turn up the heat.

"Hell," he replied, "You just don't know what *really* makes the world go 'round. Do you have a clue about the power women have over men?"

"Power?" she said.

"Yeah. If women could find a way to make men mainline that stuff, they could rule the world with a syringe. I mean they practically own it anyway, but they can't disengage their hearts long enough to really take charge."

She rolled her eyes. "You're confusing 'means' with 'motivation'."

"Means and motivation?"

"Yeah, most girls just don't think that way."

He turned and looked at her. "You think I'm crazy, don't you?"

Bonnie Jo pointed to a blacktop road up ahead. "Turn up there on that road," she said. "No, you're not crazy. Your hormonal overload isn't any worse than most guys your age. That house down there on the right."

"So you think it's only the guys that are crazy, huh?"

He slowed his old truck and turned into her drive. A long gentle curve of pavement took them through mature oak trees and up to the house. One of the nicer places around Raeford, the house had large gables and a big front porch.

"You want to come in?" she asked.

He shook his head. "I can't. I gotta get home to check on Mom."

"Is she sick?"

"No, not really—I mean, I don't know. It's just—she hasn't been doing so well since dad got killed last winter. Too much nerve medicine, I reckon."

Bonnie Jo looked off to the side and squinted. "I read about it in the paper," she said. "I mean, when your dad died."

"What's done is done," Billy said. "So, when do we have our first tutoring session?"

She gave him a sad smile and shrugged. "What's a good time for you?"

"How about Monday after I run?"

"Where?"

This was something he hadn't considered. The tables behind the Dairy Queen came to mind, but if he was seen hanging around town with her, the Lizards would harass the hell out of him, and it would definitely cost him some popularity points. He noticed a wooden swing hanging from a huge oak in her front yard.

"How about over there?" he said.

She shrugged.

"Weather permitting, it works for me."

"Sergeant Coker!"

Jarred back to reality—such as it was in Nam—Billy realized someone was calling him from somewhere in the warren of sandbagged bunkers encircling the fire-base. Firebase Echo had been home as of late for his air-borne infantry battalion. They'd been holed-up there for a month overlooking a road crossing near the A Shau Valley—'interdiction and pacification' they called it. George Custer tried the same thing with the Sioux. Billy almost laughed at the thought.

The surrounding mountains were crawling with North Vietnamese regulars, and the battalion had been whittled down to the equivalent of three lean companies of men. This was bad-guy territory, and the enemy called most of the shots. They even had anti-aircraft guns somewhere in the surrounding hills, which made re-supply choppers few and far between.

Again, someone call his name. Martin, one of Billy's men, stuck his head out of the bunker below. "It's one of the cherries," he said. "You want me to go get him, Sarge?"

"Yeah, if you don't mind. Go get him before a sniper takes his dumb-ass head off. And stay down."

They'd made him squad leader, probably by default, because had there been any competition, Billy was pretty sure he'd still be a buck private. Instead he'd spent the last three months trying to keep his men all in one piece. He figured that was the most important thing, because noth-ing else about this war made sense. He remembered how Bonnie Jo always said he was too cynical—especially when he called the Lizards egotistical jerks. If only she could see him now. He'd perfected cynicism in Nam. It was his forte, and he'd raised it to its highest form.

Martin crouched as he trotted back down to the bunker with the cherry. "Cherry here says Bugsy wants you up at the CP. Says it's real important."

Billy turned to the cherry. Dumb-ass nodded earnestly as if his role as messenger gave him some kind of authority. "If you don't stop wandering around in the wide-ass open, you ain't gonna live long enough to really enjoy this war."

"But, Sarge."

"No 'but' to it, dumb-ass. If you want to stay alive, start thinking like a soldier. These goddamn hills are crawling with NVA snipers, and they *will* put a round through that thick head of yours if you don't start using it for something besides a helmet holder."

Lieutenant Busby—or 'Bugsy' as the men called him—was the platoon leader. Billy decided to finish his cigarette. Sitting back down on the sandbag, he looked out across the mountains, wondering who he had become and where he was going when he left this godforsaken place. Other than eight weeks of Basic, nine weeks of Advanced Infantry Training and Airborne school, his résumé before getting to Nam would say he'd read a few books and did a focused study on female anatomy. It was a damned shame. Here he was just nineteen years old and CMFIC of a combat infantry squad.

The CMFIC—that's who they ask for when they want to talk to the person in charge. People often thought it was an official military acronym, an understandable assumption, but an incorrect one. Billy exhaled a cloud of smoke into the stagnant afternoon air. CMFIC was an *unofficial* military acronym that stood for Chief Mother Fucker In Charge. The real kicker was that his men actually thought he knew what he was doing. He was their squad leader, and they watched his every move, hoping he could show them something that would keep them alive just one more day. It would have been laughable had it not been so serious.

It was simply a matter of the one who'd been here longest leading the ones who'd just shown up. If it wasn't for the war, most of them, himself included, would have been down at a McDonalds by nightfall, trying to pick up chicks, drinking Old Milwaukee talls and listening to Hendrix or Steppenwolf. Instead, they were here on this godforsaken firebase, and Billy only hoped he could make a difference whenever the shit hit the fan.

Actually, he'd been fairly successful as a squad leader. He thought about it. Perhaps it was his ability to use their vices to motivate people. God knows, he had a few. And, the cherry was just a big dumb oaf—kind of reminded him of Raymond Hokes, another old Raeford High classmate. Like Ray, the cherry wasn't too bright, and Billy realized he had to find a way to motivate him—give him something to think about beside the rain, rats and mosquitoes. He figured the best way was to find something he desired, perhaps tell him about the whores in Phu Bai, or the navy nurses on R&R down at China Beach. And if his experience with Raymond Hokes had any relevance, the theory might just work.

Sex was always his prime choice as a motivator, and it was with Ray that he first tested the theory. The way Billy had it figured, there wasn't a red-blooded boy anywhere in Raeford who wouldn't sell his soul for a few hours with the right woman—his reasoning being based on his own experiences since puberty. Women ruled the world, and he, Billy Coker was their slave. Albeit a willing one, he wasn't the only one enslaved by feminine charms, and his strategy for dealing with Ray Hokes greatly depended on that assumption.

Ray always liked to start shit with anyone he found hanging around in the halls after school. Problem was he was a man amongst boys. Having failed the fourth grade twice, he was nineteen years old and the star lineman for the Raeford High Wildcats. Ray was a sum total six-foot-four and two hundred and eighty-nine pounds of pot-bellied redneck. And for some reason, he had decided to make Billy his whipping boy that year.

It was only the third week of school, and Billy had no intention of spending his entire senior year getting his ass kicked by Ray. Problem was a head-to-head confrontation with him was tantamount to suicide. Normal-sized humans had to rely on wit and guile to survive run-ins with Ray. That's how Billy came up with the plan he hoped would, as the guidance counselor might put it, 're-align

Ray's priorities' or to put it in simpler terms, 'get him off his ass.'

School let out that day as the final bell rang and the student body burst through the doors like a covey of quail, leaving the ancient hallways all but empty. Billy was on his way to the locker room, his footsteps echoing in the silence, when he spotted Ray going into the boy's rest-room. It was risky, but it was time to face his nemesis. It was time to try his new theory. And if it blew up in his face there'd be no witnesses. He would die and be buried on the schoolyard battlefield like thousands of nerd-warriors before him, but at least his annihilation wouldn't include public humiliation.

The way Billy had it figured, Ray was going to pound his head every day until he got creative and found a way to distract him. That's why he decided to ask him if he'd ever had any pussy—an exceptionally stupid question to ask Ray of all people, if he really meant it. One look at Ray and you knew he hadn't been near one since the day he was born—at least not one belonging to a human. Knowing his "agricultural" background, though, there may have been an unlucky farm animal somewhere along the way.

Billy slipped into the restroom behind Ray. Ray glanced over his shoulder and shuffled closer against the urinal. He was probably one of those delivered by a midwife in the country and never circumcised. You could always tell, because they often hid themselves, even in the locker room. Billy walked over beside him to take a quick pee.

"What the hell are you doin' in here, Coker?"

"Oh, hey, Ray. I saw you and was going to tell you something."

Ray finished and zipped up before backing away from the urinal.

"What?"

"Well..." Billy hesitated. He should have rehearsed. "Have you ever had any? You know?"

"Any what?"

Ray always seemed angry for no reason, and Billy found himself unable to muster a pee, so he zipped up and turned to face him.

"You know, pussy."

Priming Ray first hadn't occurred to him, but it was too late. The fuse was lit. Ray began stuttering, then turned and charged like a rodeo bull. Grabbing Billy's throat, he lifted him off the floor and pinned him against the wall between the urinals. This wasn't the way it was supposed to happen. Bad timing he figured, but he had to come up with plan 'B' quick or die.

"Wait a minute, Ray!" Billy said breathlessly. "Hold on a second. I need to tell you something, something important."

Ray hesitated with his fist drawn back as he held Billy there against the cold tile wall.

"What?"

His moronic little eyes came together like a pair of B-B's in the middle of his country ham face.

"What if I told you I know a girl who likes to mess around—you know? And she kind of likes you, too."

Ray's eyes narrowed even more until his brows nearly touched as he fought to focus on some shadow of a thought deep within. With this mask of total concentration covering his face, it seemed certain the cognitive overload was about to melt one of his two brain cells. Deep down in his heart Ray must have thought making love to a real girl was beyond the realm of possibility in his lifetime.

"Who?" he said.

Billy froze again. It wasn't that he didn't have in mind several of the finest specimens of female anatomy at Raeford High, but for some reason, he had a forevermore-unbreakable radar-lock on Sissy Conroy's most magnificent buns. This would never work. The mere idea was a desecration. Letting Ray have the misguided thought that he could dip into that little honey pot was totally repulsive. Death would be a better option, and for the moment, that possibility seemed imminent.

Skydiving couldn't have given Billy the adrenaline rush he had dangling there, his back against the wall and Ray's sledgehammer fist staring him in the face. He had to think. The toes of his tennis shoes barely touched the puddles of water on the floor, and Billy tried with all his might to come up with a name other than Sissy's. That was the one part of the plan he'd neglected. He needed a name—a believable one.

"Bonnie Jo Parker," he blurted.

The words no sooner left his mouth than Billy felt sickened by what he'd done. He was a loathsome jerk. He had just betrayed the girl who was going to help him graduate high school. Ray would trail her everywhere she went.

"I wouldn't touch that little pig," he snarled.

Guilt-ridden or not, it was too late to start over.

"Ray, I can't believe you would say that about Bonnie Jo. She's a little on the chubby side, but she's really a sweet person, and I think she likes you."

Billy's heart raced as he fought to catch his breath. Again, Ray's face became masked with concentration. Beyond the odor of Ray's bologna and mustard breath, Billy could almost smell his two brain cells smoking from the overload. Then slowly—so very slowly—Ray loosened his grip from around Billy's throat. His tennis shoes settle back onto the tile floor, and the smell of the urinal was like that of life itself, almost invigorating.

"What makes you think she likes me?"

It was think-fast-or-die-time again.

"I heard her say your name the other day while she was talking with some girls in the cafeteria."

Ray didn't say anything. That a female mentioned his name in conversation seemed an incomprehensible concept to him.

"I saw her looking at you in the hall, too."

Billy laid it on thick, and after a few moments the hormonal influence must have been too much for Ray's teenincy brain to overcome. He walked over to the mirror and gazed into the biggest section that wasn't cracked. With the heel of his hand he pushed his larded locks into place. Billy was frozen in place, pinned by his own fear, unable to move. Damn, Ray was ugly, and this lummox could go either way at any moment. Sucking down a deep breath, Billy took the first tentative step toward the door. Ray didn't seem to notice as he turned his head and studied his profile in the mirror. Billy bolted and didn't look back.

Sissy Conroy, the most glorious hunk of teenage womanhood in the school, owed him a big one. He had saved her from Ray, but since she was the heartthrob of most of the football team, crossing paths with her would probably never happen, at least in any significant way, such as undressing her and engaging in mad and passionate love making. She would never know how he had made Bonnie Jo her stand-in human sacrifice.

Taking another hard drag on the cigarette, Billy watched as the cherry stumbled down into the bunker. He was just another Ray Hokes. All he needed was the right motivation.

This novel is available in both paperback and Kindle editions at: http://amzn.to/1XOw1qW

Other novels by Rick DeStefanis include The Gomorrah Principle Series (Books 1 & 2):

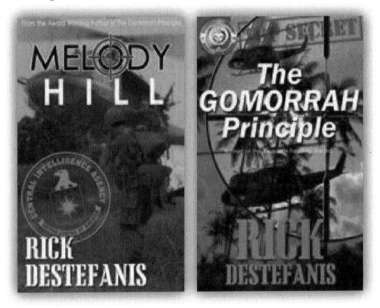

Available on Amazon.com at: http://amzn.to/1TykIj7

Made in the USA
Lexington, KY
10 December 2018